OH, TH[...]ALL

When Yourdon touched the sword he felt a subtle energy run through his bones, then a stirring of something deeper still, a hidden magic.

He saw misty images of a mighty king, of great warriors atop armored horses charging into battle. He stood a bit straighter, felt that much stronger as he raised the blade before his eyes, then lowered it again to the table. The images in his mind began to fade.

He touched the mace lying beside the sword. It too lent a strange sensation, though the sense was less . . . noble. He saw a band of soldiers, a village in flames . . . worse had happened before the flames. . . . only barbarians were capable of such atrocities.

Yourdon set the weapon back down and moved on, examining a battered morningstar. As he touched it, he watched the forming image of a young boy swinging it about, bravely facing a foe clutching a leather covered shield and a rusted sword. The sword won. He rested his hand momentarily on the hilt of his own sword, and tried to imagine what the victor must be feeling: Yourdon had never actually killed a man.

Then he picked up the dagger, and a chill swept his spine. He saw a soldier of Detimar—a young and slender soldier, very much like himself—lashing out with the dagger, striking toward the belly of a tall opponent. He wanted to be that soldier, wanted the glory and honor of killing the enemies of Detimar with this dagger, the satisfaction of fulfilling the promise the army had finally given him. And the dagger itself seemed to fit so perfectly in his hand, seemed to feel so right. . . .

SWORD OF THE PROPHETS

MARK A. GARLAND

SWORD OF THE PROPHETS

This is a work of fiction. All the characters and events portrayed in this book are fictional, and any resemblance to real people or incidents is purely coincidental.

A Baen Books Original

Baen Publishing Enterprises
P.O. Box 1403
Riverdale, NY 10471

ISBN: 0-671-87776-3

Cover art by Darrell K. Sweet

Map by Kevin Butterfield

First printing, May 1997

Distributed by Simon & Schuster
1230 Avenue of the Americas
New York, NY 10020

Printed in the United States of America

For Mathew, Kristy and Gregory

Special thanks are due and overdue to Bruce Coville,
Barbara Block, Robert J. Sawyer, Edo van Belkom,
Nick DiChario, Chuck McGraw, Toni Weisskopf,
Jim Baen, Jim Glass, Merritt Severson,
Valerie Freireich, Michael Payne, Michelle Levigne,
Dave Wolverton, Josepha Sherman, Lawrence Schimel,
Lawrence Watt-Evans, John O'Shea, Bob Gottstein,
Nancy Kress, Julia Ecklar, Andrew Zack and everyone
in the Fantastic Fiction Forum.

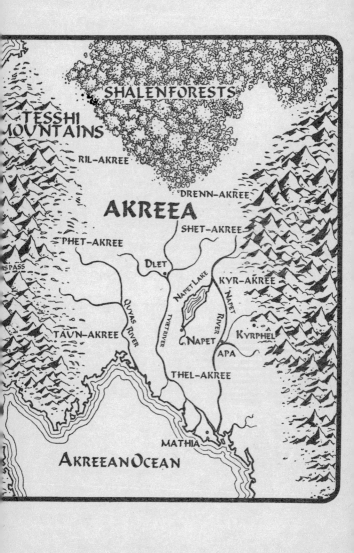

SHALEN FORESTS

TESSHI
MOUNTAINS

RIL-AKREE

DRENN-AKREE

AKREEA

SHET-AKREE

PHET-AKREE

DLET

KYR-AKREE

NAPET LAKE

...PASS

QUVAS RIVER

TAUN-AKREE

TYET RIVER

NAPET RIVER

NAPET

KYRPHEL

APA

THEL-AKREE

MATHIA

AKREEAN OCEAN

❖ PROLOGUE ❖

Yourdon Lewen stood in the doorway to the little armory shop blinking at the walls and small, rough wooden tables, including the long cloth-covered table across the room, in front of the proprietor. The man was not of Detimar, not any sort of person Yourdon had ever seen, with his squat frame, thick, unruly white hair and beard, his narrow eyes and a terribly large nose. He looked to be a hundred if he was a day. Moles and age spots dotted his baggy face and knotty hands.

The light was poor, the smell strange. Musty, Yourdon thought, and dusty, but lacking any of the accumulated regular scents that foods and hearth fires and human bodies deposit in a room. Which was odd, since this was an old village, a place that had stood at the stream forks even before the Empire had come to know the Syttrel.

Dozens of odd little shops like this one lined the merchant square, places where he'd been told a browse might find just about anything. The shop brought a tingle to his nerves. Yourdon moved ahead, tantalized.

The village was little more than a stopover, an assembly point for troops on their way to the recent Vaul ridge assault, on their way to victories and glories killing Syttrel—Yourdon's first.

"Help you?" the shopkeeper asked, a gritty voice that sounded older than many of the shop's wares.

"Just looking," Yourdon said. The walls and tables were

1

well stocked with medals, colors and flags from many armies, many battles; some Yourdon remembered only from history lessons, others he had no knowledge of. One display recalled the famed armies of Lord Renem himself, and the first great border war with the Syttrel, more than a generation ago. And everywhere there were pieces of armor.

When he reached the far central table the shopkeeper pulled the cloth covering back. Yourdon had fancied himself many things, but a warrior most of all. Here, his eyes feasted on the finest tools of war.

"You sure?"

"What?" Yourdon asked.

"Sure I can't help you?"

Yourdon looked about once more. He noticed the old man watching him with a steady eye, arms folded in front of him as he leaned back in his chair. His belly was just round enough to nudge the table.

"May I?" Yourdon asked, looking down again. His nerves were tingling, battle fire from endless training and anticipation leaking into his blood, his mind. It felt awful. And of course, incredible . . .

The shopkeeper nodded toward the table's contents. Yourdon leaned close. The first piece was a sword with a blade made of a highly polished metal, and a gold handle elaborately carved, though worn at the ridges; overall it was twice as long as Yourdon's arm, and nearly as wide where the blade met the hilt.

When Yourdon touched the sword he felt a subtle energy run through his bones, then a stirring of something deeper still, a hidden magic. He hefted the blade barely inches into the air and turned it over. Next he whispered the chant he had invented so many years ago, intended to encourage his own small magical talent, and his mind began to whirl.

He saw misty images of a mighty king, of great warriors riding atop armored horses, all of them charging into battle against the armies of darker men. He stood a bit straighter, felt that much stronger as he raised the blade before his eyes, then lowered it again—until he let the tip of the sword touch the table. Gently, he rested the hilt as well. The images in his mind began to fade.

He fancied the war hammer lying beside the sword, and the heavy flanged mace beside that, both of which Yourdon decided he simply had to examine more closely. When he touched the mace it too lent a strange sensation. With this weapon, though, the sense was less . . . noble. As he whispered the chant once more, renewing the minor spell, he saw a band of soldiers killing villagers, taking what little they had. He had not been trained this way these past many months. Only barbarians like the Syttrel were capable of such atrocities, he was certain.

Yourdon set the weapon back down and moved on, examining a magnificent two-handed battle axe, then a battered morningstar, its leather ropes quite rotted. As he touched this last piece he watched the forming image of a young boy swinging it about, bravely facing a foe clutching a leather covered shield and a rusted sword. The sword won out. He rested his hand momentarily on the hilt of his own sword, and tried to imagine what the victor must be feeling: Yourdon had never actually killed a man.

A bow and several arrows lay lengthwise, though the bow was built too thin and flimsy for Yourdon's tastes. Nothing so deadly or far ranging as the fine weapons used by the bowmen of Detimar. Then he picked up the shortest of the daggers, and a chill swept his spine. The blade was stout, made to penetrate most armor, if not very deeply. Amber jewels decorated the handle, one on each side. He admired the balance, a fine throwing weapon as well, he thought. Yourdon could hit nearly any mark, and that with a dagger not half the equal of this one.

Repeating the phrase once more, renewing the spell, he saw a soldier of Detimar—a young and slender soldier, very much like himself—lashing out with the dagger, striking toward the belly of a tall but vague opponent. He wanted to be that soldier, wanted the glory and honor of killing the enemies of Detimar with this dagger, the satisfaction of fulfilling the promise the army had finally given him. And the dagger itself seemed to fit so perfectly in his hand, seemed to feel so right . . .

But as he looked into the vision again he saw that the figure facing the soldier was changing: some of the height was gone, and the face was partially hidden now by a hood that revealed only the edges of a short, pure white beard. One arm, wielding a barbed silvery blade the length of a man's thigh, reached out from beneath a mantle and a pleated tunic. Yourdon began to feel slightly dizzy, almost numb, so he let the magic fade. The shopkeep might soon suspect what he was doing in any case, he thought, and his magic, he had long ago decided, was something best kept to himself.

Yourdon asked about the dagger's price. He didn't have quite enough. The army paid little, and his father had given him only a small traveling fund, nothing else. His father had money enough to buy the whole shop, but asking him for anything would ruin everything; it simply wasn't on Yourdon's personal list of options.

"Through?" the shopkeep prodded.

"Still looking," Yourdon said. "They are amazing. I've never seen the like. I wish I could own them all. Maybe after the war, I will come back this way."

"Yes, the war. Which war?"

Yourdon looked up, surprised. "The war with the Syttrel, of course."

"Yes, of course." The shopkeep shrugged, waved fingers at the table. "You are interested in the dagger."

Yourdon reexamined the smooth wooden grip, the amber jewels, the stirring in his blood. He saw his distorted, clean-shaven reflection scarcely nodding in the flat blade's polished surface.

"I could give you a special price," the old fellow said. "Each piece has a self, you know. I have a feel for such things. That one, I believe, should be yours."

Yourdon set the dagger down and studied the old man carefully. His mind wanted to chase after the other's last words—but he pushed this thought away, and replaced it with much larger ones. "You seem more a collector than a simple armorer," he said.

"Perhaps," the shopkeep said. "After so many years, interests change. As do one's needs. We all need to cling to something."

We do, Yourdon thought, as again his mind lingered over the other's words. The army had finally given Yourdon what he'd always lacked, what he'd always needed. He looked sidelong at the old man, again nodding. "I see," he said.

The old man shook his head. "Most men never do, especially young as you. But one never knows." He pulled the dark cloth back part of the way, then he hesitated, and picked up the dagger before covering the rest of the table. "It is yours," he said, handing the weapon up. "Give me what you can."

Yourdon quickly untied his purse string and fished most of the contents out, then handed the coins to the old man. "That enough?" he asked. The shopkeep nodded and put the coins inside his faded robe. Yourdon turned to go, then he paused. He felt a mix of emotions pressing toward the surface as he held the strange dagger again, a need to say something more. He held the dagger out. "This means a great deal to me. I thank you."

The shopkeep held Yourdon's gaze. His face seemed to have changed, gotten still older somehow, perhaps darker. "I am not surprised," he answered. "You have much in common with it. But everything you see here costs more than it is worth. They are a fool's tools, my friend, nothing more." He ran his hands tenderly over the dry cloth, straightening folds.

Yourdon stood back, squinting at the old man, considering him. "They are the tools of great men!" he corrected. "The day I first held a sword I was changed. I was never certain of anything before that. Now—now I am—"

"A fool with a sword, and a dagger." The shopkeep sighed ruefully. "Go and fight your war. I'm sure it is all you have."

Yourdon held in the doorway, blinking at the shopkeep. *All that I have,* his mind echoed, and some part of him had tensed at the thought, would not let loose. He tried to imagine what the old fellow was up to, whether he might even be joking, whether he might be mad, but it was no use—and Yourdon didn't think so. "Please explain yourself," he insisted, scowling, hardening somewhat.

The shopkeep only stared, eyes dark and unblinking.

"You will explain yourself!" Yourdon demanded. His palm tightened around the dagger's grip. He felt a tingling in his wrist, a mighty battle somewhere in the past—or possibly just ahead. "I could kill you," he said.

The shopkeep chuckled softly.

Yourdon flipped the dagger and held it by its point, held it up, ready to throw. His hand was shaking, spoiling his aim. The old man gently shrugged.

Yourdon set his jaw and slammed the door.

❖ TRIAL AND ERROR ❖

The dead and dying lay everywhere in the tall grasses of the rolling plain. Yourdon Lewen took uneasy comfort in the fact that most were Syttrel. The barbarians, dressed in billowing breeches and bright sashes, their swarthy faces and torsos painted with symbols of death, seldom wore any sort of armor for protection. They were creatures of speed and movement, zealous warriors prone to wild, glorious battle.

The armies of the Detimarian Empire were vastly superior. Yourdon wore a layered leather cuirass covered in armor platelets, a plumed helmet and greaves, making him much harder to wound; his shield and sword were larger, stronger, and made of much finer metals than anything Syttrelian metallurgy could field; and his legion's training and tactics were unmatched. Or so it was said.

Yet the barbarian tribes had held on against Detimar for so long . . .

Yourdon toed the still body of one young Syttrel warrior, rolling it over. Male, though it was not uncommon to find the occasional female among their ranks, something Yourdon had been warned about before coming to the border wars, yet something he, like many of his fellows, still found hard to accept. Here was a fine specimen, lean and muscular. His dark black hair was pulled back straight and tied behind his head, his face bore the short bushy whiskers favored by Syttrelian men.

Yourdon examined the careful, colorful designs painted on every visible part of the dead man's skin. Powerful Syttrelian magic, it was said, worn as curses on their enemies and protection for themselves. He had heard that Syttrelian gods and hexes or both could rob a man of his luck, his sanity, his life.

In the end, Yourdon reminded himself, the armies of Detimar would surely be victorious against these curious heathens. He could not allow himself to consider otherwise, out here, surrounded by death. This had been his first true battle, and nothing like what he had expected.

The Syttrel had ridden in from three sides, taking Trison's legion entirely by surprise. Yourdon saw two comrades fall within the first moments not a yard from himself. Many more followed, screaming, some dying much too slowly. Despite endless mental and physical preparation he had never imagined . . . this.

The Syttrel had finally broken off, screeching and howling as they did no matter what, and fled back into the sparsely wooded hills to the east.

Yourdon shuddered as he used the dead barbarian's breeches to wipe the blood and gore from his sword before returning it to its sheath. They needed to die, of course. Every Detimarian knew that. The Syttrel lived like packs of wild animals and knew nothing of honor. They believed in endless spirits and gods and fought with each other as often as with their enemies. Their only strength seemed to lie in their skills with arrow, sword or dagger, and in sheer tenacity. But even these strengths knew limits, as the warrior at Yourdon's feet fairly proved.

He looked about, curious, feeling a need. He decided no one was paying any particular attention to him. Slowly, pushing aside a familiar uneasiness, he bent and picked up the Syttrelian's sword, a short, flat-bladed, rather clumsy weapon, heavily battered from use.

He whispered the binding phrase and almost at once Yourdon's small magical talent began to tell him the weapon's secrets. In his mind's eye he witnessed this dead Syttrelian receiving the sword, much as Yourdon's own sword had been given to him, not a year ago. There had been another battle, Yourdon saw, as more images brightened, then faded. The barbarian had used this very blade to cut off the head of a fallen Detimarian, perhaps only days ago.

He shuddered again and dropped the sword, then kicked the discarded weapon away reflexively. He did not envy the Syttrel their weapons, or their women, or their savage lives.

Only their boots, which were of the finest leather craftsmanship. The dead warrior's feet, in fact, looked to be about Yourdon's size. . . .

He shook the notion from his head. Wearing booty taken from dead Syttrelians seemed suddenly unappealing. Like war, Yourdon thought, before he could stop himself. The army had seemed the perfect answer to most of Yourdon's problems—until this day, this moment. Until the barbarians had attacked, and changed something inside him.

He turned away, straightening his cuirass, then his belt and apron. His shield had a long dent in the center, which another soldier had remarked only proved Yourdon's ability to keep his head in a battle. He took a breath, smiled grimly to himself and headed for the wagons, deciding it was best to be prompt. Trison would be calling an assembly at any moment and he would likely not be pleased, or patient. Their fresh "victory" aside, Yourdon was convinced that something had gone terribly wrong.

❖   ❖   ❖

"We face an army of jackals!" Trison began, standing in an open wagon, wasting neither time nor originality. "But we will hunt the beasts until their numbers darken this land no more, by the True God!"

Cheers rose up through the ranks. Yourdon abstained.

"None of our scouts returned," Trison went on, getting to the particulars. "Had they, *we* would have been waiting in ambush, instead of the Syttrel." Trison drew his sword and swept the weapon over the heads of his troops. "New scouts will be needed. We will find the barbarians, and bring to them the wrath of Detimar's finest legion!" Fresh cheers erupted. "Each captain will choose a man," Trison finished.

A dozen captains' heads turned this way and that. Yourdon suddenly learned that standing next to his own captain had been an unforeseen error. He followed the others to the front of the assembly.

Trison spoke again of their mission, cheers followed, Yourdon barely heard. He had never truly fit in anywhere, never succeeded completely at anything until he had become a soldier. The legion had given him many of the things his youth, and his father, never had: direction, identity, worth. He had imagined he might even take these things home with him one day. If he ever went home again.

He had set his dreams on becoming a great and noble warrior, and now . . .

Trison turned to his first captain, who was standing just behind the wagon. "Instruct the new scouts to locate the Syttrel before sunset tomorrow," he said, his voice flat now, but loud enough for Yourdon and the others to hear. "I don't want to chase them into another region. One tribe at a time is quite enough." The captain acknowledged his orders and moved quickly away.

Trison was not as unforgiving as many, but the war

with the Syttrel was taking much too long, years too long. Many in the capitol city were said to be growing weary of a war that had started over free trade routes to the sea, and had produced no trade routes still. The barbarians seemed utterly unwilling to negotiate within reason, but the scattered, disorganized Syttrelian tribes had promised easy conquest, and the war had begun. Now, all six members of the High Council were pressuring the army to make good on that promise. No field commander, Yourdon was sure, was in a very good mood.

When the general command was given to dismiss, the first captain came around the wagon. "Follow the barbarians into the woods, learn where they are and how many they are," he told the scouts. "And be sure at least one of you survives to report before tomorrow night." His words were met by a dozen salutes, including Yourdon's. "Be sure," he repeated, adamant.

They seemed to insist on dying, these Syttrel, Yourdon thought, just as he had insisted on his chance to kill them, until he had actually done so. He had mortally wounded two enemy warriors as his training had taken over. In the heat of battle the blood he drew had given him a tremendous sense of power, and a sense of justice, at taking the lives of those who had come to take his own. Then the frenzy had ended, leaving something much less tenable in its wake.

The captain went about picking a commander for the detail, and Yourdon straightened his posture, trying to look his best. He had been chosen for minor commands on several occasions during training, and each time he had excelled. No battle plan or tactic, no lesson his superiors had taught had ever slipped his mind. The scouting mission might be a foul one, but he was sure he would fare much better if he were to command it. He would carry out the mission, by one means or another, but he had no intention of getting everyone killed. The captain picked Laren, a young solder like Yourdon, good at following orders. A trustworthy man, Yourdon thought, and with more time in the field to be fair, but he seemed no leader. He lacked insight and mental agility. Yourdon had seen him stand for ages deciding which kind of bread to have with his stew.

Yourdon shook his head but accepted the fact. Laren would not be out to get them killed, either, for what that was worth. *We will be successful,* he thought, choosing to do so. Nothing else made sense.

The captain turned and walked back to another wagon a few yards behind the first. Soon enough he returned and held out his hand. Laren opened his palm and the captain dropped the talisman into it. A simple trinket, not much more than an ordinary pebble. They were enchanted in small quantities by the High Council's own Lord Priests. Thrown out with the properly rendered phrase they could cause a fair-sized object to burst into flames. The last scout commander had carried one as well, of course, for all the good it must have done him.

Laren put the stone away, then turned to his men.

"We're already too far behind them," he said. "Move!" With that he turned and led off. They packed their horses with light provisions, hard bread and dried meat and water, then loaded a pack horse with extra feed for their mounts. As darkness gathered, revealing a bright, nearly full moon the scouts formed a line and rode southeast, through the warm night air, trailing the Syttrel into the trees.

"They've been through here, the entire army, looks like," Sireth said, pointing. He was another soldier very close to Yourdon's young age, though larger; a good man like most of them, and one Yourdon had shared ale with

many times. Yourdon had known few friends as a boy—
in Thetar mothers tended to create a family's social life,
and he had never known his. And even if he had, his
own father thought her people little better than the
Syttrel. But in the legion men were trained to depend
on each other, and friendship, or something very much
like it, seemed to come more easily.

Sireth walked his mount along with two of the others,
circling narrow tree trunks. Laren nodded to him. Trailing
the Syttrel had been a simple matter. The moon lit the
land clearly even through the sparse trees, and the ground
was soft enough to hold the impressions of several
hundred Syttrelian horses.

"Their camp should not be far," Drines said, a slightly
older man, a proven soldier, though he was noticeably
overweight these days, and talked too much of his wife
and children in Thetar.

"They move even at night," Yourdon offered, recalling
the lesson of the bloody Song Lake battle, the worst in
this war so far, he'd been told. The thought seemed hard
to imagine now, having seen so much death and butchery
only hours ago. He tried not to think about it. The mission
at hand was all that mattered now.

"No doubt," Laren said, glancing up at Yourdon. "They
seem to be in full retreat, but Syttrel have no honor, and
no need of sleep I think, nor the common sense to travel
in a straight line. We will not rest until I know where
they are. Enough lives have been lost to Syttrelian tricks."

*And those under commanders far more perceptive than
you, friend Laren,* Yourdon worried.

"We'll quicken our pace," the commander added.
"They might double back on the legion before we learn
their plan."

Good enough, Yourdon thought, nodding to himself.
Laren might yet do the job. . . .

Laren led the way, pacing the horses at a bone-jarring rapid trot. The hills were difficult at times but the forest never thickened enough to slow their pace for long. And Yourdon thought about killing.

"I know that look," a voice said in Yourdon's ear, a whispered tone. Sireth. Yourdon shrugged. He hadn't realized it showed.

"You will get used to it, the fighting, the dying," Sireth said. "Unless they kill you."

Yourdon attempted a smile.

"It's them that's the problem," Sireth went on. "Those cursed Syttrel. It isn't your fault they won't surrender and save us all a lot of spilled blood. But they don't think that way. They force us to kill enough of them to *make* them see it."

Yourdon had been taught to think much the same way during training, though it had seemed a somewhat contrived logic at the time. He clung to the idea now, telling himself that it made almost perfect sense. With Northern Sea trade increasing, ships were being lost at a rapid pace as they attempted to navigate the rocky, turbulent and cluttered island waters that separated Thetar from the open sea. Clearly, that could not go on.

"They don't fight like men," he told Sireth, letting it come out. "They fight like rabid wolves, like demons, like—"

"Like barbarians!" Sireth answered, grinning.

"Yes, barbarians!" Yourdon echoed, to some relief.

"Ahh, that's the stuff!" Sireth chortled. "And all of it true."

Abruptly Laren drew up and raised his hand, signaling the others to halt. "They are splitting up," he said, pointing. "Most seem to be turning south." Yourdon could see the tracks plainly enough, splitting in two directions as they neared a long, low ridge. Laren urged the scouts forward first, following the straight tracks until they topped the rise. Below lay a small grassy valley, and at its center, three long, dark Syttrelian tents. The scouts watched for a time but saw no one about, not even a horse.

"An old camp," Sireth suggested.

"Or the beginnings of a new one," Laren said, leaning out over his horse's mane, peering harder into the moonlit night. "Deserted for now, I say." He looked about, then pointed to Yourdon and Sireth. "You two ride down into the camp and look it over. The rest will remain here with me. This may well be a trap."

Each man nodded. Sireth set off immediately down the hill. Yourdon felt his heart pounding. *It is they who must die,* he told himself, clinging to the warrior's creed. *They are barbarians!*

They rode in at full gallop, splitting up as they entered the camp. Neither man found any sentries, or anyone inside the tents as they checked each one. Finally Sireth rode to open grasses and waved. Laren gestured, and the rest of the scouts broke cover and headed down the hill. All twelve met around the cold central camp fire.

"Some tracks leading off that way," Sireth noted, indicating the northern slope of the valley. "But the majority of them turned, back there on the hill. This may be nothing more than a diversion."

Yourdon nodded, then looked at Laren, waiting for him to take the appropriate actions, hoping he would be named.

He pointed past Yourdon to the last two soldiers in the line. "Agreed. You, go," he ordered. "Report to Commander Trison that we suspect the Syttrel have turned, and are likely to attack again, perhaps by dawn if they are as quick as I suspect. The rest of us will continue following their main force . . . until we are sure."

The two men acknowledged their orders, turned their horses and rode back toward the ridge. Yourdon watched them go, then his eyes went wide as not a hundred paces out Syttrelian arrows struck them down.

"Protect yourselves!" Laren called out, seeing it too, taking his shield from his horse's side and raising it up. Each of the remaining scouts did the same, pulling their shields free in time to deflect the small spray of arrows that fell on them next. Still more arrows fell, though none found their intended human targets. Some of the horses did not fare so well, leaving several scouts on foot. A moment of quiet stillness followed, but did not last.

The Syttrelian animal calls came next. When Yourdon got a look he saw them charging down from the tiny valley's northern slope, perhaps two dozen or more. They had given up archery and were taking a more direct approach. This had been their mission, Yourdon thought, going cold inside, to eliminate the scouting party.

Laren quickly got a line formed. The Syttrel rode straight at them, bearing down. The scouts nocked arrows to their own bows and let fly as the enemy came within easy range. A few barbarians fell. The rest rode through the line, toppling several of the scouts as they leaped from their own horses to engage the men. As always, the Syttrel were fast and fierce, but no fair match for Detimarian armor and weapons. *And skills!* Yourdon thought, priming himself, letting his body and training take over as a Syttrelian came at him. He moved to the attack, wounding the first man as he slipped past, then killing another outright with a clear thrust into the barbarian's heart. He could smell them now, their own sweat mixed with the sweat of their horses, a sour, pungent odor.

He turned to see Drines fall victim to a double assault. One of these Syttrel, he realized with a start, was a woman, young and muscular but shorter than most of the men, her figure clearly female beneath her leather-laced sleeveless tunic. As she withdrew her blade from Drines' side, another scout found her unprotected back and opened the flesh with a level swipe. She moaned and fell, then lay on the ground, back arched, agony fading from her moonlit face as life flowed from her body. Black-looking blood soaked her clothing.

What kind of creatures were these, Yourdon wondered again, to let women do their dying for them—or to force honorable men to kill their women? What kind of woman would go into battle? He felt stunned, felt the battle fire cooling quickly inside him.

A shape caught his eye. He ducked under a pass from a barbarian on his left, then came up blade first, transferring his revulsion to contempt quickly enough. He missed the torso completely, then stepped in and swung again. Mostly by chance his blade caught the Syttrelian in the throat. As the man lay on the ground gasping blood, Yourdon spit upon him. "Bastards," he said. "Cursed barbarian bastards!"

Sireth shouted. Yourdon quickly saw his predicament. Three Syttrel were closing in, and he'd already taken a wound in his left arm. Yourdon filled his other hand with his amber-jeweled dagger and rushed to Sireth's aid. He struck one Syttrel in the shoulder with his sword, then countered with the dagger as the man turned and raised iron to protect himself against another blow. Sireth dispatched one of the others, striking back when the attacker thrust inward only to blunt his blade on Sireth's heavily plated cuirass. They teamed up on the last of the trio, and quickly forced his end.

The two men stood for a moment, winded, heads

spinning. They exchanged a look of obscene satisfaction, and for a moment, Yourdon believed there might be a great warrior inside him after all. But as the shouts of battle brought his head around he was staggered by what he saw. Aside from Sireth and himself, only Laren and two other soldiers stood against nearly a dozen Syttrel. The barbarians were concentrating on the others for now. *They will get to us,* Yourdon thought. And if two-to-one becomes four-to-one . . .

Yourdon tried to enlist reason. In his mind he repeated every battle cry and noble precept his military mentors had taught him. "Syttrelian bastards!" he shouted again, desperate to refire an overwhelming rage.

Sireth had already gathered the wind back into his lungs and was charging into the flurry of men and blades just a few yards away. No thought, no doubt . . .

Yourdon stood still, suddenly, inexplicably frozen, knees shaking, heart pounding, arms aching with the growing weight of his sword and shield. His mind was spinning, thoughts reeling by. *My duty!* Yourdon thought again, as he suddenly recalled the captain's words at camp, his dictum that some one of the scouts, at least, must return with a report. *Someone must! Someone* . . .

"Laren!" he called, hoping to get the commander's attention. When this failed Yourdon began shouting, "One of us must get back to the legion!"

But Laren was too busy or too outnumbered to pay him any mind. Or the man simply hadn't the wits to decide two things at once, Yourdon feared. He would have sounded retreat by now if he had thought of it, if he understood his duty, if he had the chance to sort out—"Laren!"

He watched the commander take a cut to his thigh, then break free. "Laren!" Yourdon called yet again, but Laren seemed disoriented now, defeated. . . .

Yourdon saw movement behind him, just to his left. He spun sword first to face one of the Syttrelian ponies, rune-painted strips of cloth streaming from its neck and mane and tail. More spells had been painted high on its muzzle and across its flanks. Yourdon knew the truth at once: *The True God has chosen me!* The clarity of this sudden revelation dizzied and overwhelmed him.

He lunged and nearly fell, but caught the horse's bridle just as it tried to bolt. In an instant he was on the horse's back, then turning it, heeled it into motion.

He heard someone shouting at him, possibly Laren. He thought to turn and look but somehow he could not bring himself to do it. As if looking back might invite certain doom, as if the Syttrelian magic might somehow draw him back into the hopeless fight and take even this small glory from him, this one chance to fulfill his duty, his destiny.

Pain slammed suddenly into his back as a Syttrelian arrow found him. He reached around and felt at the shaft. The head had entered his ribs low on his left side. He clenched his teeth and pulled, and the arrow came free, along with a bit of flesh. His cuirass had blunted the point and diminished the impact. Still, his hand came away covered with blood, and the pain did not lessen. It hurt to breath, to move—to think, yet his mind would not stop, his body would not wait. He kept riding, fast as the horse would run.

Laren took a scratch from a sword point in the right thigh, then managed to break into the open for an instant. He looked up to find his troop decimated, and Yourdon getting on one of the Syttrel ponies. But instead of charging, the soldier turned the horse and started away. Laren called out, ordering the man to stand and fight. "Bastard, coward!" he shouted, when Yourdon did not so much as turn around. Instead he kept running, riding all the faster.

Laren plunged his hand into the pouch on his belt and grasped the small stone talisman, wetting his lips and uttering the empowering phrase as he did, over and over, hoping it would take. As yet another Syttrelian confronted him he threw the stone, and the man burst instantly into a pillar of orange and yellow fire. The stench of burnt hair and flesh clouded around the barbarian as he screamed curses at one of his gods and dropped to the ground, rolling wildly.

The other barbarians stopped in mid-attack to stare at the burning body, then one of them waved an arm and spoke to the others, words Laren could not grasp. The Syttrelians edged backward, away from Laren and the three men who still stood with him.

"They're waiting to see what else you've got," Sireth said under his breath.

"And when they find I'm no wizard, they'll finish us, and our duty with us," Laren answered.

Sireth nodded grim agreement. "I'd say." Laren glanced briefly about, then gave the order to retreat. The four of them broke into a run, chasing after any horse that stood near. The Syttrel overcame their surprise and started after them, but the scouts were already mounted and riding, straight for the ridge.

The barbarians would follow, Laren was sure of that. But he had a fair head start, and the Syttrel were short of horses, and he simply could not fail his mission. . . .

Either of them, he thought. *We will make it yet, and come demons or Syttrel or the True God himself, I will live to have the head of that traitorous coward Yourdon Lewen.*

They topped the ridge as a bank of clouds hid the moon and stars, casting the land into true darkness. Laren kept pushing, navigating nearly invisible trees, riding toward dawn.

Yourdon felt consciousness slipping away. The bleeding had slowed but not stopped. He had grown weaker and colder as the night wore on. As he made the crest of yet another slow rise and turned full around, he could see the first hint of sunrise beginning to show in the east. With this he felt a glimmer of hope return. He'd kept the general direction in mind, first by the stars, then by guess when clouds had arrived, while letting the pony work its way through the trees. Now the sunrise gave him bearings.

He prodded the pony and it started down the hill through the last of the trees, toward the open grasses just beyond. Soon, he thought, just a little longer, and he would have food and wine and a physician to tend his wound. He would tell Trison of the Syttrel. He would be acknowledged, spoken of as a true warrior. Even his father would hear of this, though it would likely mean much less to him. For Yourdon, it meant that the legion had been the right choice after all, despite everything that had gone wrong—had always somehow eventually gone wrong, or so it seemed.

No, he had truly done well, and no one, not even his father, would be able to deny him that. *If I can just manage to make it back alive . . .*

The pony reached level ground. Yourdon looked up and saw riders coming towards him. Squinting, feeling his blood start to race, he reached for his sword and realized he had lost it somewhere. His dagger was still in its place. Then he recognized the armor, the plumed helms, and his heart soared. They reached him so quickly, he only blinked, it seemed, and they were gathering around him, six riders, one of them a lieutenant. Yourdon displayed a feeble grin, the best he could do, and opened his mouth to speak. The lieutenant reached out and slapped him backhanded hard enough to sweep Yourdon from the pony's bare back and send him tumbling to the ground.

Yourdon drew air into his lungs. The arrow wound snatched half his breath away. "I must speak to Trison," he gasped, unable to raise his head.

"Trison does not talk to traitors," the lieutenant replied, "he executes them. Tie him and bring him along!"

Yourdon felt hands grab hold of him, and lift him off the ground.

"It seems you may live long enough to see home," Trison said, his voice heavy with contempt. Yourdon lay facedown in the back of an open wagon, as he had for most of the past two days, and focused with one eye on his commander. He could hardly move, so tight were his restraints, but this he did not mind: the simple act of breathing still caused him pain enough. The wound would heal, he'd been told, slowly.

"My liege," Yourdon began yet again, straining his dry throat, but before he could say another word Trison gestured, and the soldier standing beside him struck Yourdon across the back of the head with his open hand.

"Save your lies for the court in Thetar," Trison said through his teeth. "You are a most fortunate man, but I would as soon end your good fortune with an axe through your cowardly neck, and realize the consequences later. Your voice only reminds me of your head!" The commander paused for a moment, as if trying to gain control. Yourdon saw him look away briefly, then turn back. He leaned over the edge of the wagon, over Yourdon's ear. "When they split your throat in Thetar, I will be there to see it. Your father's tears will be my bliss."

There would be few tears, Yourdon was sure, but Trison didn't know that. His father's long prominence as a member of the Second Council had apparently spared Yourdon an immediate execution in the field. Trison's advisors had convinced him that this was best, since Dree Lewen was very much in line to be elected to one of the six High Council seats, should any of them become vacant. To make an enemy of such a man would not be entirely wise. But Trison clearly had trouble living with this.

Yourdon decided to take the commander's advice and keep silent. He had already explained what happened, that he was only attempting to do his duty, that at the moment, escape had been his only option, and the legion's as well. But Trison had no ears for this. "You tell a tale you wish us all to believe," the commander had said, "but I think even you do not!" This last was something Yourdon had somehow managed not to consider until that moment, and it had troubled him through the night.

In the three days since being bound and brought to camp Yourdon had not been able to convince anyone at all. The truth was so plain, yet they refused to see it. The battle had been so swift and so fierce, such a confusion of thoughts and events—yet he was certain his logic had been sound, his purpose clear, his courage intact . . .

But it would be his death to speak of such things again in Trison's presence, he was convinced of that now. He could see their dilemma, how in their place, he might think as Laren and Trison did—as everyone seemed to. But that brought little comfort indeed.

He wanted to hate the legion, hate Trison for his callousness, and Laren, who had somehow made it back in time to warn the legion; Laren, who was a hero, of course, in spite of himself. But even now Yourdon found it difficult. Only a few days ago they had been his comrades and mentors, the only people he had ever fit in with, or so he'd believed. It was easier to hate himself, and the Syttrel.

"We are ready," another voice said. Yourdon bent his neck enough to see one of the captains standing beside Trison now. The commander nodded. "Very well. Split the infantry into two columns. I will take the first. Have the second follow two hours behind, in case the Syttrel have yet another ambush in store. No matter what the news, I do not trust them."

The captain acknowledged the orders and swept himself away. Trison followed, apparently more than finished here. Only the soldier guarding the wagons remained. Yourdon didn't know him well, could not recall his name.

"Where are we going?" he asked. The soldier looked at him but made no reply. Yourdon asked again, and the man's expression seemed to cloud. "The capitol," he said, after a time. *Thetar,* Yourdon thought. "When?"

"Now." The soldier edged away, as if mere proximity lent distress.

"But why? Surely the Syttrel have not been routed yet!"

The soldier chuckled briefly, then he shrugged, as though the whole conversation had suddenly ceased to matter to him. "A rider brought word only yesterday. I am not surprised you were not told."

I don't matter, Yourdon reaffirmed. He waited for a time, certain the soldier was enjoying his taunt. Finally the man finished: "The High Council and the Syttrelian kings have made a peace. The war is ended."

The idea came as a shock to Yourdon, more jarring almost than the other events of the past few days. *It cannot be,* he thought, trying to understand. He had been taught to hate Syttrel, trained to fight them, to kill them. To blame them . . .

Were they simply to be forgiven their countless atrocities, their insistence on this bloody war in the first place, forgiven for what had happened to him? For what was about to?

No one in Thetar will shed tears, Yourdon mused, closing his eyes again. The soldier had moved off, out of sight, leaving Yourdon alone to contemplate peace— which seemed far more incredible than war—and the prospect of going home.

❖ A WAY FROM HOME ❖

Daylight stabbed at Yourdon's eyes as he was led out of the dungeons through the door at the top of the stairs. Fresh air began to replace the stench of himself in his nostrils, an odor that had become secondary to other concerns. He took short, shaky steps, struggling with the weakness in his limbs and the limited travel his shackles would allow.

Memories crowded all around him now in this place where the Royal Guard was garrisoned, where he had finally found something of a place for himself as boy servant to those elite soldiers, and later as a soldier himself. Since he had first realized he could never be the kind of man his father was, or wanted him to be, Yourdon had begun to wonder what else might become of him. Never had he found an answer, or anything close to one, until he had come here.

Across the yard in the western keep he had spent many a night listening to tales of glory from battles past, and those to come. There, cleaning armor, weapons, and Syttrelian spoils brought from the field, he noticed that the small magic he possessed had grown stronger, and he took it as a sign. Whether it had been his age or the weapons or a thirst for battle he could not be certain, but he had imagined himself a warrior ever since.

Until just a few weeks ago.

The small courtyard led to a greater one, and finally to the central keep, the great hall of the High Council.

"This way," his guard said, yanking Yourdon by the arm, heading for one of the side entrances. "We have to get you cleaned up first." Yourdon trailed after him, stumbling, coughing as he grew winded and tried to breathe more deeply. He had been in the dungeon since his public trial, some two weeks ago by his count, though the dungeons offered no clue as to day or night.

They entered and he found himself pulled down a long hall, then into a small room. A sunken stone basin waited, half filled with water. Fresh trousers, boots and a plain brown tunic lay on the small wooden table beside the basin. Another soldier waited in the room. He motioned Yourdon toward the basin while the first guard removed his bindings. Yourdon slowly undressed.

"You take too long," the first guard said. "Afraid of a little water?" Both men grinned, then one of them pushed Yourdon forward. He lost his balance and stumbled into the water, scraping his right shin on the basin's stone edge. He instinctively protected his side, where the arrow wound had finally begun to heal.

"I don't think his kind comes clean," the second guard remarked, bitter, tipping his helmet back so the cheek wings framed his eyes. "Stink, nor stain."

"Aye," the other man agreed, holding his nose. "The only way to get rid of that is to bury the source."

Yourdon said nothing as he began to scrub. The soap burned in cuts and sores he had not even known about, but as the burning began to subside he noticed how soothing the water was. His face must have betrayed the fact, for the guards moved in and yanked him out by the arms, then threw him into the chair before the little table. "Dress!" one of them ordered.

As he began a woman entered and removed his old

clothing. She was young but not very attractive, and she barely looked at him.

"Move," one of the men ordered, ushering him out.

The light of day had at least taken the nightmares from his mind's eye. In the dark of his cell, surrounded by straw and clothing soaked in his own excrement, Yourdon had relived the attack a thousand times. He saw the Syttrel charging, his comrades dying, his narrow escape—then the end of everything he had worked so hard to become. He had nearly died trying to bring word back, trying to do his duty, to be a good soldier. In his dreams the Syttrel followed him. They hid in every thicket and copse. Their painted runes and symbols appeared on every tree and rock, patterns that sought to drive him mad.

The guards led him down another corridor, then another until he found himself in a large antechamber somewhere near the meeting hall of the High Council, and the adjoining Second Council assembly hall.

This is all a mistake, he thought, as the guards let go of his arms. "I am no coward," he recited, realizing he had said it out loud only after the fact. The soldier nearest him raised his hand, threatening. "A coward, a traitor, and a liar!" he said.

I am not, Yourdon's mind trailed. The words grew jaded even now, words followed by stoic images, the moment of decision, or indecision . . .

If only they believed, he thought again, though it was getting harder by the day to hope for such.

The antechamber was empty but for a heavy oak table, a few chairs and a cabinet. The head of a zeret hung on the wall: one of the heraldic beasts of the High Council's Lord Priests, it resembled a big cat, pure white but for its thick, curled black ram's horns. Fierce, wild creatures, they existed solely for sport, and commanded the respect of all but the most foolish. Its glass eyes seemed to stare at Yourdon now. Even in death, Yourdon feared he saw something in the beast's expression that he would never know.

The guards were suddenly gone. Then the room's only door opened again and another man entered, dressed in lavish gold embroidered silk robes, and wearing the symbolic cloak of the twenty-member Second Council: Dree Lewen, Yourdon's father.

"You are your mother's son, I fear," Dree said first, following a long, empty silence. "You have now proven this beyond even my expectations."

He looked old, grayer in the beard and temples, and he sounded older still, though perhaps it had always been so, Yourdon thought. Dree had never been the kind of father who spent time, acknowledgment or praise on his son, or on Yourdon's mother. Dree Lewen was a man of great wealth and lands and power, all of which had occupied his life completely for years. Yourdon, consigned to servant care like most of Dree's other holdings, had never become a truly valued asset. In the end this had pleased neither one of them.

"The Syttrel ambushed us," Yourdon said, plunging in; Dree had not attended the public trials. "They are like demons. I did the only thing I could do."

"I have been informed," Dree said, briefly closing his eyes. "I do not care to hear the details of your disgrace yet again."

"I thought you might want to hear my side."

"What difference does it make? All Detimar knows what my son has done. You disgraced my name and yours before the people, the High Council and the True God. You have never risen to your station, and now, I fear, it is forever beyond your grasp." His voice was calm.

Yourdon had seldom heard his father yell; he didn't get that excited, that involved, as a rule.

"I am sure you will survive well enough," Yourdon muttered, feeling the sting now, even though he'd expected this. He had run away several times when he was young—part an act of self-martyrdom, part a reckless effort to find something else, something better—only to be returned home. Not until he joined the legion had he finally made his way clear . . . or so he had believed.

"There is to be a marriage," Dree said, looking away, examining the smooth stone walls. "Assta, daughter of the Jeffes, will wed the son of a Syttrelian king one month from now. This has brought peace, it seems, and much good will is already spreading with the news. Slaves are to be released on both sides, many executions have been stayed. I asked for your life as well, and the High Council has granted it."

The weight of his father's words settled slowly yet heavily upon him. He had prepared himself for death, for the ultimate act of injustice. Now, suddenly, he was being told that this was not to be. Strangely, Yourdon felt little relief.

"A pardon?" he asked.

"Of course not." Dree walked in a small circle, thumbing his chin as if the fate of all Detimar rested on him alone. His father had always valued form over substance. Yourdon had never seen the point.

"The Council feels your life is more than you deserve, and I find I have no argument for them. You may go, but you will have no rights as a citizen of Detimar. This leaves you heir to none of my holdings, of course, but that too cannot be helped—you must know this. You realize, I'm sure, how permanent is the wound your dishonor has caused me." Dree sighed, a truly pained sound, one Yourdon had heard many times. This was followed by a wince, as if a headache had seized the man. "It is all I can bear simply to look upon you now," he finished.

Gently smoothing his robes, Dree let a moment pass in silence. Yourdon nodded.

"No," Dree began again, "it is best that you not return home. Ever. I can give you money, enough gold to last several years, if you spend it wisely. You must use it to make a life for yourself, if you can. That is my wish, and the wish of the Council."

Yourdon heard the words and tried to understand. This was how it had always been, twisted truths, the facts arranged to suit Dree Lewen and no one else while affording him impunity at the same time—Dree Lewen, a mere servant of the fates, responsibility resting in the lap of the gods. Though occasionally, the servant seemed very much the master.

Dree had been pleased when Yourdon had gone to service at the palace, and again when he had been accepted into the legion, seemingly as pleased as Yourdon was, though he had never been quite so transparent as now.

"Was it like this," Yourdon asked, "when you sent my mother away?"

Dree's face darkened. "You have no idea."

"I do."

"She would have run off in any case, as well you know. She was a coward, too!" The rage flared, then it faded as Dree reined himself. They had spoken of this before, but the story was not complete. Yourdon had learned more from servants and gentry and street merchants than he had from his father. His mother had been Shetie, "the wanderers," they were called, a people whose small caravans brought villages and cities alike some of the finest wares, entertainers, enchanters and fortune tellers in all the land.

But their strange, mystical ways were often the source of dark rumors and much distrust. Outside of their bazaars the Shetie were not truly welcome. Some said they did not believe in the True God, that their magic was wicked and the blood of demons was mixed in their veins. Even though few believed this last, mostly offhanded insult, it had been enough to convince Yourdon early on to keep his own small magic a secret.

Yourdon saw things more clearly now. To Dree Lewen, the young Shetie girl had been little more than a fascination, and one he later tired of. He had never spoken well of her. Only in the bazaars had Yourdon heard another truth. There his own slightly darkened complexion and high-boned features, the source of ridicule throughout his youth, had become an asset for the first time, and helped to loosen the tongue of a Shetie woman less trusting of outsiders than they of her. She had told Yourdon of a kind, decent woman who tried to see the good in others— and of a lord's broken promise, something Yourdon could easily imagine.

Yourdon had never truly taken his father to task on the subject. Unfinished business, he thought, perhaps the last of it; *the only remaining bridge between the two of us.* He felt a need now to burn the bridge. He glanced up at the zeret, saw it looking back at him, taunting him, he was sure, from its grave on the wall. It was a curious thing, but with the end of all that had been his life there seemed to come a certain freedom, a feeling that anything was suddenly possible. Even the truth.

"My mother married a coward," Yourdon said, taking a tentative step toward his father. "Were you a man, you would have kept her." *And me,* he added in silence.

Dree's face changed as he focused on Yourdon, a different man, eyes suddenly filled with surprising fury. "She was a witch, a heathen, a whore!" His voice boomed louder with each word. Then the other Dree, the aristocrat, the purveyor of pretense, regained control. "It was witchery that drew me to her so deeply, and witchery that kept me spelled while she carried you. Yet when I finally came to my senses, out of the goodness of my heart, I still did not put her out, not until I was sure she could find a caravan of her own kind."

Yourdon had heard these lies before, had kept his silence. No longer. "You put her out as soon as I was weaned."

"Believe what you will."

"I think you have told these stories long enough that you believe them yourself," he said, recalling his commander's words to him.

"What little mind you had has slipped altogether," Dree said summarily, lacing his fingers together against his abdomen, shaking his head slowly, side to side. "The Shetie blood in you, of course. You have never been a right fellow. The palace physicians threw their hands up years ago. I held out hope. This, I see, was in vain."

Yourdon reached to his side, suddenly filled with the urge to draw his sword and still his father's tongue once and for all. No weapon hung there. Dree observed the action with raised eyebrows. He turned, walked to the door, and pulled it open. The guards again entered the room.

"I owe you nothing, of course," Dree said, gazing at the ceiling in mock fatigue, raising his voice as if to make an announcement. "And you must realize that you can never repay me the embarrassment you have caused, or the life I have won for you, or the money I give you freely. But I am a man of honor, and it is my hope that, by these last actions on your behalf, some small repair might ultimately be made to your character. May the True God show mercy on you."

Dree nodded to the guards, then turned to leave the room. Yourdon glanced up at the zeret, crystal eyes reflecting knowledge Yourdon could only imagine. Still, he thought he saw a glimpse. "I owe you nothing as well, my father," Yourdon said. "It is enough that I remind you so of her."

Dree paused in the doorway. "As you wish," he replied, a slight quiver in his voice. He took another step. Yourdon hadn't finished yet; one more truth remained.

"As to God, he has indeed shown me mercy, I think, for as you say, I am my mother's son."

Dree Lewen left without another word.

Yourdon leaned against the wall and slumped down to the stone walk outside one of the very last respectable inns Thetar had to offer. He had been willing to pay three times the normal rate. "No room for the likes of you!" the innkeeper had said with rare viciousness. "Not for *all* your father's gold!"

"Return here and I will have you arrested!" the innkeeper before this one had said, and the one before that.

Nearly every businessman in the city had been on hand for Yourdon's initial trial, and for the parade Trison had staged when the legion had first returned to the city. They had seen Yourdon chained in the back of an open cart like a captured Syttrelian slave. Dree Lewen was well known in Thetar, indeed throughout most of Detimar, and his son's infamy had made great gossip.

There were places along the river front where lodgings could be had, and in the western sector, though many of these were already well occupied by bugs and thieves and rats. Still, after three weeks sleeping in the city's stables and alleys those accommodations were beginning to seem less unthinkable. He had nowhere else to go.

There had never been more than a few souls in all Thetar he had called friend, and many of those had been tied to his father in some way. Yourdon had made the rounds, and had enough doors slammed in his face. In the city's eastern quarter he had gone to visit with Emiala—a girl who had once spoken to him of love, who had all but promised to wait for him the night before he left with Trison's legion—yet here he had not only been turned away, three men had followed him when he left. In a narrow street they closed the gap, and fell upon him with fists. Yourdon was not as large as any of them, but his looks and his luck had taught him to fight at an early age—the only means to quiet some of the ridicule at lessons, and the best defense when some of the losers waited, two or more, in ambush on his way home. His training in the legion had only improved his skills, and his knowledge of the cost of backing down.

The attackers had managed to knock him down hard enough to keep him there, but two of the three paid a heavy price for their brief victory, and none stayed to see if he would get back up. Most of the bruises and cuts had begun to heal, as had the arrow wound, but his ribs were still tender.

Rubbing his eyes, Yourdon rose, and felt his stomach growl. Food was less a problem. Even in the markets some merchants would not speak to him, but there, luckily, most people were more interested in coins than pretense.

He set off slowly toward the corner, pondering a direction. In his youth he had run through these same tiny, clogged streets. They were his only refuge once he had become the fool's favorite, the one to taunt. Here, he could be anyone. He recalled imagining how good the life of a city goat must be, or those of the many cats that basked in the warm sunlight. *But they will never know anything else,* he reasoned, when he had grown older. *Nor, perhaps, will I,* he thought now.

A fresh wave of depression filled his mind and body. There seemed no plan that offered hope, no chance at all. He could not escape even at night, when his dreams were visited still by dead comrades and painted, jeering Syttrel.

As he reached the corner he heard the sounds of strange music playing, strings and flutes. He looked up to see a great procession of brightly colored wagons approaching on the larger cross street. Hundreds of people had gathered on the street's edges and in the doorways of houses, or they hung precariously out upper floor windows. Headed toward the palace, Yourdon thought, realizing the direction. He stood and waited, as curious as anyone. He recognized the ponies first. Syttrelian.

They passed slowly by, two dozen heavy wagons in all, a handful of carts and at least two hundred Syttrel, many of them warriors, male and female, each of them dressed in much finer trousers, tunics and leather vests than Yourdon had seen in battle. Their dark hair was worn pulled back and tied. Those in the wagons were dressed in colorful silks, soft skins and bright linens, with finely crafted leather belts and bits of delicate lace as ornamentation. Most of the women wore bracelets on their arms and beads about their necks. Syttrel children huddled among them, their eyes big around, their mouths utterly silent. The wagons were filled with wares.

Yourdon stayed a subtle urge to retch as he watched them pass. Only part of what he felt was contempt; much as he tried to deny it, another part of the ache inside him now was something more like . . . *fear.* Even though that made no sense. *I am losing my mind,* he worried, not for the first time.

He found himself staring up at a woman, a Syttrelian warrior, who had reined her pony momentarily. She was looking down at him with a grin on her dark and slender face. Tiny wrinkles sprang from the edges of her deep black eyes and fine mouth giving a clue to her age, which Yourdon guessed was half again his own. She wore a tight, sleeveless white tunic that revealed her trim, muscular arms and torso as well as a long, irregular scar that wound its way up the back of her left upper arm, starting at the elbow. Yourdon was suddenly back in Syttre, facing his enemies. Laughter broke his trance.

One of the city's guards had paused his mount beside the woman's. He looked carefully at Yourdon, then spoke again in her ear. Her expression grew more reflective then, though only for an instant. The guard finally rode on. The woman fished a few Syttrelian coppers from a pouch on her saddle, grinned disparagingly, and tossed them down with a nod before riding on.

Yourdon felt all control slip suddenly from his grasp. He ran, turning up the least crowded street at this corner, then the next, until he found himself in a narrow cobblestone way, gasping, too winded to go on.

The emptiness had grown vast within him, a chasm easily deep enough to swallow a man whole. He shuffled ahead, then lay on the ground near the entrance to a stables, still quietly gasping air into his lungs as tears burned the edges of his eyes, though even now they would not come. Pain shot through his shoulder—a boot moved at the corner of his vision. A soldier, he saw, looking up, four soldiers in all, exiting the stables. They recognized him, of course. Three of the soldiers continued on, grunting disgust. It was Sireth who stayed behind.

"You would do well to leave Thetar for a time, until some of them forget," the other man said, bending, helping Yourdon to his feet. He faced Yourdon in silence for a moment, eyes staring blankly. Finally he said, "I will do what I can for you, if you wish." Yourdon tried to imagine what kind of cruelty this might become, what sort of trick.

"Leave?" Yourdon repeated.

"You have not fared well here," Sireth added, sounding quite genuine. "It may be best. I heard a man talking earlier today, at Dokla's inn, he was hiring mercenaries for a war in the Akreeas. Or you could try the southern province."

Yourdon coughed, then got shakily to his feet. His mind was working much too slowly. He thought he knew why. He had considered such things, of course, yet even now he was reluctant to dwell on them. "I have never lived anywhere else. I have never traveled alone."

Sireth shrugged. "An opportunity, then. Anything might be better than this." He stepped closer and checked the pack on Yourdon's back, then snorted his disapproval. "Nothing much in there. But we can fix that easily enough."

Yourdon watched Sireth pensively. He began to wonder if perhaps in all Detimar he had kept at least one friend. Was it possible that Sireth alone believed him? They had been comrades together for many months, had nearly died together. *Just one would be enough,* Yourdon thought, staring at Sireth. *Just one other.* He wanted to ask as badly as he had ever wanted anything, but he was afraid of getting the wrong answer.

"Come," Sireth said, glancing up and down the way. "Walk with me."

As the two of them went Yourdon noted the faces of those few they passed. They knew, some of them, those who watched as if he were trailing a wagonload of disease-ridden corpses behind him. Yourdon had already imagined meeting one by one with every citizen in the realm, explaining his side, but he could not yet convince anyone he *had* told, so willing were they to believe otherwise. Sometimes, in the face of such doubt, he was unable to keep himself from wondering . . .

Sireth said nothing more until they arrived in a tiny square near one of the city's oldest gates. They paused at a small, open shelter built into the wall. "Rest here for the night," he said. "Think about what you might do elsewhere, where you might live. Thetar is no place for you now."

Perhaps it never was, Yourdon reflected.

Sireth placed one large hand on Yourdon's shoulder. "In the morning I will return."

The question still begged to be asked. Again Yourdon kept silent as Sireth bid him good-bye and disappeared into the fading evening light. Then he did as asked, and rested. He watched the city grow dark, watched torches being lit, the stars coming out, until his eyes finally fell shut.

Soon enough it was morning, and Sireth was shaking him awake.

"Here," the soldier said, handing Yourdon hard breads and dried meats, a full wine skin, fresh clothes, a fresh bed roll. "No matter what you do, you will need these."

Yourdon got to his feet and checked his money pouch, found the remainder of his gold still there. Sireth had taken no payment. The two of them packed everything away.

Yourdon had no choice but to ask now: "Why?"

Sireth gripped Yourdon's arm, and looked him in the eye.

"I was there," he said. "Beside you. I saw what you saw, the hopelessness of the battle, and I know the way you fought. I nearly ran as you did. They say the painted magic the Syttrelian warriors wear can do all that and more to a weaker man. I saw as much that day. But for the grace of the True God, and being born too stupid to know when I am licked, I might have taken that pony instead of you."

So that was it, Yourdon thought, only pity, *and half of that for himself* . . .

"I see the battle each night in my sleep," Sireth added.

"I know," Yourdon quietly replied.

Sireth let go, then glanced about, as if to see whether anyone was watching him. "I wish you good luck," he said.

"And you."

A good and simple man, Yourdon thought, as he watched the other pad back into Thetar's small, choked streets. He saw such men more clearly now, it seemed, all men. The greatest enigma remained himself.

He was no longer a soldier, no longer a citizen of Thetar, no longer the tarnished son of a wealthy second councilman. He was not even supposed to hate the Syttrel anymore, even though it was their trap that had ultimately brought him to this end.

Perhaps the painted curses they wore had worked—worked well enough on him, at least. While all his training and weapons, even his dreams had failed him utterly. *The tools of fools*, Yourdon thought then, remembering for the first time what a shopkeep once said to him. *As am I*, he supposed.

Slowly, Yourdon made his way to the well on the far side of the square. He drank all he could, splashing his face between gulps, then he turned face about. A guard sat at the gate, there to check those who would enter, uninterested in those who wanted to leave. Yourdon avoided the man's eyes as he passed.

He took the southeastern road—his father's vast land holdings lay to the west—shifted his pack higher up on his back, and lifted his face briefly to the summer sun. He felt slightly cold, a chill he could not shake. The heat and light seemed to soothe him. Soon enough, the road branched again. Yourdon stayed to the eastern way, toward the mountains, because he had never been that way before.

❖ LOST IN DRA MAI ❖

He woke at midday. The hot summer sun had heated
even the dark corner where he made his bed to an almost
unbearable temperature. Yourdon dragged himself up from
the floor, from the thin mattress he kept there, then
wandered in the semidarkness until he found the door.
He burst out onto the street, stumbled and nearly fell.

The heat was even greater here; it hit him like a wave
and sent him reeling. His head pounded now, his legs
shook. He wiped his sweat-covered forehead with a damp,
grubby sleeve and tried to swallow, found his mouth
would barely function. "The fool still lives," he muttered,
squinting as he looked about. *But he needs more wine.*
Yourdon pulled at the matted knots in his long hair and
beard—the extent of his grooming—then set off across
the quiet little square in search of some.

Dra Mai had only one proper inn, so Yourdon had
been sure to solicit the good graces of its proprietor. So
close to the Tesshi Mountains, so far from everywhere
else, Detimar's easternmost village offered few of the
amenities of the west. No true market square, no decent
roads, and few local farms or vineyards. But that was
partly why Yourdon had finally come here: almost no
one else did. The village was surrounded by many miles
of dry, rocky hills where only grass would grow. It was a
land of sheep and goats, and copper and tin mines, but
little else.

He was unknown here even to the occasional visitor, at least so far, and there had only been three visitors in the seven—or was it eight?—weeks since Yourdon had arrived. All had been crude, suspicious-looking men, on their way to the hazardous Dais Pass through the Tesshis, bound for Akreea. None of them had returned.

No—Yourdon saw, as he neared the inn and spied two fully loaded pack mules and a riding horse being led by the stable boy, away from the inn—*four* visitors. And the usual curiosity mixed with the usual dread arose in his mind. *What news will the traveler bring?* Then, *Will this one know me, and begin the persecution again?*

Yourdon tried to shrug the notion off, something he was slowly getting better at. He could imagine it no longer mattered so much, what anyone said, what they thought, not even what *he* thought, as long as the wine and ale and his gold did not run out. . . .

He went inside and found an empty table; most of them were. Like all of Dra Mai the room was small, dirty and lacking crowds. The serving girl, the owner's daughter, glanced up from her duties at another table. She frowned, then moved away. Yourdon waited until she returned with bread and butter and a pot of wine.

"You stink worse each day!" the girl moaned, humorless. "It is enough to chase away the flies."

"Forgive me," Yourdon offered, polite.

"It is enough to spoil butter," the girl added more loudly, having fun with it now.

"Perhaps so," Yourdon muttered.

"It is enough to drive demons away!"

Not all of them, Yourdon thought.

She seemed suddenly to tire of the game, perhaps having played it too often. "We can't keep letting you in here, not unless you get yourself cleaned up a bit, you know that," she told him.

"And I will."

"So you say."

"Aye."

Yourdon paid her and she finally hurried off. She was a fair young woman, though her nature undercut her looks, as far as Yourdon was concerned. He had so far managed to hold his tongue, of course, great though the temptation occasionally was. Part of what she said was true, after all, and he worried her father might cut him off if he spoke his mind. He ate bread and butter, drank half the wine, and began to feel better.

As Yourdon sat back he noticed the stranger sitting at another table, nearer the hearth. A rather old fellow, for a fact, and plump for one daring enough to seek the pass. He looked up and their eyes met. There was no hint of recognition. Yourdon felt a slight relief.

Next he thought to introduce himself . . . more or less. He still had an interest in the rest of the world, and in Thetar, even if the city had no need of him. A visitor, particularly one who didn't know Yourdon Lewen, offered the only source of news.

Emptying the pot into his cup, Yourdon rose and approached the fellow's table. As he neared he noticed the man sway a bit, sitting there, eating his stew. He did not look well. Yourdon took a breath, then offered a morning's greeting and, after a pause, his name. The man seemed unimpressed.

"I am Beken," he replied, in a voice too small for his bulk. "What is it you want?"

"To talk. A diversion, nothing more."

Beken looked him over for a long moment. "Seems you've already got one of those." Beken pointed to Yourdon's wine.

"Join me?" Yourdon asked, raising his goblet.

"No, not up to it." Beken seemed to examine Yourdon

still more closely. "But I doubt you mind taking drink alone," he added.

Yourdon nodded. "I prefer it."

"Then leave me be."

Yourdon eyed him back. Beken seemed inclined to threaten, but the fire only smoldered, and did not light. His eyes, up close, looked clouded and bagged, and he carried his head as if it weighed too much for his neck.

"Do you need a physician?" Yourdon finally asked.

"Is there one about?"

Yourdon shrugged. "No."

The other man nodded and pushed his plate away, his cakes only half eaten. "It will pass, in a day or two, I trust. Then I will be on my way."

Beken didn't look hearty enough to make the long Dais Pass mountain journey even if he was well. Yourdon couldn't see the reasoning. He decided just to ask: "Why go at all?"

Beken licked his lips. "Opportunity."

"So I hear, but details never find my ears." Beken cocked his head, still sizing up Yourdon. "You wouldn't be the type to waylay a fellow on his way out of town, now, would you?"

Yourdon laughed, but the laugh quickly turned into a cough that proved difficult to quell. He gasped a deep breath and got it over with. Finally, gulping down the last of his wine, he managed a grin.

"No," Beken said, "I don't suppose you would. Very well, in my case it is simple. There is a war in Akreea and so a need for weapons, yet there are no wars here, where weapons are abundant and relatively cheap. I plan to sell the Akreeans what they need at a fine profit."

"A war," Yourdon repeated, trying to remember through the haze that lately filled the back of his head. "I have heard, of course, but . . . which war?" Then he remembered the man in Thetar hiring mercenaries.

"I have been there already, you know, on two separate journeys, and I find that tends to change. The Dral-Akree empire is an old and hollow shell. They have spread themselves too thinly and for too long. Much of their army is made up of locals forced to service, or disgruntled mercenaries, and many of their governors are beyond their control. Lately, I hear, the Thel-Akree have seized the moment."

Yourdon was falling behind. The Tesshi Mountains had kept Detimar and the many Akreean peoples mostly separate for centuries, an arrangement the High Council seemed to favor to this day, but a basic knowledge of their lands was part of every soldier's training. Akreea was many times the size of Detimar and Syttre combined. It had been a land ruled by many peoples, the names of which Yourdon knew only a few: the Taun-Akree, the Phet-Akree, and the Dral, fierce warriors from the northern forests. The Dral had come south and conquered all Akreea several generations ago. The Thel-Akree were not immediately familiar. Yourdon said so.

"They are the richest traders in all Akreea," Beken said. "Their lands lie along the fertile plains of the south-central coastal regions. Their ports are ripe with goods and markets. Traders come to cities like Mathia from much of the world. The Thel are vital even to the Dral-Akree."

"Yet they have risen up against the Dral?" Yourdon asked.

"Not precisely. As I understand, they sent emissaries to pay off much of the Dral army, then purchased a fair number of mercenaries themselves, men from all over Akreea and lands beyond. The uprising has come quickly, as have successes. I heard one story of a great battle fought not far from KyrPhel, at a place called Napet.

An ambush that took an entire division of Dral by surprise, and resulted in their complete annihilation. Such news travels quickly, and would surely serve to rally other Akreeans. In some places they say there is no resistance at all; in others, fierce fighting continues."

"As does the need for armaments," Yourdon added. Beken grinned in satisfaction, a look Yourdon had an urge to test.

"What if you cross the mountains only to be met by Dral-Akree soldiers, and they take your wares and your life on the spot? What if no one can pay you for your wares, should you live to sell them?"

"There is no gain without risk, my friend. But I think they are too busy to guard quiet mountain passes. And someone is always able to pay. No, the crumbling Dral empire has left room for a few adventuresome traders. I will be one of them. My greatest worry is that the winter winds might fill the pass before I can get across. With luck, there is still time. Without it . . .

"But I have nothing here in any case. No family any more, and no friends in years, I'd guess." Beken leaned over the table, close to Yourdon's ear. "I was a tax collector, you see."

"Ahh, of course," Yourdon said.

"Now," Beken added, "I am someone new!"

Yourdon was nodding, truly sympathetic as he repeated the phrase in his mind: *someone new.*

"You can't know what it's like," Beken required.

"Yes," Yourdon countered, "I can."

"It's a life that has taught me much about people. And the fates, I'd say. Mostly, I learned never to trust in either. But if you must, the fates will usually be fairer than people."

"I think I'd agree with that," Yourdon said.

"Never trust anyone," Beken repeated, as if the point

fully required it. "People are plain unreliable, but with enough planning, the fates might be coerced."

"Most people I've known," Yourdon agreed again, thinking about far too many examples his own life could offer; people, and fates. He wondered if Beken's advice included one's self . . .

"You seem quite articulate to me," Beken said, again considering Yourdon carefully. "What were you, before . . . this? How did you come to fall so low?" He shook his head at Yourdon's appearance, which Yourdon had lost interest in since coming to Dra Mai.

"I used to be—a soldier, among other things," Yourdon replied, again wondering if he had ever been even that. He looked into his empty cup, wished it full.

"I see. And now you are a drunken fool." Beken smiled as he leaned back. His gaze drifted to the inn's thick rafters. "What you lack is a dream, you know," he began. "Mine is to accomplish something worthwhile—just for me! To make something else of myself, my life, what's left of it. I'm still working on how, but it's coming along." He looked at Yourdon again, one eye closed. "I don't suppose such things concern you."

"They used to," Yourdon muttered. *Very much.* His mind repeated the question. *How did I fall so low?* He hadn't realized, hadn't asked that question himself, lately. . . .

"Friend of yours?" the serving girl asked, leaning abruptly into the conversation, speaking to Beken.

"Of course not," Beken assured her.

"Leave him be, or I'll come after you," she told Yourdon, glaring at him. He bowed his head slightly, then got up, collecting his cup, and moved away from the table. He looked back and saw Beken place a few copper coins on the table as he too stood up, then waited a moment, eyes closed, as if gathering himself. A

wheezing cough overcame the old man, one that seemed
to last too long.

Yourdon handed the girl his wine skin and a gold piece,
and she went to fill it. As soon as she returned he left
the inn. Staying would only tempt him to do something
he would regret, and he'd done enough of that for another
man's lifetime, it seemed. Beken stayed still and quietly
watched him go.

The heat of the afternoon seemed to have grown more
severe. Yourdon fell asleep sitting in the shade behind
the inn, and for the first time in recent memory he did
not see Syttrel in his dreams, or anyone he had ever
known. Instead, his mind's ear heard only the words of
a plump old merchant, and he saw something entirely
new.

With the approach of evening Yourdon sat outside
his tiny home and tried to get thoroughly drunk, but
somehow tonight even this, the one thing he had lately
excelled at, seemed a difficult task. Since waking his
mind had been filled with thoughts of Akreea, with
fantasies of what might wait there, beyond the mountains
he had sat idly beside for so many weeks. He had not
seen Beken near the inn again, so he reasoned the old
man must be sleeping in the stables, close to his
merchandise.

As dusk began to gather, Yourdon decided that a quiet
stroll was in order. With luck he would find Beken up
and about, and they could talk a bit more, perhaps. About
Akreea, and doing something new. Yourdon had never
fancied himself a merchant before.

He tossed his nearly empty wine skin aside and made
his way down Dra Mai's only cobbled street until the
stables stood before him. The boy was often there at
night, cleaning, or sleeping. Yourdon looked for him but

saw no one. He finally called out, first to the boy, then to Beken. Somewhere he thought he heard a moan. He called again but only silence came back. After a moment, searching about inside the stables, Yourdon found Beken laid out on the straw in the stall beside his mules and bundles of merchandise.

At first Yourdon thought him dead, waylaid perhaps, but then he noticed breathing. He gently shook the old man, which seemed to rouse him enough to get him leaned up against one of the stable's heavy support beams.

A fit of coughing took him then, which set Yourdon off on a small coughing fit of his own. When the clamor subsided the two men looked sidelong at each other. This time, genuine grins were exchanged.

"What brings you here?" Beken asked.

"Something you said to me."

Beken closed his eyes, then opened them again, waiting. "About your life. You said you had nothing here. That you had no one. Neither do I."

"Then why are you in Dra Mai?"

"Because . . ." Yourdon hesitated. "I cannot go home." Beken seemed to nod. "Where were you before? What part of Detimar is home?"

Yourdon pushed matted hair off his forehead and reached instinctively for his wine skin. He suddenly recalled his last visit with his father, reaching for his sword in the same manner. "I never had a home, it seems," he said. "But I have always wanted one."

"Ahh, well, when you have no past, you are left with only the future," Beken said, and again he closed his eyes.

Yourdon leaned closer. "I want to go with you. My mother was Shetie; I may have some merchant blood in me. Perhaps I was meant for that life all along! And I speak some Syttrel, which they say is something like the Akreean tongues.

"You are of ill health, and not so fit no matter what. You'll need help if you intend to reach Akreea. Any reasonably small share of the profits will do, so long as you do not cheat me. Lend me a sword and I will help you keep your neck as well, should trouble find us."

"A mercenary then."

"Perhaps . . ."

"You've thought about this awhile, haven't you?"

Yourdon nodded.

"But what good are you to anyone?" Beken asked, sitting up a bit straighter, coughing only once this time. "Look at yourself. I'll be carrying you before we've gone a day's journey."

"I'll do well enough, rest assured."

Beken chuckled at this last.

"It's true," Yourdon said, stern.

"Show me how you hold a sword, then," Beken told him, indicating one of his bundles. Yourdon went on his knees and worked the rawhide straps loose, then pulled some of the heavy cloth back. Inside he found only swords, many different shapes and styles and sizes, some of them in very good condition. He hadn't seen weapons like these since his days with the Royal Guard. As Beken watched he took one of the swords by the hilt and pulled it free.

A straight, narrow blade, simple craftsmanship. But he noted that the metal had a fine tension, as he tried the tip on the hard dirt floor, and the balance was acceptable. He raised the blade and guarded, then struck out at the air. Confidence swelled inside him as he realized how clearly his mind recalled the skills, even though his body was not quite up to expectations.

Another skill made itself known as well, subtly, just at the edges of his mind. His small magical talent seemed tied to objects the way lightning was tied to storms, and to some more than others. Only once since leaving Thetar had Yourdon seen the visions clearly, during his third week when a priest had come to Dra Mai in search of boys willing to follow him back. The priest had dropped his scepter and Yourdon had picked it up. With little effort he saw images of the great temple in Thetar, and a lavish ceremony in progress. A lamb was being readied for sacrifice. The priest had taken the scepter back, and the scene had vanished completely.

Now as he held the sword, as his blood ran hotter, he saw images again. A very young Syttrel warrior, apparently learning how to fight. No one had died by this weapon, Yourdon decided, for he would have seen that. He noticed Beken staring at him. Quickly, deftly, he swung the sword over his head, then brought it to rest. Beken was grinning, nodding approval.

Yourdon dug in the bundle for the leather belt and sheath that fit the sword. He found what he needed quickly enough, and tied it about his waist.

"So you are a robber after all," Beken said.

"I'm no thief. I'll give this back if you want, or keep it if I'm going with you, as partial payment."

"Any more terms?" Beken asked, frowning too much.

"No, but I'm sure to think of some."

Beken winked. "As am I."

"Then you agree in principle?"

"Do you intend to bathe?"

Yourdon grinned in satisfaction, then realized it was getting nearly too dark to be seen. "Yes," he said.

"I may need a peddler as much as a warrior, my friend. Do you truly think you would make a good merchant?"

"I intend to find out."

"No experience, then."

"None," Yourdon admitted.

"There is much I must teach you. A new language,

for one. There are many Akreean tongues, too many, but these days nearly everyone speaks enough Dral-Akree to get by on. So must you. And some Akreeans are more pleasant than others. Most do not trust each other much, and our kind not at all. Many with good reason. The Ril-Akree might run and hide, the Taun might confront us, the Quin-Akree, on the other hand, are unpredictable extremists who would kill you one day or try to convert you to their faith the next; if you are fortunate, they'll offer you the choice."

"I have never heard of the Quin."

Beken rolled his eyes. "You will. And more."

"I am a fast learner," Yourdon offered, quite truthfully. He had learned reading and writing with ease, done well enough with artistic endeavors, especially mosaics, and even excelled at boyhood games from hoops to wrestling. He'd learned the art of war, quickly, too, even though he seemed to lack a warrior's heart. In fact, he'd been good at everything he'd ever tried to do, though apparently, that had not been good enough.

"Splendid," Beken replied, "for I am likely a poor teacher." He closed his eyes again and breathed several slow, deliberate breaths. "You wouldn't have a little of your wine for myself, would you?" he asked.

"No," Yourdon answered. "I'll fetch some more." He got Beken onto some extra straw and into his bedroll before he left. The illness did not seem too severe, but in a man of Beken's age, any illness was cause for concern.

He found the inn still open and paid for a bath along with the wine. When he finished, he found he couldn't bear to dress in what he'd worn. He sent a boy to the houses of the village, instructing him to buy trousers and a fresh tunic from anyone who could supply them, and a new pair of boots from the cobbler; he realized he hadn't worn boots in at least a month. While he waited he decided to see about trimming his beard and hair, just a bit.

The boy did well enough. Finally dressed and quite pleased with himself, Yourdon strapped on the sword belt again and went out into the street.

Someone new, he thought, which was possibly what he had always been trying to be. . . .

The wine sloshed in the skin as he walked. Strangely, Yourdon had little interest in it. He had far too much on his mind.

❖ DOWN . . . AND OUT ❖

Yourdon lay awake, curled tightly in the warmth of his bedroll, listening to the wolves. From the snarling he knew they were close, just above among the rocks, and they were having a fine night. The sky was clear and bright with stars, the air was cold and still, and the mountain goat had been an easy kill, from the brief bleating Yourdon had heard around dusk.

"They will leave us alone," Beken had assured him. Yourdon expected this was true. Still, he kept his attention focused on the sounds in the night around him. His head ached from lack of wine. Tomorrow would be better, he thought, and in another four or five days, by his best reckoning, they would be half way through the long and narrow Dais pass. Or they would be dead. . . .

Already he understood why this pass had never been used for an invasion, either by Detimar or the Akreeans. In many places the rock walls were barely far enough apart to accommodate one loaded mule at a time, and certainly never a wagon. A small garrison had stood at the entrance in Detimar, a handful of men and mounts, ready to take word of any true threat to the regional garrison in Ektay; thereafter the invaders could be killed one by one as they emerged. Yourdon assumed there were similar arrangements on the Akreean side.

But legend too kept many away. It was said that much of the pass had been created by the True God himself, that he shook the earth until it split apart, and would close it again one day. The question was, when . . . ?

Not tonight, Yourdon thought, watching the stars creep past the highest cliffs. One wolf called to others. On a distant hill he heard a lone wolf reply.

Yourdon shivered and closed his eyes, and wished for sleep's brief comfort. He had neglected to bring warm clothing, but Beken had insisted he purchase a heavy wool cloak, sure to be needed. "The mountain nights can get quite cool," he had explained, "and if we are fortunate, that is all they will get."

For a man who didn't like to trust in people or fates, Yourdon thought, Beken was doing a good deal of both: trusting bad weather would wait for them to cross the mountains, and trusting that Yourdon wouldn't prove himself a great mistake. Yourdon wasn't entirely sure that either was a good bet.

For now Yourdon wore only the breeches, long sleeve tunic and leather boots he'd bought, saving the cloak for when, and if, it was truly needed, though ahead of them he had seen snow on the tallest mountain peaks. For now he had more immediate worries.

His head was not the only part of him that ached. Since embarking he had grown fatigued. *Not just the lack of wine,* he speculated. *I must have Beken's sickness.* . . . The darkness seemed to close in around him with that thought, and his shaking seemed to grow a little worse. This night, though, when sleep came, it was long and deep.

The next day the pass wound its way upward and seemed to grow more treacherous. Both men walked, leading the animals, making slow progress. The night that followed was the coldest yet, but Yourdon had begun to notice that the ache in his head was almost gone, and muscles at first sore from lack of use had begun to strengthen. Yourdon decided he was not so sick after all, but he'd begun to worry that Beken was getting worse, that he might not survive the journey.

"I am fine," Beken insisted, plodding upward through yet another fair but darkened day.

"Rain?" Yourdon asked, observing the sky.

"I hope so," Beken said, adding nothing more. With the ninth—or was it the tenth—morning in the pass frost covered the ground, and did not melt until mid-day. The clouds never broke. Yourdon took to wrapping himself in the wool cloak now, even putting the hood up over his head as the gusty afternoon grew bitter. The temperature dropped further as day's end approached, and light snow began to fall.

"I haven't seen snow in years," Yourdon said; the climate in Detimar seldom allowed it. The silent beauty of it all helped him forget the numbness in his hands and especially his feet.

"You'll wish you hadn't seen it yet, I think," Beken answered, sounding as grim as he looked. He had taken to wearing his heavy wool coat and hat. Yourdon suspected his feet were cold, too, as he had begun to falter.

"The animals lack their winter coats," Yourdon said, casting about. Beken said nothing. The footing was growing treacherous for man and beast. They had already decided it would be foolish to take turns riding the horse. The animal would only fall and break its legs, along with its rider's, on the uneven, icy trail.

"I know," Beken said, and that was that. They slept most of the night beneath a rock ledge, out of the wind, but by morning they were hemmed in by small snow drifts, and the cold was almost unbearable.

"We may not make it," Beken said, the first time he had actually spoken so. "I thought there would be time enough. I was not so far off, I don't think. A fluke, this weather."

"I know," Yourdon answered, attempting a smile. "And I thought you knew what you were about."

"You see? You trusted me, and I trusted in the fates, now both of us are disappointed."

"Then I trust you are wrong," Yourdon quipped, though even his mind seemed to be a little numb this day.

They set out again, but the old man seemed weaker than he had been, his eyes only half open, his gait erratic. Yourdon put Beken's arm over his own shoulder, and let him lean. Beken looked up at Yourdon as though he'd just discovered the daylight, but then the eyes settled back on the trail ahead, and the lids sagged once more.

By afternoon Beken seemed to be getting a second wind, but now Yourdon found himself faltering, losing the fight. Before the day was ended it was Beken who put Yourdon's arm over his shoulders, helping him go just a little further.

"Thank you," Yourdon said, as they huddled in a stand of pines for the night, shaking, wrapped in their bed rolls.

"You could have left me," Beken said in answer.

Yourdon shook his head. "I could not."

"I am right about the fates, but with you, I may have been too harsh," Beken told him.

"You are a lot tougher than you look, old man."

"I don't feel it."

"But I feel worse."

Beken coughed, just twice. "No one could feel worse."

"Nearly as bad, then."

Beken grinned feebly. "Perhaps."

They tried to get some sleep. Yourdon's feet hurt and kept him awake most of the night, a night he thought might be his last. *At least,* he thought, *I will not die alone. . . .*

The snow had stopped falling by dawn, but the winds had begun to gust, blowing the dry, fluffy drifts around, numbing the skin of Yourdon's exposed cheeks, nose and fingers. They held on to each other, arm in arm, heads bent against the icy breezes as they tried to go on.

"Next year," Beken said, after a long morning's silence, "winter will come later, I am sure."

"That is always the way," Yourdon replied, though he could barely speak now, his jaw was so cold, his body so weak. But he would not quit on Beken, and Beken, sick as he was, still apparently refused to quit on him.

Here the pass had grown wide and easy. The snow-covered rock underfoot had begun to slope downward—an encouraging sign, though at the moment it kept the footing quite treacherous. Then Beken stumbled and fell, and could not get up.

"You're too weak," Yourdon said, gathering the old man up into a sitting position, listening to him wheeze. "You will ride. I'll walk the horse. We have to try it."

"We are almost there," Beken said, waving, indicating a narrow valley the pass vanished into just ahead.

"No," Yourdon said. "Another week at least, I think."

"No, almost there," Beken repeated weakly. "The valley. I can make it."

He couldn't. Yourdon got him standing, then finally up into the saddle. Steadying himself, he pulled the horse forward. It would be dark again soon, he thought. He needed to find shelter from the wind, a place to rest, or to die.

As they moved on, the trail turned sharply left, then right, around a high rock wall. Here the ground pitched sharply downward. Yourdon led slowly, but with its next step the horse slipped, then stumbled, legs scurrying to find purchase on the steep snowy ground. Beken tumbled off his horse just as the animal seemed to right itself. Yourdon reacted without thinking—and tried to break Beken's fall.

As the two of them landed Yourdon's right leg twisted underneath him and he heard, more than felt, something give. *Somehow,* he thought, grinning inwardly, finally thankful for the cold, *I am sure that hurt.* . . .

"Roll over!" he called into Beken's ear, but the merchant only groaned in response. Yourdon heaved and managed to push Beken off of him. He didn't think the leg was broken, but he decided not to try using it. Even through the numbness brought by the cold he could feel the pain growing now. Instead he let the leg pull straight, gritting his teeth against the dull fire in it, as he used his arms to lug Beken and himself back up against the rough rock wall.

Then he closed his eyes for just a moment, and dreamed. When he opened them again he noticed the snow had stopped. The sun was shining in his eyes from between two high mountain peaks, warming him, already melting the snows enough to soak his clothing. He looked downslope into a small, snow washed mountain valley and saw two figures dressed in great, heavy coats striding toward him. He tried to move his right leg, but a wave of pain rose from the ankle, and for a moment, consciousness slipped away.

They carried him on a stretcher, a man and a boy. The mules and the horse trailed behind, with Beken riding again. Yourdon envied them their neatly sewn, heavy wool coats and caps. The man wore a full beard on his starkly featured face, the boy seemed poised to begin one. They were not quite as tall as most men he had known, and their skin was slightly darker than his own. Their hair was darker still and full of waves—not unlike Syttrel, he thought, or Shetie, though their faces were rounded, not quite so angular as Syttrel.

The horse and both mules were still loaded with their bundles and packs. His own travel sack was strung on the horse, though even from here he could see it had been opened.

All around Yourdon saw the scrub- and grass-covered slopes of the Tesshi foothills. Small amounts of snow melted in the shadows, and behind him, he saw a glimpse of snow-covered peaks. He spotted a small herd of sheep perched on a distant hillock, grazing. Yourdon glanced again at his right leg. The ankle was wrapped tightly and set with a splint. No blood still, and less pain than he might have expected. He hoped it was not broken.

They made their way further down the hillside, past more pines and another pasture, until a nearly level clearing emerged from the woods. A squat cottage stood here, appearing as the stretcher was turned—and it occurred to Yourdon that he'd seen no Dral-Akree garrison. Unless they had passed through one higher up; unless these men carrying him *were* Dral. Though they did not look the part. And as they drew nearer, the small cottage—just one room and made of daub and wattle—seemed no garrison by any means.

The house was not very big. Smoke curled from a hole in its roof. As Yourdon's eyes followed the smoke upward he noticed the tips of a few of the forest's leaves had turned the color of autumn. He had heard of this happening early, high in the mountains.

Beken spoke to the others then, all of them rattling on in a language Yourdon could not follow—though he thought he knew some of the words, or bits of them, as they hurtled by his ears. Yourdon cleared his throat and sound came out of it, a rasp, but passable. In his own language he greeted them.

Beken corrected him: "Na tsa," he said, in the others' language.

"Na tsa," Yourdon said. It was nearly the same as a Syttrelian greeting, Notsa, which he knew well. *Perhaps it is true,* he thought, recalling the ancient legends that claimed the Syttrel had come to the western realms from Akreea, thousands of years before, even before Detimar had existed. It was heresy to say so according to the laws of the High Council, but the stories never completely vanished, and Yourdon had always wondered. *Barbarians, then,* he thought, an easy assessment.

Yourdon lay back down as they neared the cabin's door. "At least we are still alive," he said out loud, in his native Detimarian.

The boy-man grinned at Yourdon. "And fortunate!"

"Yes, we are," Yourdon said, tipping his head up. He examined the boy more closely, then looked to Beken, who had dismounted and was busy steadying himself. "How do you know my language?" he asked, mostly of the boy.

"Beken!" the boy replied. "And others. They come, they stay. Until they leave, I learn. I am Besh," the boy continued, choosing his words. "This is father, Lossef." The older man stood silent, solemn, just watching.

Yourdon introduced himself correctly, certain it didn't matter. The boy seemed eager. "Yourdon. You get up?"

He didn't want to try that. His body still ached, but the toes and fingers all seemed to work. As he tried to use the splinted foot, though, he felt a rush of pain sweep up through the limb, pain that sustained itself even after he relaxed the leg completely. Slowly, much of the fire went out.

Besh nodded. "Not broken. Bad twist."

"Yes," Yourdon groaned. "Bad."

Besh smiled. "After a while, maybe better." Yourdon stared cheerlessly at the leg in question. "A while . . ."

"You are merchant too?" the boy asked.

"Yes," Yourdon said, glancing at Beken. "That I am." To which Beken gently chuckled.

"What you have to sell?" the boy asked.

Yourdon looked to Beken, who nodded, then both of them explained what was in the bundles on the mules. Besh stepped up and began to open one of the ties. Lossef wandered over and crowded over the boy's shoulder as he looked inside.

"I need to know about the Thel-Akree led coup," Beken said, taking over, though his voice was weak. "And the fall of the Dral-Akree empire. I bring weapons to sell to your champions!"

Yourdon was not certain who such persons might be, nor whether they might be the highest bidders, but he was inclined to trust Beken's wisdom. The reaction of the two Akreeans, though, was quite unexpected. As Besh finished his translations, he and Lossef looked at each other, and they began to laugh.

Lossef spoke Akreean. Beken listened, and grew pale. Yourdon looked up. "What is it?"

"They are gone," the other replied.

"Who is gone?"

"The Dral-Akree. It seems the wars are over. All the local Akreeans have their lands back."

"Just . . . over?" Yourdon pressed. "So quickly?"

Beken and the boy spoke to Lossef, and they appeared to come to some decision.

"Come, inside," Besh said. "We eat, talk. There is much to tell."

"Can I have my sack?" Yourdon asked, pointing to it. Besh nodded, though he looked slightly troubled as he retrieved it. Yourdon looked inside. His gold was all gone, but none of the bread, dates, dried fish or hard tack was missing. That did not surprise him.

"What is wrong?" Besh asked, sounding meek. For his part Beken seemed strangely silent.

"It appears I was robbed, in the pass."

"Bandits, I think," Besh offered. "We found sack, in snow."

"I had a bit of gold," Yourdon said.

Besh nodded. "Taun raid our lands sometimes."

"Taun-Akree?" Yourdon asked.

"The neighbors," Beken said. He described the Taun as more warlike than the Phet. Though they had never sought to conquer their western neighbors, having no desire to live in more mountainous lands, their limited raids were a constant worry. It had been this way for as long as their storytellers remembered.

"You need no gold now," the boy insisted, genuine. "We help you."

"The important thing is, these two will let us stay here, till spring if we need to," Beken said, though the look in his eyes reflected his guilt. The Akreeans had been paid, it seemed, though no one appeared inclined to admit it.

"And what will they want in return?" Yourdon inquired.

"Nothing, I think," Beken replied, averting his eyes.

"These two wouldn't be the types who would waylay a fellow on his way through the mountains, would they?" Yourdon asked a bit coldly. Beken shook his head knowingly.

"I see," Yourdon grumbled.

"Ahh, good!" Beken said, and with that they helped Yourdon inside, then into a chair beside the hut's small table. He put his teeth together again and let the leg trail. "Wars seem to be ending everywhere I go these days," he said in a moment, as bread, smoked meat and mead were given to him. He hovered over the mead, hesitating, but the dull throbbing in his leg urged him on.

"Good for others," Besh said.

"Perhaps," Yourdon mumbled. He drank, then ate as Beken joined him. Lossef stood by once more, just watching.

"You were going to enlighten us?" Beken asked the boy, when his appetite began to lag.

"Yes," Besh said, using the Detimarian word, then he began all in Akreean. It took a while, with Beken translating and Yourdon asking too many questions, but finally they both began to understand. Besh and Lossef were Phet-Akree, one of the great western peoples— or they had been, before the Dral crushed their rather small army and beheaded Nata-Phen, their king, long before Lossef was born. Since then they had suffered numerous Dral-Akree governors. They learned to speak the Dral dialect, to obey endless Dral laws, to pay Dral taxes and homage, and they suffered the loss of many young Phet men and women who were taken as soldiers or laborers to serve the empire.

But no more. The Dral were gone, back to the northern forests where they had come from. The Thel-Akree, from the lands along the southern seas, had ultimately driven them out.

"This was the coup I spoke about in Dra Mai," Beken explained to Yourdon. "Led by the Thel-Akreeans. I had no idea how well such a thing might work. Already the war is over. The very war we have come here to supply."

"Then we are too late."

Beken nodded.

"Do the Thel rule your people now?" Yourdon asked.

"No," Besh grinned. He chattered at Beken in Dral. Yourdon kept picking out words.

"They are merchants, not warriors," Beken translated. "The Thel bought many Dral mercenaries, and the disloyalty of the Akreean peoples came freely enough.

When the Thel's hired soldiers came to fight, many Dral went away. Those that stayed, died. Afterward, the Thel stopped paying, so their mercenaries dispersed. But the Dral left many weapons behind. Many were taken from the dead. Those who want, have. But most peoples are tired of war, for now."

"All but Quin-Akree," Besh said, deferring to Beken. "Of course," Beken answered him.

"But who are the Quin?" Yourdon asked, shaking his head. "You mentioned them before."

"A religious nation of sorts, led by their holy men. They are widely spread, but they can be dangerous."

"Thel ask Quin for help," Besh added.

"They may be sorry they did that," Beken replied. Yourdon sat blinking. "Why?"

"I'll explain later," Beken told him. "It is . . . complicated."

"I can imagine," Yourdon said. Then, running one hand through his matted hair, he said, "What do we do now?"

"Stay until that leg is mended."

Lossef leaned over toward Beken and looked in the old man's eyes, then said something in Dral. Or it was pure Phet, Yourdon couldn't tell.

"He thinks you do not look well," Beken explained. "I think he is right."

"He thinks *I* don't look well?" Yourdon gasped, staring at Beken, then making a face. "What does he say of you?"

Beken made the same face back.

"Stay winter," the boy said, sounding pleased and looking at Yourdon and Beken as if they were unexpected gifts, a treat of some kind.

"We may have to," Beken said.

"I don't want to," Yourdon told him. He was anxious to get on with his new life, with this new land. To have struggled so fiercely and come so far, only to be kept like a babe in a cradle for— "For how long?" he asked.

"By the time that leg is better, and I am rested enough to travel, the heaviest snows will be well upon us. The way down from these hills will be impossible."

The idea of spending the next four—or would it be six?—months in a tiny hut was, well . . . was the only way he could think of to get what he had paid for, since these people had his gold, like as not. He could try to console himself with that thought for now. . . .

"Don't look so stricken," Beken said, waving a hand to snap Yourdon out of his musings. "You need to learn a great deal if you are to manage in this land. Perhaps I will teach you. And perhaps by spring, the True God willing, there will be yet another war!"

"Something to hope for, I suppose," Yourdon said, raising his cup as Beken did, drinking deeply. He ate what remained of his meal, and the boy took the bowl.

"Come the time, we will go to Dlet," Beken told him, after a time. "But it's a journey, halfway across Akreea. Still, it is the greatest free city in all the land, aside from Mathia. There, I'm sure, we will yet sell our wares. Or learn where to sell them. They have many physicians, healers and conjurers there as well, from many lands. Perhaps . . . one of them can make me well."

Yourdon hadn't thought of that. He wondered if this was the true reason Beken had sought to return to Akreea, and so late in the year. If asked, Beken would say no. Yourdon was not so sure of that.

"Dlet," he repeated.

"Yes, Dlet," Besh said eagerly.

"Have you ever been to this city?" Yourdon asked. Besh seemed to grow smaller. "No," he said.

"Almost no one from his village has," Beken explained.

So that was it, Yourdon thought. The boy wanted to tag along in the spring to see Dlet. Yourdon understood, in a way. How a boy might grow tired of work, might not be satisfied with his life, his home, his friends, perhaps much more. How he might want to start over, because he couldn't just give up . . .

Yourdon wasn't sure he liked the idea, but saying no would be easier when the time came, if that's what needed to be done. They had time to work that out, if nothing else. . . .

After a little more mead and a good deal of help Yourdon moved to one of the two beds built along the wall, each one covered with soft sheepskins.

"They'll go to their village in a day or so," Beken told him. "We can't go there. Many Phet don't like outsiders. Some would call us demons, or worse. The boy's father, I gather, is neutral on the subject. The boy outright likes us, but he is a minority. I learned that the hard way, on another trip. They'll be around, one or the other of them, when they can."

Besh said something in Akreean. Beken nodded. "The prophets say, 'No man is less for what he does for another,' " he repeated for the boy.

"Bless the prophets," Yourdon said. *Bunch of infidels*, Yourdon's teaching insisted, but the thought made him smile. The Akreeans set about tending to their own stomachs. Yourdon closed his eyes and thought about spring, about Beken and doctors and a city filled with wonders, and his pockets filled with gold.

❖ TAKING TURNS ❖

When he could walk well enough to venture out of the tiny hut, into the snowdrifts and cold winds that always awaited him, Yourdon found that the temperature bothered his toes and fingers. Throughout the winter he watched the tips turn white and start to tingle as soon as he went outside for any length of time. Besh seemed to understand the condition well enough, and managed to help out a great deal. He visited the cottage every few days with food. Often he stayed, sometimes for a day or two. Neither of them asked much of Beken, who could not seem to shake the rattle in his chest or the cough that went with it.

But deprived of any other activity, he proved an excellent teacher, especially with Besh's help. Most days they talked, mostly in Dral, the language the Dral-Akree had imposed everywhere they had conquered. Yourdon learned that Beken hailed from Southern Detimar, the Wenn Lake region, and that he had never taken a wife. Yourdon admitted he hadn't, either. Then Beken and Besh told Yourdon what they knew of Akreean geography.

In return, Yourdon told the boy about Detimar and Thetar, and the war with the Syttrel—though certain details had to be left out. This helped to pass the time, but in some ways those memories made the passing uneasy. He wanted to get on with his life, whatever that meant.

Yourdon's patience, never much, was all but used up by the day he'd been able to get around again. Long before the snow had melted he was desperate to leave.

He managed to keep many of his wits, going easy on the mead and ale, but the price was awareness. And with that awareness, the desire to fill his life with something seemed to grow even more intense. It began to drive him crazy, yet through it all Yourdon could not help but notice how calm Beken always seemed to be, how sure, even when he was not. "Does nothing bother you?" Yourdon asked him one night, when his illness seemed to be winning out.

"Nothing that matters," Beken replied, leaving Yourdon quite silent for a time.

"Don't you worry we won't get to Dlet in time to do you any good?" he asked after that.

"Yes," Beken said, nothing more.

But on one particular morning, the sun warming a countryside ripe with buds about to burst and streams frantic with high rushing waters from the melting snow, he was sure the time had finally come.

He let Beken sleep as he went about loading the mules and the horse, all of whom had fared the winter well enough. Finished with that he went back to wait for Besh and his father. They were due to visit again, and he wanted to speak with them before he left. When he reentered the cottage he found Beken looking pale as usual, perhaps a bit worse. He knelt and gripped the old man's arms. "Are you ready?" he asked.

"Of course, though I am not so sure that will be enough."

"I am sure," Yourdon said, even though he wasn't.

"Only the True God knows what is to become of us this day," the merchant cautioned, his voice weak.

"He has forsaken me, I'm sure," Yourdon offered, "which should leave him more time for you."

This made Beken smile.

"Come on, old man. Let's get you up."

When they stepped outside only Besh was there. The animals waited. Besh nodded understandingly.

"You need more food, for your journey," Besh said.

"We have plenty," Yourdon insisted. They'd managed to save hard bread, dried meats and fruits and more from the generous supplies Besh had been bringing. "I only hope you can find some of my gold in the pass above, now that the snow is gone." He glanced knowingly at Beken, who pretended ignorance, then quickly added, "But truly, even that is not payment enough for all you have done."

Besh became the focus of a pregnant silence. "Your thanks is enough," he said.

Then the boy was looking at Yourdon with a strange expression on his face, one of longing, perhaps, or reverence. This was the time Yourdon had anticipated, the question he always knew Besh would ask. He had known the answer once, but he had come to like the boy more with each passing day. Besh was kind, bright, diligent—for a barbarian. Yourdon wanted to say no, but he could not.

"Perhaps we will take you with us, to Dlet," he said, smiling. But Besh grew suddenly somber. He looked up toward the high peaks of the Tesshis, then to the trees downhill.

"Thank you, but I will stay here," Besh said at last.

Yourdon looked at him with surprise.

"I have my home, family, friends, a girl promised me," the boy went on. "What has Dlet? I could not live as you."

Some of us, Yourdon thought, do not have a choice.

"I could have told you he'd say that," Beken said.

"I hope to live differently," Yourdon said. "New lands

await beyond these, a new life. I can't go back to Thetar . . . or Dra Mai. I won't."

Beken smiled.

Besh smiled knowingly; he didn't know, not really, but that was just as well. With much ceremony Yourdon got Beken on the horse, and they finally headed down the mountain.

They avoided Besh's village, then another Phet village they encountered the second day. Two days after that they were on the plains, traveling a narrow, packed dirt road, bound for Dlet.

These lands were much like the eastern regions of Syttre, covered in grasses and thin forests, the days breezy and warm, the nights sweet and cool. The journey put Yourdon in a good mood and kept him there. Beken seemed less enthused, but he seemed to be faring well enough, so far as Yourdon could tell. Beken, of course, would not say.

For two weeks they rode due east, then turned northeast as Besh had said, the safer route. The terrain grew more varied, rolling gently here only to dive low there, as streams began to appear, all running south, and the road deteriorated but remained passable. A well-traveled mostly stone road would be found if they turned slightly south again, but that way led through the main villages of the Taun-Akree.

Unlike the Phet, who had chosen surrender once the hopelessness of the invasion became evident, the Taun had fought the invaders to tragedy. Many of their warriors had been killed along with all their kings, then their kings' sons. Now, with the Dral gone, there were few clear heirs to the many Taun thrones. Fighting among factions had begun in earnest, and the wise traveler did well to avoid them.

"I would like you to tell me more about Dlet," Yourdon

said, as he led the horse and mules slowly along a winding stretch of road, letting Beken ride. "I wish to know every detail."

"I have none. I've never actually been there."

Yourdon looked at him with surprise.

"No," Beken explained. "I have been near to it, and heard much about it, but on both past visits the Thel lands to the south seemed more worthwhile. But they need no weapons there, I am certain, and Dlet has been growing in leaps, from what I've heard. That is where my optimism takes us."

"Perhaps it is time for optimism," Yourdon smiled. "After all, what else could go wrong?"

Even as Yourdon voiced the thought the answer came boiling out of the woods, a dark-clad warrior riding bareback on a gangly looking mare, lofting an angry fist over his head and howling like all the demons of the godless abyss were after him.

He looked young, no older than Yourdon, though his outgrown beard and hair and sacklike headdress made it hard to tell. It wasn't until he was only a few dozen paces away that Yourdon decided he wasn't running from anything, but was surely attacking. The rider drew a small sword from somewhere beneath his tattered robes. Yourdon tried to gather his wits. He got the animals turned and headed out of harm's way, slapping and hollering, but by the time he got his own sword out and his dander up, the other man was upon him. Yourdon ducked right, and heard the blade swoosh past his ear.

The rider drew reins, turned and started back again. Yourdon was ready this time. He stood poised, then jumped one step aside just as the attacker reached him, then ducked again. This time, though, as he came up he managed to swing his own sword. The rider arched as the edge of the blade cut into his back, but already Yourdon knew the blow had been shallow.

The rider stayed on his mount. Yourdon watched as he came to a halt and looked back, eyes hidden in shadow with the sun high behind him. This close Yourdon couldn't help but notice how ragtag the man appeared, how tarnished his narrow little sword was. He would have expected to see a battle axe or mace in the rider's hand as he charged, but the sword seemed his only weapon.

Abruptly the other man and his mare turned about in a small circle, then he rode straightaway, uphill, back into the forest. Yourdon watched him work his way up through the trees until he topped the low ridge and vanished altogether.

"No fight in that one," Yourdon said out loud, somewhat relieved. He tried not to notice how badly he was shaking.

"You wounded him," Beken said, nudging the horse out from the trees he had ridden it into. "I think."

"I did, just not badly enough."

Beken pondered the ridge. "I agree."

Yourdon began to reflect on the battle as he calmed himself. "Other than that, what did you think of my performance?" he asked wryly. "Fairly impressive, I thought."

"Indeed it was."

"Not *just* a merchant, perhaps," Yourdon added, grinning.

"Definitely not. You could have taken on a small army, I am sure," Beken said, though his chuckle made him sound less convincing.

"I could indeed," Yourdon insisted. "The Taun, I think, are fortunate they did not send one!"

Beken rolled his eyes. He turned the horse and mules east again, readying them. "I wonder where that fellow came from?" he said. "And where he has gone?"

Yourdon glanced back, as if something ominous might be hiding there. Nothing was. Still . . .

The ridge curved around nearer the road just ahead. Yourdon decided one of them ought to make for it in order to get a look at the shallow valley that lay beyond, to the south. Beken offered to get down.

Riding slow, Yourdon urged the horse gently up through the trees until the valley beyond the ridge was revealed to him. Another road wound its way through the woods below, at one point arriving at a little village—Taun-Akree, surely, and certainly where the warrior had gone. Then he saw the dust rising along the lower road, followed by faint shouts that just now came to his ears on the gentle breeze.

Easily a dozen riders in all, Yourdon guessed, or more. He watched them turn off the road and head up through the trees, toward Beken and the mules. He turned the horse and hurried back down onto the little road below.

"What is it?" Beken asked, as Yourdon rode up in earnest.

"A small army!" Yourdon disclosed. "We have to get going."

"I thought as much," Beken said, frowning as he nodded. "Skilled as you are, it makes no sense to fight unknown numbers if we can elude them," he added.

"None," Yourdon agreed, as he helped Beken back up onto the horse, then climbed up behind him. "But I don't think we'll have a choice. They are not tired wayfarers. Fresh men and mounts will have the advantage."

"I know," Beken said. "I know." He set off as fast as he could without letting go of the mules. This amounted to a stiff trot, which was not nearly fast enough. Already, when the breeze turned their way, Yourdon could hear the Taun getting closer. Beken could hear them too.

"I hope you are better than even you think you are," he said, glancing over his shoulder.

"You should never have allowed us to get into this situation," Yourdon said. "You are supposed to know better."

"I knew it was risky," Beken insisted. "What do you want of me? I did the best I could."

Yourdon thought about that; he'd done the same thing as often as he could remember, and it had turned out much the same way. "Very well," he said, panting, running alongside. "Did you have any idea what you might do if something like this happened?"

Beken grew pale. "I figured you'd think of something."

Great, Yourdon moaned, then he did the only thing he could think of.

The trail rose to accommodate a knoll; Yourdon and Beken waited at its crest, looking back. He could just make out the Taun-Akree all gathered in a clump where he had set one of the mules free, still bearing its weapons bundles. There was apparently a small local shortage of quality arms, at least. With luck the Taun would be content with their prize and return to their village to divvy it up.

"No need to wait around until we find out," Beken said. "You can't trust anybody," Yourdon quipped.

Beken bowed his head.

They turned around and started east again. The Taun realms did not reach beyond the Quyas River, which Yourdon reckoned was less than a day's ride ahead of them now. Following that into the lowlands they would find the Tyiet River, a great waterway that flowed through Dlet itself.

They traveled well into the night before they found the Quyas and made their way carefully across. As they lay trying to sleep, Yourdon heard Beken coughing again, sounding worse than ever. *Soon, my friend*, he thought, *we will find you the help you need.*

"Yourdon Lewen," Beken said into the quiet darkness, the only time Yourdon recalled hearing the man use his full name.

"Yes?" he said, staring up at clouds crossing the moon.

"I would not have survived, if I had come without you."

"Nor I, had I not gone with you," Yourdon answered in kind. Silence surrounded them again. Beken said nothing else.

Even on the river's far banks Yourdon slept poorly. He dreamed of the Taun finding them there, taking what was left of their booty, slitting their throats before he could raise his sword. He woke with the sun, feeling quite well, and wasted no time in getting up. It was several minutes before he realized that Beken was dead.

For a long time Yourdon knelt beside the grave. Everything had changed, then changed again, and nothing that was left seemed to make any sense. He said another prayer for Beken, then said one for himself. The prospect of living through tomorrow without poor old Beken, without his forgiving, knowing companion, his friend, was . . .

It just wasn't fair, to either of them.

"Look what you've done to me," Yourdon said, squinting hard to keep the tears from coming. Yourdon hadn't taken the man's advice, he'd trusted Beken to stay alive. But Beken hadn't taken it either.

"You fell short of your dreams," he said over the stones and earth that covered Beken now. "But I am glad you came this far." He stood, and took a breath. "Perhaps you have shown me how to search for mine." He walked back to where the animals waited. The trappings of a merchant.

He broke camp and started out again, toward the markets of Dlet. Beken, Yourdon was sure, would have wanted it this way.

The days passed uncounted then, though slowly Yourdon began to emerge from the trance Beken's death had put him in, slowly he began to notice the mornings, the evenings, the possibilities. The future was not entirely bleak. None of the old rules, the Detimarian rules, applied, and none of the limitations. He might even become a great land baron one day, or a commander in the army of . . . of some deserving nation. Or simply the soldier he had trained to be. Or a prosperous merchant, perhaps? An idea which still served him well enough. Cheered, he counted the passing of another four days, then suddenly his journey ended.

The city emerged from the fields and forests just as Yourdon had begun to wonder whether he had gotten lost, so rural were these lands. Beken would have been impressed, he thought, nodding to himself. Though it was at least as large, Dlet was nothing like Thetar, nor was it like any place Yourdon had ever imagined.

Walls had surrounded parts of the city untold years ago, though they lay mostly in ruins now. Cobblestone roads led through them into streets that seemed to follow no rhyme or reason as they grew wide or narrow, ended at corners, turned into alleys or emptied into squares. The buildings were a jumble as well, and followed no single pattern of design for more than a street or two. Yourdon decided the city had been built a section at a time by peoples and architects who seemed to have only culture or proximity, not Dlet, in common.

As he made his way deeper, wandering wherever the path seemed clearest, he passed simple houses and shops that could have been in any city; but there were others that appeared most unusual, their exterior wooden frames painted in pictures and symbols reminiscent of Syttrelian runes, or scrubbed so white they were hard to look at in the sunlight.

He saw far more wood and mud-brick construction than in any Detimarian city, and far less stone. In some places ornate homes and temples boasted fat towers with domed roofs, while many nearby rooftops were of wood and pitch. He found still another place crammed with ramshackle huts, built crooked where they rose more than one floor, and topped only with thatch.

A row of these last had recently seen fire, and were now the site of new unimproved construction. But what impressed Yourdon the most were the people. More varied than the city itself, he saw every sort of person and dress, or so it seemed. Most were Akreeans, slightly short, their faces many shades of darker skin, their eyes too round to be any other race—though among them Yourdon had begun to notice subtle differences, the way their hair was worn or covered, the colorful, even flamboyant ways many of them trimmed their clothing.

Armed men were everywhere. Many he saw did not seem to be Akreean at all, they were so tall and light skinned, while others bore smooth features and nearly golden flesh. Most wore shoes of brightly dyed leathers, a fashion no doubt, and an endless array of embroidered blouses, tunics and cloaks over both hose and pants.

He watched children playing, men and women tending stalls in the many bazaars and market squares, merchants and tradesmen bringing goods in carts. The stalls were bustling with customers. Busy folk, most of them—though some others, clearly, were not. Men adrift as he had been, not long ago, in the streets of Dra Mai.

For his part Yourdon seemed to pass largely unnoticed. . . .

More mercenaries, Yourdon told himself, now observing two men wearing closely cropped beards, white, heavy linen blouses drawn at the waist and red cloth caps that were sewn to an odd, floppy point over the forehead. Short gray mantles covered their shoulders, each bearing a small pattern of circles embroidered in white along the garment's edges. They carried massive swords at their sides and found little trouble ganging way through the crowded street. Several people bowed briefly as the two men passed. Yourdon simply stepped aside.

Abruptly another pair appeared, identical to the first, though these two were trailed by a taller, slender man in a dark, pleated, gold-embroidered mantle. His raven dark beard had begun to gray, as had his hair, which disappeared beneath an elaborate, layered woolen hat. He glanced at Yourdon as he passed, though his eyes did not focus. Again Yourdon made sure to let them pass.

A girl no more than twelve stood near him, holding a large earthen pot in her arms. The tantalizing smell of freshly mashed garlic and olive oil rose up all around her.

"Who were they?" Yourdon asked her, choosing the Dral words carefully. The girl seemed uneasy, eager to move on.

She tipped her head and made a sour face, as if his own scent had suddenly overcome that of the pot.

"Please," Yourdon urged.

"Quin *emari.* Holy men," she said. "Except him," she added, already backing away, pointing to the last one. The odd one.

"Ahh, of course," he answered. "And who is he?" Yourdon tried.

"That one is Rem Ana, The One!" she chirped, as if

it was something everyone knew, then she turned away, watching the man with the gold mantle vanish down the street.

Which one? Yourdon wondered silently. Then he realized the girl had gone. He decided it didn't matter. He moved on, breathing deeply now as everywhere he began to detect the smell of food cooking, a varied aroma rich with scents both familiar and strange. The tempting smells made his mouth water, and helped him to overlook the well-remembered city stench of sewage that rose from the gutters lining most of the ways.

At length, in a narrow market square, he found a small shop that seemed to sell many hard goods, including every sort of arms. It was the fourth such shop he had seen so far. But unlike the others, this one was open. Once more, though, despite trying not to, he wished that Beken was there. He shook the notion off, and opened the door. Inside there sat a well-fed, middle-aged man dressed in brown robes and surrounded by merchandise, tools, barrels, chairs, and of course, weapons and armor of many sorts. Swords hung on the walls and lay in a little pile on one of the tables, leather and metal breast plates, shields and various helmets rested elsewhere; spears, battle axes, glaives, morningstars and more rested in two of the shop's corners. Everything was quite used.

The proprietor was working at his bench on a pair of worn and battered greaves, tapping away at a bend with a small hammer. The shopkeep looked up, revealing graying beard and hair, black eyes, pouchy cheeks. "Yes?" he said, in perfect Dral. He could have been Dral, for all Yourdon knew.

"I have merchandise to sell."

"Not buying." The man's voice was flat, his manner gruff. Yourdon felt an urge to growl back at him, thought better of it.

"Please," he managed, "look at what I have. Then say what you will."

The other man was silent for a time, tapping metal. Then he gestured, a wave of his hand. Yourdon took this to mean "go ahead." He went back outside and returned lugging one of the two remaining bundles. When he pulled the coverings apart the old man rose and came near. Spears and axes, mostly, mixed with a few daggers, a mace or two. "What else?" the shopkeep asked, after looking things over.

Yourdon hauled in the second bundle containing only swords—he had been saving the best for last.

The shopkeep seemed more impressed this time. He picked up a few of the blades, looked them over, then set them down and disappeared into another room. In a moment he returned with a few gold coins. A pittance, truly, Yourdon thought, by any standards.

"They are worth much more," Yourdon said firmly.

The shopkeep shook his head. "I say no."

"Yes," Yourdon countered.

"Get out," the man replied, outflanking Yourdon completely.

"There are other shops," Yourdon said, seeing no loss in it. The shopkeep only shrugged, sat down at his bench, and went back to his tapping.

Yourdon felt the loss of yet another small battle rest like a stone in his stomach. "Very well," he agreed. The shopkeep rose again, fished in his robes and gave Yourdon the coins. Yourdon found himself looking into the man's dark eyes. As he watched, the other's expression seemed to soften.

"Not Akreean," he said. "What are you?"

Yourdon grew cautious. "Does it matter?"

"No. Just arrived?"

Yourdon nodded. "I have come a long way."

The other man nodded back. "What plans do you make?" Yourdon just stared at him.

"Of course," the shopkeep said, closing his eyes briefly, a sudden lack of interest. "I know you well enough, I suppose."

Yourdon tensed again, then realized the man must be speaking generally. He searched his mind for the Dral word meaning "perhaps" but couldn't find it.

"You'll need work, no doubt," the merchant said, just a mumble that seemed to spill out, a little splash. "There is a need for men of arms, even for you, I think. This city is like the others, like all the many realms. No place is safe, you see. Go to the Golden Axe, before your gold is gone."

He thinks me a mercenary and a thief, Yourdon realized. "I am a merchant," he corrected.

The shopkeep looked at Yourdon more carefully. He chuckled briefly, then shook his head. "As you wish," he said. "All the same, you'll find the Axe at the finger. Ask someone."

Before Yourdon could say more the shopkeep went to the bundles and began spreading things out. Yourdon stood silently for a time, watching him, sensing that the conversation had ended but reluctant to accept the fact.

What the shopkeeper was suggesting bore at least some merit. He needed an alternate plan; every soldier, or former soldier, knew that. "But there are many mercenaries here already," Yourdon said.

"Thus the need for more," the old man replied. He pawed the second bundle apart, chose a massive two-handled sword and carried it to the back of the shop, where he slipped into another room.

The mule could be sold next, and the horse after that if need be, Yourdon thought, but in truth he knew more about weaving or smithing than he knew about being a successful merchant, which was to say almost nothing.

Briefly he thought to collect a bundle and take it and the gold with him, since the old man had seen fit to scurry off and leave him here. What was a merchant without goods, after all? But he thought better of it. He didn't know his way past the corner, but those who might come after him surely would. And the market was . . . soft.

He put the gold into his leather shoulder pouch and turned to go. A dagger lay on the floor beside one of the scattered bundles. He bent to examine it, and saw that it was like the one he'd gotten from the old man in another armory he had visited, back in Detimar, the one he had lost when he was arrested and taken in irons to Thetar. He picked the dagger up with two fingers and examined the sharply tapered blade, the handle set with one amber stone on each side. Of course, there was one way to be certain. He wrapped his hand around the handle, and mumbled the short phrase that helped to concentrate the magic.

And again he saw the young soldier, a man much like himself, flashing the dagger at a slender, hooded figure, and he knew. How Beken had come by the piece Yourdon could only guess. . . .

The shopkeep was robbing him to begin with, he thought with a measure of guile, so a bit of extra payment was well in order. He hesitated only a moment, then, glancing briefly about, Yourdon put the dagger into his belt and hurried out into the street. As he gathered his horse and mule and moved steadily off he kept watch over his shoulder, worrying the shopkeep would be right there. He kept going. No one followed.

By day's end he'd settled on an inn, reasonably priced, small but adequate rooms and not too badly infested. On the same street he found a small stable. In just a few weeks his money would be gone, but for tonight the feeling was a good one. He lay awake for a time thinking about the days to come and what he might make of them—what they might make of him. He couldn't imagine either way. On the one hand he was limited only by his imagination; on the other, his imagination had never been the problem. When sleep would not come, Yourdon imagined a bit of ale might help.

After a visit to the inn's common room, sampling their rather bland brew, he decided to go in search of better. The nearby streets offered several choices. As he walked, one in particular stood out. A girl, tall and young and effectively dressed in a long, smartly cinched black tunic waited in the doorway, the look of temptation in her eyes, the promise of comfort. Yourdon had not been with a woman in . . . a while.

She beckoned to him, and Yourdon found himself overcome by a collaboration of thirsts and hungers.

I can at least try the ale, he decided.

She was not Akreean. Yourdon had never seen her like, skin nearly the color of the amber in his dagger, eyes and hair black and shining. Her jaw was wide enough to be almost unattractive to his eyes, but when she grinned at him her strangeness turned to charm.

"You remind me of someone I once knew," she said, in badly rendered Dral. She stared at him as they moved inside, and he began to feel uneasy.

"Who?" Yourdon asked, after a silence.

"He was from Detimar."

"A friend?" Yourdon asked. She smiled.

"Ahh," Yourdon nodded. "I am Detimarian myself."

"Yes," the girl replied. She took his hand and led him to a table. The room was like many others, not very large and not crowded, and dark, no windows and too few candles. Only half a dozen patrons were present, all

Akreeans, Yourdon guessed, as he nodded to the three
men seated in the corner, just behind his table. They
did not respond.

"You come to Dlet, why?" she asked.

"I'm a merchant," Yourdon answered, getting used
to it.

"Much gold, yes?"

Yourdon didn't like the sound of that. "Not much,"
he said, shifting in his chair. "Not now."

The girl leaned closer. Her smile had vanished. "I buy
once, from Detimarian merchant. We all did. No more."
The three men from the corner had gotten up, and were
moving closer. "Detimarians come to Akreea to find
victim," she went on, leaning back again. "We pay once,
for southern salt. We got barrels near full of sand."

Yourdon wasn't surprised; most Detimarians who came
here would consider these people little better than the
Syttrel—heathens, barbarians. Especially visitors of more
recent times, who were likely ignoble sorts to begin with.
Some might have considered it their duty to take any
advantage they could. Of course, *they* were not here to
pay the consequences. Yourdon took a breath, cleared
his throat, then pretended a confident frown.

She watched him, waiting for his reply.

"I have cheated no one," he said.

"You are Detimarian," the girl replied. "You cheat.
Now, *you* pay." She waved a hand at the men. "Nobody
like your kind," one of the three said over Yourdon's
shoulder.

Beken, Yourdon thought, *I did not learn enough from
you.*

The girl got up. Yourdon stood just as the men reached
for him, but all three sets of hands found purchase. They
held him fast while the girl pulled out a long narrow
dagger and stabbed out with it. Yourdon flinched

instinctively—but felt nothing. When he opened his eyes he saw she'd cut the leather strap on his pouch.

His coins rolled out onto the table. Suddenly all three men at once let go of him and grabbed for the coins, following the girl. Yourdon stumbled, then turned and bolted out into the street.

In a way it was ridiculous: he had committed no crime here, yet he was being held accountable for one, at least in part. *You are closer to home than you think,* Yourdon told himself, as he ran fast as he could down the street at first, then more slowly as he grew fatigued. He ended up nowhere near the inn he was staying at, lost, utterly, in the seemingly endless maze that was Dlet.

He felt the dagger still pressing at his waist, and he thought about what might have been, had he stayed and fought them for his gold. But even now he counted the odds. Impossible. *Four to one . . .*

He watched every person he saw, careful of the look in their eyes, the notice they gave him as he entered a plain square dominated by a graceful stone building. A temple, perhaps, Yourdon thought, observing the many spires on its rounded roof. He had seen others like it in Dlet. Outside on the steps leading into its main entrance there stood four swordsmen, each wearing the odd hats and short embroidered mantles of the Quin-Akree. He'd seen them several times now throughout the city, but still he knew nothing about them.

The men eyed him steadily as he crossed the square. Yourdon stayed clear of them. The little girl had called them *emari,* holy men. Still, he thought he could trust no one in the city, perhaps in most of Akreea, though he hoped things were not so dire.

The adjoining street became an alley, then another street, though this one bordered on water, a "finger" of the Tyiet River that pointed deep into this part of the city. Small boats of several types floated along fortified wooden banks. Inns, shops and a large boatworks stood among the buildings that lined the banks on either side, some of them brightly lit inside by candles and oil lamps. Yourdon started up the near way, his mind still reeling as he considered his circumstances again—as he remembered the armorer's words, and his own. He peered across the narrow waters to the jumble of tattered buildings there: *A finger* . . .

He didn't see the other man cross his path until they'd walked full into each other.

He was very tall, unusually trim and neat in a fine linen coat and a carefully sewn leather cap. His long beardless face was cast in a sneer. He pushed Yourdon backward and started shouting at him. Most of the words made no sense.

"Pardon," Yourdon said in Dral, when the Akreean paused for breath between rantings.

"What are you doing?" the man demanded, now in Dral.

Yourdon bowed his head. "Walking."

"Walk elsewhere!"

Yourdon glanced to his right, the direction this fellow must have come from. They stood before an inn. Yourdon couldn't decipher the sign. "I look for the Golden Axe," he said. "I am sorry if—"

"The Axe?" the other boomed. He looked sidelong at Yourdon, then bunched his face into a scowl and extended one hand, indicating the inn's massive oak door. "There!" he scolded, adding, "Cursed outlanders."

Yourdon nodded. The other man stood watching, waiting. Yourdon attempted a grin and went inside.

What he saw was not what he expected.

❖ WHO GOES THERE ❖

Unlike the place he had just left, this common room was large, crowded, and well-lit by metal oil lamps set on every table. As many sorts of people as he had counted on the street could be counted here, though he saw no Quin at all. He tensed as a figure moved slowly towards him. A woman, he saw, as she passed close by—Syttrelian, he was almost certain. She paused to look at him. Her subtle grin, her dark eyes, seemed almost familiar to him. He watched her vanish out through the door into the street and tried to dismiss the idea. Syttrelian women tended to look much alike. Still . . .

He guessed the room's other patrons numbered fifty or so. Most appeared well-armed and formidable. One stood out from the rest, an Akreean sitting in the far corner, his back to the walls; an older man, showing his years but still built stout enough. He had plenty of gray mixed with the black in his long, bushy beard and ample curled black hair. He wore a neatly cut white silk tunic, open at the neck and chest, and a flat woolen cap dyed purple, which even in this land was rare—such colors were usually worn solely by royalty, since the dyes were made only from murex shells. His eyes were dark and narrow, his hands thick and kept folded in front of him on the table. Yourdon drew nearer, searching for a place to sit.

Several others were crowded around the corner table,

89

scurrilous sorts, he wagered. As the angle changed Yourdon noticed a very large dagger, sheathed in finely carved leather, lying on the table beside the big man's hands.

Yourdon felt himself becoming the center of attention. His skin prickled with apprehension as he sat. Since leaving the Tesshi foothills he had grown ever more convinced that whenever something didn't look good, it probably wasn't. He had already trusted a woman tonight, and paid the price; he trusted no one now, finally, truly. A small, very dark skinned man wearing a dark linen coat and a dagger nearly as large as those carried by the Syttrel suddenly appeared in front of Yourdon. He bent forward, one eye drawn nearly shut, ale heavy on his breath. "What brings you in here?" he asked. The voice was low, the words spoken in a peculiar Akreean dialect, not Dral exactly, though Yourdon got the gist. "A pot of wine?" he offered, holding quite still.

The man didn't blink. "Plenty of that anywhere."

Yourdon glanced past him to the corner, found all eyes looking back. He decided to do exactly as the armorer had suggested. "I need work," he stated. "And soon."

The man before him stood back, glanced over his shoulder, then began to chuckle. The bigger man at the corner table grinned, deepening the many lines on his face and exposing a fine set of teeth.

"What kind?" the little man came back.

Yourdon wasn't sure of his answer, so he turned it back around. "You know," he said.

The other man nodded, gripped the hilt of his formidable blade and made an agreeing hum somewhere deep in his throat, then he pointed a thumb over his shoulder. "You just go see him," he told Yourdon. "Banlae Tfa." With that he stepped aside, and waited. Yourdon got the idea he wasn't expected to dawdle. He got up and walked straight to the corner table, then took the only empty chair, the one directly across from Banlae. He tried to ignore the other two men at the table, one left, one right, two of the largest and best dressed swordsmen Yourdon had seen in Dlet.

"You wanted wine," Banlae said, in perfect Dral.

Yourdon nodded, and a tankard was placed in front of him. He sipped, grateful.

"Who sends you to me?" Banlae asked, hands still folded. The man gave nothing away, so steady was his gaze, but Yourdon was sure a certain amount of respect would be wise.

And honesty. He told Banlae about the shopkeeper.

"You know something of weaponry, then?" Banlae asked.

"I do."

"And how to fight?" Banlae made his lips grin.

"Yes."

"Where did you learn?"

"I was a soldier in the Detimarian legion."

"Detimar, you say? You are a long way from home."

Yourdon only nodded.

"You do not look like most Detimarians. Part Syttrel, perhaps?"

"No!" Yourdon refuted, shaking his head. He lowered his voice. "Part Shetie."

"Ahh. I know so little about them, but Detimarians make excellent mercenaries, most of them."

"They are the best-trained soldiers in the—"

"Yes, yes of course," Banlae interrupted, barely waving one hand. He glanced knowingly at the other men present.

"I have seen battle," Yourdon responded, feeling inadequate somehow. "I fought the Syttrel."

"And lived to tell about it, clearly," Banlae chuckled.

Everyone chuckled.

"They are a savage people."

"Of course they are," Banlae replied. "They make good warriors, too, you know." He took a breath, let his attention wander before adding, "Though they are often a bit . . . *shrewd*, for my tastes, I think."

"Then again," Banlae said loudly, "we Dral are not so fond of most anybody else!" Another round of laughter followed. Yourdon sipped his wine.

"This one is a waste," the man seated at Yourdon's right said in Dral. He scowled. "No spine. He is no warrior."

"Not true," Yourdon said quickly.

"It is," the other man replied, slow. "No spine at all." He stared Yourdon in the face, waiting.

Not true, Yourdon insisted, fighting an urge to doubt himself, feeling a welcome swell of ire for his efforts; his mind grew sharp as his muscles tensed. He didn't like where this was going, but there was no way out, and he had not forgotten many hard won lessons in the cost of backing down, lessons learned in the legion. Banlae was watching both of them, utterly placid. Yourdon could hear men behind him, moving, closing in. He knew he had only one option here, either way.

Just don't think about it, he told himself. "I've spine enough for the likes of you!" he responded, sliding his chair backward, rising and wrapping his hand around the hilt of his sword. The other man rose as well.

"You stand no chance here," the other said.

"No? I am surprised a man with such poor judgment has lived so long," Yourdon taunted, quoting from many attentively witnessed barracks brawls. *A warrior*, Yourdon thought, *not a merchant!*

Swords rang out as they cleared their sheaths. Banlae raised his hands—and both men paused to look at him.

"Enough!" he said, flashing a mildly pernicious grin. "I believe him. What point would there be to a lie? Or to die for a lie?" He looked straight at Yourdon. "Answer the question."

Yourdon swallowed. "None."

"Have you a horse?"

"And a mule," Yourdon replied.

"Ah!" Banlae grinned fully now. "Wonderful."

"Why?" Yourdon asked, watching the other swordsman sit first, following after.

"I find countless men who can use a sword, but horses and asses are hard to come by." Banlae seemed to pause for a moment of reflection, then he leaned forward slightly, candor removing his grin. "Listen carefully, friend. Many are in need of men willing to put a reasonable price on their lives, and their talents with a sword. They come to me, most of them. I will put you on the list. Like a wheel, it goes round, until your name comes up. If you cross me, you will be killed. If you do well your name is put on the wheel again, but that is always up to me. The pay is several times what you'll get anywhere else in Dlet, I assure you."

"You need only live to collect it," said another man's voice from behind, quite nearby. Yourdon did not turn around. He gave his name, and Banlae produced a parchment, then began to write. Yourdon relaxed a bit, partly the wine, partly the ease with which he and Banlae seemed to be proceeding. He was beginning to feel almost good inside, and he felt no desire whatever to claim he was a merchant.

"Very well," he agreed.

"Good. Now, get out," Banlae said, face briefly stolid, then the grin was back. "Return tomorrow night. I may have something."

Yourdon nodded. He found no one in his way as he

94   *Mark A. Garland*

rose and turned to go. As he left the inn behind a sense
of achievement lingered within him, tainted by the
directions in which events seemed to be pushing him,
but pure enough for now. He found his way back with
little trouble.

He slept well, rose late, and spent the remainder of
the next day walking the streets of Dlet, investigating
alternatives. He asked wherever he went, but there was
no work to be had, at least not today. And most of the
work, he admitted, he would not endure in any case: a
stable hand, a dock hand, a laborer in one of the mill
districts, a servant to one of Dlet's wealthier families.
No tradesmen needed him, nor merchants of any sort.
There were simply too many people in Dlet, and too
many of them were Akreean. . . .

By the end of the day Yourdon had toured nearly half
the city, learned to speak a handful of new Dral words,
and worn himself out. With the evening his melancholy
threatened to return. He ate from his remaining
provisions, then made his way to the Golden Axe, half
expecting nothing, or at best a job no man in all Dlet
would want. He had all but convinced himself that he
had built his hopes on clouds by the time he arrived.
But as it turned out, Banlae Tfa had come through.

"Understand, you are offered this opportunity as much
for your mule as for yourself, but a swordsman is needed,"
Banlae said, almost cavalierly. "There may be other duties
as well. The man you are replacing was both servant
and protector. But you are new to me, and poor, so you
will do whatever is required."

There were fewer people in the room this evening.
Two men lingered at a nearby table, carefully looking
on, but no one was seated at the corner table except
Banlae. His massive dagger still rested beside his hand.

The man had been a mercenary since before the True God had created the world, Yourdon was certain of it. He was also, Yourdon presumed, one of the few Dral remaining in Dlet.

"I am listening," Yourdon replied.

"A talent in itself," Banlae said. "But first I will listen. If you have concerns, say of them now. I will not hear so well later on." Banlae leaned closer. The table creaked under his weight. "I promise you that."

"No concerns," Yourdon stated, clarifying it for both of them. "What am I to do?"

Banlae sat back. "A mother and her daughter, both Kyr-Akreeans, have arrived here in Dlet. They are traveling to their home in KyrPhel, in the easternmost realm. The journey will take several weeks, the way might be treacherous, but they are willing to pay well enough for a reliable escort."

Yourdon found himself pleasantly surprised, and pleased—protecting women was certainly a noble task—but he had already begun to wonder just how precious these women might be, and what, exactly, Banlae meant by "treacherous"?

"How many escorts in all?" he asked.

Banlae's eyes grew large. "You will need assistance?" Yourdon had expected something like this. "I rely on your judgment," he said, bowing his head slightly. When he looked up he saw this had had the desired effect. To suggest that Banlae did not know what he was about would be a mistake, and one Yourdon did not intend to make.

"They have a paladin with them, as I understand it," Banlae said, smiling just a bit. "Another man was along as well, but he and their pack mule both took ill after drinking questionable waters in the southern foothills. These people have no great enemies, at least none that

I know of. The Quin are a possible concern, their disputes with the Kyr are long-standing, but your main concern will be bandits and the like. This should not trouble one so able as you."

Banlae was watching Yourdon closely, his large head tipped to one side. Again, there was only one answer. "I am most confident," Yourdon affirmed.

"You will be provided with everything you need for the journey there and back. Your wages will be waiting here with me when you return."

That was apparently something else one did not question Banlae about, though the urge to do so was strong. Yourdon could only agree—or walk away. He nodded once.

"Come ready to leave in the morning," Banlae instructed him. He provided Yourdon with a map, neatly drawn on a small scroll; it showed nearly all of Akreea, from the Tesshis to the hilly country that nearly surrounded KyrPhel, then the mountains and the great inland desert beyond. Yourdon tucked the map away. He sensed it was time to leave.

"Good night," Banlae said, cordial enough, as Yourdon turned away. No one else said anything at all.

The rest of the night seemed to take forever to pass, and sleep came only briefly. In part Yourdon was surprised at how excited he seemed to be, but the more he lay awake, thinking, the more reflective he became. He had suffered many doubts and setbacks, in Thetar, in the legion, in Dra Mai, and in this new land—even while sitting at a table across from Banlae Tfa—but some part of him had never been willing to give in. Not completely, not permanently . . .

Still, he needed something to pin his hopes on, and it seemed Banlae had provided that. It was a good feeling after so many bad ones, even if there was no way of telling whether morning would bring about its end.

When the sun finally rose Yourdon hurried from the inn. He was waiting at the stables when the master arrived. He packed his horse and mule with what little clothing he owned and headed across town. He knew he was too early, but he intended to wait at the Axe until Banlae, or someone, arrived. As it turned out, they were waiting there for him.

Both the mother and her very young daughter wore travel robes and veils, but they were obviously quite beautiful. And clearly Akreean, though their features seemed finer somehow than most of the women Yourdon had met here. They wore subtle colors on their faces that made their eyes look big and deep, and beneath their veils he caught a glimpse of rich black hair, braided in the back and laced with golden thread. Their manner spoke of grace, even as they simply stood and talked with the three men who waited with them.

Two of the men Yourdon recognized as Banlae's. The other, certainly, was not. He was an older fellow, built thin but hard, graying hair pulled back in a short ponytail, eyes narrowed among deep wrinkles that seemed to know the expression well. He wore a neat brown tunic, tawny boots and pants, but the clothes were cut at all the corners in a rounded style, and the tunic was edged in a black pattern that was striking.

Three horses and one mule stood in the street behind them, each heavily loaded. As Yourdon reached the assembly the men began at once shifting some of the supplies to his mule. Yourdon simply stood there, quite still, eyes fixed on the women. For an instant he became lost in their presence, and came around only when Banlae himself emerged from the inn.

"Pella," he said, introducing the older woman, "and Flene," he added, nodding toward the girl. Yourdon guessed Pella was perhaps five or six years his senior, while Flene could have been no more than ten. The girl showed Yourdon a practiced smile many a woman in Detimar would have envied. She had learned it from her mother, Yourdon saw next.

"And this is Tremet," Banlae added, "the paladin I told you about." The older man only frowned.

"Good day," Yourdon said, bowing to each of them.

"Good day," Pella replied, followed by a nod from Flene. Tremet said nothing. If anything, his frown seemed to deepen, but something about it was reminiscent of Beken, he thought. Yourdon decided to get right to business.

"I expect we'll take the southeast road," he said, taking out his map, beginning to unroll it. "Nearer the Thel-Akreean regions. I am told—"

Tremet reached out and put his hand on Yourdon's map, forcing Yourdon to lower it. "You are to take orders, not give them," Tremet said, using a remarkably deep voice. Yourdon looked at Pella and realized he was on his own. The paladin said nothing more as he turned, bowed once in Banlae's direction, then headed up the street, trailing his horse and the other mule. Pella and Flene made their farewells brief, then went directly behind him.

Yourdon's eyes met Banlae's, and the big man grinned. "Sleep lightly if you cross *him*," he said.

Yourdon nodded. He gathered reins, and hurrying followed the others through the maze that was Dlet, until they were beyond the city's walls.

Yourdon ended up riding lead while Tremet trailed, which allowed him to keep an eye on everyone. A general silence prevailed for the rest of the day. Pella and Flene spoke to each other now and then, and to Tremet less often, but by the time darkness had begun to settle Yourdon had decided Kyr-Akreeans were a plainly unfriendly people. *Weeks,* he thought dismally, reassessing the journey ahead.

With evening they made camp in a wide moonlit clearing along the edge of a shallow stream. The women had a small tent which Yourdon helped Tremet erect. Next they asked Yourdon to help gather wood for a fire. After that he sat and rested, quietly, while Pella and Flene fixed their meal—fresh dark bread, beans and a spicy but enjoyable sausage. The others began a quiet banter as their bellies filled; most of it Yourdon could not understand. This didn't seem to matter, as they made no attempt to include him in any case. Finally he stood.

"I'm going to bed, I think," he said, using the Dral phrasing. "I feel I will not be missed."

"Ahh, good," Tremet replied.

As Yourdon stood up he accidentally kneed Flene's arm, causing her to drop the small, perfectly sewn doll she had been holding. When Yourdon picked it up to give it back to her he felt the magic stir quietly within him. With only the barest effort he conjured the image of a family gathered together, a room filled with people all bringing gifts to the girl: a small box that might have been made of ivory, a roll of material that must have been silk, the doll. . . .

Flene's birthday, Yourdon gathered. He gave the doll back and started away.

"Wait," Pella said, shaking her head briefly at the paladin. "This is not proper. Please, sit again and talk with us if you will. I am told you are from Detimar. We have never known your like. Tell us something of yourself, your land."

"Yes," Flene added, her young eyes sparkling in the firelight as she leaned forward. "Tell us everything!"

Yourdon wasn't about to do that. But he did return

to the fire. He explained a little, fictionalizing where he thought it best, stumbling in his still limited knowledge of Dral. He said his father was a rich and powerful man, but left it at that, and he told them a little about the legion. When they asked why he had come to Akreea he spouted something about adventure and opportunity, because he didn't have a proper answer. As quickly as he could, Yourdon turned the focus around: "I am told you left your home seeking asylum."

"Then you were told enough," Tremet said sharply.

Pella and Flene both fixed Tremet with a dour stare. The paladin frowned, stiff-jawed.

Pella turned back to Yourdon. "Yes," she said. "The Dral were cruel at times and never to be trusted. My husband was killed when the Thel helped our people try again to drive the Dral out of KyrPhel. He would have taken my father's place as sultan of KyrPhel one day."

"I am sorry," Yourdon said, thinking of his charges as royalty for the first time, though he had begun to suspect as much. He had guessed the women were from a wealthy family; he had that in common with them, in fact, though the similarities seemed to end there. But a princess' heart could suffer like any other; Pella's wound had not healed, he could see that plainly as she spoke.

"At the time my father decided it might be best if Flene and I went away, to safety," she added, stopping there.

"Were there many of you?" Yourdon asked, picturing a great stream of refugees, women and children, fleeing Dral retribution.

"There were no others," Tremet said, sitting forward, stirring the fire. "Why would there be?"

"You few are the only ones that escaped?"

"I was chosen by the sultan himself!" Tremet boomed indignantly. "I did not . . . *escape!*"

"My husband led the army in their first attempts," Pella said quickly. "My father feared the Dral might ultimately seek reprisal through his wife and daughter. He never thought the city might fall, but he worried attempts might be made on our lives if we stayed. Tremet is one of the finest guardsmen in all KyrPhel. He was ordered to travel with us . . . along with poor Lapan, who is no longer able."

"Do you ever plan to go home again?" Flene asked, round eyes gazing up from beside him. It was almost as if she knew, somehow. She didn't, of course. She was a sweet, innocent sort, much like her mother.

"I don't expect to," Yourdon answered, looking away.

Flene tipped her head. "Why?"

"Flene," Pella said, touching her daughter's arm. Then her eyes glanced up, found Yourdon's as he turned again. "He may not wish to say."

Astute, Yourdon thought. He was becoming convinced that he had never met anyone quite so able, yet so kind. He hadn't known many such people, except, perhaps, the occasional Shetie. "It is a life I have no need of now," Yourdon answered.

"What do you have need of?" Tremet asked.

Yourdon knew what to say. "This fine purpose your need offers me."

Pella donned an almost secret smile. Tremet's face only darkened. "Our need may cost you your life, if the Quin are of a mind to trouble us," he said.

"Tell me about them," Yourdon urged. "I know little."

"It is best, perhaps," Tremet said.

"The Quin have no lands, unlike the Kyr, and the Thel, the Shet, the Taun," Pella explained, frowning again, briefly, at Tremet. "Though most agree they came from central and eastern Akreea, ages ago. Nevertheless, the Quin are tightly bound by their faith in the Five Gods, and are led only by their holy men, such as Rem Ana."

"The One," Yourdon said, repeating what the little girl had told him on the streets of Dlet.

"So he claims," Tremet mutters.

"He and his people helped drive out the Dral," Pella continued. "But only because they have no tolerance for those who do not share their creed."

"And who are the Five Gods?" Yourdon asked, though not entirely certain he wanted to know.

"Surely you know of the Gods of Naldisa?" Tremet began, warming somewhat, as if Yourdon's ignorance made him somehow more palatable. Yourdon shook his head.

"Nearly all Akreeans believe in them," Tremet said.

"They control the energies of universe," Pella explained. "Which in turn combine to form the Gods. All consciousness, all creation flows to them, and back. But many Akreean realms have their own ways of worship, their own prophets and customs. Most, like my people, are tolerant of the others. The Quin are not. They believe their strict practices and prophecies to be the only true path, and they consider those who do not believe, their enemies."

"Rem is the problem now," Tremet went on. "He will not let the Quin rest. For some the wars are not over, they go on."

"I've seen him," Yourdon noted, "in Dlet."

"I am not surprised," Tremet said. "The Quin have a grand temple there."

"Rem does not like my grandfather," Flene said in her gentle, pensive voice.

"It's true," said Pella. "The Quin are prone to violent acts. Bands of them have challenged nearly every realm. Years ago my father rode with his army to the aid of the Shet-Akree, a smaller realm to the north of Kyr. It was a young Rem Ana who led the Quin there. They were badly beaten, despite Rem's attempts at sorceries. Yet somehow this only strengthened Rem in the eyes of his followers. He is said to possess much greater powers now, a dark magic perhaps stolen from the Gods. Not everyone believes this."

"Many do," Tremet said, stirring the coals at the edge of the fire. "He still claims to be The One." Pella and Flene both nodded.

Yourdon squinted at them as smoke, thick with the smell of pine, clouded past his eyes. "Which—One?"

The others traded glances. "Quin prophecies tell of the coming of a man who will be killed," Pella began, "but who will not die. He will command the Shreeta Crystal, and through it, receive the truth, which will be made clear to all Akreea. He will lead the Quin into a new era, and a new land of their own."

Yourdon was losing track. Prophets, prophecies, resurrections, and now . . . "I'm afraid I have never heard of this crystal, either," he apologized.

Even little Flene rolled her eyes.

"Many have claimed to know the power of the Shreeta Crystal," Tremet said. "Many other fools believe in its power much. It is best no Quin ever comes to possess it."

"Tremet does not believe," Pella said. "But most do. Especially the Quin."

"Yes," Flene grinned, "but my grandfather will never let the Quin have it!"

Yourdon briefly closed one eye. "Then it's real?"

Flene looked at him as though he were the child, and not her. "Oh, yes! The Shreeta Crystal is at the palace. I have seen it, sitting in its box, round and beautiful."

"And safe," Pella added. "In truth, no one can say that ours is the real Crystal, though many believe it is. My father has never been able to find any powers within it, even though he is a mage himself. But that is not the only test, and he does not want to take chances. The Quin have said that only a Quin, chosen by the Gods, may know the ways of the Crystal."

Yourdon watched the fire again. "My mother's people sometimes use crystals, and many other stones and jewels," he said, thinking of it. "They say the crystals help them to see the future."

No one said anything. The silence lasted for a time. Yourdon was getting tired now, truly tired. He decided on a prophecy of his own. "If we meet with trouble we'll likely need some sleep, all of us," he said, getting up once more.

Everyone agreed, even Tremet, who stood as well, then moved toward Yourdon. "You sleep first," he directed. "I will wake you when it is your turn to watch."

"I'll help check the animals first," Yourdon said, thinking it wise; he had managed to get Tremet talking to him, and he hoped to build on that progress. Tremet nodded.

Not such a bad man to work with, Yourdon admitted, as they set off together toward the stand of trees down near the water's edge, where the mules and horses were tied. Even now, as they walked, Tremet would not let Yourdon at his back out of habit. But such a man, entrusted for so long with such precious lives, would learn wisely never to let his guard down. Never to trust anyone . . .

"Your sultan chose well, when he chose you," Yourdon told the paladin.

"I must hope Banlae did the same," Tremet remarked; Yourdon had not expected Tremet to be impressed by flattery, even if it was the truth.

The nearly full moon shone brightly overhead. The night air smelled cool and fresh. Yourdon noticed he was beginning to feel quite at ease. But just as they reached the horses crazed shouts of men rang out in the darkness, freezing Yourdon in his tracks. A band of riders thundered out of the trees on the far bank and into the stream, galloping through the water, weapons drawn. In the moonlight Yourdon could see them clearly enough, five in all, wielding swords and battle axes, three dressed in coats and two in leather cuirasses, and one of these last wearing a simple iron-framed leather helmet.

Yourdon looked to Tremet only to find the other man had already mounted. As the riders left the stream Tremet turned and rode to meet them, his sword in one hand and a small, rounded shield taken from his saddle in the other. Yourdon reached for his own mount and struggled to pull the reins free of the branches. The sharp ring of sword on sword just behind him sent a chill up his spine as he leaped up and heeled the horse to motion.

One of the raiders already lay on the ground, apparently the victim of Tremet's first strike as he had rushed past, but the others had turned to engage the paladin. As Yourdon charged he watched the first of the remaining bandits reach Tremet, swinging his axe in a frantic manner. Tremet dodged the weapon easily enough, then used the opening to render a deadly blow to the axe man's gut. As this second victim fell to the ground the other three bandits converged on Tremet in a flurry of rapid strikes and shouted oaths.

Yourdon circled behind, and drew one bandit away from Tremet. He blocked Yourdon's first blow with his sword, then came back with a battle axe. Too high. Hugging the horse's ribs with both legs, swinging his sword in one hand and his dagger in the other, Yourdon found himself backing off, unable to do more than defend himself. He stole a glance toward the others and saw

Tremet go down, silently, then lie still on the ground. The other two bandits turned away from him and rode to aid their comrade.

It occurred to Yourdon that all the gold in the world had no value to a dead man. He couldn't imagine what these men might be about. They were too skilled to be simple highwaymen; a band of seasoned mercenaries out for profit, more likely. But the little caravan was bringing no valuables other than Pella and Flene. . . .

Whatever they wanted, they would kill him soon, and then they would have it. Which meant the only sane solution was to break off and ride into the woods, saving at least himself and possibly the women, by allowing the inevitable. Yet somehow, just now, as the other two swordsmen moved to flank him, he could not clear his mind enough to make the choice. He could hardly think at all as he continued to let the rage of battle fill him.

He urged his horse backward, trying to keep out of striking range as all three of his foes fell on him at once. They quickly forced him back again, draining his strength, until he realized he had reached the edge of the clearing and camp.

He was suddenly aware of Pella and Flene beside him, moving up as if to stand with him. What courage, Yourdon thought. Then he thought that perhaps they intended to surrender—though already it was clear such a plan would not work: one of the swordsmen had broken off and started toward them, sword held high.

Just as he swung his blade the air itself seemed to ignite with a bright blue fire, quickly forming a shimmering sphere of swirling flames that surrounded the two women and spread to encompass Yourdon as well.

The bandits fought to calm their horses. Rapid chatter passed between them, then all three men seemed to decide at once. They howled in concert, chose targets, then urged their mounts ahead. But as their swords struck the blue halo they each recoiled.

The force shook their bodies as well and swept the three men from their saddles. Yourdon glanced down and saw the look on Flene's face, a grin almost too large for her young features to contain. He shook his head. *How ... ?*

Then Pella touched Flene's shoulder, and the girl's expression quickly sobered. Both women started backing away again, shaking their heads side to side at Yourdon. Whatever they had done, they could not apparently do it again. The sphere of light began to fade. Yourdon watched the other men getting to their feet, gathering their swords and horses. He took a deep breath, swallowed hard, and raised his own sword once more. The ache in his hand and shoulder made him wince; the blade seemed to have tripled in weight.

He heard another rider approaching just as his heels dug into his horse's haunches. *More bandits,* he thought, feeling his heart sink. He struck at the nearest bandit all the same, momentum carrying him. The blow was high and served only to dash the helmet from the other man's head.

Yourdon saw a second bandit turn toward him and move in just as the approaching rider, no more than a thin, dark shape against the moonlight, light cloak flapping, charged into the gathering. *It is hopeless,* Yourdon thought, fending off first one man's axe, then the other's sword. He had come so close to turning his life around, had fought only to have it end in the grip of misfortune. His best hope was that he could end the life of at least one more bandit before—

He heard a shrill battle cry followed by a much lower howl, and looked up to see the one bandit falling backward, clutching at his chest. Now the new arrival engaged the next nearest bandit, drawing him off Yourdon, then deftly leading his attack using a long, narrow sword, and finally wounding him mortally with two rapid thrusts of a slightly shorter, curved blade. Yourdon was left finally one on one. It took only a moment to finish the fight. He turned his mount to face the other rider, who was waiting silently now just a few paces away. A slim, steady form, bathed in moonlight. A woman.

"I would enter your camp," the rider said. The words she used sent a cold chill down Yourdon's back. He had not heard anyone speak in the Syttrelian tongue since . . . the war.

She urged her horse forward alongside Yourdon's. He could see clearly the familiar, slightly aged Syttrelian features of her stark, yet somewhat attractive face. She had a dark look in her eyes, a grin on her face. The same look she had shown him when he raised his eyes to her on the streets of Thetar, as she paraded grandly through the city that had cast him aside—when she had taken pity on a pathetic gull and tossed a handful of coins to him before riding on.

A small charity, much smaller than this. . . .

"You were in the Golden Axe, a few days ago," Yourdon said accusingly, certain now. He realized he had begun to shake. *From the fight,* he told himself.

"I was?" she said, feigning candor. "Perhaps," she added. "I am Tasia," she announced, turning to Pella and Flene. Mother and daughter stood beside the horses now, staring up.

"Please, come and let us thank you," Pella said. "Yourdon will take your horse."

"I will, of course," Tasia answered. She dismounted and handed up her reins, then the three of them walked back toward the fire, leaving Yourdon in the dark.

❖ ANOTHER FACE AND TIME ❖

The ground yielded to a depth of several hand breadths, then hard clay interfered. *Enough,* Yourdon thought. With only swords, daggers and a small axe taken from his pack mule to dig with, they would be all night making the grave much deeper. When Tremet's body was laid to rest and covered over, Tasia helped Yourdon drag the bodies of the raiders from the clearing into the trees, a gift to the wolves.

"You fight . . . well," she told him, as they let go the last pair of cold, dead hands and started back toward the fire. Yourdon objected to her tone, one of surprise. Still, he felt compelled to return the compliment, as it was only true.

"And you," he said, as they neared Pella and Flene. The sweet smell of cured sausage cooking on the fire drifted to them, causing Tasia to sniff the air like one of Thetar's street cats. Yourdon glanced at her, and saw the concentration on her features. She went straight for the meat, then sat devouring it: Pella had guessed right, their new acquaintance was famished.

The two Akreeans talked with Tasia, speaking briefly about who they were, where they were going. Each time Yourdon glanced at Tasia he caught her looking back at him with deep, dark eyes that revealed nothing. *Cold,* he thought, reminding himself how unnatural and barbaric this female warrior was, of how strange she must be in many ways.

Yet she was almost beautiful, he decided, not for the first time, as he examined her face and figure more carefully in the glow of firelight. The two impressions seemed not to fit together in his mind.

He agreed with his earlier assessment, she was at least ten years his senior, and a bit too muscular, certainly not the sort of woman he would fancy. Still, the boldness of her manner and carriage was alluring in a strange, unsettling way. The fact that she was Syttrel, however, outweighed everything else. He had heard the stories told by many a Detimarian soldier in legion camps at night. The Syttrelian female warriors were said to make love just as they made war—much the same as men did. Yourdon half expected her to attack him at any moment, though whether she might draw her sword or strip off her tunic he could not predict. He found her looking at him again, and realized that either idea frightened him more than he cared to admit.

She finished her meal while telling Pella how honored she was. "I had no idea I was coming to the aid of such a noble pair," she said. "I have heard of KyrPhel, a rich and beautiful land, though I have never been there. You must be glad to finally be returning."

"And for that we have you to thank," Pella reiterated. "Were it not for you, we might never have survived."

"You are very brave," Flene added, almost a squeal.

"All true! And I thank you," Tasia replied, grinning at the others with altogether too much satisfaction for Yourdon's tastes.

"I recall there were two of us fighting the brigands— three to start," he pointed out, adding his own smile, attempting to dull the edge his tone implied.

"Oh, yes, you were quite brave as well!" Flene told him, nodding vigorously.

"Indeed, you are a fine soldier," Pella agreed, bowing

her head toward Yourdon, smiling at him, a very pleasant smile, Yourdon noticed. "Banlae chose well," she added. "We owe our lives to both of you, and to Tremet, of course, who was both protector and friend. His is a great loss."

"Agreed," Yourdon said, then silence fell as each of them remembered. Yourdon had only just begun to appreciate the paladin, and now he was gone. *Like Beken,* he thought. *Like everything.* The inference was absurd of course. . . . Still, it was a disturbing trend.

"I never knew him, but I am sure his was . . . a hero's death," Tasia said. She glanced only briefly at Yourdon as she spoke, but long enough to leave little doubt about the thought that had crossed her mind. He remembered well the Detimarian soldier speaking in Tasia's ear in Thetar, telling her about him as he looked up from the street. It seemed she remembered, too.

"What was that remarkable blue light I saw?" Tasia asked, apparently choosing not to mention Thetar just now. "I have never known the like."

"Nor I," Yourdon said.

"Flene has the gift, like her grandfather," Pella explained. "Though hers is yet quite small, as is she. Tufan had been teaching her the spell these past few years. She has memorized the chants, and when there is time to concentrate, she repeats them, building the spell a little at a time, gathering the forces she needs from within herself, and from the world around her. The layering is the key. It is like pouring a ladle of water into a pail, then pouring another, until finally the pail is full. One ladle makes only a little splash, but the entire bucket is capable of a great dousing."

"Can she do that again?" Yourdon asked. "We have a long journey yet ahead of us."

"Yes, in a few days," Flene told him.

Pella nodded. "Six days at most."

"A wonderful talent indeed," Tasia remarked, almost singsong. "Is there a talisman involved?"

Flene shook her head. "No, but one day, perhaps. That is a talent yet to be learned."

Tasia nodded.

"What are you doing here?" Yourdon asked.

Tasia looked at him, eyes wide, but said nothing.

"It is a simple question," Yourdon prodded.

She turned to Pella and Flene. "I was following the road along the stream, just as you were, seeking a good place to rest the night. I heard shouts."

Yourdon stood and stirred the fire with a pliant limb, then he looked up, and threw the stick down. "No, what are you doing in Akreea?"

Tasia's eyes widened. "What are *you* doing in Akreea?"

Yourdon's narrowed. "You first."

Tasia seemed to study him a moment, tipping her head slightly and to one side. She settled back, legs crossed beneath her, took a deep breath and wrinkled her nose. "I am a merchant of sorts," she said.

He found himself wondering what sort of merchant she was, since he knew of no easy markets, and since she had room for nothing but necessities on her mare; he'd noticed that much, at least, when he'd tied the animal up. "A merchant must have something to trade," he said.

Tasia shrugged. "I do, from time to time."

"It must be an interesting life," young Flene said, still wide-eyed.

"It pleases me," Tasia answered. "I came to this land to seek my fortune, and perhaps a bit of adventure as well."

"Plenty of both west of the Tesshis," Yourdon replied.

"Ah, but no longer," she corrected. "Killing Detimarian soldiers was a worthwhile diversion, but with the war over, I grew bored. I felt in no hurry to go back to my village; and your cities—loud and filthy, and unfriendly, as I have seen—did not impress me, either. Akreea promised to be more . . . interesting."

He watched her watching him, waiting for his reaction; he gave her none.

"You like your war?" Flene asked, innocent curiosity.

"Some enjoy killing more than others," Yourdon said, keeping his voice level. He waited for her reaction now.

"There is no joy in death," Pella said, as she sat studiously wiping the cooking pot clean. Yourdon was struck by the purity of the act, and her tone; he wondered how the princess felt about doing for herself, sleeping by herself. She could endure so many hardships, yet surely she desired better, for herself and her daughter. He tried to imagine his father behaving so, and could not.

"There is great joy in victory," Tasia said, then she looked up at Yourdon. "And pain in defeat."

"What do you know of pain?" Yourdon asked.

"More than you realize."

"I doubt that."

"You would doubt yourself," Tasia said sharply.

"And you would fool yourself," Yourdon snapped back.

"Have you two met before?" Pella asked.

The two warriors looked at her. "We have," Tasia told her. "Briefly . . ."

She seemed to be playing with him; he didn't see the humor. His mind found a handhold. "You never told us—what it is you trade?"

She shrugged yet again. "Artifacts," she said, "Akreean artifacts." Yourdon did not understand the Dral phrasing, but Pella and Flene helped to clarify.

"The Akreeans have many rich cultures, each with many sacred or personal objects they hold dear," Tasia went on. "The Dral tended to be collectors of such things, and traders, among themselves. Many items have been lost and scattered: idols, jewels, medallions, beads, ceremonial pottery, even weapons held as sacred because of who owned them, or used them, or created them. I have found it worth my while to hunt these items down, and return them to their rightful peoples."

"For a nice profit," Yourdon said, pressing.

"For a usually handsome fee, yes."

"Twice handsome, I'd wager," Yourdon snorted. "And if the rightful people cannot afford your price, do you sell to the highest bidder?"

"You have no kindness in you," Tasia said, lifting her chin.

Yourdon wasn't having any of that. "Syttrelians are thieves, as anyone knows," he said, pointing a finger at her. "They take, they do not give."

"You are wrong about that, my good fellow," Tasia said, sounding now like a mother scolding her child. "You must know a lie when you hear one."

"As well as the truth, but you would likely know little of that!"

"You never told me why *you* are here, in Akreea," she came back, suddenly terse, dropping the act she was putting on for her hosts. It caught Yourdon off guard, but he felt some satisfaction at the unsettling effect he was finally returning.

"Why should that concern you?" he asked.

"It must be an interesting story," Tasia said, as coyly as possible. "To have come so far, and from so low, you must be a remarkable man . . . or lucky."

Or neither, Yourdon thought, but he tried not to let it show. "I came as you, a merchant, seeking my own fortune. I had none, as you well know."

She shook her head. "Ha! You had barely two legs to

stand on. I felt sorry for you, which I deemed better than disgust at the time. Perhaps *that* was a mistake."

"Enough!" Yourdon said. "No Syttrelian woman is fit to judge anything about me, nor any other man—save her own poor husband, should there be such a fool."

"Syttrelian men are not like you, they have true courage."

Yourdon wanted to explode, but some part of him knew that to do so would be to play directly into this demon woman's hands. She was too clever, too ruthless, and was probably enjoying baiting him. Yourdon desperately attempted calm, then tried to turn the tide of battle.

"Aye, a man might require great courage to come to your bed, but that is a different matter."

"Courage," Tasia said, "and stamina." She grinned, then glanced at Flene, who was listening avidly and blushing. She was letting them go, perhaps to take the measure of these strangers in her company.

"What stories you tell! You are as quick with your tongue as you are with a sword."

"You will never know," Tasia replied, licking her lips. "But thank you."

"I meant no compliment."

"Too bad."

Yourdon stood boiling. He turned away, lips pressed together.

"What of your merchant tales?" Tasia asked, hounding him now. "Here you are, a soldier still. Can it be you came to Akreea because that is one thing you can never be again in Detimar? But perhaps your people were right."

Yourdon winced, gritting his teeth. Again the woman had found his belly exposed! He felt a pressing need to turn things around.

"I don't believe your tales of artifacts," he said, turning

on her, taking a step toward her. "You have failed as well, or you would not know to speak as you do. There is no merchant or buyer in all Dlet who has need of a man from Detimar, or a woman from Syttre. Banlae offers the only answer, as you know well enough, else you would not have been at the Golden Axe that night."

"I go many places, many more than you, I think," Tasia said, almost affable. "Much can be learned from some of the mix of visitors at that inn."

"Aye," Yourdon said, seeing his chance, "but a woman is likely to learn only one thing in there, and earn money the same way."

Tasia's face went stiff as she scrambled to her feet. "I should cut off your head and hang it from my saddle!"

Yourdon basked in her ire. "You would find my head does not come off so easily," he said, taking another step toward her, too caught up in the challenge to worry about where it might lead. "But the heads of heathens do!"

"No," she said directly, placing her hands on her hips, taunting. "That would cause these fine women to endure yet another burial, and even a fool such as you is not worth that."

"And burials are something the Syttrel are all too used to. That is why your people surrendered."

"It was *you* who surrendered!"

"How can you deny the truth? We finally killed enough Syttrelians to force reason upon you, and a truce."

"So the truth is plain as always—Detimarians are ruthless butchers, and all butchers are cowards."

"Butchers?"

"Your people cast you down because they could not bear to see their own faces in yours!"

"Your people are thieves and liars. A nation of barbarians no more civilized than the wolves and jackals that tend your dead!"

With that Tasia gripped her sword. Yourdon reacted in kind, feeling the solid reassurance of the hilt fill his palm. He waited, still keen enough to control the urge to draw the iron free. They stood no more than three paces apart, jaws set, silent but for the breath snorting through their noses. Pella squeezed herself almost in between them. She cleared her throat loudly, fetching their attention.

"Tasia makes half a point: If you kill each other, who will accompany us to KyrPhel?" she chided, looking from one to the other.

"If I am forced to kill him, I will fulfill his task," Tasia said.

Yourdon leaned to Pella. "No need to worry over that."

"Surely you must have had other plans," Pella said, looking to Tasia. "And there has been enough killing already today." No one seemed eager to disagree with this last.

"And I have been frightened enough for one day," Flene said, standing nearer now, nosing in. Her voice was thin and quivering, her eyes baleful and puffy. "If you don't stop, I'll cry, and I won't be able to stop."

An act, Yourdon guessed, but a very good one. "We are all upset and tired," Pella added. "Wouldn't you both agree?" Tasia capitulated, and stepped back once, as did Yourdon. Pella and Flene smiled privately at one another, then Pella put one gentle hand on Yourdon's sword arm, while Flene did the same to Tasia.

"Let the night pass. When we are rested, we can all talk more, in the clear light of day."

"She makes good sense," Tasia murmured, just as Yourdon was about to.

"As always," Yourdon told Pella, bowing briefly to her, hiding his scowl.

Pella stepped away and put an arm around her

daughter, drawing her to her side. Tasia held out her empty hands, a gesture of good will. All three women smiled pleasantly at one another. Too pleasantly.

"I have to check the other horses," Yourdon said. He turned and stalked away, and noted that two of the bandit's horses had wandered back into the clearing. They were grazing on scrub near the trees where the other animals were tied. They proved easy enough to collect.

As he stood checking knots and tying new ones his temper began to cool. He felt a slight amazement, mixed with a touch of embarrassment, at the hostility Tasia had provoked in him—more easily than the worst of his boyhood hecklers or even his father ever had. He recalled the way he had felt the day of his first encounter with the Syttrel, how it had shaken him, the death and the blood, the female warrior he'd seen slain when the scouts had been attacked. A woman much like Tasia.

He had not been certain he could have killed the woman himself, had it fallen to him, but he knew differently now. Given the chance, forced into it, he could do whatever needed to be done, he thought. Some part of him wanted to retreat from this darkness taking form inside him like some magically conjured beast; but another part, like a lost sibling suddenly found, felt it a rare satisfaction. . . .

He finished tying the extra horses, then walked around Tasia's, looking it over closely. A fine beast, he thought. No Syttrelian runic curses were painted on this animal. In fact, the mare was of a breed common in Detimar . . . as were its saddle and pack frame. He spied a large, slightly curved, nearly sword-length dagger tucked into the animal's pack, the kind possessed by nearly all Syttrelian warriors. The weapons were a part of their owner's identity. He had vivid memories of comrades dying by these weapons, and of Syttrelians dying with their precious blades still clutched in their hands.

He thought to touch the hilt, almost habit now with all weapons he encountered. At first he deemed the idea a sour one, but by the time he'd checked the other horses and given it a bit more consideration, an idea began to sweeten in his mind. He looked toward the fire, saw no one coming his way. He untied the rawhide strips and drew the dagger from its scabbard, then began his chant. There would be images he was sure, of war, of Syttre, but he was interested in what the dagger could tell him of more recent times. The spell seemed to follow his will. Yourdon suddenly thought himself back in Thetar.

He recognized the inn that filled the cloudy vision, though he had never been inside. Tasia leaped from her pony onto the nearly darkened street and sauntered in. Yourdon decided this was well after the public Syttrelian arrival he had witnessed, for the crowds were gone. He watched her, dagger on her hip, enjoying the fine wine so common in Detimar—enjoying a great deal of it, in fact. By the time she stumbled out, shooing a handful of late night would-be suitors away, she seemed surprised to notice her pony was missing. Wandered off, no doubt, Yourdon reasoned, or someone had decided such an animal might make a fine possession. After all, it must belong to a Syttrel, which made taking it no real crime. . . .

Already, Yourdon's bit of conjuring began to fade. He renewed the spell, speaking the chant over and over—not finished yet. Now Tasia wandered the streets for a while, until she seemed to decide on a just solution to her problem.

The mare was a fine one, saddled and loaded with bags of fruit. Yourdon guessed its owner must be inside the public bath that stood only a few paces away. In fact, the young tree farmer was just exiting the building as Tasia mounted his horse and started away. He shouted at her, "Thief! Horse thief!" Which brought a number of men to the bath house door. She didn't stop.

Yourdon saw an image of Tasia sleeping the night behind one of Thetar's smaller theaters, then the magic was gone.

"More!" Yourdon said out loud, eager for every incriminating detail. "I must see more." He tried again, straining, feeling the effort in his mind and body, sensing his limits, yet forcing himself all the same. Finally something much too vague began to take shape before him.

Tasia, he thought, riding like the four winds . . .

A hand gripped Yourdon's shoulder as the images vanished once more.

"You would steal something so sacred from me!" Tasia said, putting her other hand on his, then made it clear she wanted the dagger back into its scabbard. He complied. She pried his fingers free. He let her. He had her now.

"It seems I was right about you," he said, glaring into her eyes. "A thief after all. Small wonder you disliked Detimar's greatest city. You did not leave Thetar by choice, you were chased out on a stolen horse! This very animal!" He slapped the mare's haunches, causing its hooves to stir. Tasia was staring at him in obvious dismay.

"Not true," she stammered.

"It *is* true," he hounded her. "To stay in Detimar would have meant prison or worse for you."

"You are out of your mind!" she said, gathering her wits. "How would you get such an idea? I—I bought this horse! The Detimarian bastard who sold it to me claimed he owned it. When I realized—"

"A thief, *and* a liar!" Yourdon cackled, refusing to let her finish.

"You are a fool. You have no idea what you're saying!"

"No fool," Yourdon said, sobering quickly, narrowing his eyes. "You drank too much and lost your mare, so you simply took another from a bath house, expecting naked folk would be slow to chase you down. You see, I know exactly what I am saying."

"How—" Tasia stopped herself, snapped her gaping mouth shut. Her eyes danced in their sockets. Again, she managed to regain some of her composure, though not quite all of it. "You are making all this up. A Detimarian would say anything to justify his deeds— which I hear is especially true of you."

Yourdon wasn't about to let her go, or get caught again. He decided to tell her, since the telling didn't matter now. "Flene is not the only doer of magics hereabouts. I have a gift as well. It is a spell I use, easily renewed. I am able to see the past through the things that were witness to it. Your sacred blade gives you away, Tasia. Admit that what I say of you is truth."

She knew it was so, he could see it in her eyes, the eyes of a trapped zeret.

"Your magic is as pathetic as are you!" she accused him. "Cursed, demon Detimarians! Cursed heathen!"

"You are the heathen, my barbarian friend," Yourdon told her, but as he did he heard the echo of his father's voice, speaking of his mother. He pushed the thought aside. This wasn't the time, and he was right, after all.

"Coward!" she screamed. "Coward! Is there nothing you will not hide behind?"

"Thief!"

"Coward!"

"Please! Stop!"

It was Pella, followed closely behind by Flene. They had crossed the clearing unnoticed. Pella put her hand out to Yourdon while Flene went past him to Tasia, and extended hers to the Syttrelian. "There is not a creature in all these woods getting any sleep tonight," Pella said. "Including the child."

"You don't want me to get sick, do you?" Flene admonished.

Yourdon and Tasia shook their heads. They glanced at each other, silent.

"Very well," Pella said. "Not another word from either of you until morning."

She stood nearer, waiting, hand out, until she got the nods of agreement she wanted, and a hand in return. Then the four of them went without another word back to the fire, to their bedrolls. This time, the respite seemed to last, though rest came more easily than sleep.

Sunrise brought with it a bitter restraint, a mood finally eased only when Flene asked Tasia where she was going next.

"To Dlet," she answered, finishing a bowl of boiled wheat and barley.

"But you were there only two three-days past," Yourdon said.

"I have been out hunting," Tasia explained.

Yourdon knitted his brow. "You have no catch."

Tasia wiped her bowl clean and set it down, then chewed a piece of dried fruit. "Not so," she said. "Two highwaymen last night, and a hare the morning before this."

Yourdon snorted once, then went back to his own breakfast. Flene sidled over nearer Tasia, eager to know more. "KyrPhelian women rarely do such things," she said.

"Rarely," Pella echoed, seeming to take an interest as well as Tasia began the telling of her exploits with a bow.

Yourdon listened for a bit, making faces, then he

decided to go and get the horses. As they broke camp and loaded the animals he was forced to listen to still more of Tasia's bragging—about the golden cup she had discovered in the farthest eastern hills and returned to the Ril-Akree, and the ten rings, once worn by the mage priest of the Drenn-Akree, and found on the thick fingers of a dying Dral commander in an abandoned hill fort, deep in the Shalen Forests. Flene was especially enthralled.

"You are surely the bravest woman in all the world," the little girl exclaimed. Pella seemed to note the look in her daughter's eyes, not that it was all that different from her own.

"Won't you come with us, to my father's palace?" Flene asked, as they gathered reins. Tasia smiled with obvious satisfaction, but her look was distant, or distracted.

"That is not such a good idea," Yourdon said, speaking up. "You do not know the Syttrel as I do."

"But they are not my enemies," Pella said. "And I gather they are no longer your enemies either. Nor should you be hers. And we have lost Tremet. You are most capable, I am sure, but I would feel that much better for Tasia's company. Provided you two can get along."

Yourdon said nothing. The trouble with Pella was she made too much sense.

"As you wish," Tasia answered, apparently at a loss as well.

"Wonderful!" Flene exclaimed.

Pella smiled. "My father will be grateful," she said. "You will be well rewarded, I assure you."

"All the better," Tasia said, though Yourdon was sure she had expected as much.

"I would know something first," Tasia said, as she mounted her horse, then waited for the others to do the same. "I continue to wonder why you were set upon by those bandits last night? They may have had ransom on their minds, or they were simply trying their luck, hoping you carried something of value, perhaps, there in your packs? If so, I have a right to know what it is."

"Just the question a thief would ask," Yourdon said, almost casually. "You wouldn't be planning to waylay anyone on the way out of town, would you?" he added, quoting an old friend.

"If you are so frightened of me, don't sleep."

"You frighten no one," Yourdon answered her. "I am simply—"

"Simply a coward," Tasia snapped, nearly gleeful.

"Thief!" Yourdon countered.

"Butcher!"

"Barbarian!"

"By the Five Gods stop it!" Pella shrieked, at a volume that seemed to surprise even Flene. Pella gently pretended to clear her throat, then let the silence linger a while. "We cannot travel all the way to Kyr like this," she finished.

"Can't you two be friends?" young Flene asked, her voice soaked in sorrow, all of it genuine this time.

"Perhaps you could simply keep from speaking to each other?" Pella offered, though it had the ring of a decree. Yourdon saw Tasia's rigid nod of agreement. He followed in kind.

"Very well," Pella acknowledged. "We'll see how long this lasts."

Flene giggled softly. Yourdon urged his mount forward to take the lead. The rest of the day passed in silence, as did that evening. The day after that Pella took to riding nearer Yourdon now, nearer Tasia then, chatting quietly. She told Yourdon a bit more about her people, her lands, her daughter. He imagined she said much the same to Tasia, though she did seem to speak especially softly to him at times, and to look at him with eyes that seemed to grow ever kinder. He tried not to think too much of it, deciding that was best.

Flene followed her mother's example, shuttling back and forth like a junior diplomat. Yourdon enjoyed their company, but the silent tension between Tasia and himself did not seem to lessen. At times Yourdon couldn't help but feel caged, almost like an animal being kept for slaughter, though he took some small comfort in the belief that he was having the same effect on Tasia. By the fourth day, though, he began to wonder how either of them could survive the weeks ahead. That night, he lay awake, worrying until very late.

He was convinced there could be no truce, and he was fairly certain Tasia felt the same way. He imagined the journey could end only one way: One of them, it was clear, would have to go, and soon. He did not intend it would be him. Then he decided it was worth attempting to talk about, just one more time.

"There is something I would discuss," he said, near the end of the following morning as they neared a village Pella was sure lay just at day's end. But he could not continue. At that moment the road led out of a copse of trees into a large field of flax, and everyone fell silent as they looked straight across to the clearing's far side, to where an army plodded toward them.

❖ FAR ENOUGH ❖

"They must number at least a hundred," Yourdon said, straining for a better look at the approaching forces. "Nearly all cavalry, what I can see of them." Followed by wagons, but these last were difficult to see in the shifting cloud of dust all around them.

"They may let us pass," Tasia said, peering into the distance. She already had her hand on her sword. Yourdon prepared to draw his, but held fast while the others coaxed their mounts into a closer gathering.

"And if they do not—" he began, watching the soldiers, still trying to make out detail.

Tasia drew her sword. "If they do not, we will die."

"You sound almost eager," Yourdon muttered.

"Perhaps you would rather run," Tasia said, not quite under her breath.

Yourdon turned, bristling, freeing the iron in his own scabbard. Tasia pulled her mount back a pace, as if to face off against him.

"Please!" Pella snapped, moving her horse forward a step and pointing up the road, "we have other things to worry about."

"I'm just trying to get him motivated," Tasia said in a charming manner.

"It's not working," Pella replied.

The troops kept getting closer, the colors of both men and standards slowly emerging. "If only we knew who

126

they were," Yourdon said—to nods all around. But it was Flene who saw. She grew suddenly excited, her head bobbing about, tipping side to side as she watched from her saddle. Abruptly she squealed, a sound that startled everyone, including the animals, and her horse bolted straight toward the approaching men.

"Flene!" Pella yelled, digging her heels into her horse's flanks, riding after the girl. Yourdon had a faint notion that he was about to do precisely the wrong thing, but stronger was the fear that Tasia would act before he did, and have that to use against him. He dug in his own heels only to find Tasia lunging ahead at the same instant. Yourdon bent over his horse's mane, urging it faster, pressing to gain the lead. Tasia began yelping at her mare, then whistling in its ear. They raced up the road neck and neck—straight into the maw of the waiting troops.

But as they closed the distance Yourdon heard cheers rising up from the ranks ahead. He looked to see Flene draw up in front of them, followed closely by Pella. They were being met by a rather short, robust, thickly bearded man wearing a large, bright cloth headpiece and mostly white garments bearing dark embroidery. He sat atop a great war horse dressed in gaudy skirts, its reins covered in bright trailing fabric. As Flene dismounted the fellow scrambled down from the war horse and hurried to her side. He swept the young girl up in his arms, and Yourdon heard the cry of Flene's shrill voice rising above the voices of the men. Then he understood the word that she kept shouting: "Grandfather!"

"My daughter speaks well of you, as does my grand-daughter," Tufan said, as he walked with Yourdon through the camp. He seemed a pleasant enough fellow, if a bit too well fed and pampered, even now dressed in brocade and flat silks that had no place in the field. His beard was trimmed just so, his dark hair in one braid and covered with a fanciful silk headdress. His jewelry—rings, bracelets and a gold and jade pendant—were worth a small kingdom by themselves. In this he was like Yourdon's father, a man who wanted for nothing in this world, but Yourdon had already begun to see that the similarities went no further.

Already he saw Tufan as a man quick to smile and slow to judge, and he apparently lacked Dree's talent for animosity, had retained instead a stubborn streak of human compassion. Not surprising, when Yourdon considered Pella and Flene. "I could speak highly of them as well," Yourdon said. "They do you great credit."

Tufan nodded with broad satisfaction. "I do not get to meet many heroes. It is pleasing to learn my many fears were never true. I had expected my family to return two weeks ago. I couldn't wait, so I decided to ride out and meet them, but each day there was no sign. After more than two weeks on the road my worst imaginings seemed all too possible. Until this day."

"I can understand your concern," Yourdon said, gazing across the camp. Pella sat on a short backless chair beside one of the supply wagons. Flene sat on another just in front of her, letting her mother fuss over her hair.

"Tell me, what do you think of my daughter?" Tufan asked. Yourdon looked at him, found an amiable expression on his face.

"She is a wonderful woman," he said evenly.

"Indeed. Nothing more?"

Yourdon shrugged. "Perhaps."

"Of course, but I'll tell you, she does not want another husband just now. You must understand that. I cannot blame her."

"I knew," Yourdon said. "I know." Though, as he had

gotten to know her he had thought, more than once, that one day she might feel differently. That perhaps she was already beginning to.

"To your credit, she badly needed a friend, and that is what she calls you," Tufan continued. "So, I do the same. Banlae will pay you upon your return, but I wish to give you this as well."

The sultan dug in his robes and produced a small velvet sack, held it out. Yourdon took it and pulled the string loose, found a stack of gold pieces inside. "Thank you," he said. "You are a . . . a most generous man."

"He is indeed," Tasia agreed, just over Yourdon's shoulder. He spun around and fixed her with a scowl. She hadn't been there a moment ago.

"She was given the same," the sultan smiled. "We are grateful to both of you."

Tasia grinned and walked on, apparently headed across the camp, toward Pella and Flene.

"She seems a fine, strong young woman, that one," Tufan remarked. "And good with a sword, I understand. Pella tells me you two know each other. Do you have feelings for her?"

"Oh," Yourdon muttered through his teeth, attempting calm, "you can't imagine."

"Good! All the better. My daughter has extended the hospitality of the palace at KyrPhel to her, and we extend the same to you."

"Is she going?" Yourdon asked, still watching Tasia striding away from him.

"She has declined for now. Apparently she has business in Dlet. I thought you might persuade her."

Yourdon nearly winced. "I too have business, but once I've seen Banlae, perhaps."

"Of course. The invitation is an open one."

They left it at that.

Dinner consisted of a pig, freshly slaughtered just for this occasion, a strange, clear wine, and fruit desserts. Yourdon slept in a tent with two of Tufan's men, neither of whom spoke Dral clearly enough to make good conversation. Which suited him. The day had been a long one, and he hoped to get an early start in the morning.

When he opened his eyes the sun had just risen; the soldiers had not. He got up quietly, then spent an early hour readying his horse and mule, shifting supplies to the sultan's animals, then he ate with the soldiers that were just getting up. He couldn't help but notice Tasia's absence as he walked through the camp. He smiled to himself—for a warrior, she slept late enough.

When Pella and Flene came out of their tent they greeted him warmly. Pella looked to her daughter, waited for her to speak. "I will miss you," Flene said.

"As will I," Pella told him. She put her arms around him and held him a moment, let Yourdon hold her too. He tried not to misconstrue any part of the gesture, but letting go seemed a difficult thing. Next he briefly hugged Flene. After a moment he asked them to be sure and let Tasia sleep.

"Oh, she is gone already, back to Dlet, I think," Pella replied.

"In fact, she asked us not to wake you," Flene explained. "She said she would make sure Banlae did not think you dead, and give your wages away before you arrived."

Yourdon's jaw went rigid. "Tell your father I said good-bye," he sputtered, turning in a circle, finding a direction. "I must go!" He set off at a run, crossing the camp toward his horse and his mule.

It was late morning when Banlae Tfa arrived at the Golden Axe. Yourdon had been waiting, pacing the walk, since dawn.

"Ah, I see my faith in you was wise," he said, booming the words as his jumbo frame came to rest just short of ramming Yourdon head on. "And I suppose you'll want your wages. Well—"

"She's been here, hasn't she!" Yourdon said, saving Banlae the trouble.

"Who?"

"And she told you I was dead," Yourdon finished.

"I have no idea. You don't look dead. A bit ragged, perhaps, from such a journey no doubt, which could explain your mind." Banlae clutched his chin with thumb and fingers, considering, then he took a big breath. "Come inside, we will get you a drink, some bread, and the silver I promised you. You will emerge a new man!" He pushed open the door, then put one large arm around Yourdon's neck and hauled him inside.

As they neared Banlae's usual corner table Yourdon noticed someone already waiting there, one of the conspicuously dressed Quin *emari* swordsmen. As Banlae approached the Quin stood, turned and bowed from the waist. He was as big as Banlae, and likely as powerful, though his face was lacking the Dral's inherent cheer. Yourdon noticed the man's left eye drawn close as he bobbed back up, a wary look, but as the moment passed he began to think the condition might be permanent.

"Kdosh!" Banlae called to him, acknowledging the other's deference. "A joy to see you, and your ripe purse, I trust."

"I have been waiting half the day," Kdosh replied. His voice was harsh and rumbled as if from overuse, but for all that his speech had a dragging, almost whining quality to it.

"Unlike you, I have been busy half the day," Banlae came back, tipping his head. "The worst of it is, you will have to wait a few moments more, as I have a bit of business to conclude with this fine fellow here." Banlae thrummed Yourdon twice on the top of his head with an open palm. Yourdon fought to keep a moan from escaping past his lips.

"How long?" the *emari* asked, short of a demand.

"A—few—moments," Banlae repeated slowly, as if that might help, then he went round to his chair against the corner, and stood there, staring at Kdosh, waiting, the familiar mild grin fading from his lips.

The Quin finally turned and walked to another table, then took a seat there, kicking his massive curved scabbard aside as if teaching it a lesson.

"Tell me of your journey," Banlae instructed, while producing a handful of silver pieces from a belt pouch hidden beneath his outer robe. Yourdon wasn't sure how much the coins were worth, he'd never seen their like before, but he believed the amount was substantial. He smiled calmly as he began his tale. When Banlae asked if there had been any trouble Yourdon recounted the episode with the five highwaymen; he mentioned Tasia as well, though perhaps not so prominently as he might have. He could think of few things less palatable than owing his life to a Syttrelian—other than owing it to a Syttrelian woman, then admitting to it in public.

"I will receive a messenger from Kyr-Akree soon, perhaps as soon as tomorrow," Banlae told him, leaning forward in a confidential manner. "I am sure your story will be on his lips. If all that you say is as you say, I'm sure I will have another task for you. Return to me then, and I will see that you do well." He paused to grin. "Though not so well as I."

Yourdon's mind was already working on possible negatives. His life had taught him that things could always go from bad to worse, and that questions like "What else could go wrong?" usually had an answer. Even as Banlae spoke, a question came to mind.

"What if the messenger does not arrive?" *What if Tasia intercepts him and pays him to lie?* he wondered after that, but he was beginning to sense the craziness in his thoughts. Tasia was taking over his mind. . . .

"I have faith in my sources," Banlae explained, though by his expression he clearly doubted the need to. "You have nothing to worry about. Do you?"

"No."

"Good. Now go, and enjoy Dlet as it should be enjoyed, with your pockets full!"

Yourdon stood and nodded once, then he turned and strode toward the door. The *emari*, Kdosh, rose immediately to take Yourdon's place at Banlae's table, putting himself squarely in Yourdon's path—or Yourdon in his. The two of them stood face to face for a moment, though the Quin's large nose came roughly even with Yourdon's head. For a Quin, the man was a monster.

Yourdon decided Kdosh was not about to step aside. He thought about standing his ground as well, but deep in his gut he felt an urge to just let it go, just this once, because there was nothing here worth killing or dying over. He looked around. Almost no one was in the Golden Axe this morning. Still . . .

Yourdon looked up to the Quin's dark eyes. "Your turn," Yourdon told him, stepping aside, waving the *emari* on as if granting him permission. The Quin uttered a minor grunt and ushered past.

The room was full of empty tables. Yourdon sat at one of them and spent the first of his wages on a pot of the inn's best wine and a bowl of thick, satisfying stew crowded with pork and carrots and beans. Cheese and fresh fruit followed, then figs and pistachios. He breathed in the rich aromas between mouthfuls, savoring the

experience. He had a few things to do before day's end.
A visit to a good clothier was first on his list, then he
would find a new place to stay, a place more amenable
to one who had lived in perhaps the finest house in all
Thetar. And then . . .

Then he would attempt to invest his spoils.
Somehow . . .

He finished the last of his meal and wine, tossed a
silver coin on the table—more than enough, he thought,
smiling to himself—then he yielded to an urge and
glanced toward the corner. The *emari* and Banlae were
still talking, and both were looking straight at him. Their
eyes strayed as he met their gaze. Yourdon decided he
was in much too good a mood to let these two bother
him. He headed for the street.

By evening Yourdon had arranged to house himself
in luxury.

He took a suitable furnished flat that featured several
rooms, including a large dining room decorated with
warm tapestries and a few paintings—most of them
depictions of heroic men and comely women, or the
Five Gods of Naldasa—and complete with a long table
surrounded by benches and stools. Yourdon imagined
adding Detimarian-style couches on which to lounge
while eating and discussing business. . . .

His father would have given a dozen slaves the task
of caring for himself and the house, but Yourdon had
been under the care of too many servants in his life,
many of them cruel or foolish or miserable, and all of
them requiring a certain amount of care in return; he
thought he might feel differently one day, but he had
no stomach for them now. Nor would his purse bear
the burden.

And there was no need: he found that several families
living nearby, many with servants of their own, were

only too happy to launder his clothes and supply him with the most wonderful meals for what he was able to pay. He sold his animals and bought a gelding, a fair excuse for a war horse, well trained and outfitted in a proper saddle, bridle and aprons. Then he went hunting for a bit more furniture.

By the end of a week he was nearly ready.

He had not forgotten his mercantile hopes entirely; the idea of adopting a completely new and different life, one far removed from that of a warrior or even a plutocrat's son, far removed from the baggage his life had saddled him with, had lost none of its appeal. Still, he knew the change would not come easily, not in the face of the resistance he had met, the distrust and even hatred of outlanders, and some Detimarians in particular, in this place. But he thought his plan a good one. The Yourdon who had made the rounds many weeks ago was not the same man, and he intended to make that clear.

There was no theater in Dlet, not like he had enjoyed growing up in Thetar, but minstrels and storytellers were common enough. Yourdon hired several, then went to one of Dlet's largest market squares and began inviting merchants and even a few craftsmen to his house for a feast. Some would hardly speak to him, but many said they would probably attend. Encouraged, Yourdon spent lavishly, exhausting what remained of his wages and the gold Tufan had given him. He saw to nearly every detail of the preparations himself. He tried to imagine every conversation, and in his mind he rehearsed his part in them, over and over again. Finally he chose the wines and ales by tasting enough of them to make the rest of that day a total loss. But then the night arrived.

He waited, confidently, in a house filled with food, drink, and glorious entertainments. No one came.

❖   ❖   ❖

"There is a certain . . . wariness, shall we say, of most outlanders," Banlae said, nodding sympathy.

"I've noticed," Yourdon replied, sitting across from the big Dral at his usual corner table, the first time in nearly two weeks Yourdon had been to the Golden Axe.

Banlae folded his thick hands and grinned. "When mercenaries helped these people win their lands back, it was a different story. Now, attitudes have completed a circle. I think most Akreeans share in this. Fortunately, I am not afflicted." He looked about the room as if to make a brief survey, then he grinned accomplicelike at Yourdon. "But it happens I have something for you. A wonderful opportunity. I was waiting for you to show up here, on your own. I'd almost decided to take your name off the list, but here you are."

"Go on," Yourdon said, less than elated. Banlae seemed not to notice.

"A guard is needed, and as I understand it, you would spend most of your time right here in Dlet. You were asked for specifically, in fact, following a conversation I had with a man you met the other day—Kdosh, that *emari* holy assassin, or whatever they claim to be." Banlae smiled at his own remark.

Yourdon's mind caught on the other's allusion. "Then they are not what they seem?" he asked.

"Ahh, they are whatever they are, just as you or I." Banlae took a deep breath, let it out all at once. "No one is who they seem to be at all times, of course. What I do know is that one of their most prominent leaders has need of added security, and it seems he would favor a non-Akreean, such as yourself; someone with few . . . local loyalties, other than profit. Quite sensible, I believe. And profit is exactly what they offer. As fine a wage as I have seen, to the right man."

Banlae reached abruptly across the table and put his

large hands on Yourdon's shoulders. Yourdon had all he could do to keep from jumping as the other came at him, then all he could do to keep his posture.

"The right man," Yourdon repeated.

"You!" Banlae said, grinning broadly.

Yourdon only looked at the bigger man.

"What have you to say?" Banlae prodded.

"I have heard many things about the Quin," Yourdon offered truthfully. "None of them good."

"Ah, yes, from those KyrPhelians you met," Banlae said, "All of it true, quite likely, but none of it important. Since my people went running back to the Shalen Forests, most Akreeans have mixed feelings at best, even for each other. Most distrust the others, or hate them outright. Many manage to keep their differences to themselves while they rebuild their lives. But others, like the Quin, are always ready to state their claims, and have never done less! Myself, I would rather know another's mind, than wonder at it."

Yourdon sat thinking about this, agreeing with it.

"The Quin want the world their way," Banlae went on. "Tell me, who does not? The difference is that many Quin are willing to do nearly anything to get what they want. But as long as they make no secret of the fact, you and I can deal with them as we require."

Banlae was making good sense, as usual. As long as you knew where you stood, it was relatively easy to watch your back. Yourdon shrugged. "What must I do?"

"Tomorrow you will go to the Quin temple in the city's eastern quarter. Are you familiar with it?"

"I've been past it, once."

Banlae nodded satisfaction, as if surprised their meeting was going so well. Yourdon wasn't certain how to take that.

"Good," Banlae went on. "As always, you will see me,

once a week, and I will pay you in Thelian silvers."

"Who am I to guard?" Yourdon asked, growing still warier of the big Dral's expression, concerned that things were about to go from bad to worse yet again.

"His name," Banlae replied, "is Rem Ana."

He looked much the same as he had the first time Yourdon had seen him hurrying down the street with his *emari* and a few disciples. He wore a long, white tunic sharply accented by a light brown, gold-embroidered mantle, topped by a tall woolen hat dyed in several shades of blue and brown. His dark, graying beard and hair made him look older than Yourdon guessed he was. Some of the intensity Yourdon had seen in his eyes that day was missing now. Here, at home in his temple, Rem Ana seemed completely at ease.

The temple itself was a truly ancient stone structure composed of several large halls, each with upper and lower levels, each divided into dozens of rooms, from what Yourdon could determine. It had surely been home to many faiths, and would be to many more. Yourdon had been touched by a sense of timeless wonder as he strode down the dark stone halls, until finally he emerged into a foyer. He went through a set of double doors swung open wide, and found himself amid the splendor of a grand hall, a room that featured a high ceiling of sculpted arches. The walls were covered by colorful tapestries, and rugs lay everywhere on the floor, thrown here and there as much for style as function. Richly painted pottery, some of it enormous, decorated the corners, and in the center of the floor itself white stone had been laid, a path that led directly to Rem Ana. The Quin faith did not seem at all a spartan one.

Yourdon imagined this might once have been a dining hall: at the far end of the room the floor rose slightly to a wide platform that crossed from wall to wall, a fine place to set the head table. Now it was occupied by Rem, who was seated in a massive curved chair, finished in ivory, which seemed to have been carved all from one piece. Four *emari* were seated near Rem, two on either side. A long, squat table stood before them on which numerous scrolls had been laid, their ends trimmed in gold. A woman, head covered by a veil, knelt before the table. Yourdon watched as she raised one of the scrolls to her lips and kissed it. Rem smiled softly at her, then she rose and moved away, leaving the room through a side entrance.

"Approach," Rem said, beckoning with one thin hand. Yourdon did so. The *emari* who had led him here stayed behind. Yourdon stood before the table glancing down at the scrolls, sacred writings of some kind. He shook his head. Yourdon had little interest in what they might contain; he had no need of Quin philosophy, as he was still trying to work out his own.

"You are Yourdon of Detimar?" one of the *emari* asked. He was Kdosh, the same odd giant Yourdon had seen talking with Banlae before. Yourdon bowed his head. "I am."

"My life is in your hands," Rem said, in a moderate voice, each word carefully rendered, as was his small smile. "Do you know of my needs?"

The question caught Yourdon off guard. "Yes," he answered, "you need a protector."

Rem grinned more broadly, almost a Banlae grin. "And do you know why you were chosen?"

"I . . . think so," Yourdon replied.

Rem leaned forward in the chair. He rested his elbows on his knees, then laced his fingers together and rested his chin atop them. "There are those who might wish me harm, you see, perhaps even a few Quin. . . ." He lowered his voice to a conspiratorial whisper. "So, you see, I need someone like you to bring balance to my guard. You can do this for me?"

"I can," Yourdon responded, as he knew he must, though indeed he thought it true. From what he had seen and heard, Rem Ana always traveled with many guards, most of them hand-picked *emari*, and he was often surrounded by throngs of devout followers. No one could be safer, it seemed. And there had been no trouble involving Rem in Dlet that anyone could tell him of—Yourdon had asked. So vigilance would likely be his only task. Still, he decided he might gently test the waters: "You have many friends as well."

Rem glanced at Kdosh, then raised his head off of his hands. "And I trust you will become one of them," he said.

"Perhaps," Yourdon said, as cordially as possible. There was something about the holy man's voice that seemed familiar to Yourdon—his tone, his control—something about his manner. Something that lent weight to the grim picture Tufan had painted of the man.

"Only perhaps?" Rem queried.

Yourdon didn't budge. "Yes."

"So, a staid and cautious man, and reliable, Banlae tells me. I am encouraged by all this, you see. You might do well."

Rem was still smiling thinly as he sat back again; Yourdon was not sure what it meant, but the expression finally made him realize who Rem reminded him of. Like the voice, Rem's countenance was not physically the same, but the manner and intent were precisely like Yourdon's father's.

. . . I will never escape him, Yourdon realized, though he also saw the small advantage that came from familiarity.

"What is on your mind?" Rem asked. The older man's

eyes held Yourdon's gaze now, though the more Yourdon stared back the more he felt Rem was looking into the middle of his mind.

"I have heard you are a sorcerer," Yourdon answered, testing again, two-ways curious.

Rem smiled more broadly now. "And would such a thing trouble you?"

"Not at all."

"Of course it is true. I have a few talents, gifts from the Five Gods, part of my calling. I have been chosen to lead my people, and the powers the Gods express through me are the single greatest worldly sign of that truth. You will see, and you will learn. But you are right not to concern yourself with such things now, as my followers would tell you. Only those who bring injustice, those who denounce the light, need fear me.

"I do not destroy, that is not my calling. I am here to build, to restore to the Quin their divinely sanctioned place in this world, and the dignity they have lost. I have been granted the power to raise a kingdom in the name of the Five Gods."

"They say you can raise the dead as well," Yourdon said, as respectfully as any man could. Rem Ana, Yourdon had already decided, was not a modest man. He fully expected the prophet to list his many feats of deathsway and other magics; to his credit, Rem's expression did not change as he glanced to either side again, and said, "I do as the Five Gods command me, nothing more."

So like Dree, Yourdon thought again. A pawn of the fates—or the Gods, this Rem, though surely he was not so helpless as he pretended. Still, it often took such men to achieve great things, or to maintain them, as his father had done. Yourdon was not such a man, he was at least as certain of that now as he had ever been, but he understood the breed, their singular values, their endlessly scheming methods, their narrow, yet frequently shifting loyalties. In his own mind Dree Lewen had always thought himself a reasonable and completely justified man, Yourdon knew, just as Rem Ana must. *Just as I did.*

Of course, everyone makes mistakes. . . .

"I understand," Yourdon assured the Quin. "In turn, I shall do as you command me." The words had always pleased his father, and seemed to have the desired effect on Rem as well.

"What do you know of our faith?" Rem asked him, settling back into the chair, giving the question a casual air.

"Only a little," Yourdon said, curbing a desire to wince. He was certain he had just left himself open to a flood of ecclesiastic dogma, but he saw little choice.

"Ah, you see? That is just enough. At least for now." Rem wore a slightly different grin now—almost a smirk. "Welcome to our circle," he finished. "Welcome to the hope of Akreea, and the promise of the Quin."

Yourdon nearly made a face, cleared his throat instead. He took his place in the second seat a few paces to Rem's right side, as the fifth *emari* now directed him. The man who had been seated there rose and went to stand beside the knee-high table, while an attendant turned and headed back to the room's main entrance. Others waited there. One by one they came forward. The faithful, Yourdon gathered, here to ask for mercy or offer their praise to the Five Gods, and Rem Ana.

Already Yourdon thought he knew their prophet perhaps better than they; even so, he didn't know what truly filled the heart, or moved the soul of this man the Kyr-Akree and many others seemed to fear so much. He wasn't sure he ever wanted to.

He sat watching the ritual, all the while reminding

himself of Beken's words, Never trust anyone. He wasn't about to. He had his eyes open wide.

He imagined Rem saw the faithful and the power they brought him in much the same way Dree saw his own vast holdings and his seat on the ruling Council, as the means to his ends, as the tangible pieces of his largest dreams. Whatever they were.

In Thetar, the priests served the True God selflessly, or most of them did. Rem seemed no such creature. But Yourdon had not been raised to know selflessness, and this world seldom favored those who practiced it. That realization had always left a sour taste on Yourdon's palate, but one he was slowly learning to accept. As long as he managed to maintain Rem's apparent regard for him, and the compensation kept coming with it, he and Rem would likely get along.

More of the faithful came and went, and Yourdon let his mind imagine the style Rem's wages would keep him in, the possibilities it would ultimately bring to him, the life it would keep him from. But there was more, he decided; he remembered only too well the man he had been when Beken had found him. Rem and his *emari* commanded a great deal of respect, something Yourdon never had. Now, perhaps, it would be denied him no longer.

The last of Rem's waiting disciples finally approached, an older, frail woman, who spoke of a sickness afflicting her daughter, who was with child. Rem said he would ask the Five Gods to favor the girl. The woman wore a look of bliss upon her face as she departed, leaving the chamber in silence.

"I will not need you tomorrow," Rem told Yourdon as he rose, and gathered with the others. "I intend to stay in my chambers for prayer and meditation. You will return the day after, early, and accompany me on my walk through the city. That is the way it will always be. Whenever I am out, you will be with me."

Yourdon bowed in response, ignoring a faint remembrance of his boyhood as he did. Rem walked slowly, deliberately toward the side entrance and disappeared through the draperies.

"He will have many appointments," one of the *emari* warned, pausing as he passed. "Come rested." He didn't smile, he didn't say anything else. No one did. They were not like the Detimarian officers he had known, these *emari*. A stolid bunch. He was sure even Commander Trison had a better sense of humor.

But as he wandered after them, out through the chamber's main door, he realized this was not entirely true. He heard them talking among themselves, then saw two men glance back over their shoulders, a sour little sneer bending both their features.

Not a good sign, Yourdon thought.

But no matter, he quickly insisted. Attitudes could only cause just so much damage. And that was likely all the two *emari* were about. . . .

He had gotten by in spite of what others thought of him for most of his life. A grim accomplishment, but one worth noting. And worth turning around.

❖ A GLIMPSE OF DARKNESS ❖

When Rem Ana went out for the day he did not stop until evening meals were on the city's tables and everyone around him was beyond exhaustion. Seemingly tireless, obsessed, he swept from one house to another, from one small meeting to the next, hearing, speaking, *working*. This last was apparent in the prophet's every act.

Always he was trailed by specially chosen followers, men and women of all ages, who carried his scrolls and ointments and potions. The entourage began the day by paying Rem and the Gods homage, then always they kissed his left hand, where he wore a large gold ring set with a brilliant round crystal, a bauble apparently regarded more as a talisman than a decoration. Next they would set off, Rem leading the way, the rest hurrying to keep up.

Always Rem spoke in the carefully worded phrases and measured tones that comprised a talent Yourdon could not help but admire. And always, Rem Ana was The One.

Yourdon kept his place just to Rem's left and one pace behind at all times. On Rem's right went Kdosh, while the attendants went behind and two more *emari* walked five paces in front of the procession, always alert, eyeing the crowds and selecting, from the many who tried, those worthy to approach their master. The worthy were never disappointed.

145

If they were sick he promised healing, if they were frightened he brought them calm, so powerful was their faith in what he said. Or the influencing spells Rem used. Yourdon could not be certain.

For a man whose neighbors claimed he was possessed by evil, Rem began a chant that called out for intervention through the powers of the Gods. A moment later the unfortunate soul was writhing on the ground while others poured water on him, as the *emari* quickly instructed. Yourdon had to help hold him still to prevent injury. A trick of the mind, Yourdon wondered? But momentarily the man's body began to glow with a radiant heat that forced Yourdon and the others to back away. They watched as the water on the man's flesh and clothing began to steam. The man screamed, then lay still, eyes shut tight. Rem lingered, speaking prayers with the others, until the man's eyes opened again.

"He is saved," Rem announced, bending, kissing the man on the forehead as Kdosh lifted his weakened torso near the prophet's lips. Cheers erupted in the street, and continued as the crowds parted, lining Rem's way as he passed. Whatever had ailed the man, Rem had succeeded in routing it. Yourdon was convinced of that.

Then on to a woman who had lost her husband to sickness, where Rem quoted from a scroll, saying, "All life is of the Five Gods, and returns to them, to all creation, so that life might be born anew." A small crowd of family members gathered around the woman and sang a hymn of praise. When it ended Rem said, "One day, we each will join with your husband's spirit in the Five Gods of Naldasa, enriched and enriching, strengthened and strengthening, ending yet beginning." Yourdon stood fast while all around him people fell to their knees, yielding to Naldasa and praising Rem's words, then Rem himself, as if he were one of the Gods.

"Faith binds us, carries us, challenges us," Rem said as he often did. He never qualified the phrase, leaving application instead to his audience—which always seemed to work in the prophet's favor.

Heathens, Yourdon thought, still likening Akreean behavior to that of the Syttrel, or trying to. In Detimar, the True God, son of the True Goddess, had been worshiped by the people since the world had been created. Detimarians were the chosen people, the bearers of truth, in a world rife with barbarians . . . such as these.

But it was not Yourdon's place to save these people from their ignorance, even if he thought it possible—and he didn't think it was. Akreeans, especially the Quin, were the sort of small-minded zealots who would present a challenge even to one of the First Council's Lord Priests.

As they went Yourdon tried to determine whether Rem was an absolute believer in the Five Gods, or more a believer in himself; Yourdon thought it was a little of both, though probably more of the latter. Nevertheless, Rem was a highly skilled manipulator, and a man whose obvious power caused Yourdon to grow less smug in his assessment as the day wore on. By evening Yourdon's regard for the holy man had deepened considerably, and so had his fear. He wondered what it might have been like if his father had wielded such power.

At their longest stop, in a square filled with Quin, Rem Ana spoke a grand invocation, both promise and prophecy:

"I will find forgiveness for you when I travel into the presence of the Gods. I will bring to you the word of the Gods, and the justice of the ages—when I am returned!"

He waited for the rolling murmur of the crowd to pass.

"A far distant evil will strike me down," he continued,

"but I will live again, and in so doing bring the might and destiny of the Gods' word to our people. This the Gods have promised you. This I, The One, promise you."

"The One!" each and every Quin present shouted, as well as some Akreeans who apparently were not Quin at all. *No,* Yourdon thought, *my father never commanded devotion like this.* Perhaps not even the Detimarian First Council and their Lord Priests had ever known the like. The moment moved even Yourdon, and the realization made him a little uneasy.

Upon their return to the temple, and the return of the scrolls to their special table, the others began to disperse. "You may go," Kdosh said, the only time the colossal *emari* had spoken directly to Yourdon all day. "Return the morning after next, at sunrise."

No comment, no thank you, no "good day." Yourdon said he would.

As he turned to go he found Rem walking toward him, then standing in his path. "I would speak with you," the prophet said, clear and calm. Yourdon waited while Rem signalled one of his *emari*, who quickly collected a stool from one side of the room and placed it directly behind Rem—who then sat, eyes fixed on Yourdon.

"What will you tell your friends, when you see them?" he asked. "How will you speak of me?"

"I have no friends. Is that not one reason you hired me?"

"Ahh, of course," Rem said, adding the briefest grin, a flicker of something larger, perhaps. "And if you should gain one, what will you say?"

"I would say you are a remarkable man," Yourdon assured him. "That you have many devoted followers."

"I do as the Five Gods command, nothing more, you see," Rem said but again Yourdon wondered whether Rem interpreted the mind of the Gods the way Dree reckoned the mind of the fates. "I see," Yourdon offered. "The gods do seem to favor you."

Rem eyed him more cautiously. "Sometimes," he replied.

"Or do they fear you?" Yourdon asked, unable to resist. "Does your God fear your holy men?"

"I doubt it," Yourdon said.

"I know of your faith," Rem said, a distant look. "Yours is a false God, you see. Most of them are. You must realize that, or you will, one day. For me, Naldasa is truth. There is no fear, understand, only hope. When you accept the words the Quin prophets have given this world and its people, even the people from the darkness beyond the mountains, you will be rewarded, this I can promise."

"I'll think about it," Yourdon said, thinking in fact of saying the same things back to Rem, swapping Gods around. He felt it would not be in his best interest just now. And he had a nagging notion that the strange and able prophet was saying many things at once.

"Of course you will," Rem said, then his expression changed yet again, to one of satisfaction. "And a journey of the mind often finds a destination. You may well think forever, you see. Yet that is not what I expect."

Yourdon stood, lost for a reply. He didn't like being outflanked by Rem. He shuffled his feet, then Rem beckoned Yourdon's ear closer with one long finger.

"I must tell you . . . I feel I must. It might help you to consider something, but if I tell you, truly listen, and try to understand." He paused, wearing as concerned a look as Yourdon had imagined him capable of. Then he went on, "At times we are called upon to make great sacrifices for the good of all. These times, all Gods, of all peoples, watch us carefully. It is my hope that if you are called one day, you will find the courage to accept such an honor."

With that Rem smiled. Yourdon didn't like the look anymore than he liked the sound of Rem's last remark, one reminiscent of Tasia's, her sharp attempts to call his bravery into doubt. He straightened his shoulders. But he wasn't sure that was the worst of it.

"You may trust that I will serve you well, as long as the wages match the task. And so long as I am told the truth." He stared at Rem this time, waiting for a sign that would give the other away, but none appeared.

Rem sat in silence for a time, then he rose and nodded, cordial. "Good day," he said simply, then he slowly swept himself away.

Yourdon found himself alone in the great, silent chamber, surrounded by wall tapestries. The Five Gods themselves might be hiding behind any one of them, he thought, kidding himself. Rem might be many things, a true prophet in touch with great powers, a great pretender in league with the darkness, a lunatic serving only himself, but he was a powerful man in every sense. And cunning, there was no doubt.

The KyrPhelians seemed to understand that very well, as did the Quin-Akree, in their own way. Yourdon wasn't about to do less. Not if he was to avoid making some dangerous mistakes. He let the day replay itself in his mind as he found his way out, and home.

The next day went quickly, but the day after, accompanying Rem on his rounds again, seemed to vanish in a whirlwind of motion, prayer, and praise. Then two days with no work, two days in which Yourdon felt more bored and adrift than he had in . . . a year, perhaps. The newness of it all, he thought, trying to rationalize, the commotion, the sense of purpose, that stimulated him. But such explanations, while real, seemed somewhat lacking.

On their fourth outing Rem spoke directly to him, something he rarely did, but once again he mentioned sacrifice, great, personal sacrifice; and Yourdon began to worry.

"If Rem makes you uneasy, I will attempt to find someone else," Banlae said with a sigh, raising his eyebrows, gazing about as if he'd already begun the search. The inn was strangely quiet this night, but the hour was not yet very late. In a while, Yourdon thought, the crowd would thicken. "I never said that," he replied. "The work is good, and Rem has done nothing I cannot abide."

"Aye, such problems," Banlae teased.

"I don't trust him."

"Good!" Banlae said with zeal. "I trust no one." *Of course you don't.* Yourdon took a breath. "Agreed, but there is something about him. I can't say what, but the more I am around him and his *emari* the more I don't want to be. He speaks often of sacrifice as the only means to salvation, speaks so directly to me, I mean. And his warrior priests, especially Kdosh, do not seem a lot. They seem proper and devout, yet they are up to something. What did you call them once, holy assassins?"

Banlae flashed a knowing grin. "I said that?"

"Perhaps," Yourdon muttered.

"So, then, you think much of what Rem says may be beautiful lies?"

"I do, but nothing of him can be easily dismissed. He is a talented mage, I have seen him do his special sorceries—no deathsway, no dead men walking the earth again, mind you, but the near-dead and near-lost brought around. And he has spells which grant him considerable influence. But my concerns go deeper. He is building a nation, make no mistake; one I may not want to live in. He pays special attention to young men of fighting age."

"He means to fight a holy war for the Quin homeland."

"No doubt, but I do not wish to take part in it."

"Nor I, I assure you," Banlae agreed, "yet there are two things I would tell you." He paused, seemed to search the inn's ceiling rafters for a proper thought, then, "First, Rem has expressed his great pleasure with your appointment, a boon to both of us, you'll agree."

Yourdon waited, but Banlae did not continue. "And?" he finally prodded the Dral.

"And . . . there is no one else willing to hire you just now. Not even at half the wages Rem is willing to pay."

"You are sure?"

Banlae sat back in his chair, then he gently chuckled. Others, seated nearby, chuckled too. Yourdon realized his mistake. "Of course," he said, picking at a nagging thumbnail. Banlae was making typically good sense. Rem had done only good these past two weeks, or so it seemed. And after all, even if Yourdon didn't want to be a mercenary forever, and even though he knew the Quin's "homeland" included KyrPhel, just now there were no reasonable alternatives.

Still, every time he imagined what his father would have become, possessed as Rem was with powers of sorcery, something inside him grew cold and hard. . . .

"I can manage, of course, for a time. What you say is true. And Rem intrigues me, after all, I cannot deny that. But if you hear of something else, even at lesser wages, tell me you will keep my name in mind."

"Oh, yes, I will," Banlae answered, suddenly so sincere Yourdon thought to doubt him. Which it seemed was the proper instinct, as Banlae looked about and chuckles began once more. Yourdon was beginning to worry about Banlae almost as much as Rem Ana and the *emari*, though for different reasons.

"Take no offense, I seldom have such ill-mannered fun," Banlae said, "but with you it comes too easily at times."

Outflanked again, Yourdon thought, keeping a moan to himself. He favored Banlae with a rueful stare. The effect was not what Yourdon had hoped for. Banlae took one look, and broke out laughing.

Yourdon held his tongue. He knew he should be laughing along with the others, but he couldn't quite get there.

"I will do what I can," Banlae said, more serious.

"That is all I can ask," Yourdon said curtly, getting up, turning to leave the Golden Axe.

"And a fine day to you as well," Banlae bellowed after him. The rest of the inn's patrons echoed Banlae's regards.

Yourdon kept walking. He was due at Rem Ana's temple at sunrise.

By the time he woke the next morning he was already late. He rushed to dress, then hurried through the streets, forgoing breakfast, arriving just in time to meet the Quin leader as he was exiting the temple on his way to the waiting many. Yourdon immediately took his familiar place to Rem's left, one pace back. The prophet paused to find Yourdon with his eyes, then he nodded. "I knew you would come," Rem said without inflection. "I knew it." Then he turned to those who had been chosen to tend him this day, his usual complement. "The prophecies tell of this and more," he said loudly. "They tell of the nonbeliever, as you see, and of this day. They tell of the great sacrifice."

A deadly hush followed. Yourdon found everyone staring at him now as if he had grown a second head.

"Could you explain . . . a little?" Yourdon asked.

"Know the truth, and all will be explained," Rem responded, quite solemn. *Which means nothing.* Yourdon sighed, silently. Next Rem looked to the others and gave them a blessing of some kind, repeated several times and rendered in a most obscure Akreean tongue. He glanced at Yourdon as he spoke, then looked to his people again. The faithful nearly gasped in apparent awe. Yourdon didn't understand the significance—which was beginning to get on his nerves.

Rem switched phrases then, chanting and holding his hands above those gathered, waving the crystal ring. He repeated the words, "tapat deshi," which were followed each time by an audible moan from the crowd. Yourdon saw them getting glassy-eyed, and wondered how they could be so convinced of anything, anyone. But he began to feel it himself then, a sense of mild distraction and growing tranquility that settled over his mind like a soft silk veil. *Like Syttrelian runes*, he thought, his mind suddenly drawn to the notion—one that brought him no comfort. He blinked and tried to shake it off. Which seemed to help a bit.

"The day begins," Rem announced suddenly, as he turned and began a brisk walk across the little square, then into the streets beyond. Everyone quickly followed.

He made only four stops this morning, all of them to console those who seemed to need it the most, two older women taken deathly ill, a man with an injury to his arm that would not heal, and finally a boy of nearly soldiering age whose faith seemed in question; his parents had died in a fire two days before. The fog in Yourdon's head ebbed and flowed, but by noon, following yet another blessing, Yourdon had begun to feel particularly slow witted.

He tried to concentrate on something basic, and began focusing on the crowds. Wherever they went the people of Dlet stopped to stare, hundreds of them; most wore a look of adulation—for their prophet, of course—which extended to Yourdon and the others with Rem as well. Even while Rem went alone into an old mud and brick house, where the city's physicians had placed a sign warning of a killing disease, Yourdon enjoyed the respect of passersby.

Not to be discounted, he told himself, pushing his still tenuous misgivings further into the back of his mind.

Rem emerged soon enough and continued on down the way, though he seemed more lethargic now, so much the slower was his pace. Directly they entered a large and busy market square. Here people crowded near, calling out to him, calling him "The One!" The *emari* drew closer to their sage as the Quin from across the marketplace led the growing crush of followers. Yourdon closed in as well.

When Rem made no attempt to stop or speak to them, the *emari* began pushing people back, some of them quite roughly. When this proved not enough the holy warriors drew their great curved swords and began waving them threateningly.

Yourdon helped, drawing his own straight blade, holding it in the air while using his free hand to bat at those who came near. Then a pair of hands jutted out of the crowd and pushed him back hard. Yourdon spun, then stumbled and fell into Rem. He reached and grabbed at Rem, who was nearly toppled, and both of them stumbled briefly. Yourdon managed to take hold of Rem's left hand, but as his hand closed around the other's Yourdon felt the crystal-set gold ring beneath his fingers, and the touch aroused the magic within him. He held on, and he saw something there. Someone . . .

As Yourdon quickly spoke his own private chant the image grew clearer, and he saw that the man before him did not look like Rem at all. He saw someone with Rem, the someone who stood before him, it seemed. This fellow wore a gray, lifeless face that made some part of Yourdon's mind grow cold. He let go and blinked the hollow cheeks and blank, staring eyes from his mind just as he heard the shouting start. When he looked again Rem Ana's head was coming off.

A blade flashed, trailing ruddy bits of bone and flesh. The head fell backward toward the ground as the torso jerked free. Black blood ran from the neck and sprayed from the tumbling head in thin rivulets, spattering a mother and two children as they screamed and tried to step away. The head rolled across the ground as feet leaped back to let it pass.

Yourdon looked down and saw the blood on himself now, as he tried to break free of the trance that held him. The blood on his tunic felt cold when he touched it. He stared at the decapitated body as it spasmed on the ground at his feet, then he watched the head leap again as an older woman screamed and kicked it away from her feet.

"Assassins!" Yourdon heard, part of an exploding ruckus of shouts and cries all around him. He spun finally, sword at the ready, searching for a target. But Kdosh was suddenly in front of him, grabbing his arm. "Your sword!" he shouted, wildness in his eyes. He reached out and tore Yourdon's weapon from his hand, nearly tearing fingers with it. As he tried to look down Yourdon felt a sharp, stabbing pain at the base of his skull, and he entered into darkness.

Daylight stabbed at Yourdon's eyes as he was led out of the dungeons, through the door at the top of the stairs, and into the fresh air. He took small steps, hobbled by the weakness in his limbs and the clumsy weight of his shackles. Memories crowded his mind as two men, part of the ad hoc mercenary force that made up the city of Dlet's private guard, led him through a series of narrow, high-walled outdoor walkways, until they emerged in a small courtyard. Since coming to and finding a throbbing knot on the back of his head the world had swirled around him like a desert storm. He had barely begun to cope.

Neatly carved stone tables and benches rested here or there among the yard's many thriving shrubs and trees, a gentle contrast to the old, blackened, fortified stone walls that surrounded them. "Sit here," one of the guards said, pushing Yourdon toward a table from behind. His knee struck the edge of the stone bench and he nearly fell. The guard grabbed him and planted him squarely on the bench.

He had been in the dungeon since his public trial, more than a week ago by his count, though these dungeons, like those in Thetar, offered no clue as to day or night. Nor did the guards offer any information. Yourdon had protested repeatedly during his brief trial, but here as in Detimar, no one in Dlet seemed willing to listen to his story. No one quite believed.

Partly he could not blame them, as he had little enough story to tell. He remembered Rem Ana's head tumbling to the ground, the screaming that followed, and then . . .

"You do not look well." The voice came from behind him. Familiar. Yourdon tried to place it as he craned his neck to see who stood behind him. The guards backed away, apparently allowing a bit of privacy. It was Banlae Tfa, splendid in a rich, colorful brown and cerise tunic and a new, many layered headpiece that all but hid his thick, curly hair.

Yourdon sat staring at the big Dral, eyes wide. *The first friendly face I have seen in how many days,* Yourdon thought. Then he decided "friendly" was probably not the perfect word.

"Can you answer?" Banlae said, staring back.

"I will never look as good as you," Yourdon grumbled.

"Ah," Banlae grinned. "And few would argue that!"

Yourdon was buoyed slightly by Banlae's mood, typically superior, mildly jocular. He wanted to explain his side, tell Banlae that he hadn't killed Rem as he had been accused, but he had no idea what had really happened in the market. Since his trial he had spent his days thinking of how far he had come, how hard he had tried, only to end up where he had started: imprisoned, accused of a crime he had not committed—at least as far as he knew—and despised by half the population. He had seen this last in the eyes of the Quin present at the trial. A mob, threatening to erupt, a city without the slightest empathy for him. But that hadn't changed either, had it. Almost nothing had, he brooded, *perhaps not even myself*. . . .

The reality of his plight had left him empty inside, bereft of energy and hope, a mood equalled only by the darkness of the dungeon they had put him in. His lifelong war against the fates had resulted in yet another lost battle.

Akreea had been his hope for a new beginning, a new life. Filled with ideals and determination, he had given it everything he had. . . .

"I'm sure you have had many visitors," Banlae said calmly. "Well-wishers and the like. I hoped you would not mind one more."

"I love to entertain," he answered grimly.

"As do I," Banlae agreed.

This was not Dree, after all, Yourdon reminded himself, attempting to gather enough sense to field Banlae's eccentric wit. In the warmth and fresh air of the courtyard he thought it might even be worth a try. After all, Banlae had come here for some reason or other.

"Feel free to use anything of mine," Yourdon jested.

"A generous offer. If only the city had not seized it already," Banlae chortled, enjoying himself.

Yourdon tired of the banter. "When is my execution to take place?"

"With luck, on the day that follows your natural death," Banlae replied. He looked about, confirming the locations of the guards, then he leaned closer to Yourdon and lowered his voice. "There is to be no execution." He grinned broadly. "Only imprisonment. You are a lucky fellow."

"You have never been me," Yourdon answered.

"True. The Five Gods have favored me there."

"About my execution," Yourdon prodded.

"It seems that not everyone in Dlet is entirely offended by Rem Ana's untimely death. As you must know, many Akreean peoples do not agree with the Quin's extreme views, or their desires to impose those views on others. They want no part in his plans, much like you and I. So they see his death as a respite. Everyone knows a war will be fought at some time, but many would prefer the distant future. Even Dlet's city council has been at odds over what to do regarding Rem. Since my countrymen saw fit to run off to the north again, he has made Dlet his home, and Quin have been gathering here ever since. I would not have been surprised if the council had come to me, requesting I commission someone to do precisely what you have done—er, were accused of doing. What *someone* has done. I understand you claim innocence?"

The question surprised Yourdon—the first true sign that not everything was the way it had been in Detimar. He thought it mattered little whether Banlae believed him or not, but it mattered very much that he had asked.

Yourdon explained his version of events yet again. Banlae nodded, not the least bit bewildered. "Anyone might have killed him, certainly. Perhaps one of his own people. Who can say? In any case, you have less to worry about than you think."

"How?" Yourdon asked.

Banlae raised his brow. "I know nothing of the customs

in Detimar, but here in Dlet the court magistrates gather testimony from every source available before the accused is brought before them. Well, it seems almost no one came forward. Even the *emari* who were with Rem declined to appear. It is as though the events in the marketplace had occurred in the middle of the night. I cannot explain it, and neither could the magistrates.

"Only a handful of citizens who had been present claimed that you *may* have slit Rem's throat."

"May have?"

"Yes, but each of them admits to being confused at the time, unable to concentrate, and each told a somewhat different story, I understand. Strangest of all, it seems Rem's body, and his head, disappeared from the market! No trace has been found. So you see, curiously, there is no evidence."

"He is a sorcerer, you know," Yourdon said, his mind suddenly filled with the images he had seen when his hand had touched the prophet's ring—the bleak, pallid stranger he suddenly looked upon. He recalled how clouded his own mind had been, too. He thought to tell Banlae about the vision, but that would require explaining his own magical talent, and Yourdon thought it best not to do that, not now. He couldn't make sense of the images in any case, though not for lack of trying. The other, though . . .

"He may have used some kind of persuasion spell, or a spell to fool the eyes. I too felt confused that morning, but Rem was using a chant, one I'd never heard before that."

"And you think there is a connection," Banlae mused, nodding.

"Possibly. Probably."

"Many have said that Rem has great talents with illusion and other tricks of the mind."

"Then that is what happened," Yourdon agreed.

"I'm sure the Quin ran off with him, expecting the head and body would somehow rejoin to fulfill the prophecy of the resurrection," Banlae supposed. "Many believed Rem to be The One."

"Rem said so, constantly," Yourdon confirmed.

"As well I know," Banlae replied. "But the facts are that you—or someone—may have done the city a favor by ridding it of the holy man, and that, along with the lack of evidence, weighed in your favor. After you were given your chance to speak, the court made its decision. You might simply have been set free, but because of a desire to avoid provoking the many Quin within this city, and the rest of Akreea, the magistrates felt it wise to keep you under lock and key. After all, one outlander does not matter so much in the scheme of things, and the Quin must be appeased, at least within reason."

"I see," Yourdon said grimly. "So sending me to prison seemed the most reasonable thing to do."

"Yes!" Banlae said, with a raucous smile. "Ahh, you are as bright a fellow as I have always suspected. Someone must suffer, after all, and who better? A likely suspect, a stranger from Detimar, distrusted to begin with—and someone no Akreean is likely to speak in favor of. Everyone agrees, and no one objects. What would you do?"

Yourdon frowned at Banlae.

"Were you them, of course."

"I understand," Yourdon moaned.

"But there is still more," Banlae insisted. Yourdon looked at him, waiting. Banlae grinned broadly now, an almost evil look that seemed no strain on his countenance. "I . . . objected!"

"To what?" Yourdon asked, realizing even as he said it, saying it anyway. He could not believe his ears.

"I have a reputation, after all. If I thought you had betrayed my trust you would have been dead long before your trial. I don't deal in second chances. I have never chosen wrongly, and never have I disappointed anyone willing to pay for the services I provide. My name is of immense importance to me, and either you or someone else has soiled it. A cleansing is needed."

"So you spoke in my defense? Publicly?"

"Of course not. There are ways more subtle. But my mind was made known. And there is more I can do. I was prepared to supply witnesses who would say you did not kill Rem, but when so few accusers showed there was no need."

"I am pleased that you believe in me," Yourdon confided. "I don't seem to have much luck with that sort of thing."

"I believe in *me*," Banlae returned. "And I chose you. To accuse my agents is to accuse me in turn. I have never much liked the Quin. No Dral ever has. They've been far too much trouble for far too long. If Dolett Bon had put them all into slavery when he had the chance—"

Banlae stopped himself, eyes darting to one side momentarily. "But enough daydreaming," he said with a sigh. "For now, at least, you will not die. Next, perhaps you will be set free. As soon as I can arrange it. That will be a more difficult thing, but with time and persuasion, great feats are possible. For now there is enough doubt surrounding your guilt to repair much of my reputation, and to predict your eventual release. I can recover from the rest. With luck, so will you."

Luck, Yourdon thought again. In keeping his neck this second time he had likely used up all that he had.

"Banlae, I—"

"Ah, you wish to lavish thanks upon me. No need.

After a few weeks in Dlet's labor prison you may wish I had let you die. You may die anyway."

"You are a cheerful fellow."

"Indeed, so good day to you, and if by chance I never see you again, good-bye, and may you fare well among the Gods."

Banlae rose abruptly, smiled once more, then padded off across the yard and was gone. Yourdon sat still, a bit stunned. He didn't have much time to contemplate. The guards appeared at his sides and yanked him to his feet. They led him away to a dungeon he had not seen before, a vast room filled with perhaps a hundred men.

As the guards clapped the heavy wood and iron framed door shut behind him, Yourdon looked into the faces of the others. Crude, caged torches were fitted into the mortar in the walls, flames blackening the low stone ceiling. The smell was a thick mixture of feces, sweat and rot.

Every man stared quietly back, then mumbling began among them. Yourdon couldn't make out any of the words, or clearly, any of the faces. Then he heard a man shout in his direction. Yourdon looked up as someone jerked a torch free from its notch and started toward him.

❖ FARTHER AWAY ❖

The man's face was hideous to look at, a great knot of a nose amid cheeks covered by sores where the whiskers barely grew. A leer pulled his mouth open on one side, revealing a few snaggled teeth. He was of average height and build otherwise, dressed in a shabby tunic and ragged pants that had never been anything grand. He held the torch too close, forcing Yourdon to pull back as the heat singed his eyebrows. When Yourdon turned to move away two other men grabbed him, one on each arm.

"Who're you?" the ugly man asked, a rough and gritty voice, a sloppy Dral. Yourdon gave his name. Several heads nodded. The man looked closely again. "You the one killed Rem?"

"I was there," Yourdon answered, not sure whether he should.

"And you killed him?"

"No."

"He did!" another man insisted.

"You like trouble, that right?" the ugly man asked, his head tipped almost sideways.

"No, not me. I've seen too much of it."

"Good. Very good. I got trouble for you, if you want," the ogre answered, making a fist in front of the torch. "Some men die in these prisons, or in the mines, or the work houses. Some never see a second day."

Yourdon didn't like being threatened, but he was sure

164

there was nothing in here worth dying over. For all he knew he was one against dozens, and he had no idea yet what the stakes were, for them, or for himself.

"I mean no one harm," Yourdon said. The ugly man looked to his friends, then he laughed for a time. Suddenly his face went slack. He cocked his right fist and drove it into Yourdon's jaw without a warning. The two men holding Yourdon's arms let go just then, let their captive collapse backward to the damp, rush-covered floor.

Yourdon gathered his wits and lifted his head. There they all stood, waiting. Just behind the man who had hit Yourdon there stood another man, a scrawny fellow, much older and grayer than the rest; he was dressed in rags like the others but apparently was in good spirits; and he was grinning like an idiot. When their eyes met the older man began signaling Yourdon, waving a flat hand toward the ground. The message was clear enough: *stay down*. Yourdon decided to take that advice. He slumped back and lay still for a moment. When he finally looked again the others were talking among themselves, moving away, apparently not so interested in him anymore. He got up slowly, then edged hands and knees toward the nearest wall, where he sat.

The man who had attacked him kept turning an eye to Yourdon for a time, then he seemed to forget. Which was precisely when the older man who had signaled to Yourdon decided to come near. He sat down cross-legged on the floor, facing Yourdon.

"Toeplo," he said. Yourdon wasn't familiar with the word, and he hesitated to ask. When he said nothing the older man repeated the word, adding, "You?" Yourdon realized it was his name. He repeated his own.

"I am Quin-Akree," Toeplo said next, and Yourdon blanched. He fought the urge to brace for battle, he didn't think the old man alone posed much threat. But how many others were there, locked in here with him? What would they do to him? Yourdon glanced past the old man to the ogre who had hit him; he and his friends were staying away. So were the rest. Toeplo seemed to notice Yourdon's gaze.

"He is Gieffa," he said. "Not Quin. Which is too bad. Gieffa holds sway over most, Tesen does over the rest." Toeplo pointed again, this time to a man in the room's far corner, only a shape.

"And what of you?" Yourdon asked.

"I am pleased to meet the man who killed that lying snake, Rem Ana!"

Yourdon's eyes opened wider. "You are?"

"Yes, of course."

The man was grinning the way he had before, the way a man with a fatal fever might, just before he slipped away. "A liar, you say. And why is that?" Yourdon asked, despite a notion he should not.

"It is obvious. Only I can call myself the greatest mortal Quin of all!" Toeplo's voice grew louder as his eyes grew wider. "The rest are all pretenders. I am The One!"

"But I thought Rem was The One?"

"Don't ask me to believe such a thing! They are crazy. All crazy! So unfortunate. Yet I thought you sane. After all, it was you saw fit to remove his blaspheming head."

"But I—"

"Now all Akreeans shall see. He claimed to know the way back from death, back to life. I have been there many times, myself, and come back again. And I have never seen him along the way." He licked his smiling lips and didn't quite tuck in his tongue.

Yourdon tried to sort him out. "Many times, you say?"

"Indeed. This world has no power over me. Nor does this city! If I die in here, I will only come back to life again."

"How many times?" Yourdon inquired.

The old man thought a moment. "The next will be my ninth resurrection, I think. Possibly tenth. I need someone to keep a ledger. You, perhaps! But only if you convince me you will not behead me as well. My sleep would be brief, but my death would be a painful nuisance. I'm not sure I understand your mind after all. What did you say your name was?"

"Yourdon, and I would have thought one resurrection would be enough."

"Agreed. I am doing something wrong, but I don't know what." Toeplo seemed to ponder the question deeply.

Yourdon studied the old man's face as it twitched in the dim light. "Do the others in this dungeon also think you are The One?"

"All say no, but all of them lie. Akreeans cannot be trusted. Even some Quin, and there are a few." He seemed to study the others briefly. "They know the truth in their hearts. And they'll leave you be. The Quin in here were imprisoned because Rem arranged it. Perhaps one or two who would slit your throat because of what you did; most will only kill you for what you do."

"That's . . . that's reassuring."

"And so true. Say what you will, I know you took Rem's life to preserve my honor. That is why the Gods have sent you here to me, where you might serve your master. Stand at my side, and I will speak well of you to the Five Gods!"

Yourdon didn't know what to say. The old man seemed gentle enough, and passionate, certainly, but he wasn't making great sense, and probably couldn't. Apparently there was a reason why the man grinned the way he did. Still, Toeplo had saved his life, very likely, by warning him against Gieffa. Yourdon felt he owed him something for that.

"What does that mean, exactly?" he said.

"You wish to do so?"

"I may."

"The Gods be praised!" Toeplo sang, head tipped back, his voice echoing around the room. Yourdon couldn't help but notice that no one was paying any attention.

"What did you say your name was?" Toeplo asked again.

"Yourdon! My name is Yourdon Lewen."

Toeplo rubbed his whisker-covered jaw. "No," he said at last. "I'm sure that was not it."

"Well it was," Yourdon insisted.

"Very well," Toeplo said, moving on his knees. He found a spot on the wall near Yourdon, then sat and closed his eyes. He fell asleep almost instantly. After a time, exhausted, his jaw still throbbing, Yourdon did the same.

He awoke to a clamor and looked up to see men crowding just to his left near the room's only door. He heard the guards shouting, then the gathering moved backward slightly, and clamor turned to mild frenzy.

Yourdon stood and discovered a number of guards had entered the room with bowls and a great wooden bucket full of cooked grains. More buckets appeared to contain water. Toeplo suddenly brushed past, scurrying into the crowd of men, wending his way to the food. Yourdon thought to follow.

"The prophet eats first, the prophet eats first!" Toeplo kept shouting, but no one took any notice. Toeplo finally reached the food and water and waited, flexing knotty fingers, until a guard offered him a filled cup and bowl. He snatched eagerly at both, but his grip was not firm. As he turned to go the bowl slipped free, spilling its contents of gruel down the front of Gieffa, who was just getting his own bowl filled—and who in turn managed to spill his gruel down the back of another man as he tried to jerk the bowl to safety.

"Crazy old fool!" this last man bellowed, knotting his dirty face, an expression Yourdon was sure must be a painful one. Gieffa reached for Toeplo, but as he did the man with the sodden back put a hand firmly on his shoulder and turned him half around. Yourdon was almost certain this was Tesen, the other man Toeplo had pointed out the night before.

The two of them began shouting at each other in a dialect that Yourdon could hardly follow, but the essence was clear. It seemed the argument was an old one, the gruel but a spark amid so much dried kindling.

Abruptly, Gieffa reached out and pushed Tesen with both hands. Tesen pushed him back. A chorus of shouts rose up around the room as others cheered their champions on. Some of them began pushing each other. Yourdon looked toward the guards, expecting them to intervene. But they had set down their buckets and bowls, along with broken loaves of bread, and were now backing out the dungeon door in a deliberate manner.

The pushing grew more excited and spread to the edges of the gathering. Then a man close to Gieffa managed to get both leaders' attention long enough to point. They followed his finger to Toeplo. "It's him what did it!" the pointing man shouted. "Was that fool!"

"Aye, it's always him!" came another shout.

Yourdon realized there was apparently far more history between these men than he had imagined, and none of it pleasant. Several men began pressing in toward Toeplo, and Yourdon saw the wisdom in standing as far away as possible from the old man. But as he tried to move, Toeplo moved with him and grabbed his arm, then announced, "My champion will defend me! The Five Gods will give him the strength to smite you all! None shall last this day but those who are chosen."

Not again, Yourdon thought grimly.

Then Gieffa reached out, grabbed Yourdon and pushed him straight into Toeplo.

"I am The One! I am The One!" the old man sang, quickly recovering. Yourdon wondered how Toeplo had survived even a day in here—how either of them would survive another.

"Step aside," Gieffa said, leaning his large, pocked nose into Yourdon's face. "I've a score to settle with your crazy friend here. Or I'll settle it with you instead."

Yourdon did as Gieffa suggested. He watched the cranky ogre grab a handful of Toeplo's gray hair, then yank it back and forth. "Sick of you!" Gieffa started shouting at the old man. "Sick of your crazy mouth, your crazy face! Likely have to kill you this time."

"Go ahead, you will see, I'll be back," Toeplo snapped, grinning that way again, like a crazy fool. It seemed everyone here thought Toeplo was a fool. Yourdon knew exactly how that felt.

"No more. Going to break your little neck!" Tesen snarled, teaming up with Gieffa. "You don't care anyway."

"Fear me, all betrayers," Toeplo insisted. "I will rise again!"

Yourdon didn't think so. And somehow he couldn't just stand there any longer.

"He's a crazy old man, as you say," Yourdon told the others, edging slightly nearer. "Can't you just let him be?"

Gieffa let go of Toeplo and swiftly struck Yourdon in the jaw again, in nearly the same spot as before. The blow sent Yourdon stumbling backward into another man, who shoved him hard—straight back at Gieffa. Someone hit Yourdon in the face again, this time not quite as hard. He focused, saw another fist coming and ducked, then he struck out at the nearest figure. He kept throwing punches until no one was throwing them back. As he turned he realized the entire room was embroiled in the fight. Gieffa had Toeplo fast now. Yourdon watched him get both hands firmly around the old man's neck and begin to squeeze. No one stood in the way. The old man was being murdered, then and there.

He slammed into Gieffa's back and felt the other man buckle, heard breath heave from his lungs. As Gieffa let go of Toeplo and turned, Yourdon held onto the ogre's tunic with his left hand, pulled, and drove his right fist hard into the ugliness that was the other man's face. The force of the blow sent them both to the floor. Yourdon, flushed and full of battle's rage, scrambled to his knees and grabbed Gieffa with both hands, then he flipped him over onto his back. Blood drained from the man's enormous ugly nose, forming thick droplets on his heavy whiskers. His eyes moved but would not focus.

Suddenly Yourdon was being hauled to his feet by other men. He tried to block the first punch he saw, but those that followed seemed to come from everywhere. Then the door burst open again and a line of guards came rushing through, each with a small, smooth mace in his hand. Yourdon found himself left alone for an instant as men tried to step aside. When someone tried to grab him again Yourdon managed to tackle the first guard to pass him. He tore the mace from his hand, then turned and began bludgeoning the men who had teamed up against him. He sent three of them to the floor before he was struck in the leg and back at the same time. Then the guards had him fast, dragging him away.

They sat along a wall, at least twenty men that Yourdon could see, each one chained to the next in a row that vanished from sight where the corridor curved away, not twenty paces in either direction. Yourdon recognized no one in the line other than the man chained beside him: Toeplo.

"You are a great hero," Toeplo said, as Yourdon rolled his eyes. Even now, without waiting for an answer, the old man had put on his grin. But he was looking about as if he'd lost something dear. Yourdon thought maybe he had. "I don't think so," he replied, struggling to sit so the chain would not press into his side.

"Then you must think too much," Toeplo said.

"Or not enough. I've done some foolish things in haste."

"Ahh, then when you have more time, you must always do wise things?"

Yourdon considered that. "No, not always."

"See? You'll do fine! You have good instincts, by the Gods. And smarts, plenty of smarts." He looked around at the others chained along the passageway, at the chains themselves, then at Yourdon and the bruises Yourdon knew were there, even though he couldn't touch them with his shackled hands. "Bad luck," Toeplo added, "but good instincts. You should listen to you more often."

"I seem to foul everything up," Yourdon sighed, letting his melancholy rule his speech, feeling a need, and no energy to repress it. "I always have. I keep telling myself that somehow, somewhere, things will change, and my life will start to fit together. But they don't seem to."

"Sometimes it is you who are right, and the rest of creation, short of the Gods, that is wrong."

"A hopeless state, nonetheless," Yourdon said, noting that this last came from a man who apparently justified his entire existence that way.

"Hopeless, unless you see that you need only change the mind of creation."

Yourdon shook his aching head. The whole thing sounded simple enough, to a mad man. "Very well," he said. "And just how is that done?"

"I don't know. But one day, the Gods will tell me." Toeplo grinned. Yourdon did not.

The guards came and got everyone up. They dragged the line of prisoners before the jailor, separating each from the next one in line as they made them stand before a squat, aging fellow whose grim, dark face seemed set in a permanent scowl. He sat on a worn bench at a small table on which rested a cup of wine and nothing else. He listened to the guards as Yourdon came to him.

"You have caused more trouble in one day than most of these others in many," the jailor said, in a deep but wobbly voice. "What have you to say?"

Toeplo, standing directly behind Yourdon, crowded his way forward. "He is my champion!" he said, excited about it. "He has been sent by Gods themselves."

"Let him talk," the jailor said, meaning Yourdon. He waved at the guards to pull Toeplo back.

"I am The One!" old Toeplo insisted, struggling. "I am immortal! I am The One!"

"You and half the other Quin we get in here, now shut him up."

"He is my champion!" Toeplo said again, extending a hand toward Yourdon's shoulder. "We are not afraid of death." A guard grabbed a hold and yanked him back.

"You people spoil my appetite," the jailor said, looking to the guards, shaking his head.

Yourdon felt an urge to strangle the old man himself. He tried to think of something to say on his own behalf. "What he means," he began, still thinking . . .

"Enough, enough!" the jailor growled. "We have no use for crazies in the mines. Put them both in the hole. We will deal with them later."

"But—" Yourdon managed, before a fist struck him low in the back, sending a wave of pain radiating inward. "Shut up and move," the guard behind him said.

"But—" The fist struck again, harder, forcing wind from Yourdon's lungs. The guard had him fast and was ushering him from the room, dragging Toeplo behind. Yourdon didn't get to say another word.

Through the four narrow slots in the center of the door he could hear Toeplo, in another chamber, somewhere nearby. Sometimes he would call out to the old man in the darkness, and Toeplo would call back, though words were difficult to make out. Often Toeplo could be heard talking loudly to no one at all.

Most of the time Yourdon sat on the floor, unable to see even his hand held up to his nose. He had no sense of day or night; only the visits of the guard who brought the food marked the passing of time. Yourdon supposed the food came once a day, no more than that. He used a knuckle-sized piece of stone he had found, groping in the blackness, to scrape a groove into the wall where he usually sat, one for each meal. The blinding light of the guard's lamp briefly illuminated the little room each day. Four walls, one of them rounded, and there a deep hole had been cut into the earth. The smell explained its purpose. On his first day, crawling about, Yourdon had nearly fallen in.

The days since had been spent mulling over all that had come to be his life. He still seemed to be losing every bit of ground he won, momentum turning into misfortune. *All my dreams,* he thought, *all my promises, unfulfilled.* Truly this was worse than being spit upon on the streets of Thetar, worse even than drinking oneself to death in Dra Mai. He remembered sitting there at the inn, talking to Beken, and wondering how he had fallen so low. Yet now he had fallen lower still, the result of events he could not fathom, at the hands of enemies he did not understand.

"Don't trust *anybody*," Beken had told him. Good advice, that. He had learned as much as a boy, trusting his "friends," his father, or later still, the girl he had come to know. He had trusted in his comrades in the legion only to pay the price of that mistake. But even Beken himself had let him down. Just when Yourdon had found a friend he could truly rely on, the bastard had gone and died on him!

With Rem, Yourdon had been more cautious, trusting only that, eyes open, a business arrangement could be carefully maintained. Yet this had proved an utter disaster, the ultimate lesson in foolishness. Even Banlae had been fooled—or he had been a part of the plot from the beginning, and Yourdon had been fooled twice over. . . .

People could indeed be crueler than the fates, but he could rely on neither, that was clear enough.

"You don't even trust yourself," Yourdon said out loud, swimming in self-pity now, drowning in it. He still could not put the scouting mission behind him, the unanswered questions that night had raised, the doubts heaped upon him by so many until in his dark prison his dreams were filled with dead Detimarian scouts, all marching after Yourdon, led by Rem Ana.

He wondered whether he could even trust his magic. He could not get the face he had seen in the market out of his mind, the face of a man he had thought was Rem, but who, it seemed, was not. If he trusted in himself, in his magic, in his instincts, he had to believe that the Rem he saw beheaded was not Rem at all, which left him to wonder who—or what—he had seen die that day. Who had he been with in the days before? What was the truth?

All unanswered questions that could drive a man mad, if that hadn't already happened. . . .

Toeplo called out. Tears came to Yourdon's eyes, there in the darkness. Until finally he slept again.

When he woke he tried to think of young Besh, at home in his village in the Tesshi foothills, tending his flock and starting his family. He needed thoughts that would chase away the altered images of Syttrelians and Detimarians and Quin—but then it occurred to him that perhaps the boy, Besh, or his father Lossef, had given him and Beken away to the Taun . . . That perhaps he had trusted in the Phet-Akreeans only to fall prey to a plot designed to make of Beken and himself a sacrificial offering to the marauding, neighboring tribe . . .

He slept again, and this time his dreams ran to images of his youth, to young Yourdon Lewen alone amid so many people, free of his home, his father, his life as he ran and hid in the streets of Thetar. Trusting in a better future. All that he had.

Petting stray cats.

Toeplo was somewhere nearby, shouting again at demons in the darkness. Yourdon stood at the door, head thrown back, and shouted at them too.

By the third week he had stopped thinking about magic and dreams, about every bad thing that had ever happened to him, and he had stopped crying, too. The sense of urgency had been lost, a change of heart or mind, he mused, or a symptom of atrophy. He felt utterly numb.

Yourdon Lewen had never been willing to give up completely, but that was a person he could only imagine now. There was nothing left to hope for, he would argue, if his senses should attempt to rally one more time against the hopelessness. He rehearsed the moment in the darkness.

"What will Yourdon think?" he asked.

"No one cares," he answered.

"A curse on you all," he said.

Toeplo called out and Yourdon called back, but the words were only sounds now, from both of them. He imagined the old Quin had enlisted the aid of his many Gods, and was shouting with joy as his spirit soared, ready to leave the dungeon, saved. But the sound drew no nearer, nor further away.

Yourdon spoke to his own True God again and again, but by week's end he had forgotten even his prayers, as the constant night began to come alive. . . .

The creatures made a sound like iron scraping iron, waking Yourdon with a start. He saw them standing in a circle around him, glowing in the darkness as though they were cut from bits of moon. Maidens, Yourdon saw, focussing. They wore Syttrelian robes that lay open at the front revealing smooth, rounded breasts. But their faces were not quite right, more like the features of a Shetie. Each wore a sword in a black leather scabbard tied about the waist.

"What do you want?" Yourdon asked, moving his mouth, hearing the words in his mind but not in his ears. Still, he thought the visitors seemed to understand. They opened their mouths to answer but only blood poured out, running down their chins, wetting their breasts and soaking into their robes. They spoke, but only a gurgling sound emerged.

Blood-stained hands reached out to him, and Yourdon shrank back as he saw that each finger ended in a long, thin shaft of polished bronze, the points filed sharp. He tried to scream at these magical Syttrelian beings, these dark mages who were certainly more powerful than any he could imagine. How had they found him here? What did they want of him? He tried to warn them off, but still his voice would not function well enough. They nearly had him now.

Yourdon rose and tried to lunge through between two

of them. He failed. Bodies moved to block his path. Hands lashed out. Yourdon sought to upend the two nearest creatures. He managed to grab one around the leg, the other by the scabbard. His own magic flickered, yet he saw nothing at all. But as the figures pulled away Yourdon began to wonder. . . .

They circled slowly, rattling their long metal nails at him. He lunged again and began his chant. This time he wrapped both hands around one of their weapons. Again there was nothing, no past, not even the present. *Not real*, he insisted. *Not here!* And with that, they were gone.

Yourdon lay still, heart pounding, chest heaving, his eyes filled only with darkness once more. He drew a deep breath and tried again to call out. This time the sound came forth. When he finally stopped he heard the scream of another, somewhere not far away, and he wondered if Toeplo had been visited too.

The meal came, and he couldn't remember if he had already made a scratch for this day. He made two, just to be sure. . . .

Finally he slept once more. When he woke this time Rem Ana was sitting at his side, holding his severed head in his lap. Yourdon jumped up, then stumbled, weak and dizzy. He lost his footing and fell, then tried to roll over. He looked up to find his visitor rising, moving nearer, still wearing the gold, crystal-bearing ring on his left hand. The head did not bear the strange face Yourdon had seen for an instant in the market. This was Rem himself.

Yourdon crawled backward until the dungeon's far wall met his back. He kept staring at the ring, unable to take his eyes off of it even as blackened blood oozed out of the head and dripped away between Rem's fingers. He tried to crawl back further into himself then, into his own mind, into darkness, and realized he met a wall there as well. He could retreat no further, it was just not in him to do so.

Then go forward again.

He bit into his lip, stood up and kicked the head free with his boot. When the body just stood there, Yourdon gritted his teeth and grabbed hold of its left arm and hand. He spoke his chant again, clutching the ring and the cold dead fingers with all his might.

Yourdon waited, concentrating on the spell. No visions appeared. Nothing happened. He let go, then closed his eyes and opened them again, and saw nothing at all. As the rush left him he collapsed facedown on the rank, damp floor. Finally Yourdon slept again, until lamplight exploded all around him, the regular meal arriving.

He could see out into the corridor as his eyes adjusted to the light. Another guard was passing by, walking backward, dragging something large. *Toeplo,* Yourdon realized, as his food and water were set down and the door was pulled closed again—as he realized he hadn't heard any shouting in a very long time. Crazy old Toeplo. Finally immortal, Yourdon thought. *And I have lost yet another friend. . . .*

Yourdon ate his bread and gruel and drank his water, and promptly began to retch until most of it had come back up again. Something inside him felt about to burst, something he was certain he could not live without.

"I'm not a coward!" he shouted out loud. "I'm not a fool!" But no one listened, no one believed, no one thought it mattered. Except one.

"What will Yourdon think?" he asked.

"No one cares," he answered.

"A curse on you all," he said. "I care."

He sat in the still darkness counting scratches on the

wall, then made a new one. He had forgotten the day before, hadn't he? And so had made another. Then he threw the stone into the little pit. He didn't need to know anymore.

Light blinded him. He strained to see a man wearing a fine linen tunic and a small, round hat standing before him, a scroll in one hand, a grimace on his face as he wriggled his nose in apparent distress. *Not real,* Yourdon tried to tell himself. *Like the others. Nothing there . . .*

"Yourdon Lewen," the man said, handing his lamp to the guard standing just behind him, then holding up the scroll. He read from the parchment. "By decree of the courts of the city of Dlet you are on this day . . . released."

Yourdon coughed, swallowed. "What?" he tried to say, his mouth forming the word. His voice produced only a garbled rasp. The official shook his head in dismay. In carefully spoken Dral he said, "You are free to go."

❖ SOMETHING WORSE ❖

"No, I cannot take all the credit," Banlae said, gnawing a long loaf of dark bread and sipping at his mead. The Golden Axe was quiet so early in the day, as Yourdon had hoped. Banlae bit off another chunk of bread, swallowed it nearly whole. "The Quin, or at least some of them, seem to have played a part as well," he added. "Perhaps a larger one than most would believe."

"But why would the Quin ask for my release?"

"Precisely," Banlae said, looking as close to troubled as Yourdon had ever seen him. "None publicly claim to have done so, but I have many sources, and this is what I hear. Who can fathom the likes of the Quin? We Dral never could." Banlae raised his eyebrows and bit off another mouthful. When it was gone he said, "If everything happened just as you say—and I prefer to believe it did—then perhaps some of the Quin are aware of your innocence, and are feeling a twinge of guilt? Of course I doubt that. Infighting, I would guess; it's the more likely explanation. One Quin faction suspects another of attempting to take control in Rem's absence, or they suspect each other of stealing the body, or of the killing itself. Your release might well be a means of aggravation, or a show of strength. Or worse, an attempt to rally the many factions to a single cause."

"I don't like the sound of that," Yourdon said quietly.

"You shouldn't. Consider: The death of one of their

181

greatest holy men has left countless Quin in an uproar. As a martyr, Rem has proven himself at least as inspirational as he was while he lived. All that is needed is a focus for the faithful's hatred, a spark to ignite the great pile of kindling Rem's life and death have heaped together. Your release might accomplish this."

"That doesn't sound any better," Yourdon muttered, head sinking down between his shoulders as he imagined the implications. He tried a swallow of mead, found it bitter. "I may have been safer in prison."

"Agreed, but the city's fathers are concerned about this as well. If too much trouble arises you may find yourself back in their prisons, for the good of all." He grinned thinly at Yourdon with this last, then let the expression expire.

"I think I would rather face the Quin," Yourdon groaned.

"Perhaps," Banlae nodded. "In any event, I had the magistrates convinced they were punishing a man who was most likely innocent. Myself!"

"Your reputation," Yourdon elucidated.

"Exactly," Banlae said. He extended one hand toward Yourdon. "And you, in turn. They only narrowly decided to sentence you in the first place. I nearly had your freedom won all on my own, but the magistrates needed an extra nudge. They still do not have a killer to blame, and one is needed, and some of the city's Quin could riot at any time—not that things were different before." Banlae rolled his eyes.

"In any case, I do not know where that nudge came from, but I have told you what I suspect. Were I you," he added, leaning nearer, "I would not question my good fortune so harshly. Or loudly. Or often."

"Very well, I understand," Yourdon said. "What do I do now?"

"Ahh, but you are a free man! That is up to you. But

again, were I you, I would become very small for a while, lest your name arrive on too many lips. Time will explain a great deal, I think. I will see to it."

Banlae drew a small leather pouch from beneath the table. He produced a few pieces of silver and some coppers, then Yourdon's amber-studded dagger. "Your personal weapon, I assume, and the wages you earned during your brief employ." He set everything in front of Yourdon. "And a few more coins, most of what the gelding and the mule brought when they were sold— minus the city's taxes."

"Thank you," Yourdon said, as sincerely as he could . . . the gelding had been a fine animal. He took the dagger and the money, grateful for both. "And I will work to repay any debt I owe to you, as well as your trust. I need some time, I think, but soon—"

"And that you shall have. I can't use you! There remain many questions in many minds. And even if one presumes you did not kill Rem, it is no small thing that he *was* beheaded while in your care. Not much of a recommendation for your services, I am afraid. You do understand."

Banlae wasn't grinning now, and the truth was obvious. Yourdon hadn't given the subject much thought. "I do," he said.

Banlae tipped his head, examined what remained of the mead. "Perhaps in a few weeks. A few months at most. In time a new leader will emerge to guide the Quin, or several of them will, and the problems they cause will get worse; or they will get better, who knows. But the people of Dlet will forget much of what went before, no matter what. We will see each other then."

Yourdon stood and nodded once, slowly. "Thank you again," he told Banlae. "I have heard much and from many about the evils of the Dral, and yet—"

"When you have met one Dral, my friend, you have not met them all."

Not truly a friend, Yourdon insisted; he was not to be trusted any more than Rem, or not at all, as Beken had cautioned, but . . .

"Is it true, then," Yourdon added, trying to smile, "that you are one of the few nearly decent men in all Akreea?"

"Ah, yes, but only when it suits me."

"Suit yourself," Yourdon said.

Banlae looked away. Yourdon went back out into the street, and began to make the rounds. He found no work, but the situation was made worse by his recent fame—much the way things had been in Thetar after his inglorious return. There were many who would not so much as speak to him.

For three days he tried, sleeping at a small inn not far from the river's finger. The temptation to go into the common room and stay there until he couldn't think or see was as great as it had ever been in Dra Mai. He fought the urge, determined to salvage some tiny bit of dignity, just enough, he hoped, to keep him going another day . . . another night. He'd been through worse, alright.

The last place he tried was a small, aging stables on the edge of the city, a broken-down place owned by a man who seemed in even worse repair. His name was Lapo, and he was nearly blind. When Yourdon gave his own name the man seemed to take no interest. "Start over there," he said, pointing to soiled straw piled deep and smelling ripe, and covering half the stable floor.

"Of course," Yourdon said, taking a breath. He went to work, putting his back into it, clearing away the mess and spreading fresh straw. By day's end his back had informed him of the mistake. Prison had left his muscles weakened and robbed him of his endurance. But his enemies had given him something in exchange. Even horse manure smelled better than the dungeon, was more real than the darkness, was much easier to endure than his dreams. He and Toeplo had both died in the dungeons, but it was he who had come out alive, had come back from the dead.

Lapo's wages were meager. Yourdon wasn't sure he could survive on them even with the little extra he had left from the money Banlae had given him. And Lapo didn't speak much other than to grumble. Still, for now, Yourdon thought, he would make do.

At night, aching and exhausted, a good meal and one cup of red wine in his belly, he slept better than he had in ages. *I will make the best of this*, he promised himself, but some days his promise seemed hard to keep.

His wages proved too small to afford a room at the inn. Lapo, for all his gruffness, offered to let him sleep in the stables. He heard himself accept, but after a few nights spent there among three restless horses and Lapo's incessantly whining dog, he found himself questioning the wisdom of his decision.

Breakfast was cooked wheat or barley bought from a woman who lived nearby, a woman who also did weaving, which Yourdon found a valuable service indeed. Some mornings there was milk from her goat as well. This morning she was away visiting someone, somewhere, and she had taken the goat along. He sat glumly lamenting the loss, then decided this alone was reason to be glum: *What have I come to?*

He didn't like questions any more than answers.

Lapo didn't turn up all day. Yourdon did very little work. He stood by the stables' open doorway for much of the afternoon just gazing into the little street at passersby, most of them poor as he was, or nearly so. Dlet was much like Thetar in that respect, home to the very rich and the very poor. Since coming to the city Yourdon had already been both, and knew which he preferred.

But at least these people, most of them, knew where they were going with their animals and carts and children; they knew who they could trust, who they were. . . .

No Lapo meant no wages forthcoming, so when the shadows grew long Yourdon decided he'd done enough. He started toward the markets, hoping he could find a dinner bargain among the many stalls, and perhaps a bit, just a bit, of ale. He was nearly there when a voice from behind called his name. A woman's voice. He recognized it even before he turned around.

"Tasia?"

"So," she said, her grin wide and full of guile, "you remembered."

The look in her eye made him grow tense; he heard the blood begin to pound in his ears. Only battle had ever affected him so. He didn't know whether to greet her or draw his dagger.

"Of course," he admitted, while his mind attempted to rearrange itself in a more defensive posture. The woman had made a fool of him easily enough before. He did not intend to fare so poorly again.

"I followed you for a while, to be sure it was you."

"Why?" Yourdon asked.

"To say hello, of course, to someone familiar . . . and to tell you how awful you look." Same grin.

Yourdon knew it was true, his clothes were filthy and he smelled of stables, his face and hands were soiled, and he hadn't shaved since going to see Banlae, weeks ago. By contrast Tasia looked quite well, dressed in a worn but smartly tailored tunic and billowing breeches, her hair all gathered to reveal the curve of her neck. In fact, she looked . . . great.

A shiver crossed his shoulders. He refocused, and

examined instead the sword she wore at her side. And her boots, which were of the finest leather craftsmanship . . .

"Have you no better entertainment?" he asked.

"Not at the moment." She changed her look, more reflective. "Seldom, in fact."

"How sad," Yourdon quipped.

"You misjudge yourself. What could bring greater pleasure to a Syttrelian warrior than the misfortunes of a Detimarian?"

Yourdon only stared at her, too weary and hungry and filthy to mount a proper offensive. He had an urge to start shouting at her, at Syttre, Detimar, Akreea and all the Gods there were. But he worried that once he began he might not be able to stop.

Tasia's expression changed again, seemed to soften. She tipped her head, examining him further. Yourdon waited for the next insult.

"You do look truly awful," she said. "I have heard of your exploits among the Quin. No work for the protector who failed so badly? Or . . . did you succeed?"

Again Yourdon held his tongue, though this required nearly biting it off. Tasia seemed to read his look.

"Ahh, you would rather not talk about Rem," she said. "Of course. I can hardly blame you. It doesn't look good from anywhere."

"Leave me alone," Yourdon said, gritting his teeth, sensing the edge of reason very near.

"I thought you might need a little money. I can give you some coppers." She looked at him just as she had in Thetar, and he realized he felt much the same as he had then, lost and alone on the great city's streets. Her coins had driven him away then. He pushed down the urge to let them now.

"I don't need your money," he said. "Or your taunts." He kept his eyes steady on hers, unblinking.

She smiled satisfaction, or something like it. "I'm not going to get you rattled, am I," she said. "You're spoiling all my fun."

"Then the day is not a complete loss," Yourdon replied.

Tasia giggled at this. The sound caught Yourdon by surprise. He was suddenly pleased he had not lost control.

"Where were you headed?" she asked.

"Looking for a meal," he said truthfully.

"Then perhaps you will let me buy you a decent dinner, so we can trade insults on a full stomach. I would do the same for anyone. Wouldn't you?"

"Why?" he asked. "Why bother?"

"Why not?" She placed one finger over her pursed lips. "Are you so afraid of me?"

Coward, she had almost said, trying to bait him again. Yourdon saw it in her eyes. He couldn't let it work.

"I don't need your meals," he said, firm. "We will each buy our own food."

"Very well, but I buy the ale."

"As you wish," he said, attempting to sound as graceful as possible. She seemed pleased as they started off together down the street toward the nearest inn.

Tasia ate nearly as cheaply as he did, opting for the stew rather than roasted pork or fowl. Yourdon began to wonder whether she was perhaps not quite so well off as her manner implied. Finally he asked.

"I've managed a few transactions, enough to keep me well," she said. "But I intend to do much better. And soon. Tell me, what are your plans? Or does 'stable boy' now describe you in full?"

The caustic grin was back, but she was watching him carefully, awaiting his answer.

"I know several words to describe you," Yourdon said.

"Flattery?" Tasia asked, batting her eyes.

"Of a sort." Yourdon looked away, trying not to smile.

at her. He sat chewing at a bit of meat and watching four men pass by the table, all of them stooped over and poorly dressed. Laborers of some sort, he thought, mill workers, or wood workers, by the wood dust clinging to them. They looked at Yourdon and Tasia with cold, narrowing eyes, then kept watching as they sat at a nearby table. Not Quin, Yourdon decided, as they turned their attention to the innkeeper. A mix of Akreeans from anywhere, not at all uncommon in this city. "Friends of yours?" Tasia asked.

"Or yours, perhaps. I'm sure a thief has many enemies," Yourdon added, sensing the line only after he had crossed it, then pleased that he had.

Her face hardened. "No more than a Detimarian coward enough to butcher holy men."

"And the Syttrel make no enemies?"

"We don't go begging!"

"You begged a war with Detimar."

"Such lies! Detimarians would not admit the truth even if they spoke it! And you call the Syttrel liars."

"You are *both* infidel swine," a man's voice called out from the next table. One of the four laborers, who all had their cups now and were again paying all their attention to Yourdon and Tasia.

"Only he is," Tasia said. "I am a . . . a royal princess!"

"You will all be made to pay," a second man said, not buying it. "For what you have done, and what you would do, all your kind."

"I don't think they like outsiders," Tasia said loudly. "We make them look bad."

"You have your own lands, go back to them," another of them said, and he spit on the floor beside the table.

"While you can," the first muttered.

Yourdon had seen this kind of hatred before, in the eyes of a woman snatching his money pouch away, the faces of innkeepers in Thetar, and here, and those of many others. He'd seen something like it in his father's eyes, more than once. He was getting tired of it.

The only sensible thing to do was walk away. The one thing he couldn't do was run. No matter what.

"May we finish our ales?" he asked, sounding glib, hoping to make light of the situation. He glanced at Tasia, frowned her to silence. No matter. His tone was wasted.

"If you wish it to be your last ale, drink well," the first man said, looking quite as serious as he sounded. He had on a dark green coat, a hole torn in one side, and dark green pants that suggested all his clothing had been cut from a single cloth. And some time ago.

"Look," Tasia said, leaning close to Yourdon, speaking low, "these types usually won't push it all the way." She flashed an innocent grin. "Especially with a woman. I'll handle them. You just relax, and watch how it's done."

"Oh, please," Yourdon muttered.

Tasia stood up and fixed those at the near table with an angry glare. "You just let us alone, and we'll let you alone," she told them. "If outlanders brought you trouble, take it up with those that wronged you. I've done nothing, and likely he hasn't either." She flashed Yourdon another grin. "But don't any of you lay a hand on me or I'll cut it off!" With that she pulled her straight dagger from its sheath and waved the narrow blade at them.

All eyes were open wide. At least one of the four seemed to take her seriously, and leaned back as if he thought her dagger might somehow reach that far. The other three exchanged glances, then the nearest one, the green one, laughed. "She looks good standing up," he said, "for a heathen."

"She'd look better yet laying down," another man answered as if they'd rehearsed the lines. At this all four of them broke into a chuckle. They mumbled to one another, then seemed to reach some sort of an accord. Green stood up then, followed by the other three, and each of them managed to produce a dagger of his own.

"You, friend, stay in that chair a while," the first man told Yourdon.

He stood instead and pulled his own short dagger free. Tasia stepped back and drew her sword, the only long blade among them.

"You don't scare anyone with that," green clothes said, approaching straight on, though the others seemed content to stay behind him. They were not soldiers any of them, Yourdon was certain of that, but they had worked together before, doing just this sort of thing—to other outlanders no doubt, or other Akreeans that did not suit their tastes. He decided Tasia was probably right, they might not have killing on their minds, but anything short of that was possible.

"When am I supposed to relax?" Yourdon asked in Tasia's ear, then he began to sidle right, away from her, so as to work his way around to the other side of the table.

"Not right now," she said, scowling. He had an urge to gloat, but that would have to wait. One man, dressed in a uniform brown, circled to meet him. Everyone in the room had taken an interest in the dispute, another dozen men in all, but none of them seemed eager to join in. Not yet, at least. Yourdon looked around, checked the door. No one blocked the way. He was about to suggest the two of them start in that direction when the man in green feinted toward Tasia, testing her reactions.

She stood her ground, holding her sword steady in one hand, her dagger in the other. Her opponent jabbed a bit closer, grinning with one side of his face. Still, she did not move.

"She's plain too scared to breathe!" he bellowed at her, garnering another round of chuckles from the others—a few of the nearest patrons as well. All three men faced her now, spreading out, waving their short blades at her. They jabbed, giggling almost like children. Tasia remained motionless even as one of the men seemed about to try circling behind her.

Yourdon moved forward far enough to give pause to the man circling his side of the table.

"She *is* scared, isn't she," the man circling Tasia said. He took another step, then again, placing himself almost far enough behind Tasia to put him out of her sight. Yourdon began to wonder about her. . . .

No, he thought, remembering what he had seen of her talents in a moonlit clearing, not so long ago. He concentrated on the man he would have to overcome in order to get to her.

"Have to cut them both," Green said, jabbing, striking Tasia's sword, producing a pale ring. He showed her his darkened teeth again. "Get her arm," he told Brown as he and the other man with him both thrust their blades at her face. She blocked them and stepped back just as Yourdon's opponent made his move. Yourdon switched hands with his dagger and blocked the attempt. The other man's eyes darted right toward a flurry of sudden movement. Yourdon looked up to see Tasia spinning around, squatting as she went, one foot under, one out in front. She swung her sword and caught the man who was nearly behind her off guard. He put his arms out instinctively to block the attack. Tasia's blade struck flesh then bone. He pulled his hands away and dropped his dagger, then started howling as he cupped one arm in the other only to watch blood spurt between his fingers.

Yourdon looked back, found his man briefly mesmerized by the scene. He stepped forward. The other man snapped to, but Yourdon was close enough now. He grabbed the man's wrist, raised the arm, then flicked his dagger underneath and down putting a long, shallow slice into the man's ample belly. The fight went out of the Akreean as he stumbled backward, gaping at his gut, then fell into the same chair where he'd sat a moment ago.

Yourdon rushed past, around the table. Tasia was backing toward the near wall now, fending off jabs by the other two men. Yourdon snatched up Tasia's chair and heaved it at the nearest man. As the other faltered, Yourdon moved in and wrapped his arm around the man's neck, then bent him backward. He put his amber-set dagger to the fellow's chin. "Let go of your blade, right now," he said between his teeth. He scraped at his prisoner's beard with the edge of his dagger, and the man dropped the weapon at once. The other, poised like a battle sculpture, was taking a moment to consider.

Tasia touched his dagger with the tip of her sword. "Outlanders aren't worth dying for," she said.

He moved cautiously away, walking backward. She followed at first, then let him go.

Yourdon stepped back and heaved his captive toward the others. The man stumbled but didn't fall.

"Get out," Tasia told them. "Just get out."

Yourdon sighed and looked at her. "*I* was going to say that."

"I know," she answered. She put her dagger away as she watched the others help their gut-wounded friend get to his feet. Blood pooled on the floor between his shoes. The man with the bleeding hand was the first out the door. Tasia and Yourdon stood well aside and let the rest pass. No one else in the room made a move or spoke a word.

"I don't think they're going to drink their ales," Tasia said, still breathing hard and a bit shaken, like Yourdon;

though she still had her wits about her. She put her sword away and ambled over to the other table, then lifted a cup. Yourdon followed, and raised a second cup to hers.

"You were . . . impressive," she said, looking at him over the brim as she took a sip.

He said nothing at first. He hadn't thought about it, and he wasn't sure he wanted to. Still . . . "Should I apologize?" he asked her, suppressing a swell of giddiness.

"That is up to you."

They drained their cups, then headed out into the street, deciding it was best not to linger. In silence they walked, until finally they arrived at Lapo's tiny stables.

"Home?" Tasia asked, her expression hidden now by the night.

"Yes," Yourdon said, waiting for the barb. None came.

"You sure you don't need anything?"

He didn't answer, he couldn't.

"I don't suppose you do," Tasia said.

It wasn't true, what the four men had said of himself and Tasia. It seemed the rule, in fact, that most of what people said about others wasn't altogether true. Often, it was just convenient to think so.

"Why did you stop me on the street today?" he asked.

"Should I apologize?"

Yourdon shrugged.

She tipped her head to one side. "Tell me why you went to the inn with me?"

Yourdon smiled. "I was bored."

"So was I."

He heard her faint chuckle join his own in the darkness. Then no sound at all. Boredom had not been a problem for either of them this evening.

"Had enough now?" Yourdon asked, asking it for both of them. Tasia nodded. After a while she turned to go.

"Good night," she said, a whisper.

"I will see you about, I'm sure," he replied.

"Ahh, such a comfort," she chided.

"I know."

"If you do, what will you say?"

Yourdon pondered the question. "Plenty."

"Good."

He had no idea what to do next. Part of his mind still wanted her to get away, to leave him alone, but another part of his mind and right now all of his body wanted her to stay. The best he could manage was to keep still.

He watched her walk up the way, until she vanished from sight. Dlet was a big enough city, he thought. One might easily go weeks without seeing a particular face. Which was probably all for the best.

Almost, he believed it.

He went inside and found his spot in an empty stall. It seemed less accommodating tonight, as stiff shafts of straw bit through the blanket into his back, and the sound of shuffling hooves joined with the aroma of fresh dung to offend the senses.

But he was exhausted to the point of not caring. He covered himself with a second blanket against the cooler temperatures the early autumn night was apt to bring, and quickly drifted off to sleep, and dreams.

He was shaken suddenly awake by hands that grabbed him and held him fast while rags were tied tightly around his face, covering his eyes and mouth. More rags went around his wrists as they were gathered against his abdomen. He struggled, which earned him a brief flurry of heavy hand blows, most of which landed on his back and sides, forcing the wind from his lungs. Then he felt himself being hauled away.

❖ FLINCH ❖

The hands set him down hard. A cart, he decided, as the world began to move beneath him. He struggled to free himself but the rags at his wrists were tight enough to hold, and those covering his face kept him from using his teeth. He imagined working the bonds loose if he kept at it. And if those who had taken him let him live that long . . .

The ride seemed to last forever and grew markedly rougher after what seemed like half the night. Then all motion abruptly stopped. He felt the hands again, hauling him out of the cart, then dragging him until finally they sat him in a chair. Next the rags on his face came off.

He counted three men, all standing around him in a darkened, windowless little room. These, surely, were Quin. Each wore a crude version of a ceremonial mantle complete with Quin embroidery. Aside from that, none would have stood out in a crowd in Dlet, though one, the one standing in front of Yourdon now, seemed a bit short—or the other two were rather tall.

Yourdon decided this room was the extent of the hut; it was not unlike the one he'd stayed a winter in, on the eastern slopes of the Tesshis. A small table had been moved against the wall, one other chair with it. A large chest and several smaller ones accounted for the rest of the hut's furnishings. The chair Yourdon was sitting on felt as rickety as the other one looked. He struggled with the rags at his wrists again, but with his hands on his lap, he couldn't move them much without the others taking note.

"You know who we are?" the shortest one said, in Dral, and in a way that made Yourdon think he should know the answer. He didn't. He shook his head.

All three Quin looked disappointed.

"We are the Thae Quin Tae, the pure, the chosen."

They stared at him, waiting for something. Yourdon had heard the term while with Rem, but he still didn't know much about them. Only that the Thae were an extremist sect within the Quin, one even Rem did not seem altogether pleased with—though he had stopped to speak with most Thae whenever he passed them, and a few of them, Yourdon thought, had followed him around the city the day he had been killed. "Is there something you want?" he asked.

"We want justice!" they all said, nearly singing it.

Yourdon was afraid to ask: "From me?"

"From he who has slain our greatest prophet, Rem Ana!" the short one insisted, nostrils flaring. He paced the packed dirt floor a moment, huffing, causing the candles on the table to flicker each time he drew near.

"But I have done nothing," Yourdon said. "The tribunal has set me free."

"Of course!" the short Quin boomed. One of the others sat at the little table facing Yourdon. "We helped to arrange this," he said. "We control your life, and your death. Even Banlae Tfa's requests for your release were only considered, but our request was granted."

"Perhaps the decision had already been reached when your request was made," Yourdon suggested meekly.

"You cannot see," the short one said. "You try to understand what has happened, even your own actions, but only we know the truth. You are but a tool in the hands of the Gods. You have served them. You have no will of your own."

"I have often wondered about that," Yourdon said, not quite understanding what these Quin were talking about but beginning to believe that perhaps they did. "Why am I here?"

"To complete your journey, and to face true justice," the tall standing Quin repeated. "Your trial was no more than a joke played on our people by the city of Dlet. But the Gods willed it so. Every Quin knows this. The truth is in our hearts. The evil is within yours. No dungeon can remove your guilt or clean away the stain of blood upon your hands, any more than you can change your past."

As the taller Quin spoke, waving his arms about, Yourdon saw his own amber-set dagger in the belt girdled around the other man's tunic. The shorter man had a large dagger; the seated one appeared to be unarmed.

"We will have our own trial for you, Yourdon Lewen, and then we will carry out the only proper and merciful sentence: death."

Yourdon blanched. A lot of this wasn't making any sense, and he wanted it to. "If you believe that, why didn't you appear at my trial and insist the magistrates take my head?" he asked. "Why didn't your people come forward?"

"You are ignorant of the prophecies, and so you should remain, but I will tell you we could not allow you to die slowly in the mines. And there are questions we would have answered, privately, here, now."

"What questions? What can I tell you?"

"All that you know."

Yourdon had been trying not to imagine the worst, but now he saw that these three men, though not killers by trade, were likely capable of anything in the name of their faith. The shorter Quin took a step closer and leaned near to Yourdon's face. He closed his eyes briefly, as if summoning his resolve. When he opened them Yourdon noticed his hands were pressed together, fingers turning white. The other two Quin had grown suddenly more restless, seeming to know what was to come next.

"By serving as the assassin of The One you have fulfilled the prophecy," he said. "You were chosen to carry out his execution so that he could return from the dead and lead our people into the future. Yours was a dark but sacred calling. That is why you must die by our hand, and no other. It is your right, as Rem himself has told us."

"He who is chosen for death be cleansed by death, first in giving, then in knowing," the Quin in the chair said, apparently quoting prophecies. The others mumbled a brief response, heads bobbing in unison. Yourdon didn't like the sound of it at all. He glanced down at the rags around his wrists and tried again to move them, but it was no use.

"The honor is a great one," the nearest Quin continued. "Rem taught us that his assassin would be a man from a distant land, an infidel, and that has come to pass. Now we grant you your only hope of redemption. Be truthful with us, and the Five Gods will know your name."

"I already have a god," Yourdon said, *though once again, he seems to have forgotten me. . . .*

The Quin reached out abruptly and slapped Yourdon across the face, hard enough to take the sight from his eyes for a moment. As the darkness brightened he saw all three Quin standing close in front of him now, their faces intense. *Or insane . . .* But he was beginning to think as much of most Quin, and a number of others as well. What had Toeplo said? "Sometimes it is you who are right, and the world that is wrong." Yourdon needed to believe that now.

"The infidel will tell us who his friends are, and what they hope to do next," the shorter one demanded, barking in Yourdon's face. "Now that Rem's death has come to pass, all those responsible must be removed, the land must be cleansed."

"Was it Banlae himself who put you up to your crime?" asked the Quin on the right. "Was it someone else, offering riches enough to buy Banlae?"

Yourdon said nothing, all he could do.

"There is another possibility," the Quin on the left said. "Perhaps he took Banlae's money to protect Rem, then took double from someone else to kill him. Perhaps even Banlae does not know."

"If so, he will be as pleased as the Quin when we take your head," the short one in the middle replied.

"Justice is rendered by the Gods," the left one said, growing more intense. "Rem Ana yet lives, struck down by your hand, raised up to Naldasa, and returned to us, to life. You will not be so fortunate. Without sacrifice, you will die forever."

There was that word again, Yourdon thought. He could see the passion of the others' belief clearly on their faces. Yourdon had heard Rem tell of his immortality countless times while guarding him; it had seemed a somewhat bizarre, fatuous bit of mythology. But these people spoke as if they knew Rem's tallest tale to be fact. *Knew* it.

"Answer!" the short Quin shouted, striking Yourdon again, much harder this time. He saw a night sky filled with shooting stars, then light slowly fading back, but in the darkness his mind's eye recalled the moment in the marketplace, just before Rem had been killed—or apparently so.

He had been unwilling to trust his own instincts, or his own magical talent, as he had held the prophet's ring and felt his powers stir—as the face of Rem had changed to that of another before him. A face like death itself.

Rem had boasted of his sorcery at every turn, even to Yourdon, and had claimed power over death many times. But deathsway magic was an old and sordid craft, and Rem would not be the first mage to practice it, on either side of the Tesshis. Still, to perform such on oneself . . .

The images of the three Quin and the tiny cottage again filled his eyes. He tried to move his face, and the pain forced a groan from his throat.

"Speak!" And again the Quin struck him. Yourdon felt his jaw about to explode. He waited out the darkness once more, following the thoughts that stuck in his mind. He had to be right. Nothing else made sense. "Trust your instincts," Toeplo had said. Almost as good as Beken's advice, especially when put together. . . . How could he trust someone like Rem to die? How could he have trusted him to show up at his own funeral? After all, by planning for the future carefully enough, one could become a most reliable prophet. The fates might be coerced. . . .

"I don't know," Yourdon mumbled, realizing as he did that the left side of his mouth was swelling up. "I didn't do it. I don't know anything." Though he was beginning to wonder at a great deal. . . .

"The truth is your only hope for redemption!" one of the taller Quin shouted, an almost desperate volume.

. . . And if Rem had not been there in the market, if he'd somehow played a trick on nearly everyone, then he had certainly set the whole event up. And he'd set Yourdon up as well. An outlander, the perfect culprit, no matter what had really happened.

Yourdon remembered the chant Rem had used as he and his crowd of escorts had set off that day, "tapat deshi," followed each time by moans from the crowd. They had grown glassy-eyed as even he had sensed a veil of tranquility settling over his mind. *Like Syttrelian runes,* he thought again, reminded of it now. *All part of the plan.* . . .

"I have given you the only truth I have," he said, his mind still back in Dlet. . . .

Rem had gone into a house alone just before the procession had reached the markets. Yourdon wasn't sure who or what had emerged, but he no longer thought it was Rem Ana. The prophet had truly used him, just as these Thae Quin claimed, though even they did not understand how.

The revelation wounded Yourdon in a way he had thought impossible now. Eyes open and forewarned, he had become the tool a fool yet again, and so a fool himself. *Rem is more like my father than I had imagined.*

Another blow stung Yourdon's face, backhanded this time.

"You *do* know something! And all that you know, you will tell us, by all the Gods I swear it!"

Yourdon let the Quin shout. He barely heard the words. They did not truly understand what was going on in their world, or likely the next, but he suddenly realized there was something to be learned from them. Despite their limits, they did not hesitate to act as they saw fit. They were attempting even now to make the world fit their expectations, instead of waiting for it to favor them. Even if they accomplished nothing, they would go away knowing they had tried. They were like Beken in this. And Toeplo, no doubt.

The world had never been kind to Yourdon Lewen, but you didn't let that stop you. You didn't let yourself down, or let your own god down. You didn't let the Taun catch you on the road, any more than you let the images that came in the darkness of a dungeon take your mind.

You couldn't let anyone drag you down, and when they did, you had to make them let go.

"I am no one special," he said. "I swear it."

"We know you spoke with many people in Dlet, merchants, craftsmen," one of them said, Yourdon wasn't sure who.

"Tell us why?" another asked.

"I looked for work," Yourdon said, his left cheek swelling between his teeth as he parted them.

"A lie!" a Quin argued, grabbing a handful of Yourdon's hair, yanking hard. "If we must we will cut the truth out of you!"

Yourdon was sure he could never convince these three that he hadn't killed anyone in the market that day, or that the Rem who was killed was probably not Rem at all, but a man who had likely died already, perhaps days before. These men didn't seem to know any of that. In fact, Yourdon was beginning to think they knew nothing more than what they had been told.

Once again, he did the only thing he could think of. "You are fools," he said, low in his throat, achieving a rather menacing growl. The word felt good going the other way for a change. "Fools, idiots, and heathens." He raised his voice. "You dishonor your own gods, but Rem dishonors them more. I will tell you nothing!" And with that, he spit in the nearest Quin's angry face.

Rage burst across the other man's features. He brought his fist back and pounded Yourdon in the side of the head with all his might, then he moved to strike again, but already the other two Quin had begun shouting at him. Yourdon let the pain and darkness that filled his mind be his ally now. He let his head fall to one side, let his body slump forward, utterly limp. As the Quin stood back Yourdon let himself topple out of the chair.

He felt hands upon him again, more gentle this time,

straightening his flaccid body on the floor. He did not resist as they turned him on his side. He barely breathed. He waited.

"Your methods are poor," one of the other Quin said, or it was something very close to that—they had ceased speaking in Dral. A brief argument ensued, most of which Yourdon could not gather, though he was sure he understood the outcome to include an agreement on some other kind of torture, something more effective, no doubt. They tried to wake him, shaking him hard enough to bounce his head against the hard packed dirt.

His mouth felt nearly swollen shut. He didn't dare so much as groan or swallow for fear they might suspect. Then he thought he heard one of the Quin mention a well and water. The sound of the door opening, then closing, followed as someone went outside.

Yourdon sensed one of the remaining two Quin still kneeling over him, then felt a hand touch his upturned left shoulder. He couldn't wait any longer. He opened his eyes just enough to let in a trickle of light. A man's midriff appeared just two hand breadths away, and tucked into the man's tunic belt, Yourdon's own amber set dagger.

He feigned a choking fit, started flopping on the floor, coughing and gagging, eyes closed tightly again. Anxious curses issued from the Quin. The nearer man leaned still closer, put both hands out. Yourdon opened his eyes and reached with both his bound hands for the dagger. He wrapped one palm around the hilt and pulled the short blade free, then he pushed it back. The Quin twitched and drew back, and fell gasping to one side. He was quickly replaced by the other man who chose to launch the toe of his boot straight at the side of Yourdon's head. Yourdon flinched and lashed out, cutting into the soft leather of the boot, into the flesh beneath. The Quin yelled, lost his balance and fell. Yourdon leaped up and fell on him. With his wrists still tied together he was forced to use the dagger in an underhand motion. He landed on the Quin headfirst, then used his right shoulder to pin the man while he plunged the blade into the other's soft middle. The Quin grabbed at Yourdon's arms before he could make a second thrust. The short blade twisted as the two men rolled to one side, and its sharp tip pierced Yourdon's left side, nicking the ribs not far from his old arrow wound.

Yourdon flexed, teeth clenched in pain and rage, then he got the dagger straight again and forced it forward. With the second thrust the man beneath him was still. The short Quin came bursting through the door carrying a bucket of sloshing water just a moment after that.

Yourdon, chest heaving, face swollen and side bleeding—but grinning like a madman—was ready for him.

The wound only bled when he moved about. Yourdon wrapped his side as best he could using torn strips of the Quin's clothing, then he went outside. Deep forest surrounded him. The cottage had been built years ago, by the look of it, and no one had come here in many seasons. He found the well not far into the trees. The smell of sulphur was strong, but he tasted the water and decided he could drink it.

Close by, he discovered the cart he had been brought in, but the horse had apparently run off. Yourdon searched for a time, but there was no trace. Finally he decided, blood seeping through his wrappings, that he'd best go back inside and rest.

Dragging the bodies outside the following day proved a poor idea, as the wound on his side bled all the more, but he was sure leaving them inside might prove an even bigger problem if he stayed any length of time. And it appeared he might have to. He needed to rest, and he needed to think. He didn't know where he was or which way he'd come, or for all of that, what awaited him if he managed to find his way back to Dlet. Rem himself, perhaps? Or more of his stewards. Or worse . . .

The Quin had brought a little food: bread and dried meat. He ate, sucking on small pieces, overcoming the ache even this caused in his jaw and cheek, then he slept. When he woke he was hungry again, so he ate a bit more, then rested through another night. The day after that he finished what little remained of the food, then he sat outside, feeling a little better, enjoying the deep woods morning, the smell of the trees and moss, the coolness of the early autumn air. Like Detimar, Southern Akreea had no true winter, but parts of the year were cool. Right now, however, the gentle breeze felt good against his swollen face, which finally seemed to be going down. His side was getting better, too, and had not putrefied. "You will live," he told himself.

With the night he slept once more, and dreamed about finding the real Rem, about wrapping his hands around the man's narrow lying throat and holding them there, squeezing until—

He woke believing it had been true, that Rem was dead along with every hoax and scheme he had ever been guilty of. But the cottage walls brought reality back as Yourdon stared at them. He rose and rubbed his face, felt the thickness of his beard, and wondered if he would ever get a proper shave again. His dagger was sharp enough. *As soon as the face is a little less tender . . .*

When he stepped outside into the gathering light of morning he heard hoof beats.

He saw a single horse and rider coming up the little trail through the woods at a slow canter, drawing near. Yourdon clutched his dagger tightly and moved ahead. He hid behind the nearest, fattest tree he could find.

There he waited, peering cautiously around the rough bark as the rider emerged from the stray limbs and encroaching brush that lined the path. He watched the lone figure dismount, details vague in the early dawn. The traveler slapped the horse on its rump, sending it trotting past the cabin on its own while its rider moved on foot, and took cover among the trees.

Yourdon let the intruder come straight to him. He was just about to strike when his target seemed to catch his movement. The other turned, sword in hand. Yourdon dodged, then held fast. He recognized her now. . . .

"I went looking for you round the stables," Tasia said, in a most cajoling manner, which doubled Yourdon's suspicions.

"Why?" he asked evenly.

She looked at her boots, began scuffing the toe of the left one in the dirt. "I guess I realized you may possibly have saved my life the other night. I wanted to say . . . something."

"In truth," Yourdon offered, "saving you only made us even."

"Ahh, well, but we can't have that, can we," she answered, glancing up at him.

Yourdon tried to frown in response. "How did you end up here?"

"You weren't around. Anywhere. So after a while I started asking after you. It was easy enough to find people who'd seen you being hauled away. One woman had been out looking for her husband, and the beggar that keeps the corner north of the stables was awake. They told me what they saw, and which way the cart had gone. It sounded like you might need a little help."

"Well, I didn't need any," Yourdon said. He couldn't help a small grin.

"That is apparent," she said, looking at him, then she paused to glance at the cottage and the woods surrounding it. "And what happened to your friends?"

"In a neat little pile, out there." Yourdon pointed to an area just beyond the cottage, where the ground dropped away into a small hollow.

"The woman I spoke to thought they might be Thae Quin Tae," Tasia noted, as a look of concern touched her features.

"They would have agreed."

Tasia's look clouded still further.

"That is bad?" Yourdon asked, noticing.

"It's enough to worry about."

"They were not trained, but they were quite serious."

"No doubt, but I wonder what they would want with you, other than sport? Hard feelings about the trial? After all, you are of no value to anyone, perhaps even yourself."

Yourdon saw the grin she failed to hide. He began plotting revenge at once. But he told her what had happened, beginning with the Quin's questions, then recounting what he had seen in the market when he'd touched Rem Ana's ring. He needed to talk it out with someone, and Tasia knew more about this land and its people than he did.

Finally he explained his suspicions about Rem.

"Rumors of his imminent resurrection are spoken everywhere now," she agreed. "And his skills with the bodies of the dead, and the minds of the living, make for fascinating stories at many a gathering. I have heard that Quin everywhere are prepared for his return, with sword in hand. It is a plan worthy of that one," she added, shaking her head. "That is how his mind works, I think."

"One roguish mind understands another?" Yourdon countered, springing at the chance. She stuck her nose in the air, accenting the tiny wrinkles that gave away her score and one-half years. Yourdon thought to make fun of this, too, but he rather liked the look on her.

"You don't really know anything for certain," Tasia continued, mostly serious. "You are running from enemies you aren't sure of."

"I'm not running, I'm thinking. There is a difference."

"I see."

"I was brought here, you'll recall. This was not my choice. And I still don't quite know where 'here' is."

"I do!"

Yourdon leaned against a tree, his mind wandering off. "What are you thinking?" she asked, giving no quarter.

"I have to turn this all around. I'm tired of being everybody's fool, tired of losing, of making mistakes, of doubting myself when I should be doubting the rest. I am as tired as I am going to get."

The look on her face made him realize how taut his voice had suddenly become. He took a breath, let it out with a low sigh. "Do you have any food?" he asked. She nodded, then went to her horse. In a moment she returned with dried fish and flat bread. They headed toward the cottage together.

"I need a lot of answers," he said, as they sat at the little table. "I would have asked the Thae, but none of them had the grace to live long enough."

"How thoughtless," Tasia said. "Or careless," she added.

"Whichever, I expect I'll have to go to Dlet's Quin leaders to learn anything." He grinned. "I think I can make them talk."

They stared at each other for a long moment, then Tasia sat back in her chair, and her head bobbed once, a decisive nod. "Very well," she said. She looked up, a wicked look on her features. "I'll make you a proposition then. I think we can help each other."

Yourdon eyed her sidelong. "How?"

"As it happens, I am going to need help in acquiring a most valuable artifact, an item that there is an excellent market for. In truth the Quin, among others, would pay almost any price for it. There are many . . . difficulties, but together I think we can succeed."

"Go on."

"You, in turn, need my help. You have to find out what is going on so you can get yourself out of the middle of it, and without getting killed. I might even agree to help you, first."

"Hmm. It sounds so easy," Yourdon said, dubious.

"Not at all. Obtaining the artifact I'm interested in will be risky, and will involve some rather, umm, questionable means; but you are in a great, soupy mess, and I would guess that the whole truth about Rem will not be easily won, or countered. Fair enough. But we must agree in full. No late questions, no second thoughts, no going back on your word."

"Or yours," Yourdon added.

Tasia nodded.

Another silence followed as they stared at each other, lips pursed, faces cast in moody concentration. She was serious, he thought, or as serious as she could likely be. Worse, she was probably right. And he didn't have much to lose, after all. Still . . .

He tried not to think too much. He needed the help, he knew that, and he could do whatever he had to in order to pay back the favor, no matter that he wished it didn't have to be. Her conduct reminded him a little too much of his father's, in a way, and Rem's, but it felt different somehow. And what choice did he have? He said, "Agreed, because there is no alternative."

"That is the reason I suggested the alliance," Tasia replied without pause.

"You said my needs would come first?"

"We must travel far to find what I am seeking," she said, nodding. "Your troubles seem to be here in Dlet. We'll deal with them first, then you will keep your word to me."

"Fair and done," he told her, pleased, but still uneasy. "How far are we from the city?"

"Two days' walk." She looked him over. "Maybe three. I will not have my mare hitched to that wreckage." She jerked a thumb toward the door, indicating the little cart that rested outside. He didn't blame her.

He drew up his tunic, edged the cloth aside and showed her his wound. "We will have to go slow."

"It's healing," she observed.

"Good."

"Still, since I am undamaged, our bargain favors you already," Tasia noted.

"I'll make up for it."

"I'm counting on that."

She walked, let him ride most of the way. A kind and civil gesture, Yourdon thought, and one he knew he would never live down.

Yourdon and Tasia arrived in Dlet under cover of darkness, quietly entering the near empty streets. They made their way through the back ways and alleys unimpeded, until they arrived outside the Quin's lavish temple—the only place Yourdon thought it made sense to begin. Just as before, two *emari* stood guard outside, back-lit now by the twin torches that burned on the temple's stone face.

"They'll know you," Tasia cautioned. "Whether they know you were taken by the Thae or not, they are not likely to let you pass."

"I don't intend to give them a choice," Yourdon said.

"They make loyal priests and followers, but I have long wondered just how good they are as warriors."

"I only know what I hear."

"Which is?"

"It's best I tell you later," Tasia whispered. Yourdon shook his head, then he took a breath. *Someone new*, he reminded. He still had no clear idea what that was— but he knew what it wasn't. "Left," he said, pointing to one *emari*.

Tasia nodded, pointed right. "Me first," she said. "You follow." Before Yourdon could object she stepped out of the shadows and strolled across the little square, straight toward the temple doors. Yourdon waited only a moment, guessing, then went after her.

Her walk took on a remarkably feminine quality as she neared the two *emari*. They watched her as she stopped just in front of them, and glanced back.

"He is a pig!" she said—of Yourdon. "He will never marry me! I should cut out his tongue, then his heart, then cut off his—"

"But my sweet!" Yourdon called out to her. "Come back with me, and we will talk."

"Heathen!" she told him, adding a private grin for the guards. She put her back to them and drew her dagger on Yourdon.

"Barbarian!" he said back.

"You see," she told the *emari* on the right, confiding in him over her shoulder. "You see how he talks to me? Do not the Gods of Naldasa tell us to honor one another?"

The guards looked at each other. "They do," one of them said.

"Especially one's mate," the warrior priest added. "You have studied the scrolls?"

"She would do better if she studied me," Yourdon said, reaching out, grabbing her left arm.

"No!" she screeched, pulling away hard. As her hand came free she stumbled backward into the *emari*, but as she did her right hand grasped the hilt of her sword, and the sound of straight iron leaving a scabbard rang out through the quiet night. Freed, the blade spun as she did, traveling outward in an expanding arc, hammering the nearest warrior's sword and scabbard as he sought to pull his weapon free.

"Don't!" she said, bringing her blade up to his face, but the other *emari* had drawn his own great sword and was turned on her. She managed to block his first thrust. Then Yourdon was there. He pressed the tip of his dagger into the second man's back, then took hold of his sword arm with his free hand. "No more," he said, prying the big blade free of the *emari*'s sweaty fingers, then holding it on him.

Tasia had returned her attention to her opponent, ready for anything. The man only stood there, eyes twitching about wildly. His hands were held in clear view, away from his scabbard.

"Inside!" Yourdon commanded them. He pushed his man to get him moving while Tasia waved her sword at the other, indicating he should follow. The four of them walked quietly inside, entering the temple one by one. As Tasia reached the threshold the man in front of her grabbed one of the two great wooden doors and swung it at her. The instant Yourdon turned to look he felt the man in front of him pull free.

The first warrior's hands grabbed Yourdon and nearly ripped his sword free. Yourdon yanked, pulling the other man off balance, then used his knee to counter the motion. Freed, he lashed out with the captured blade. The blow found the *emari*'s side. Yourdon watched him stagger back, then fall. Tasia stood over the other man. He lay motionless on the floor, a great bleeding welt on his forehead, just below the hairline, where Tasia had apparently struck him with her sword's blunt-ended hilt. Yourdon wasn't sure he would ever wake up.

"We have to keep going," she said.

"To the reception hall, I think," Yourdon replied, stepping over the prone, yet still breathing *emari* at his feet. He pulled the man's scabbard free and put it on. "I know where it is."

"Then go," Tasia said, letting him lead the way. In a wide hallway they passed a group of Quin disciples, all of them women and children. Yourdon avoided their eyes, and they each kept to themselves.

"Someone will hear of what those people just saw, and soon," Tasia warned. "Even if they did not know you, no one the likes of us would be found here."

"Especially the likes of you," Yourdon chided, seeing his chance again.

"You are not so popular either," she replied. Yourdon grinned and set off again, moving carefully through the quiet corridors. They emerged in a pediment where Yourdon expected to find the doors to the reception hall. Instead they found only flat masonry, and in the middle of the floor a pool filled with a black liquid that seethed and boiled, and gave rise to wisps of steam. Yourdon sniffed, but detected no scent.

"I had no idea your memory was so poor," Tasia scoffed.

"It isn't." Yourdon chewed at his lip, considering. He stepped forward. *Trust your instincts*, he told himself. He began reciting his magical chant, concentrating on his magic, then he plunged his hand into the dark liquid.

His hand struck only the hard, block floor, and his eyes saw a circle of ordinary stone all around his fingers. He stood up and walked across the smooth stone to the place where the reception room doors should have been, then he touched the wall. Most of a door appeared almost

at once, as well as a vague procession of those who had
come and gone here. He turned around and saw Tasia
staring at him in wonder.

"Illusions," he said, turning again, opening the door
to the great hall beyond. The room was clearly visible.
Tasia joined him as he entered. No one occupied the
room.

"Rem was a better sorcerer than I thought," Tasia said,
turning away, looking out over the floor. "I still see the
pool."

"*Is* a better sorcerer," Yourdon corrected, walking back
out. "And I agree. He may even be here."

"In one form or another. . . ."

Yourdon looked about, trying to recall. "This way,"
he said after a time, and they were off again. They
rounded another corner, still very near the assembly room,
and ran straight into a second pair of *emari*. The smaller
of the two was not familiar, but the larger man was. The
largest Quin Yourdon had ever known, Kdosh.

Again Tasia had her sword up first, but Yourdon
managed a very close second. They steadied their blade
tips close to the throats of both their opponents before
either of them could get a weapon ready.

"This, I think, is the fellow who cut off the head of
Rem Ana, or some fellow," Yourdon said, waving the
tip of his captured sword at Kdosh. "And likely the one
who carried the body and the head away afterward. He
even wears the ring!" Yourdon exclaimed, as he gave
Kdosh's hands a closer look. On the third finger of the
emari's left hand was a small ring set with five tiny crystals,
but his right little finger was adorned with a much larger
ring, the same single crystal ring Rem had worn, or it
was quite identical.

Doorways marked both sides of the hall only a few
paces ahead. Yourdon and Tasia exchanged nods, and

ushered both their captives toward them. They entered what seemed to be a guest room, a place to sleep but lacking personal belongings. As soon as the *emari* were relieved of their swords Yourdon pulled chairs together and bade them both sit.

Kdosh put his hands together in his lap. Yourdon looked the ring over again. He decided he had to know. "Take it off," he said, pointing. Kdosh, silent but for a malicious glare until now, made a grumbling noise deep in his throat.

"That is no way to treat an old friend," Tasia told the huge warrior priest. "Do as he says." She pressed the tip of her sword into Kdosh's ample left shoulder. The *emari* struggled briefly, then the ring came free and he handed it up. Yourdon held the bauble in his palm, then spoke his special chant and let the magic fill his head.

He saw Rem at first, entering a house alone, meeting with a man who sat blank-eyed in a chair, no breath entering or leaving his chest—the man Yourdon had seen in the market. Rem removed his ring and placed it on the other's pallid hand, and the hand twitched. As Rem stood back the image faded. Yourdon renewed the spell and witnessed the murder itself yet again. And Kdosh, he saw, just clearly enough, moving quickly in the misty conjuration, raising his great sword and bringing it across, just above the shoulders of the man who was not truly Rem. Yourdon chased the spell away.

"Why?" he asked of Kdosh, throwing the adornment in the *emari's* face. "Why was I chosen to take the blame for Rem's execution?"

"You were right?" Tasia asked.

"I was right."

"Where is Rem now?" Tasia prodded the Quin.

"And why go to all that trouble, set up the switch, then me, then stay away from the trial?" Yourdon added.

"Why was Yourdon released?" Tasia tried.

Kdosh didn't move.

"This is awfully one-sided," Tasia said.

"I know. Tell me, what do the Thae and the *emari* plan to do now?" Yourdon asked, leaning into the Quin's forbidding face. "Answer just that."

Kdosh suddenly grinned at Yourdon. "The Five Gods will answer all your questions, just before you meet your final doom."

"You ask too nicely," Tasia suggested.

"Only once more, by the True God," Yourdon swore. "Then you will regret your silence."

The warrior priest looked up, and spit in Yourdon's face. Yourdon had an urge to strike out at the other man with all his might, but he knew how that trick worked. Instead he turned to the second man.

"Perhaps this other fellow will be more talkative," he said, smiling. He put the sword away and took out his short stout dagger, then he raised the smaller *emari*'s hand. He held the man's fingers against one of the blade's fine edges. "How many are you willing to part with?" he asked.

Movement flashed at the corner of Yourdon's eye. Kdosh hit him like a loaded wagon, knocking him off his feet into Tasia and down onto the stone floor. He realized the dagger was still in his hand and managed to keep from stabbing Tasia with it. Kdosh sought to grip Yourdon's right arm—but missed. Luck landed Yourdon's first blow on the giant man's forearm, where the blade sank to the bone. The *emari* howled and jerked away, but Yourdon, blind with fury now, followed after him, stabbing with the dagger at any part of Kdosh he could reach, striking once for each day he had spent in prison, each night spent on the streets of Dlet, each time he had been chastised by his father or his friends or Tasia or himself—until Tasia's voice brought a flicker of present back into his raging mind.

He fell back, gasping, collecting his wits. He realized he was covered in Kdosh's blood, as was the floor and part of a wall the two had rolled near. He looked up at Tasia—who was staring at him, eyes wide, waiting to see where his thoughts were now.

The second *emari* was still sitting in his chair, holding his hand where the knife had apparently cut his fingers as Kdosh had lunged. A few drops of blood had dripped onto his boots. Yourdon stood up and walked slowly toward him. He held his bloodied dagger in the smaller *emari*'s face, and examined the look in the man's eyes, the fear. "You had better tell me what I need to know," Yourdon said, seething, forcing the words out between his teeth, "or even your gods will fear me for what I will do to you."

"Yes . . . yes!" the man said, trembling, dripping more blood as his hand began to shake. "Yes, I will tell!"

❖ THE PRIEST AND THE WARRIOR ❖

"The beheaded one was not Rem," the man admitted quickly enough, still staring at the bloodied body of Kdosh with eyes that held a mix of horror and dismay. Yourdon had seldom seen a more severe reaction even among men on the battlefield—as severe as his own during his first battle, when the Syttrel had attacked the legion. He glanced up at Tasia and felt the familiar churn in his gut; he tried to put it out of his mind. Tasia looked back at him, curious.

"It's nothing," Yourdon said. He turned again to the *emari*. "Tell us who you are."

"Dapna," the man answered, shuddering a little as the word passed his lips.

"Tell us more about the man in the square. And tell the truth. I will know. The ways of sorcery are well known to me. I saw his true image with a spell of my own."

"He was a 'dotri,' a man who had died, just the day before." Dapna spoke slowly. "Rem used powerful spells from the Gods to bring the body back to life, but not the spirit. He has done this before."

"Deathsway magic. What about me?" Yourdon pressed.

"You were chosen from the first. You are not Akreean, which the prophecies have foretold."

"At least according to the prophet Rem," Yourdon corrected. "Many of his predictions happened as only he said they would, and by his own hand."

"By the hands of many," Dapna responded, head down. "We brought you to your doom."

"I have yet to thank you for that."

"But we helped set you free again," Dapna quickly added.

"Banlae and the Thae Quin Tae did most of that," Yourdon argued, lifting the man's slightly pouchy chin. "Or don't you know?"

"Perhaps they believe they accomplished more than they did."

"Perhaps."

"Where is Rem right now?" Tasia asked, surprisingly sharp, while Yourdon pondered the Quin's last words. She seemed to have run short of patience already, no doubt in part because neither she nor Yourdon knew how many other warriors were about in the temple, or how long it would take for them to find this room.

"In hiding," the *emari* said, utterly crestfallen now, speaking as though the words themselves caused him terrible pain. Yourdon could only assume the hand hurt more.

"Where?" she followed.

"I know where he was, but not where he is. He travels, as do the many *emari* who share his greatest moment, and his dream, the dream of a Quin homeland and the justice that has been promised us by the prophecies." The Quin seemed to perk up a bit as he spoke.

"So I have heard," Yourdon told him. "But how, exactly?"

"Rem and the *emari* are building a Quin alliance that will finally unite the many tribes, and offer Rem an army of faithful warriors to command."

Dapna's mood had changed still further as his own words seemed to remind him of what was at stake. "No matter what I say, what you do, none of this will change. The One will fulfill his destiny."

"So the *emari* are all privy to his plan," Tasia speculated, sucking at the corner of her lower lip. "They know, yet they go along. When will Rem return?"

"Very soon. I don't know the day."

Yourdon frowned. "What is he waiting for?"

The *emari* hesitated. Yourdon pressed with the dagger. "The Shreeta Crystal," Dapna revealed, swallowing hard.

"Do you know where it is?" Tasia said at once, eyes going wide.

"In the hands of Tufan, the sultan of KyrPhel. Rem has promised he will have the powers of the Crystal when he completes the prophecy."

"You mean when he turns up again." The other only nodded. "Tell me more about the Crystal," Yourdon insisted. "What powers?"

"You do not know?"

Yourdon nearly pierced the man's flesh.

"It brings to a chosen few the voices of the Five Gods themselves, and the ability to command great energies, upon their favor," Dapna sputtered.

"No, I want to know exactly what it can do. How does it work? What has it done before?"

Dapna only looked at Yourdon as if the question was beyond him. Tasia cleared her throat.

"I know a bit," she said. "The Crystal is made of five small, separate pieces of darker stones set inside a larger, clearer crystal sphere. It has been kept by many ancient holy men, most of them men of great power."

"All of them," Dapna boasted. Tasia ignored him.

"Countless wars have been fought because of it, or with it. The Quin who holds the Crystal and the ability to use it holds the power to rule in the place of the Gods. Or so the Quin believe."

"So Rem means to rise up from the dead, then take possession of this crystal—then he'll start a war with the Kyr-Akreeans," Yourdon said, following now. Tasia nodded.

"All this and more," Dapna insisted.

"It is a plan that almost assures him of success," Tasia added. "But for years no one has known for certain where the Crystal was. It was lost during the Dral occupation, or . . ."

Yourdon examined her face, the look of careful consideration that had fixed itself there. She seemed unsure whether to go on, which made Yourdon all the more curious. "What?" he insisted. "I must know."

"Or some of them were lost. There have been many 'crystals' in recent times, and many Akreeans who held them, all hoping to gain by claiming divine powers. Most are purely fake—the people and their crystals. But many rumors have been heard these past few seasons, especially quite lately." She turned toward Dapna. "They say the Sultan at KyrPhel has the true Crystal, just as our friend here says."

"That is what Pella and Flene told me," Yourdon confided, concerned only with putting all the pieces together now. "They said Tufan acquired the Crystal in order to keep it out of Quin hands. A wise decision, it would seem." He waited for Tasia to say something; instead she was silent, as if keeping her tongue in check. He waited.

"Under most circumstances," she said in a thin voice.

"What does that mean?"

"How does Rem plan to get the Crystal?" Tasia asked.

"There are Quin everywhere, you see," the *emari* began, using the phrase Rem seemed so fond of, apparently paraphrasing his leader now. "Believers in every land, in every city. Even in KyrPhel. Even in the palace itself."

"They are going to steal it somehow," Tasia said with a frown, as if this last had soiled her somehow.

Yourdon fixed her with a discerning stare. "It takes a thief to know one, I am told."

"It would take a fool to think anything else," she countered, staring back at him. "Rem must have been planning this since the Dral went back to the Shalen Forests. And it seems a good plan indeed, if he can make it all work."

"I have seen part of the sultan's army," Yourdon said, in a mood to scoff now. "They are well-trained and well-armed. And Tufan himself is an able man by most any measure. I wonder how even Rem could hope to steal such a thing from his very house?"

"But he will!" Dapna said, almost a cheer.

Yourdon thought not of Tufan now, but of his daughter, his granddaughter. There were too many possibilities.

"Rem is ready for war?" Tasia asked.

"It would be difficult to field enough men to march on Tufan," Yourdon said. "Pella and Flene told me their's was the land's greatest city, with the largest, strongest palace in all Kyr-Akreea."

"KyrPhel is the key to the region, of that I'm sure," Tasia said. "And I agree, to take it by force would be no small task, Crystal or no."

"He will have two armies," the Quin said, boasting again, apparently finding great comfort in this. "One Quin, but another as well. Tufan can only hope to slay the first. Even the finest soldiers cannot do what has already been done."

"What does all that mean?" Yourdon asked. Dapna only smiled. "Tell me!" Yourdon demanded, pressing yet again. The dagger lay against the flesh just below the Quin's left ear now.

The Quin gulped, eyes straining toward the blade, but he stood his ground. "You two must figure this out for yourselves. I have told you enough," he said. But

Yourdon still had one unanswered question, and Dapna was still the only man who might know.

"You say the *emari* helped set me free again. I want to know why? Why bother? The Thae Quin Tae wanted to know who had paid me to kill Rem, so they don't know what you know, which is that I didn't do anything."

"Of course," Dapna said, grinning now despite everything. "Rem was right to choose you. He chose the perfect fool."

Yourdon lost what little calm he had achieved. He withdrew the dagger, turned his hand sideways, then balled his fist around the hilt and struck the Quin in the face. His knuckles came away throbbing, but the Quin's eyes were out of focus, head bobbing.

Yourdon pulled his fist back for another go. He struck lower this time, putting all his weight into a close abdominal blow. Then he stood back panting through his nose and waited while the Quin came around. Dapna blinked, looked up and tried to get his hands raised, feebly guarding his face.

"Speak now!" Yourdon demanded, hovering.

The Quin coughed, nodding, then used his arms to hold his stomach instead. "You were freed . . . because it is you who will steal the Crystal," he wheezed.

"That's impossible," Yourdon scoffed instantly.

"Yes, but that is what all Akreea will believe. For this crime you will be hunted down and killed by the *emari*, who will recover the Crystal and present it to Rem. All will finally be as the prophets tell. You cannot change these things. You cannot fight the Gods."

"I see no Gods here, only trickery!"

Dapna closed his eyes. "Yet the prophecies are fulfilled."

Yourdon stood silently a moment, heaving furious breaths in and out. The Quin was right, he had been the perfect fool ... yet again. But he had a lot of company. Five Gods, for a start. "By the True God," he said through gritted teeth.

"What now?" Tasia asked, innocent, though Yourdon was certain she would have ideas of her own.

"I'd like to kill this one," he said, flipping one thumb at the seated Quin. "But ..."

"But you are just going to wrap him up and leave him here, aren't you," Tasia remarked, clearly testing now.

"Unless you would like to kill him," Yourdon said, testing back. She smiled grimly, but shook her head.

Yourdon looked about. The room featured no tapestries, and the rugs were too thick to work with. "We need something to bind this one with," he said. He looked at the body on the floor. "We could use Kdosh's breeches," edging a smile.

"You don't have to take his pants off for me," Tasia replied. They moved instead to the room's only bed, used their blades to cut the linens.

When they had finished they stood together near the door, listening for movement in the hall. Finally they opened the door and took a look, then edged their way out. They got nearly to the main entrance before one of the temple's priests spotted them. He let out a frantic, howling oath. Others would come, Yourdon was sure, but this *emari* chose not to wait for them. He charged, wielding his great blade with considerable deftness. Yourdon backed away. Tasia glanced accusingly at him, but then she saw the look in his eyes, the nod. She followed, backing off. Just before the swordsman reached them Yourdon turned and started to run. Tasia did the same. But instead of continuing they each stopped short and spun full circle.

The *emari* tried to bring his blade to bear, but as he arrived between them Yourdon and Tasia each came around, dropping, swords going before them, catching the priest in the sides and back at nearly the same time.

They left him there and set off again, fast as they could go. In just a moment they reached the main doors again, then slipped out into the quiet little square beyond.

Darkness covered them as it had before while they moved through the streets. Soon they were again outside Dlet, resting at the edge of the copse of trees where Tasia had left her mare, and waiting for first light to touch the distant, eastern sky.

"It seems a cruel trick of the fates," Yourdon said, shaking his head, "that after all I have been through, Rem is not only still alive, but he intends to steal the Shreeta and make me appear guilty. Again!"

Tasia sat and listened, surprisingly sympathetic. "You are having a bad run of luck," she said. She slapped at a mosquito on her neck. Yourdon looked at his hands, found one biting him as well, slapped it dead. He stared at its flattened corpse. *Not an impossible fate,* he mused.

"What do you think he meant by two armies?" he said, not really expecting an answer.

"What did he say . . . ? 'Even the finest soldiers cannot do what has already been done,' " Tasia repeated, going along.

"Could he raise an army of men like the one I saw beheaded in the market?"

"Perhaps," Tasia said. Her eyes opened wider. "You can't kill a dead man."

"Rem has had time to prepare such a spell, certainly, if he is capable of one."

"But where would he find another army?"

Her expression suddenly changed. Yourdon thought he saw an idea swirling behind her eyes. "What is it now?" he asked rather cautiously.

"There was a great battle fought not far from KyrPhel,

during the final days of the Dral empire, at Napet. An ambush, just beyond the city's edge near the southern tip of Napet Lake. The Dral's northward marching forces were caught off guard. They say none of them lived. All of them were buried there." She waited, eyes narrowed. "Just a few day's ride from KyrPhel," she finished.

"An army of dead Dral would be the perfect tool," he agreed. "And Rem will stop at nothing, even that, I believe. He can't. I didn't know him long, but I know his type. He is more interested in the Five Gods as a form of power, as a means to his ends. Like most of his *emari*. What they believe is secondary."

"Even the Quin might be better off if he were not allowed to realize all his plans," Tasia said. "But it is possible things are not as bad as they look. I would assume the Crystal is well guarded. Stealing it will not be an easy task."

"Still, we should warn them."

"Before you do, there is one thing you should know," Tasia muttered, almost under her breath.

Yourdon looked at her. "What is that?"

"The Shreeta Crystal," she said, "is the artifact that *I* am after, and for which you are sworn to help me."

Yourdon felt her words like blows. His mind began tallying the implications immediately; none pleased him in the least. He could see the truth of it in her face even now as he tried to control his and his tone. "You never told me that," he stammered.

"You needed my help. You didn't ask."

"And you needed *my* help!" Yourdon erupted. "You said 'obtain' an artifact, you never said you meant to *steal* it. Or who you meant to steal it from! You would have me betray the only people in this whole heathen land that I have any respect for. People you know as well as I. Flene looks up to you, she thinks you a hero!"

Yourdon shook his head in a fit. "By the True God, they are the only people who look up to me, instead of down, and you—I should have known better than to bargain with a thief!"

At this last Tasia leaned away, as from the heat of a flame. Yourdon saw the surprise in her eyes and realized how loudly he'd been shouting. He didn't care. *What's done is done*, he thought, but that didn't mean there wasn't plenty more to do. "I must go and warn Tufan, tell him what I know about Rem, and help him if I can. How can I do that if—"

"I know, I know," Tasia said, leaning nearer again, but wary. "But you haven't heard me out. If you'll calm down I will tell what's on my mind. It is not what you think."

"Threats won't help you," Yourdon countered. "Keep them to yourself."

Tasia weathered the remark, apparently serious.

Yourdon sat silent, steadfast.

"Only a coward would be so frightened of mere words," she said after a time.

"Does it matter what lies have you to tell me now?"

"It may," Tasia said, hardening now, but continuing. "For one, when we made our bargain I didn't know for certain that the Crystal was at the palace at KyrPhel, and I didn't know when I helped you defend Pella and Flene on the eastern road. I only learned as much these past few days. Anyway, I can still go without you. I know I'm welcome there."

"You won't be if I tell them what you want."

"You can just get out, you know," Tasia replied, turning bitter. "Go back to Detimar. You should have done that a long time ago. Just turn around and leave all this behind."

"No." Yourdon looked away. "My life isn't ever going

to be that way again." He thought he ought to challenge Tasia further, or walk away from her, at least, but he saw no point in either. "Speak," he said. "Tell me your mind."

"I think we can still help each other. Kyr-Akreea is the only stable realm in the east, which has helped to keep its neighbors from falling apart, and next to Thel currency their coins are the most valued among the money changers—more reliable in central Akreea than the money Dlet makes for itself. If Rem destroys Tufan and the other Kyr rulers it will ruin what little trade has been restored, and the effects will be felt throughout most of Akreea, even in Thel. Most of my plans require at least a little stability. In any case, if Rem comes to power over much of that region, doing business will become a hazard, I'm convinced of that. Especially for outlanders. The Shreeta Crystal is not the end of my journeys, I hope; it never was.

"And the Crystal will still be there, of course, for perhaps some other day. That is, if we're in time to help Tufan keep it. Meanwhile," Tasia grinned, "I expect the sultan will be quite generous with those who help him through these troubling times."

Yourdon thought out her words, and he couldn't help but notice that she was making a good deal of sense. He saw this as one of her most annoying traits. "Possibly," he conceded, fidgeting too much. "Perhaps."

She pulled one foot back with both hands and tucked the heel under her other leg, then she smiled at him with a flare of mockery. "Besides," she said, tipping her head a little, "I find it interesting that you are willing to leap to Tufan's aid, and fight back against Rem Ana, for him or for yourself, or both I suppose. It is almost more than I can believe."

"And I am not supposed to find your sudden glut of good intentions hard to believe?"

Tasia tried to keep her features stiff, but they gave way to another, less biting grin. "Well then, we will just have to trust each other."

Yourdon's mind reeled. He couldn't possibly, not in this lifetime, not even in the next! Not after all that had happened to him, and all that might, all she had already done. And yet . . .

Yet some part of him *wanted* to trust her, no matter what, as though that was the only choice he could live with now. Even if he didn't dare.

If Beken were alive, Yourdon thought, *this would kill him.* "Trust," he said, offering the word as if handling a sharp knife from the wrong end.

"Yes," she said.

Yourdon felt ill. He took the advice of an old crazy man. "Very well," he said, still painfully. "I agree."

Tasia looked at him a moment, then she stood and bowed to him, smiling all the while. "Courage, convictions, trust," she said. "By the many gods, I am impressed!"

Yourdon fixed her with a doubting eye.

"I make no joke," she said. "In fact" —she pressed a straightened finger to his shoulder— "it is just possible that some Detimarians, even you, are not heathens and cowards after all."

"Thanks," Yourdon said, shaking his head at her, still wondering at her agenda. "Thanks a lot."

"Aye," she replied. "But now what? KyrPhel is nearly four weeks' ride. I have a mount, and you do not."

"We'll go back to Lapo's stables," Yourdon said, taking care to avoid her eyes, "and we'll—er, um—*borrow* one of his horses."

The three young men were *ta-emari,* none more than two years from becoming full *emari* warrior priests. One, called Dlase, came forward, crossing the antechamber, pausing at the center of the room. The riders had arrived breathless on sweat-bathed horses that had been ridden so hard they might not survive. But Dlase seemed to stop breathing altogether as he looked upon the figure standing in the doorway at the other end of the room. After a long moment Dlase began to shake, then he fell to his knees and burst into tears.

"Rem Ana!" he called out, his voice echoing up from the rough stone floor. The two men who had arrived with him acted in kind, then echoed the cry: "Rem is risen! Praise the prophets! Praise the Gods!"

"All is as I foretold," Rem responded, slowly crossing the distance to Dlase's side, then touching the young man on one shoulder. "Know that it is true," Rem continued in a clear and soothing voice. "Feel my hand upon you, flesh and bone. Sense the strength of the Gods within me, and within you."

"The Gods are with us!" all three *ta-emari* replied.

"Indeed," Rem said. "Now rise, and tell me what news you bring. I am sure it is most important."

More important than the lives of those who sent you, he cursed under his breath, since the presence of the messengers threatened many of his plans and defied one of his decrees. Moreover, it meant something had likely gone terribly wrong.

Rem waited as Dlase slowly raised his head. "It is the *emari* of the temple who have sent us to so sacred a place," Dlase started.

"A secret, sacred place," Rem corrected, sensing that his features already betrayed the annoyance his practiced voice sought to conceal. Which only made him all the more impatient. "Now, speak quickly," he said.

"The sanctity of the temple at Dlet has been violated," Dlase repeated. "And one of the *emari*, Dapna, was placed under a powerful spell, one which forced him to betray you."

"A spell?" Rem marveled, drawing a dubious eye nearly closed.

"Yes, my lord. The intruders killed Kdosh before Dapna's eyes. They wounded many others before they escaped—another of the temple's priests died of wounds even as we made ready for our journey. The others barely prevented Dapna from taking his own life to end his shame."

Possibly a spell, Rem thought, though somewhat unlikely. That kind of sorcery, akin to much of what he practiced, was nearly impossible—especially compared to a convenient lie. Dapna had been a cousin to Kdosh, and probably a mistake from the first. He had a weak mind, a flaccid will, all of which even Kdosh and years of *emari* training and preparation had never quite made up for. Rem had never regretted him more than now. "Is he here?" Rem asked.

"He is, my lord," Dlase answered, speaking as well as his nerves would allow. With that Dlase glanced back at his two compatriots. "We brought him with us, so that you might know his words, and so that he might begin to atone for what he has done."

And so that I might take my anger out on Dapna, instead of the rest, Rem added in silence. The *emari* were not fools, most of them anyway. The prophecies told of what could be, but it was up to those who understood them, those who understood the world, to see them fulfilled. One way or another. Power was not often given, it was acquired.

None of the *emari* doubted Rem would learn the secrets of the Shreeta Crystal once it was in his possession, then use it to change the face of Akreea. And while Rem had not truly accomplished his own resurrection, the illusion would leave him unchallenged among the leaders of the Quin. And he *was* a formidable sorcerer in his own right, something no Quin was wise to forget. Regardless of the level of their faith, they each saw Rem as the power to reckon with. Most of the *emari* desired the future Rem promised nearly as much as he did, and none sought to make themselves an obstacle.

But not, it seemed, Dapna. . . .

"Do you know what was said?"

"We do," Dlase replied.

Rem nodded. "Then tell me how I have been betrayed." Dlase took a breath and plunged ahead, recounting everything they knew Dapna had told the two intruders in the temple, and including the identity of one, a man many had recognized with no trouble at all. As Dlase went on, Rem's stomach began to turn. The cousin of Kdosh, it seemed, had talked a great deal. The implications roiled in Rem's keen mind like the nightmares of a fever, impossible yet growing, multiplying, feeding on themselves. He had expected the worst, but this seemed worse than that, so devastating was the potential—and so unreasonable, *so unfortunate!*

"How could this happen?" Rem finally snapped at the *ta-emari*, as well as the handful of personal guards and servants that attended him now. The plan had called for Yourdon Lewen to quietly exist, living in filth, doing nothing, content to await fresh blame in Dlet. Which was exactly what he had been doing, the last Rem had known. "Who was the woman with him?"

"We do not know, but we have learned that Yourdon was taken from Dlet by several Thae Quin Tae," Dlase began again, explaining that Yourdon and the woman had returned, but the Thae had not.

Rem cursed silently. The Thae had always been a nuisance, but a tolerable one, and at times they had proven their worth as agitators, able to provoke a mob or spread a rumor, or die for the Five Gods during the final Dral battles. *Still dying,* he thought, from the sound of things. Rem hadn't expected them to do anything quite so insane in Dlet. . . .

Nor had he imagined Yourdon breaking into the temple, learning so much, then escaping unharmed!

"Every attempt was made—" Dlase assured.

"Not so," Rem moaned, trying to come to grips. He had worked hard and relentlessly, waited most of his life, done everything right. Each detail had been carefully, patiently planned, yet now it had come to this! He had never imagined a destiny that did not find him as the greatest living Quin leader, yet on the eve of his day, his time, such trouble as he could not imagine had arrived.

Yourdon and his friend will tell everyone, he thought, though he forced himself to wonder at the same time just how devastating that would be? And what could be done about it? He had always considered himself a resourceful individual, had proven it time and again, though this situation would surely put him to the test.

"Have you searched the city for them?"

"They are gone, my master," Dlase said, bowing his head. "Gone to warn Tufan in KyrPhel, of course," Rem said out loud, and saying that he felt his temper flare, witnessed his fist slamming into his thigh before he could control it. The action had been correct, if not the target. He moved the leg a bit, wincing slightly, then he put his hands to his face and rubbed his eyes.

"Go about the grounds," Rem told one of the attending *emari.* "Gather everyone here to me. I would hear their thoughts. We have much work to do." With a nod the warrior priest vanished out the door. Rem lifted his head then, preparing to speak to the others in attendance. They were his inner circle, and knew most of what he knew, but that did not automatically exempt them from doubt. He needed to tell them what he would tell the people; he needed to tell himself. *You have always been in control. . . .*

"We must decide what is to be," he began. "We cannot fail in our great and holy task. *I* will not fail, for our day is still at hand! The Five Gods will provide the answers we seek, and the future will yet bring the prophecies to life!" *And if they do not,* Rem assured himself, *I will find a means myself.*

The room was filled with bobbing heads. Rem turned away, and most of the others present began to talk among themselves. "What of Dapna?" the young *ta-emari* inquired, as Rem's following began to gather.

"Bring him to this room and leave him. I would speak with him."

Dlase bowed agreement. Rem dismissed him and his comrades to the task. When the three young men were gone he turned to Kwshan, a well-muscled *emari* still waiting beside him, Kdosh's permanent replacement, now. "Find out everything Dapna can tell you," he instructed.

"Do you wish to punish him?" Kwshan inquired. "A public torture, perhaps?"

"No. He was Kdosh's cousin, and he has always tried to please. It is not his fault that he is too weak, or too foolish, or both. It is simply his poor fortune the Gods made him that way. I am not without compassion or mercy. When you have finished with him, cut off his head cleanly, then bury the remains in the hills."

"As you wish," Kwshan replied, sounding sympathetic. He turned and headed toward the door. Rem watched him go, then retired to his own chambers. He sat brooding, waiting for his *emari* to gather there and counsel him. He needed to determine the best possible remedy, and they could help him, or they would. But already from the sea of nightmares a vision had begun to form.

In his initial panic he had been overwhelmed by the loss of so vital a step in his plans, his hopes to pilfer the Shreeta Crystal before staging his resurrection. But now, as he considered his options more rationally, he was forced to ask himself how significant the placement of that step had been. For one, the possibility was real that he might rally the many Quin tribes without it, that his "resurrection" and his message, all resting firmly on the groundwork he had laid these past few years, might be enough. At least for a time. For another, if he could hold Quin attentions and loyalties long enough, he might yet manage to take the Crystal by force.

As the *emari* came to his chambers and sat at his table, the idea continued to take shape in Rem's mind, a plan that seemed to solve several problems at once.

He would still try to gather his army, as many men as he could, then travel to the Apa River Valley, the battle ground where a combined Akreean force had crushed the Dral garrison there. This part of his plan would not change. Enough dead Dral lay buried in mass graves there, and none of them dead too long yet. These would provide a second army, slow and awkward but relentlessly obedient, and nearly large enough by itself. His problems would become apparent early on, when he tried to seize control without the Crystal. But if that could be accomplished, the rest would follow.

It is the only choice, he thought now, as the idea unfolded before him and began to seem more friendly. He put his fingertips together as he looked at the other men around the table. Time would be of great importance—the need to move swiftly and masterfully was obvious, the need to inspire as he never had before—but together his two armies could take KyrPhel, capture the Shreeta Crystal, and assure his conquest of all Kyr-Akreean lands. The sultan Tufan was said to be a mage of sorts, but nothing noteworthy had reached Rem's ears, despite many quiet inquiries. The sultan's head would itself make a fine second trophy.

And if the Gods showed favor, Rem thought, he would find Yourdon and his new companion in the palace with Tufan, and he'd be happily rid of them all!

He focused, subduing reverie for a moment as he noticed his chamber table full. The *emari* waited for him to speak. He nearly didn't know where to begin. Then he favored the time-tested approach.

"The Five Gods have spoken to me in a vision, and the answer has been made clear. Send the messengers forth." Rem grinned satisfaction. "Tomorrow, I rise!"

❖ EYES OF WONDER ❖

Yourdon woke to warm sunlight and the gentle chatter of birds already getting on with the day. He felt hungry . . . and lucky. Tasia slept just a few paces away, on the other side of faint embers that had been a strong fire the night before. One day ago, as usual, she had been the first to rise, and not for the first time he had paid the price. Now, at last, he saw his chance for redress.

Rising silently he went on his toes, round the coals, until he hovered over Tasia's sleeping form. He held his own sword in one hand and her long, ceremonial dagger in the other. He raised both blades above her head . . . and struck them together with a heavy clang that pierced the quiet morning and made Tasia's eyes spring open wide. She sat straight up, eyes darting. Yourdon stood laughing heartily.

Tasia leaped to her feet, opened her mouth, and let out a howl sufficient to frighten whole legions away. Yourdon turned and started running, deftly dodging trees and shrubbery, but Tasia stayed close behind.

"You will not survive this day!" she shouted after him.

"I could have put a snake in your bedroll, as you did mine," Yourdon reminded her.

"It was a harmless snake," Tasia countered.

"Then *you* should have slept with it!"

"You have my blade," she said, shifting her attack.

"Have it back!" Yourdon cackled. With that he leaped

over a great fallen tree, then turned to face her. He raised the giant dagger and let it fly. The tip of the blade buried itself in a tree just behind Tasia, only a hand's breadth to her right . . . if that. Tasia scowled heavily, then pulled the weapon loose with both hands.

"I am lucky you have bad aim," she said.

"You are lucky I have good aim."

"I will send you to your God bit by bit!"

"I'm likely to need all my bits if I'm to be of use to Tufan, or yourself. Or have you forgotten?"

"A few bits," she corrected, walking toward him, "would not be missed."

Yourdon tried grinning at her. She grinned back cold as the peaks of the highest Tesshis.

"Do all Syttrel suffer such delusions?" Yourdon asked, outwardly calm, inwardly pleased that this would likely be their last day on the road—which meant there would not be another night. . . .

"We've earned them," she answered.

"You have earned a reputation," Yourdon said, while holding his nose between finger and thumb.

Tasia jumped first, and Yourdon bolted again. They ran out of energy a few moments later. Exhausted and breathless, they followed each other warily, keeping trees in the way, back toward the camp. A silent truce had been declared by the time they arrived, one of many. They finally gathered cautiously at the fire and ate a quiet breakfast, nearly the last of the dried fish, a fairly fresh loaf of flat bread and a brick of cheese—these last purchased from a man met on the road, carting a good deal of both to a nearby market. Only two days past they'd gotten a skin full of goat's milk, but this morning the milk had spoiled; water-thinned wine took its place.

"A good day to travel," Yourdon said aimlessly, eyeing the clear skies, warming in the morning sunlight. Tasia only nodded. As they broke camp and prepared to set out on the road the silence grew heavy. There was nothing more to say about the weather; it had been fair the whole four and some weeks since their journey had begun. Only twice had it rained, and neither storm had brought cold weather with it.

The road ahead, then.

"They make fine gravel, these Kyr," he said of the crushed stone that lately covered the way. "We'll be there soon."

"We could reach KyrPhel by midafternoon," Tasia replied, quite neutral.

"Perhaps."

She sought safe, idle conversation as he did. *Just as well*, he thought. There had been no formal agreements during the past few weeks, as they had kept their steady pace toward the Kyr provinces, but conversation—and certain subjects in particular—had been regularly avoided. At times the temptation to start railing against everything the other stood for was difficult to refuse. Yourdon didn't want to fight. For him the urge was tempered by the words of the woman who had stolen his purse at knife point, the words of angry men at an inn just weeks ago, calling both him and Tasia heathens and telling them to get out. The way he'd been treated by his own father. He was sure she had her reasons as well.

Tricks and jokes seemed to let some of the tensions pass, but this morning, so close to their goal, the usual banter seemed especially inadequate. If not intolerable. *Keep your head*, Yourdon cautioned himself, nearly saying it out loud as he mounted, then urged his horse out onto the road beside Tasia's. He wasn't sure, but she seemed terribly restless.

"There is a question I would ask," Tasia said.

"Yes?" Yourdon welcomed the chance.

"It is something which has troubled me through all these many days we have camped together. Something . . . personal."

Yourdon ventured a guess: he had made no advances toward Tasia, deciding at the outset of their journey that such a move would be ill-advised for both of them, and possibly quite dangerous. But one night, as they had prepared to go to sleep, the tension between them seemed to find a voice all its own. Unspoken words seemed to pass between them. The potential was there, as near and intriguing as tomorrow, yet quite unknown. He didn't want to think about it; he couldn't help thinking about it. But he wondered now if she had taken his restraint as an insult—an idea which brought a smile to his lips. "Yes?" he cooed.

"We have spent many nights together, yet apart."

"Yes?"

"There are things I would know about you."

"Of course."

"Do all Detimarians snore like sleeping swine?"

Yourdon's mood inverted along with his smile. "To keep unwanted beasts away. And it seems to work well enough."

Her eyes twitched as her mind searched for yet another volley. Yourdon took considerable pleasure in the moment; it was not often he took the lead in these contests, but he was getting better at it. She glared at him, consternation knitting her brow, then abruptly her expression changed and she began to laugh. A genuine, growing, helpless laugh.

"By the gods," she muttered, shaking her head.

Yourdon's mind understood and reflected the humor instantly. His laughter fueled hers, and the two of them wound up gasping, hanging on their reins.

"There must be *something* foul you have neglected to say about me," Yourdon said, as control began to return.

"No, I think not!" she chuckled. "I will have to use some of them over again."

"It is fortunate we managed to run out of journey just when we ran out of insults. I am growing tired of the old ones."

He waited for her reaction. She ignored the opening he had left her. "As am I," she said.

"Here, the fates are cruel enough," Yourdon offered, sobering considerably now. "At home, the fates have less sway, so people seem always eager to make up for the lack."

"More cruel than I?"

Yourdon was mildly surprised at his answer, "Yes."

Tasia nodded. "As well, life in Syttre is not so easy. A young girl must choose between two lives, that of a mother and a wife, or that of a warrior. Choose either, and you might regret the loss of the other."

"You can't . . . change your mind?"

"Syttrelian men do not change theirs. Most would hold me in the highest esteem, especially those who have fought alongside me, but few would ever want to hold me long in their arms, at least not as a wife. Such a woman has many virtues, but chastity is never considered one of them."

He watched her expression. It was she who was leaving herself open now, baiting him, perhaps. Or she simply wanted to talk. Wanted it enough to take a chance. He knew exactly how that felt.

"Still, you at least look like the rest of your people, and you gained the respect of some, in one sense at least, by earning your place as a warrior. I cannot claim the first, and the Syttrel took the second from me."

"You are a little darker than most Detimarians, but I always saw that as one of your finer qualities."

She smiled at him. Yourdon explained that his mother had been Shetie, that his father was a brutal man, though not in the physical sense. He wanted to keep going, wanted to dump everything he carried inside him as if he were a ruptured aqueduct, but he managed to stop himself somehow.

"Do you hate him more, or . . . me?" Tasia asked, when he fell silent.

Yourdon looked at her. Strange as it seemed, he thought he sensed her mind almost completely. "When I call you a heathen I hear the voices of hateful, unthinking Akreeans; I hear my father speak of my mother. The old insults were made up for us, I think." Tasia looked at him with a strange, unreadable expression, though Yourdon thought he saw a glimmer of something like wonder . . . or possibly it was satisfaction.

"We should at least make up our own," she said, adding a smile that made the words count for much more. "My father was killed in battle, just as Flene's was."

"Fighting Detimarians," Yourdon stated.

She nodded.

"So there was no one, no husband?" he asked after a while.

"No. Then, or now. But that doesn't mean I enjoy being alone."

"No one does," Yourdon said, finding a softness in her eyes that made him wish so many nights on the road had not been spent that way. He wanted to say so, but he was sure he didn't have to.

They rode in silence for a time after that. When they spoke it was about the countryside, the warm, bright day, the rolling, rising hills of forest, scrub and pasture. Kyr villages appeared, first one, then another while mountainous hills grew larger up ahead and to the south. Soon the road bustled with ox-drawn carts and foot traffic.

As the sun reached its zenith the hills loomed large indeed, and stood watch over a great valley, which seemed filled with the city of KyrPhel.

The reception was held at sunset in a grand hall that featured a vaulted, sculpted ceiling supported by dozens of colonnades, each one meticulously beveled. Rich tapestries hung from the walls and thick rugs warmed the smooth stone floors, while enormous works of delicately painted pottery decorated the corners. Several tables, only knee-high and surrounded by fat silk pillows, made up the furniture. Yourdon searched the walls for the heads of beasts but found none. The custom seemed a Detimarian thing, he decided, having seen none anywhere in Akreea, even in the heraldry.

At the head of the room rested the largest table, and upon it a feast as grand as any Yourdon's father had ever set out. Servants carried wine, roasted foul, steaming soups and fresh pastries to everyone in attendance and the hall was filled with well-attired people.

"You have gone to too much trouble," Yourdon said, sitting next to Tufan, speaking loud enough for everyone nearby to hear. Pella and Flene sat on Tufan's left, Yourdon, then Tasia, on his right. For the moment they each seemed more interested in feasting than talking. The sultan smiled warmly. "Your arrival merely supplied an excuse for all of this. We get too few."

Yourdon ate and drank to contentment, then listened while minstrels played odd stringed instruments and bells in the center of the room. As his belly filled and the wine disappeared the day began to catch up to him. He started to drift in a warm, distant daydream of Detimarian feasts he had attended as a boy—a daydream replaced by another, more personal image as he felt Pella lean against him, not for the first time.

He opened his eyes when Tufan slapped him suddenly on the back.

"You would sleep through my hospitality?" he asked, the lines deepening on his round, somewhat fleshy face.

"Forgive me," Yourdon said.

The sultan stared gravely at all his guests, bringing a halting silence to the table. Everyone waited, as if the worst might happen at any moment. "Then sleep all you wish!" Tufan abruptly shouted, slapping Yourdon on the back again. Everyone jumped—while Tufan sat laughing. He joined by the others at the table, including Adsa, the commander of Tufan's royal army. He had taken the seat beside Tasia, and seemed to enjoy the company. He was nearly her age, Yourdon guessed, and and seemed to be an able fellow in most respects. And courteous. He had been only too kind to Yourdon and Tasia since they had arrived—especially to Tasia.

The commander leaned and whispered something in her ear, and she laughed—or giggled, perhaps—acting almost silly. Yourdon had never seen her behave quite so. He shook his head, attempting to chuckle at them both as their laughter and their eyes turned to him. . . .

"My father has a wonderful sense of humor," Pella told Yourdon, squeezing his hand. "I hope you don't mind."

"Forgive my dullard's mind," he said. "The journey was long."

"We are tired from so many days and nights on the road from Dlet," Tasia said quickly enough, fighting a yawn of her own as she explained. "But especially Yourdon, who stayed up during the night, guarding the camp while I rested."

Her vexing grin said more than they knew, but Yourdon understood well enough. He hadn't dared sleep too soundly at first, not with Tasia's penchant for practical jokes; later, though, when turning one's back grew less hazardous, they had taken turns with the watch, as any two soldiers would.

"He is very brave," Pella told one and all.

"So I have heard," Tasia remarked.

Yourdon's fatigue was strong enough to overcome the urge to escalate the little challenge Tasia seemed to offer—an offer made mostly in fun, he knew, but with Adsa so close and cordial, Yourdon began to wonder. Or it was a wish to encourage Pella's most friendly manner that stilled his tongue—he wasn't sure. Perhaps none of it meant anything, he told himself, Adsa's behavior, or Pella's. Perhaps the Kyr were simply a very friendly people, and he was somewhat jaded. . . .

He yawned, and felt the sleep of ages coming on as his mind sought to flee the issue. They had been shown their rooms earlier, lush and inviting rooms, with soft beds surrounded by plush rugs to replace hard ground and damp bedrolls and the tiny, mostly miserable little inns or stables they had slept in when they could. He daydreamed of the luxury just ahead.

"You do look haggard," Tufan said, nodding understandingly. He finished the wine in his chalice, then turned his head to either side, examining the mostly emptied plates. Then he looked to Yourdon once more. "Very well, you are welcome to retire at any time. But before you go I would know of the trouble you mentioned."

"The reason for our visit," Yourdon affirmed. Upon arrival he and Tasia had urgently asked for an audience, but neither Tufan nor Pella would hear of it before a proper feast had been offered. Now, their meals accomplished, the sultan's curiosity would not wait.

Yourdon began, explaining as best he could. He and Tasia had used their long journey to speculate at length on Rem's overall scheme. They had a few likely scenarios, most of them grim.

"Even now, you may have a few trusted people around you who are in truth the servants of Rem Ana," Yourdon explained, causing many heads to glance warily about the table.

"If Rem can obtain the Shreeta Crystal, then stage his return from the dead," Tasia went on, "he will become a danger to every non Quin throughout eastern Akreea—but he will begin with you."

As they spoke the sultan's face took on a look of puzzlement. He glanced restlessly about, hesitating as his daughter's eyes met his, then Adsa's.

"You have heard of this?" Tasia asked first.

Tufan cleared his throat. "What you say rings true, but I fear Rem must have changed at least part of his plans. You must not know."

"Know what?" Tasia asked.

"He appeared not four weeks ago, no doubt just when you began your journey here," Pella said. "Rem Ana is already returned from the dead, and calling on all Quin well enough to fight to join him in his holy quest."

"He has proclaimed their right to their ancestral lands," Adsa added. "As we knew he would. And the right of the Quin as the Gods' chosen people to rule the spiritual lives of all Akreeans."

"And their ancestral lands lie mostly in Kyr-Akreea," Yourdon said, clarifying. The Kyr all nodded.

"But there was never any attempt to steal our Crystal," Tufan remarked. "It remains quite safe."

"Rem would know we questioned his *emari* at the temple in Dlet," Yourdon said. "He must have guessed we might come here and warn you of his plans. Has anyone offered to buy the Crystal from you, or threatened you for it?"

"No," Tufan assured him. "But if he has an army, and wishes to acquire Kyr-Akreea badly enough, then he must lay siege to KyrPhel at some time. If he wants the Crystal he might intend to take *it* by force as well, which gives him twice the reason to attack."

"I agree," Tasia said, glancing at Adsa. He held her gaze a moment, then looked up.

"I will prepare all our defenses," he proclaimed. "KyrPhel will stand strong." He rose as if to go about the task at that very moment.

"And I will help you," Yourdon said, watching Tasia stare quite attentively at Adsa. "If you wish," he added, deferring to Tufan. "I have had a great deal of training in the tactics of battle. The wisdom of Detimar's greatest commanders. All mine to offer you."

"How fortunate we are," Pella said, fairly glowing as she nodded approvingly to Yourdon.

"Oh, indeed, victory is certain now," Tasia said, wrinkling her nose at Yourdon, then getting serious in front of the KyrPhelians. "All the same, I have some Syttrelian tricks that may be of use. Perhaps I could explain them to you."

"A people known for such," Yourdon muttered in kind.

"I think I would enjoy hearing of them," Adsa told Tasia. "Have you any command experience?"

"Some," she smiled.

"Wonderful, all of it," Tufan said, obviously pleased as he looked from side to side. "I am a peaceful man, someone who enjoys the simple, pleasing life of a rich and happy sultan. Rem is just the sort of fool that might ruin all of that. I do not intend to let him. When the Quin come, we shall be ready!"

"There is something else," Yourdon cautioned. "We think Rem plans to use his knowledge of deathsway magic to raise a second army of dead." Eyes clouded all around the table. Yourdon let the idea settle a moment before he continued.

"I still do not believe such a thing is possible on any large scale," he said. "We have priests skilled in battle magics in Detimar as well, and bringing movement to a corpse is not beyond some of them, but building numbers of able warriors from the dead has never been done."

"Your god does not allow it," Tasia said, almost scolding him.

"And your gods are not capable," he returned. "We do not ask ours."

"Rem is known for such powers," Tufan said in between them, apparently quite concerned again. "What you say *is* possible, if Rem has fashioned a spell that is strong enough, if he himself is powerful enough, if he has invested enough in the proper chants, and if he can find a good supply of dead soldiers—of which there is no shortage in many parts of Akreea. But the longer the dead lie, the more difficult it is to raise them, and the more pathetic they become. After a few winters even the bones begin to rot, so the corpses become worthless."

"We will fight the living and the dead," Adsa announced boldly, eyes glancing again at Tasia as he did. But Yourdon noticed him steal a glance at Pella then—who, Yourdon realized, was watching him in return. *Not me*, he thought, before he put it out of his mind.

Pella turned back to Yourdon then. The look on her face did not seem one of passion, he was sure, but it was certainly filled with warmth. She did seem glad to have him around; Yourdon couldn't imagine tiring of being with her. The rest was too much to contemplate just now. He decided to take a road he knew. "To a brave man," Yourdon remarked, raising his goblet to toast the commander.

"To another, I'm sure," Adsa returned.

"Yes, yes, well and good, but both of you can only

fight the living," Tufan informed them, still distracted. "Remains raised in such a manner cannot be stopped by mortal means. Only sorcery can oppose sorcery. I will have to build a countering spell against his army of the dead, and hope it will not be needed."

"My father is a most talented mage," Pella said in support. "He will do whatever is necessary."

"But we all have our limits," Tufan insisted, apparently not disposed to brag just now. "I should know the lean of Rem's spell before I attempt to spell against it. It is not so simple."

Pella looked suddenly concerned, and Flene looked utterly disheartened. Tufan looked about, then he grinned, though this time the expression lacked luster. "That would be the best way, of course. But we have no way of knowing, so I will simply have to guess."

For a time the table was quiet. There seemed nothing more to say, just now. At last small talk began again, and Yourdon noticed Tasia and Adsa speaking to one another. He turned to Pella, but he seemed to have run out of things to say. *I am making too much of all this,* he told himself.

As the evening ended and the guests dispersed Yourdon made his way to his chambers, alone. He washed his face and hands in the basin, then sat on the bed to relax. He hadn't been there long, when he heard someone in the hall outside, then a knock at the door. He opened it to find Pella waiting there.

"I wanted to speak with you," she said, coming close. A hundred thoughts went through his mind, from admitting to complete insanity to a night filled with passion. He tried to silence them all as he smiled warmly at her, waiting.

"My husband would have done as you are doing, if the Gods had spared him. But we are all glad you are here, and Tasia as well. It is with joy and confidence that I have come to grant you a position as advisor to Adsa himself, with the rank of second commander, if you will accept it. I have my father's blessings in this. We do well to put ourselves in your hands."

"What of Adsa?" Yourdon asked, not sure how to qualify the question. Not sure he should.

"He is a good man, worthy of his post," she said, with an expression Yourdon found suddenly unreadable, but certainly complex. He decided not to pry any further.

"I accept, with gratitude," he said, and he felt a touch of pride swell within him. She had not come here to lavish him with physical pleasures, but what she brought was at least as desirable to Yourdon. He bowed to her, took her hand and kissed it gently. Then he had a thought.

"You need not inform Tasia," he said, licking his lips. "I would like to tell her myself, in the morning."

"Oh, no need," Pella replied. "I believe Adsa personally offered her the same honor, and she has accepted as well."

"Of course," Yourdon said flatly. *I can just imagine,* he added in silence.

"Good night," Pella said, looking at him, then she turned and left. Yourdon closed the door and went to bed.

Morning saw royal preferences aligned more to Yourdon's. Not only Pella, but Tufan as well seemed inclined to speak more to Yourdon during breakfast. Afterward, as they went out to meet all of Tufan's highly trained and splendidly outfitted soldiers, even Adsa tended to favor Yourdon's ear when he spoke—to Tasia's subtle but apparent displeasure.

As they all walked out into the vast central courtyard Yourdon could not help but express his approval. In the field, months ago, Tufan's men had been dirty and a bit weary. Here they wore the same linen corselets, each covered by bronze scales that extended over the thighs, and the same bronze helmets complete with colored horsehair plumes, but every thread was clean, every bit of metal was polished to perfection. Most were mounted troops, some four hundred or more. All of them were equipped as archers or with spears and javelins, yet all carried shields and swords as well. Another two hundred or so straight and ready foot soldiers rounded things out.

A formidable force, but it was clear that Tufan, as well as Adsa, were not convinced these numbers would be enough. They said as much as they walked along, greeting their captains. Yourdon let them talk, just listening. Tasia said nothing either as she trailed Adsa, but Yourdon expected she would speak her mind soon enough.

They toured the fortifications next. The city itself was defenseless, having grown too large for its walls, but the palace was all but impregnable. Stone walls, built mostly on solid rock, were ringed at the top by parapets and battlements, and at all the corners stood narrow towers with open turrets. A smaller, inner wall stood thirty paces beyond the outer one. The main gates through the two walls were set at either end of an arched, stone enclosed walkway, above which ran a narrow, hidden walk. From there men could rain axes, arrows or hot oil down upon anyone who breached the outer gate.

"The attack will come from the west," Tufan insisted, as he and Yourdon stood at the top of one of the two gate towers. They faced due west, overlooking the city that filled the central valley. He turned once, a full circle, and was rewarded with a clear view of the entire horseshoe valley in all directions. Tufan drew Yourdon's attention to the east.

Well behind the palace the heavily forested eastern hills rose, nearly straight up in places, just as they did to the right, where they curved around to form the valley's southern rim. Beyond the eastern hills stood mountains as foreboding as the Tesshis, but, as Yourdon understood it, with no known pass through to the deserts that lay beyond.

Between the palace walls and the nearest slopes lay great open, cultivated fields, where no man or mount could easily hide. Adsa was particularly fond of this feature—his idea in part, it seemed, and a good one.

To the north, as Adsa took pains to point out, the hills curved as to the south, but there they crested early, then fell away to the plain, allowing the city of KyrPhel to trail off northward around the lower edges of nearly vertical walls of rock.

"That is why the palace was built here," Tufan explained. "If an enemy attempted to attack down from the southern rim, or from the hills behind the palace, they would have to come over mountains, then contend with the thick forests that cover the hills, the sheer drops, and the rock slides—if they were lucky enough not to get caught in one. It would be difficult to move an army of any size down such slopes, or even to position one, and impossible to bring along siege engines large enough to threaten our walls. Then they have the open fields to cross."

"And there is no advantage to attacking from the north unless the broader eastern roads are blocked," Adsa pointed out. "A direct approach is the only sensible one. Easy routes, level ground, and the buildings of the city itself provide at least some cover. That is where they will come."

Yourdon nodded, pressing one thumb against his lips,

still looking. "How will you protect so many people?"

"At first word from our spotters of an approach by unfamiliar forces much of the city's population will flee into the countryside, and the rest—the old, the sick, and those with very young children, will take refuge within the palace walls," Adsa explained.

"Even your citizens are well trained," Tasia said, her first words since climbing the battlements.

"We feel it is essential," Adsa replied, smiling at her.

"I would say you have done all you can," Tasia came back, nodding graciously to the sultan and his commander. "If the Quin come, they will be well met."

Yourdon let it go. He was still wondering, still troubled. "Rem is shrewd," he said. "He will not saunter up with a few hundred zealots and expect to get inside the palace. And I know of no magic that can work to good effect against walls such as these. If he comes, I suspect he may bring many hundreds, and that they will be well prepared. There are enough weapons and siege engines in Akreea, both Dral and others, to supply any army with whatever it might need. And I worry about Rem's deathsway army; more than some of you, perhaps, but I think with good reason."

"There has never been a Quin force larger than a few hundred, not even during the Dral withdrawal," Adsa reassured him.

"That is true," said Tufan. "And their soldiers will not be armored or trained as ours are."

Yourdon frowned and stole a glance at Tasia. "I said the same once, of my legion in Detimar, just before the Syttrel attacked us by surprise and nearly routed us."

"The Quin are not Syttrel," Tasia said.

"No," Yourdon admitted, "I agree, they are not. But there has never been anyone like the Rem we are expecting."

"Perhaps," Adsa allowed. "It must be considered."

"As to Rem's deathsway warriors," Tufan went on, speaking to Yourdon, "they remain to be seen, and dealt with. With luck and a little skill, we will turn them as well, if they appear, I think. I intend to prepare most of a countering spell, then complete it when I know better what I am fighting.

"But you have been in Rem's circle. I value your opinion. We must take every precaution, and I must work very hard. Beyond that we can but wait."

"His opinions must be tempered with a knowledge of his past," Tasia said, flashing an evil grin at Yourdon. "He has been called a . . ."

He fixed her with a cold eye.

". . . a very cautious man, by some."

The very look she had expected.

"What do you mean?" Adsa inquired, quite serious. Tasia mocked Yourdon's glare with one of her own.

He didn't see the humor. *I'm no coward*, his mind insisted, *and if you dare to say so in front of Tufan and Pella, I will—*

"Nothing, really," she said. "Caution is wise."

"Have you anything else in mind?" Tufan asked, giving Yourdon a chance.

In fact, he did. "Yes," he said, gathering his thoughts. "A Syttrelian ploy, in fact. One used against armies and scouts alike. If the city would provide cover for an invader, then once they are here, would it not do the same for a force fielded by the defender?" He looked slowly from the sultan to Tasia, smiling just enough. As the other man considered the idea it clearly began to take.

"It *is* a Syttrelian tactic," Tasia said, attempting to salvage something. "If such a force is to be deployed, I should be among them."

"Let us talk more of this," Tufan said. The tour seemed

about to end up where it had started in a reception room in the southern keep, an upper floor chamber with splendid balconies.

"I have the whole of Kyr-Akreea to worry about," Tufan explained, as they entered the room and gathered about a table set with wine and cheeses and a sweet porridge Yourdon had never before encountered. "If KyrPhel were to fall, disaster would follow throughout the region. So it is not only for my people, but all of eastern Akreea that I believe Rem, or any Quin attack will begin and must *end* here. It is not enough that they simply fail."

"Agreed. They must be stopped," Adsa said.

He looked at Tasia and she smiled at him yet again. Yourdon shook his head.

"Perhaps above all," Tufan said, a more brooding voice, "Rem must not obtain the Shreeta Crystal. We should have a second plan, I think, so that if an attack does somehow succeed in breaching the palace walls, the Crystal can be hidden or protected somehow. I have placed a spell upon it where it now rests, one which makes it difficult to see, but Rem can counter such a spell, I am sure."

"There must be many hiding places in a palace so large as this," Tasia said, looking about. "Towers, dungeons, bedrooms, and passageways between."

"We should assume that any area might be searched, if the impossible were to happen," Tufan explained, looking to Yourdon as if he expected something. Yourdon felt a need to justify the sultan's favor. *Think of something!*

"We might bury it under the palace," Adsa suggested.

"Unless Rem has a way of seeking it out, a spell of some kind," said Tufan.

"Or a ballista could be positioned at the top of the eastern wall," Tasia said, jumping back in. "If the need arose, the Crystal could be placed into the cup and released to the fields beyond, where it could later be retrieved."

"An interesting wonderful idea," Adsa commended her.

"Yes, interesting," Pella echoed, though Yourdon was almost certain he detected a faint, sour note in her voice. She was looking at him just as Tufan was.

"And retrieved by the first rider to reach it, I think," Yourdon said, eyeing Tasia unkindly. She shrugged at him, nose up slightly. He turned to Tufan. "What if the Crystal were not here at all? Is there some place it could be taken to in secret, and hidden? A detachment of your most trusted men could remain to guard it until you send for their safe return."

Tufan pursed his lips. "Yes, there is," he replied. "I may know of just the place."

"Then perhaps you and I could speak of this in a more private place," Yourdon said, looking hard into Tufan's eyes.

The room contained a small number of servants and two guards. And Tasia, Yourdon thought, deciding extra chances need not be taken. Tufan glanced about, seemed to understand. "Of course," he agreed. "Come with me. Adsa, you will begin seeing to the placement of our catapults and ballistas, and to preparations in the town as well," Tufan said. "Perhaps Tasia would agree to go along? And there is the matter of the separate force, which I hope she will agree to command."

"Sure you don't need me right now?" Tasia asked, fixing Yourdon with a curious stare.

"We'll manage," Yourdon said, enjoying this sign of the ruler's favor perhaps a bit too much. But he was sure, things turned around, she would do the same. "You may . . . go." He smiled happily.

Tasia's expression changed abruptly to one Yourdon

had no trouble reading at all. As they all rose Tasia approached him, then stood very close. "You don't trust me, do you?" she asked, just above a whisper, hiding her face from him.

Yourdon couldn't tell if she was playing. He tried the easy answer. "I suppose I don't."

He saw yet another look in her eyes, doleful, as if she'd lost a friend. She turned and said nothing at all as she started away. *It is an act,* Yourdon told himself, almost certain he was right. He followed as the others filed out of the room. When they reached the hall and parted ways Tasia turned to him.

"Then I don't trust you, either," she said. "If it comes to a fight, and the fight goes badly, I expect you will turn tail and run just as you did once before."

Her mood startled him. "You must know better by now," he told her.

"I thought I did."

Yourdon stood in silence as she turned and moved away. *She must know better,* he thought. Or he had been quite wrong. . . . He realized the others were watching him and tried to move on. "The Crystal awaits," he said.

"You must tell me more of your relationship with her," Tufan insisted. "It might make interesting conversation."

"Aye, it might," Yourdon muttered. Tufan nodded, a grin on his face, then he spun slowly on his heels and started down the hall. With luck, the sultan would let him hold the sacred Shreeta Crystal, and he would be able to try his own small magic spell on it. He could only begin to imagine what that might reveal.

❖ CRYSTAL CLEAR ❖

The small room was lit only by the lamps Tufan and Yourdon carried with them when they entered. A single guard, Motan, attended them: young but disciplined in his manner. Tufan said he could be trusted as Adsa was. He waited by the open door while Tufan led Yourdon to the table in the center of the room—apparently empty, until Tufan paused to utter a spell. Now a simple wooden box rested there. Tufan produced a brass rod bearing a carved emblem on its tip, the royal seal, to be used when the Crystal was placed back inside. The imprinted wax already on the box had not been disturbed.

"The place to hide the Crystal is up in the eastern hills, behind the palace," Tufan said. "There is a small trail, barely wide enough for one rider, which leads past a series of caves along a small ridge." Tufan turned the box in his hands, then removed the pin that held the latch.

"Only one cave is large enough to enter. It burrows into the ridge wall, well back from the edge, on a flat escarpment. The forest obscures the entrance until one nears the caves themselves."

"These caves must be well known," Yourdon remarked.

"Yes, and no. Few Kyr have been there. It is a place of meditation, considered sacred by many. And it is a place for determined lovers. But the trail is difficult and without reward for most."

"Can a proper guard be left there?"

Tufan nodded. He tugged at the lid, cracking the wax.

"Is there a way for them to flee with the Crystal, if necessary?"

"The ridge curves around into the southern hills, but there is no clear trail. Still, if need be, a few riders might manage. I will choose the men myself." Tufan lifted the lid, then raised the box up in both hands. "Two squads, a dozen men in each. Motan can lead one of them. You will see to the rest."

Again, the sultan's trust in him gave Yourdon a feeling of great satisfaction. "I will, as the True God is my witness."

"As you wish," Tufan acknowledged. He nodded toward the Crystal. Yourdon reached in and lifted it from the box. "As you can see," Tufan said, "It is the true Crystal."

Yourdon held the Crystal gently and peered into its smoky depths, to the five smaller crystal spheres trapped inside. He had never seen anything like it, anywhere. He turned slightly from the sultan's view and finished his silent chant, then he waited for the magic to work. Slowly the images formed, numerous and changing. He saw many men and women attending many ceremonies as great rulers used the Crystal, holding it high, summoning their peoples to war.

If nothing else the Shreeta seemed an ideal means of rallying the masses.

Yourdon renewed the spell and waited for the coming of the Gods. Instead he saw another image, the carnage of a bloody war, the Crystal carried before the marching troops. . . . But the Crystal fell into the nearly vanquished hands of the enemy! As the images changed again he saw its new owners fight and die, fight and kill.

Always, it seemed, this Crystal had been used as a tool of war, as a kind of weapon against peace, yet it had not the power to slay anyone directly. And nowhere did Yourdon see the Gods. He began reciting his chant out loud, again and again, looking for the presence of divine beings, of great sorceries. He saw only one man who could wield magical power, but his was a dark kind of sorcery, much like Rem's, and seemed to owe nothing to any immortal force gained through the Shreeta.

"What is wrong?" Tufan was saying, as Yourdon's mind cleared enough to let him hear the sound through his trance. "Are the Gods speaking to you? What language do you use?"

Tufan was genuinely excited, apparently suspecting a revelation of some kind. Yourdon thought that a reasonable explanation, but he shook his head. "No. It is a simple spell I learned, many years ago, one I seem to have a knack for. It helps me learn more about a thing. The events that have surrounded it."

"Ah, yes, splendid!" Tufan replied. "You will have to teach me this spell. I have tried many times to feel the Crystal's powers, to discover its secrets, but nothing has ever come of it."

"I am not surprised," Yourdon muttered.

"But why?"

"Because nothing will."

Tufan frowned. "What have you learned?"

Yourdon took a breath, "The Crystal itself is quite unremarkable, I think. I am still trying to understand what I saw, so that I can put it into words, but I saw no gods, no energies. There have been countless battles fought over it, that is certain, but I fear the Shreeta Crystal, like so many legends, is only what people make of it." *And like so many lives,* Yourdon thought, reflecting as he spoke.

The sultan was staring at him.

"You have never found its secrets because it has none,"

Yourdon clarified. "The Crystal has no powers of its own."

Tufan nodded, suddenly keen. "Then it is not the true Crystal. I have been keeping a worthless amusement."

"No, Tufan." He put the Crystal back into the box. "I believe this is the Shreeta Crystal the others seek. It is very old. Many generations have kept it, all of them believing in it. Its origins must be very ancient indeed. I cannot fathom them."

"I have always wondered, you know."

"I have no doubt. My spell has always shown me the truth," Yourdon said.

"But if that is so, then we have much less to worry about," Tufan considered. "Even if Rem were to capture it, he could not use it to turn the Five Gods against me."

"It is enough, I think, that the Quin believe he can."

Tufan stood silent, thoughtful, for a time. Yourdon gently closed the lid of the box. When he looked up he could see Tufan now understood.

"He needs only their belief to wield the power he requires," Yourdon added.

Tufan nodded once. "In either case, he must not be allowed to possess this Shreeta. And there may still be a means to utilize the Crystal, even if no one has for generations. And Rem may discover it, given the chance. How can either of us be certain?"

Yourdon acquiesced, though he did not believe this last was true.

"In a few days I must speak to my warriors, and to the people of KyrPhel. They will all be told. I will have you at my side, along with Adsa and Pella. They must be prepared for what may come."

Again, Yourdon felt the warmth of the sultan's confidence, the glow of his appreciation. He had never felt quite this way before, so entirely free of the past. Once more he swore an oath to Tufan, as he watched the sultan place the pin back in the latch. He melted fresh wax, and pressed his seal against it.

"In a few weeks, when we have finished our preparations, you will take the Crystal and hide it in the caves," Tufan finished and turned about, signaling Motan to lead the way back out. "Then we will wait, and hope we are wrong."

By midmorning several days later Yourdon and two dozen of Tufan's most trusted soldiers, Motan among them, had struggled up a steep entangled trail and reached the small plateau cut into the high hillside. The caves nestled there, far back among the trees as Tufan had promised. A clearing of sorts had been fashioned by previous visitors. Some of the trees had been felled, and much of the undergrowth cut, though no one had visited for some time, Yourdon guessed. The forest had begun to rebound. He had the men cut and trample the area in front of the cave, to deprive anyone who might approach of cover.

Most of the cave openings were very small, but one's rounded mouth was nearly half again as tall as a man and several paces wide. Perhaps twenty paces inside the roof dropped sharply, and the cave became no more than a black gash that disappeared into mountain rock. Yourdon carried the box containing the Crystal to the back of the cave and set it to one side on a mound of rock. Next he had rugs brought in and laid on the cave floor, then over some of the other rocks, places to sit for the men.

"You are in command, Motan," Yourdon told the soldier, who had remained mostly silent during their journey up the trail, just as he had in Tufan's presence: a dutiful and trusted servant to a good and grateful sultan. Tufan managed to inspire such loyalty in all his men, indeed in most of the citizens of KyrPhel, but especially in his inner circle, his attendants and commanders, his family. This was how Yourdon had always thought it could be, between patrician and lord, lord and servant, father and son. . . .

"There is room enough," Motan said, looking about. They each held an oil lamp. Yourdon set his down, nodded. It would be cramped, but if the weather were to turn, all two dozen men could sleep within the cave. Of course, most would spend little time there. Already they were spreading out, finding positions at the edges of the clearing. The biggest question on the minds of many was how long they would need to remain here? Some, like Motan, had families in KyrPhel.

"Not a comfortable place," Yourdon remarked, as a cool, damp draft from the cave's darkest depths brushed his face. Three soldiers entered carrying food and water and wine taken from the mules. Motan directed them to one side.

"It will do, I think," Motan replied. "I have endured much worse."

You serve your people well, Yourdon thought, as he bowed acknowledgment to the other man. Motan bowed in kind. They walked together then, discussing defensive plans in the event of an attack, and Motan showed Yourdon the way that led to the southern ridge, a place of hills and cliffs at least as steep as those that surrounded him, Yourdon thought. And a journey he hoped no one would have to make.

In all, the plan remained a good one.

"The Crystal is in your hands now," Yourdon told Motan, when they had nothing else to say.

"I leave my city in yours," the other replied. Not mine alone, Yourdon thought, but Motan's meaning was clear. And Yourdon was getting used to it.

It was nearly dark when he returned back down the

hillsides and arrived within the palace again. He headed immediately for the kitchens in search of a meal. He found a meaty stew and plenty of breads, which satisfied him well enough. When he finished he decided to retire early for some much needed rest. He'd spent most of his days these past few weeks helping train Tufan's men in Detimarian tactics, and helping ready the people of KyrPhel for possible exodus. There seemed no end to the work, but it helped him feel better about the future, which was not to be dismissed. And it left him tired enough to thoroughly appreciate a good night's sleep. Tonight would be no exception.

He started up the hall and found Tasia waiting for him, alone. She had been training with the new, secondary force, and working with Adsa the rest of the time, though Yourdon still could not decide if there was anything private between them. Adsa seemed to spend a good deal of time with Pella as well, after all. Pella seemed cordial toward him, but nothing more. She seemed the same way with Yourdon, most of the time. Whenever Yourdon and Tasia wound up in each other's company they usually just stared at one another, as if something needed saying, but there was nothing to say.

"You are back safe and sound?" Tasia asked, a bit too chatty.

"So it would seem." He attempted to pass. She moved to block his path.

"Tell me all about it."

"There is not much to tell."

"You don't have to tell me where the Crystal is. I just want to know if you touched it. You've had weeks, and today, wherever you went. You must have tried."

"Why?"

"Did you use your strange little magic on it? Is it truly the Shreeta?"

Yourdon looked closely at her. "Tell me why you want to know?"

"Tell me first," she said, seeming impatient. "You owe me that much, I think. What did you see?"

Yourdon felt suddenly uneasy. "Tufan could have told you. He was there."

"I asked him," she said, making a face. "He put on such act. He said you saw nothing at all of gods or powers, and yet the two of you go to all the trouble of hiding the Crystal away just the same. Apparently he does not trust me, either, thanks to you! So now it is you who must tell me."

"Once more I would ask why?" Yourdon replied, growing even more suspicious of her enthusiasm.

"Because I have a right to know."

"Not good enough."

"I am simply curious," she replied, irritated now. "Who wouldn't be?"

"Perhaps." Yourdon could see the look in her eye, one of interest, or concern, but mixed with something else—a touch of madness? She had promised not to steal the Crystal, but how could he be sure any promise was something a Syttrelian would keep? Why else would the Crystal's authenticity mean so much to her? She had been seeking the Crystal for some time, and was no doubt speaking some truth, but he sensed there was much more here. Something that went way back.

Realization began to take form as his mind started sorting the events of past weeks in an entirely different order. *The proper order,* he was suddenly certain. *So obvious,* he thought. And so incredible he hadn't seen through her by now. It was entirely possible that Tasia had known more than she had let on, perhaps all along. That she had been attempting to use him, use his talent, in ways he had clearly not imagined.

"You knew, didn't you?" he accused her, stepping closer to her now, looking into her eyes.

"Knew what?" she asked, unflinching.

"You must have known all along that the Crystal was rumored to be here in KyrPhel, and you planned to have it from the start. That is why you came after me when the Thae Quin Tae took me into the forest," he went on, almost as fast as it popped into his head. "You only rescued me because you hoped I might be able to use my magic to tell you whether Tufan's Crystal was the real one. Once I helped you steal it!"

Yourdon waited for the denial, ready for it. They faced each other in silence for a moment, then Tasia let a disturbing little grin touch her mouth, a grin she tried to hide behind her limp hand. "Perhaps," she said softly.

Her brazen display only served to provoke his imagination more. "After which," he went on, giving voice to a flood of speculations now, "you decided you had little choice but to help me with my Quin problems. It gave you a lever to use against me, and I might not have lived long enough to spell the Crystal for you otherwise."

"Were you always so clever?" Tasia said.

"Then you deny none of this?"

"You don't know quite everything," she replied. "You give me a bit too much credit. But who else, other than you? Who better? We were both invited to visit the palace, after all. When we learned the sultan and the Crystal were in danger from Rem, it seemed the perfect reason for a visit. In fact, *I* was going to insist we come and warn Tufan, but you suggested it even before I could. I simply smiled at my good fortune."

"But how could you expect I'd go along? You told me in Dlet that you were out to steal the Crystal. What if I hadn't believed a thing you said after that?"

"I took a chance."

"And I made a mistake."

She wrinkled her nose. "You are a Detimarian."

Yourdon didn't see the humor. "You knew Tufan had the Crystal even when you rode into the clearing that night, when the bandits attacked, didn't you!" He let his anger fill his voice, holding nothing back now. "That is why you were at the Golden Axe."

"No," she said, to his surprise. "The Axe is a place where one can learn many things. I saw the bandits ride out after you, and I could not help but wonder if the women might be carrying something valuable, or that they might bring a good ransom by themselves. Which I think was likely the reason for the attack. Somehow the bandits learned that the women were royalty, or at least wealthy. I deal in artifacts, not people. I had heard rumors, like so many others, but only learned about the character of Tufan's Crystal later on, in Dlet."

Yourdon saw another wrinkle here. "What if they had been carrying valuables? What then? Would you have killed me, or Pella, in order to have them?"

Tasia looked surprised. "The women would never have been harmed," she said. "In truth, I thought the bandits would kill you as they did the paladin. Things don't always work out as you hope they will."

"I won't let you steal the Crystal," Yourdon promised. "And I won't help you learn its secrets."

"You don't have to. I told you I wouldn't take it, and I won't. Can't a person be curious? You're acting like a complete fool, you know. All worked up over nothing. Don't you think?"

Yourdon could not find the words. He was losing a battle against the rage inside him, and possibly another with the Syttrelian who seemed never to tire of taunts. He wanted to reach out and—

"No! You are a liar!" he said coldly. "And a thief. You have lied about everything else, why not this?"

Tasia set her jaw. "I'm telling the truth."

"You wouldn't know the difference!"

"I don't have to answer to you," she retorted, finally losing her composure. "And I will not!"

"Yes you will! I should go and tell Pella and Flene what kind of woman you really are."

"As if you are fit to judge anyone. As if Pella would look at you the same way if she knew you better!"

"Would Adsa look at you with anything but contempt if he knew the truth?"

"Leave Adsa out of this!"

"Leave Pella out of this!"

Tasia stared at Yourdon, clearly frustrated, her eyes seeping outrage like a wound letting blood. Yourdon kept up the attack: "Tell yourself what you want, but it won't change what you are."

"And the world will always know what you are," Tasia snarled, at least as furious as Yourdon now.

"No one needs you around," Yourdon declared. "It is you who should go, not me. Why don't you take your lies and get out, just go back to Dlet. Or go back to Syttre if even they will have you. Stay, and I fear the worst might happen."

"So," she countered, "the coward is also a fool. Or perhaps only a fool just now."

Yourdon set his jaw and reached for the hilt of his sword. His palm wrapped solidly around it, but he held back. Tasia put her hand around her sword as well, then shook her head. "You will die," she said.

Yourdon glared back at her. "One day, I'm sure."

"It is not a fair contest, since I must catch you before I can have at you," she said.

"Enough!" he called, feeling the words like daggers.

He wasn't thinking clearly anymore. He didn't want to. He drew his sword and stepped back as Tasia's blade cleared its scabbard in nearly the same instant. They faced off, circling in the cavernous hallway, eyes fixed on one another. Yourdon had lost the war between Syttre and Detimar once; he had no intentions of losing it again.

He waited for an opening while keeping his guard up. She left none. Several times more they circled, never so much as flinching. Then Yourdon saw the look in her eye change just slightly. She was going to strike; he knew it. He took a breath, ready . . .

"Ah, there you are!" Tufan shouted from behind. Yourdon dared not turn and look, but Tasia's eyes flickered as she ventured a glance over his shoulder. She backed away two quick steps and straightened up, and Yourdon did the same.

"I was told you had returned," the sultan said to Yourdon as he drew near. "We must talk of your mission, every detail, and there is to be an assembly tonight. I insist that you attend." Tufan lent a knowing grin. "We will speak of Detimarian battles!"

"There are many great Syttrelian battles," Tasia offered, still holding her sword, point down, as if some small animal might be threatening her feet. "Perhaps—"

"Yes, perhaps tomorrow or the day after Tasia could recount them," Yourdon interrupted, holding his blade mostly behind him now. "Or some other time."

"Ah, a fine idea, and one I think Adsa would enjoy. You are a most equitable man," he told Yourdon—whose boyish grin caused Tasia to fashion a grisly scowl.

"Did Adsa say as much?" she asked.

"No," Tufan replied. He tipped his head. "Have I interrupted your practicing?" he asked then, eyeing their swords.

"Oh, yes, um, yes," Yourdon stammered.

"Yes, of course," Tasia concurred, though her look had not changed.

Yourdon bowed toward Tasia. "She is quite adept, but I was just demonstrating to her that she has much to learn."

"Ahh, of course," said Tufan. "But I'm certain she needs very few pointers, and now I need you. And Pella has been asking about you as well. You will forgive us, Tasia? Or would you like to come along?"

Tasia looked as if she might burst, so red and furious was her expression. Yourdon only smiled again.

"Are you well?" the sultan asked her, noticing. "You look upset."

"No," Tasia said. "I am . . . fine."

"Go and rest," Yourdon suggested. "We don't need you. Really we don't." He turned away from her.

Behind him he heard her put her sword back in its scabbard, heard her stalking off down the hallway, talking to herself. Which was all he could have hoped for.

Tasia paced in her room, still outraged, still wondering what she would have done had Tufan not happened along when he did. And what she should do now. She had nothing to be ashamed of. She'd told the truth when Yourdon had asked it of her, part of it, at least . . . before and now. Yet he had only gotten angrier, had only demonstrated the limits of his nature, and an utterly pathetic sense of humor. The man truly was a fool, and perhaps a coward as well, though she doubted this much more than she would ever let on to him.

"Bastard!" she said out loud, pacing harder. She thought of going to Adsa, now, before Yourdon could do any harm. But if Adsa had truly wanted her around he might have asked for her at the assembly tonight—or something. He seemed to show as much interest in Pella as he did in her, and not enough in either of them. Not that Tasia fancied herself the commander's mate, especially, but she at least considered herself worthy, and she wanted him to make that clear. Apparently, he had not. The man was nearly as pathetic as Yourdon Lewen!

She drew her sword, spun precisely and lashed out at a chair, cutting well into the wood. The blade stuck and she had to wrestle it free. When she finally succeeded she kicked the offending bit of furniture halfway across the room.

I have to get out of here for a while, she told herself. *Away from all of them. I have to think!* She was certain that if she laid eyes on Yourdon again any time soon she was likely to do something quite regrettable—and Adsa as well, now that she thought about it. In Yourdon's case, however, she might be doing KyrPhel a favor. *What possessed a man like that to think he could lead an army. . . .*

On their journey here for those many days and nights on the road, and more than once since arriving, she had almost come to see something likable in the young Detimarian. . . . And she had thought, more than once, when he had looked at her or chased her or run from her, that he . . .

She had always been able to sense what was within a man, yet just now she could only wonder what she had been thinking of. What she was thinking of!

She ran her sword back into its scabbard and left the room, pounding the heavy wooden door shut behind her. She kept walking through the palace halls and out into the labyrinth of courtyards, until she'd made her way to the palace stables. She found her horse easily enough, put the mare's blanket and bridle on, then she added her bedroll, so she wouldn't be without it, just in case. Then mounted and rode out through the gates, into the city.

People passed everywhere around her, many carrying great baskets on their heads or in their hands, others pushing carts, all finishing the day's business as night began to surround them. She found the main routes too crowded, the people's stares unnerving. After a time she turned left, heading south toward the city's nearest edge. When she reached the outskirts she sat staring out across the fields and up at the steep, moonlit slopes of the ridge beyond.

There, she thought, *is a place to think, to be alone.*

She heeled the mare forward, across the open ground that lay ahead, then she started up the first narrow, gullied trail she could find. The horse had a time of it, but Tasia helped her choose her way, let her go easy, until they reached a point more than halfway up the great slope, where a wide ridge swept from somewhere high and behind her, and continued on toward the higher hills that loomed behind the palace, east of KyrPhel.

Here, on the flat rocky ground and surrounded only by knotty trees and silence and darkness, she began to feel quite at ease. She walked the horse to the ridge's rounded edge, then dismounted and stood there, gazing down at the valley below, watching the fires of people moving about in the streets, the glow from the palace itself. She had missed dinner entirely, she realized, and she'd neglected to bring any food. She wasn't hungry.

"It would serve you right if I *did* steal the Crystal," she said to everyone below.

Another choice was simply never to go back down there. But that sounded too much like something she might accuse Yourdon of doing. The sultan and Adsa had entrusted her with the counterforce, after all, and unlike Yourdon, she did not intend to run away from her duty. Nor from Yourdon. To leave now would not profit her in the least. Only him . . .

Although, the way things looked, she might not gain very much for her troubles in any case. Not if Yourdon had much to say about it, and not so long as Tufan and Adsa were not obliged to appreciate her. But . . . *Oh, curse the gods!*

She decided to camp on the ridge for the night, under the cool, constant stars. She built a small fire against the chill the clear night had brought, and to discourage mountain cats. As she sat and focused again on the valley below she saw that movement had increased in the city's streets. Hundreds of torches had been lit and seemed to be gathering in clumps everywhere. She kept watching, noticing too that in the palace itself, torch-lit commotion on the walls seemed to have increased. No sound reached her ears, she was too far away, but slowly, as the fires began to gather across the city's northern sectors, the significance grew clear.

Already? she wondered, not quite willing to accept the possibility. She and Yourdon had been in KyrPhel for only a few weeks, and just over four weeks before that when they had left Dlet. There had not been time. Even for Rem. Still, she had a solid feeling in her gut, a bad feeling. . . .

She stood up, heart quickening, and turned to gather her horse. In the woods beyond she heard a subtle noise, the snapping of a sprig, the rustle of branches. Some sort of animal, a mountain cat perhaps, she thought, eyeing her suddenly nervous mare. Then sound became movement and the woods were filled with men. Warriors, she saw, as they approached her, each of them drawing iron. They all wore the embroidered mantles of the Quin.

❖ HOW CLOSE, HOW FAR ❖

"Their force is twice the size we expected," Adsa told Tufan, obviously displeased. "How can there be so many fools!" The two men stood in Tufan's antechamber, joined by Yourdon, Pella and Suta, one of Adsa's commanders. The mood was anything but bright. Runners had been to every corner of KyrPhel. Much of the city's population had been gathered and were even now being escorted north, toward the many villages, fields and woodlands that filled the countryside all the way to Shet-Akreea. The old, the weak, the very young, and all those unable to fight were being gathered within the palace walls.

"Rem moves quickly, perhaps too quickly for any man," Tufan said, a grim speculation, and one Yourdon didn't think the sultan truly believed. Still, it was a question surely everyone in the palace must be asking himself. Already, with the coming dawn, great clouds of dust kicked up by Rem's approaching forces could be seen near the farthest outskirts of the city. Scouts, the most recent to go out, had arrived with word only a short time before. It could only be assumed that earlier parties had not lived to report what they had seen, something Yourdon had no trouble accepting.

"Rem's *emari* were at work gathering his armies even while he was supposed to be dead," Yourdon reminded Tufan.

"Apparently they were quite successful," Tufan answered unhappily.

"And he has managed to conjure his army of the dead as well, I think. I sense his spells even now."

"Rem would have come past Napet," Adsa speculated. "If his talents with deathsway magics are as great as you suspect, he might have raised many Dral from the massive graves there."

"Hundreds, perhaps," Tufan agreed, looking even more concerned. "I must go to the western tower and prepare. I have nearly finished building my countering spells. . . ." He trailed off for a moment, as if some more pressing thought had filled his mind. The trance seemed to lift then, and he finished, "But on such a scale, against such dark sorceries, I cannot say what effect they will have."

"You can say what you feel will happen, at least," Pella insisted. "You can tell me what your heart tells you."

"It will take all my strength, my daughter." Tufan looked into her eyes. "Rem has had years to prepare, and he is a master of the art. I have had only a few weeks, and I am no master. I cannot undo what he has done. I can only hope to add to the spells he has cast, to make them into something that no longer has any power. And still my spells cannot even be completed until I have had a chance to better sense his own, to comprehend. Then I will need time, and luck. I do not intend to let you down, I promise you that."

"I know," Pella said, putting her arms around him. Then Pella drew back. She turned toward Yourdon but looked past him to Adsa, where her gaze seemed to linger, then she swept herself from the room.

"There is no word from Tasia?" Tufan asked, looking from one face to the other.

"None," Adsa replied. "I am worried."

"I'd wager she's in no danger, wherever she is," Yourdon

assured him, all too certain of it. "But I would like to know what has become of her as well."

"We cannot wait," Adsa insisted, a chastened look on his face. He turned to his second commander. "Suta, you will take Tasia's cavalry. We will need to employ all of our stratagems to survive this siege. Wait for the signal, then do whatever is required."

"I understand," Suta replied. The young commander vowed his fealty and promised Tufan victory, then he bowed from the waist, first to Adsa, then deeply to Tufan. Yourdon had known a hundred men just like him, soldiers in the Detimarian legion, loyal, fearless. He had known one especially well. He watched Suta follow where Pella had gone.

"I too was once that sure," Adsa said, after the soldier had gone.

"Aye," Yourdon said, mostly to himself, somewhat relieved to hear the other say what he had been thinking.

"We have little time left to prepare," Adsa said then. "They will have at least half a day of good light left when they attack."

"They will fight by day, and by night," Tufan explained. "With an army of dead, the fighting will go on regardless. Creatures of the darkness need no light. He will be in no hurry. I think. Rem can take his time, as well as take some chances."

"I will go inform the men on the walls," Adsa said, excusing himself.

"Go with him," Tufan bid Yourdon, touching his shoulder. "We must trust in each other to find the means to save KyrPhel. Adsa has my greatest confidence, but he will need you. My warriors believe you are wise and capable, a gift sent by the Gods from a distant land. Adsa is in command, and you must promise to respect his authority, but he will listen to you. He will not say so, especially in front of my daughter, but he is glad you are here, too."

"He thinks a great deal of Pella, doesn't he?" Yourdon asked, evenly as possible.

Tufan was silent a moment, then he raised his brow and tried to grin. "We all do," he said.

Yourdon nodded. Trust in each other, his mind repeated. He didn't like the sound of that. Of course, he couldn't let it matter. "I will fight at his side, and we will turn this threat, I swear," he said, feeling pride swelling once more inside him—a feeling so rare until he had come to this land. He felt determined to justify Tufan's faith in him, no matter what that meant. He bowed to the sovereign, then went after Adsa to take his place among the battlements.

❖   ❖   ❖

Adsa and Yourdon had already worked out their positions, both of them up high where the men could see them, Adsa near the southwest tower, Yourdon near the tower at the northwest corner. Tufan would be above Adsa in the taller southern tower, where he could hear the sultan calling out. A soldier was to wait in the northern tower, prepared to start the signal fire on Yourdon's command.

As Yourdon made his way down the hallway, anxious to reach the walls and see what awaited in the growing dawn, a voice from behind him called his name. He turned to find Pella catching up.

"I must ask something of you," she said, her voice lowered to a breathless, shaky whisper. She drew very near. "A small task, but one that means more to me than my own life."

"Certainly," Yourdon assured her, somewhat startled by her apparent distress. "Anything."

"I fear for us all, but for Flene most of all. You were

willing to fight to the death to protect her once. I would ask you to protect her now."

I had little choice, Yourdon thought, recalling the night the bandits had attacked in the river clearing, but he only nodded. "What is your wish?"

"Take her to the caves in the hills. Leave her there with Motan and the others. My father would not so much as consider it; if he sent his family away it might be seen as a sign that he expected the palace to fall. When all the Akreeas were at war it made sense to send us away, but not here, not against Rem.

"But if the palace should fall and we should die, Flene will be heir. Her survival is vital. And even if it was otherwise I would ask. I cannot bear the thought of what Rem might do to her. I cannot bear to lose her as I lost her father. In the hills she will be safe, while I remain at my father's side.

"If Rem is the victor, then Motan can flee with Flene. Stay with her yourself if you can, for she could ask for no better, nor could I."

Yourdon reeled at the implications. He could not refuse Pella her request, nor could he forget his promise to Tufan to stay and help Adsa defend the palace. But another thought nagged him now. *In the hills . . . safe.* He heard Tasia say the words in his mind—wherever she was—and sensed a growing hardness in his gut as he imagined the consequences.

He had not seen her since their argument, had considered this a blessing, but he could well imagine that she would turn up in time to accuse him loudly and repeatedly of running out on his duty to Tufan, of taking the young girl to the caves so that he could hide there with her, behind her perhaps, a coward no matter what, irrefutably. . . .

"Please," Pella asked, taking his hand and squeezing

it so tightly Yourdon thought to yank it away. "Save my daughter. Promise me you will."

"I do promise to take her," Yourdon said, almost in spite of himself, feeling his insides twist a little tighter. He could not deny her this any more than he could deny Tufan's wishes. But the palace had an army and Adsa to defend it. Flene needed him, as did Pella. "I cannot bear the thought of Rem getting hold of her either," he said.

"Once you have gone I will tell my father what I have asked of you. He will understand. You will not be dishonored by this deed," she added, as if she'd read his mind. But his thoughts were not so hard to guess, he imagined. "I will see to it," he said, settling on the idea. He hadn't promised to stay with the girl, not precisely, and there was still time before Rem's forces reached the palace walls. He could not be in two places at once, but he could possibly come close. "Where is she now?" he asked. Pella quickly led the way.

Flene had a large soft leather bag, drawn with rawhide, already packed with clothing. Yourdon found her dressed in riding breeches and holding a bedroll much like the one she had used on their last journey together. She seemed quite glad to see Yourdon, and ready to leave; apparently she and Pella had already said their good-byes.

"I have more than a squad of men, my personal guard, ready to ride with you," Pella said. "Take them. They will serve you well, and serve Flene should the wrong hands find her. Use the main gate. You will not be stopped."

Yourdon stood silent, waiting as mother and daughter held each other one more time. "I will see you again," Flene said, more confident than her mother seemed to be, though the woman did her best to hide her doubts.

"You are quite courageous," Pella said. "So much like your father."

"And Yourdon," Flene said, smiling up at him, making him feel briefly immortal. Her mother nodded, then let her go. Flene came to Yourdon's side and took his hand. "Soon, she will be returned to you," Yourdon promised. He led her away.

The men Pella had promised and two extra horses were waiting in a small courtyard near the stables. They formed a line behind Yourdon and the girl, then crossed the grounds to the inner gates. Without a word the guards let him and the others pass, as if they knew exactly. He looked for Adsa as he entered the passage between the walls, then continued through the outer gates. He expected to have need of a story—their procession was in plain sight, and he was certain Adsa did not know anything of Pella's concerns—surely something would need to be said.

But no one hailed them. Pella had no doubt summoned Adsa to a final meeting or some such; Yourdon could only smile.

He led the troop through the streets of KyrPhel, circling left, then left again, observing the last of the city's citizens loading carts for the journey out. Pausing in an empty square he called one very young and wiry soldier aside. "You know where we are going?" he asked.

"I do," the soldier replied.

"Then listen. I want you to remain here. Hide yourself well. Witness the battle as it unfolds. I should return soon enough, but if I am detained I will need news. Wait until near next nightfall, then be prepared to follow our trail up into the hills and tell me everything you have seen."

"As you wish," the boy answered crisply. He turned away from the line and trotted his horse off into the near alleys, into darkness. Yourdon turned away and continued to the eastern edge of KyrPhel, where he pushed the horses to a gallop across open ground, passing into the shadow of the eastern hills. He kept pushing as he reached the trail and started up. When he looked back he could see dark shapes looming at the western edge of the city, great rising clouds of dust. A chill swept his spine as he left the coming battle behind.

In a clearing only a short walk from where they had found her, Tasia came face to face with Rem Ana. As she was pushed, stumbling and unarmed, into the campsite she saw two long, elaborate Akreean-style tents, though no details or colors were visible in the darkness. She found Rem waiting for her, standing in the center of the camp, where his men were busy building a central fire. As the flames grew she saw that he was smiling at her, apparently quite pleased to have her here. She saw this as a bad sign.

"Who are you? Why do you trouble me so?" she said, feigning ignorance. She looked him over more closely as she stood before him, as the flames brightened. He wore a long, dark, pleated tunic and a hooded mantle that covered his head and hid much of his face in shadow. His entire beard was pure white. She couldn't help but wonder how he'd done that.

"Who are *you?*" Rem asked, looking at her closely, as if something in her eyes might even now be giving her secrets away. A spell of some kind, she worried. Rem had long been known for his talents for bending or embellishing what the mind perceived. This was the effect the runes were said to have on those who did not possess the protection of Syttrelian blood in their veins. People like Yourdon, she thought, finding him filling her head. Then she caught herself and made his image go away.

"I am a trader, passing through, on my way north to Shet-Akreea," she said.

"But you have nothing to trade."

"I seek something to trade."

"Perhaps," Rem said, walking slowly around her, folding his arms limply across his chest. "But I am inclined to believe no one these days. Especially outlanders. Now, you will tell me your name, and I will tell you mine."

"Lewena," Tasia said promptly—too promptly.

"As you wish," Rem said. He lingered a moment, then seemed to nod to himself. Next he turned and gave a brief command to one of his men, a tall *emari* nearly Rem's height, one of several men who had been hovering just behind Rem's left shoulder. The other turned at once and hurried away. Rem waved a finger at the next man.

"I have seen her in Dlet," this other *emari* said. "She is Syttrel, I think."

"Her name?"

The *emari* shook his head. Rem waved him off, then turned again to Tasia. "A nuisance. Please sit, and be comfortable," he told her, indicating a spot on the ground just in front of a massive tree. "Soon, I will have more questions for you."

Tasia stepped away twice and sat, then pressed her back against the tree. Two *emari* stood guard over her. She watched carefully as others moved about the camp, counting less than thirty men in all, most of them warriors, though at least three appeared unarmed. Advisors of some sort, she guessed. Rem walked with several others from one tent to the next, apparently concerned with some detail. He remained inside for a very long time, then he emerged and sat at a small table that had been set up not far from the fire. A fire that could be seen half a realm away, Tasia thought, watching flames lick at leaves and branches above.

Apparently Rem believed he had nothing to hide, or fear.

A commotion drew her eye. She watched as a rider entered the camp and leaped down, then spoke to Rem. The conversation was brief. A moment later the rider remounted and sped off, back into the darkness the way he had come.

Quiet descended again, and stayed for a while. Finally another rider arrived, and did much the same as the first. Much later a third rider arrived, confirming a regular interval, but when he dismounted he spoke much longer with Rem, then he came straight toward Tasia and looked in her face. She could see him well enough, and realized the first light of dawn was beginning to seep into the forest. He was dressed in KyrPhelian robes. Tasia thought she recognized him, one of the servants at Tufan's palace, perhaps, or one of Tufan's guards without his uniform. As he looked at her his eyes grew wide, then he turned and hurried back to Rem, his chatter sounding more excited. Rem nodded him silent. Then he rose and made his way to her with the other man in tow.

"This is Daco, from KyrPhel, a spy," Rem grinned, extending a hand toward the other man. "He was originally going to attempt to steal the Shreeta Crystal from within the palace, until that idea became much too well known. But you know about that, do you not? You were with Yourdon Lewen at the temple. The two of you killed Kdosh and questioned poor Dapna, then you came here to warn Tufan."

Tasia watched his mood darken quickly. He looked suddenly about to bite her. "Admit to your many crimes," he said. "The Five Gods will accept no less, and neither will I."

"I am sure I have never been to your temple," Tasia said, because she didn't know what else to say. She tried to concentrate on what it might be like to wrap her hands around Daco's neck and squeeze until his eyes popped out—or cut off his ears and feed them to him, or—

"I am told by some that Syttrelians are thieves and liars. It seems these things are true."

"I am told—" Tasia started, gritting her teeth, but she stopped herself. To bark back or admit what she knew would only hasten her fate.

"You will tell me all the secrets you know," Rem said. He hiked his robe up slightly, then dropped to a shallow squat and glared at her. The composure was gone now, from the face, the voice. "I would know where the Shreeta Crystal is being kept, how many men guard it, and any obstacles that might keep me from it."

"I don't know," she replied, looking away. He struck her hard across the mouth with the back of his hand. *I'm going to look like Yourdon did when I found him,* she thought without cheer. The pain faded and she looked up. *Something,* she thought. *I need to tell him something!*

"I have seen the palace defenses, some of them, but that is all I have."

"Then describe them," Rem said. He stood up again and began reciting a jumbled phrase under his breath. She watched his hands move subtly, the same motion several times over. Soon she began to feel the effects of his spell on her mind. Like a moment ago but stronger, more painful. She rarely got headaches; this one had already begun to make up for those she had missed.

"Now, what is in your mind?" Rem asked, adamant.

"A sword," she said, straining against him. "A sword that I might use to cut your throat!"

"Indeed?" Rem said, sounding almost amused. "And what of my *emari*?"

"I would kill them as well, if they insisted."

This drew a faint chuckle from several of the warriors,

those standing within earshot. She concentrated on withstanding Rem's spell.

Rem spoke his chants again and Tasia's headache grew a little worse, limiting her choices.

"Describe the defenses," he commanded. The words seemed to fill her mind. "Yes," she said, putting her hands to her head, acting as though the spell were nearly killing her—which was not nearly far enough from the truth. She gave in a little, trying to save her strength, and told him most of what she knew about the size and type of the sultan's main forces, then she described their deployment inside the palace walls. She even told him of the many catapults and ballistas that had been pressed into service, but she made no mention of the special cavalry she had been asked to command. Here, at last, she held the line. After all, she could not truly say what had become of them. . . .

She finished speaking, still head-in-hands and moaning softly, pitifully. Which seemed to work. Rem did not immediately renew the spell, she observed with great relief. This, however, was short-lived.

"Now," Rem said, "you will tell me where the Crystal is."

"I don't know," she whined. "Truly, I don't."

"You do," he insisted, growing visibly angry now. He set about chanting again, waving his fingers almost frantically. Tasia waited for the pain to increase, for control to slip away. The pain wasn't as bad as she thought, and she held on, somehow. After what seemed like a very long time Rem stopped and stared at her. Her head throbbed as if horses had trampled over it, her stomach felt twisted inside, her mind was foggy, incredibly sluggish, but her thoughts remained her own.

"Where is the Crystal?" Rem asked yet again.

"You are wasting your time. It is not at the palace," Tasia said, a truth that he would not believe. He did not. He asked again, but she only looked up at him this time and showed him a painful smile.

"Very well, if it is not there, where is it?"

"I sold it back to the Gods."

"Enough!" Rem shouted. "Tell me what I want to know. You cannot fight me for long."

"You can work your spells on a Syttrel as long as you like. They won't work," she said hoarsely, realizing it as at least partially true.

"I will make them work!" Rem shouted, face red from his efforts and his anger.

"Just as you came back from the dead," Tasia teased, still hurting, bitter enough not to care about the consequences.

He brought his hand back to strike her, but a call from one of his *emari* gave him pause. The warrior priest seemed to have found something quite urgent to report. Rem moved away and the two of them spoke momentarily, keeping their voices low, then Rem motioned to Tasia's two guards, who immediately flanked her, one on either side. They placed their hands on the hilts of their great curved swords and she swallowed hard in anticipation of losing her head.

But the men did not move. Rem and the warrior who had beckoned to him joined Daco the spy, all of them speaking together. The warrior gestured toward the valley below, then toward the mountains, east. As a gentle breeze stirred by the sunrise came gently toward her she could almost hear their words.

Abruptly Rem turned and shouted a series of commands, then he turned to Tasia and her guards and ordered all to follow. Soon nearly everyone in the camp had formed a loose assembly. They set off, trailing Rem through the woods. They arrived very near the spot where Tasia had been captured.

Below, still in the distance but closer than Tasia would have imagined, a great ocean of dust washed the sky beneath the already climbing sun. Rem's army was entering the city unopposed.

But Rem's attentions were not on this sight, she began to realize as she studied him. He was huddled with Daco and the *emari* who had just brought him here. She followed their gaze to the far hills, to where the valley wall curved and rose out beyond Tufan's great palace. A small gash was barely visible in the trees as she squinted, eyes straining for a better look. Another cloud of dust rose up there, high on the eastern ridge, tiny compared to the storm kicked up by Rem's forces but clearly visible.

Rem nodded, then he moved again nearer Tasia, so as to look upon his marching forces. "There is nowhere they can go for help," he said, to no one in particular.

"Agreed," the *emari* answered. "Not in time. Perhaps it is the sultan himself, escaping with his family."

"Not before the battle has even begun, not Tufan," Rem replied, apparently quite sure of this. "Though you may be half right. Any band of citizens might attempt to escape into the hills."

"There are caves in those hills, on a small plateau," Daco told Rem. "A safe place to hide the royal family, perhaps."

"Perhaps. Still, to send his family into hiding so soon would bring despair to Tufan's troops, to all who knew. But what of gold or jewels . . ."

His voice trailed off, as did his focus. They stood about for a time, all apparently watching the army advance into the streets of KyrPhel—all except the warrior who stood directly behind Tasia, hand on hilt. Tasia guessed the army's numbers at well over a thousand, possibly closer to double that, though it was difficult to tell. She knew that no one in the palace had expected a force so large.

"Or perhaps—" Rem said suddenly, spinning, facing Tasia. "Is it possible I did get some truth out of you after all? When my spell was strongest you said that the Crystal was not at the palace. What if you were right?" He turned to Daco again. "You say these caves would make a safe place to hide?" Daco nodded. Rem turned once more and summoned all his people around him.

"Kwshan!" he shouted, to an *emari* wearing a more brightly colored mantle than the rest. "Take all your men and ride to the rim, that way. Try to reach the eastern hills if you can." He pointed toward the faint dust plume still visible on the hillside. "There," he said. "And bring Daco. Find the caves he speaks of. Whatever you find there, bring it here to me."

"At once!" Kwshan replied enthusiastically. He turned at once to comply. In only a moment he had rounded up some twenty other warrior priests, then all of them headed back through the trees toward the camp. Soon they came riding through, making a symbolic, sweeping hand gesture as they passed Rem on their way toward the high eastern hills. Only three *emari* remained, along with the three advisors. All of them waited silently while Rem watched Kwshan go. Tasia decided her chances would never be better. And in any case, she'd had just about enough.

She could hear her *emari* guard just behind her, very close, could feel his breath faintly touching the back of her neck where her pulled-back hair did not cover the skin. She turned and threw both arms around him, squeezed, then put one foot behind his legs and pulled it in. The priest went down first, hard and flat, head bouncing off the rocky ground as Tasia braced her wrists. He somehow kept his grip on the hilt of his sword even as Tasia's forehead bounced off of his. For an instant she was dazed. Then she saw his eyes, still out of focus.

She pulled her hands out from under him, then reached without looking and wrapped her hand around his. She pulled and rolled off of him all at once. As the sword came free she turned it, using both hands, and wrenched it loose from his grip. The *emari* seemed to recover fully then, eyes suddenly fixed upon her. She jerked back and swung the great blade, and he died. She was expecting the other two *emari*, but as she turned to face them, she found only one of them running at her, nearly arrived.

Tasia rolled left, crouched, then blocked the first strike as the warrior tried to finish her quickly. She stood up and struck back, wielding the great blade with a strength that clearly surprised the *emari*, who suddenly found himself on the defensive. He took a step back, gathering his wits. Tasia advanced and swung hard against his sword. As the other's blade went right she pulled back and thrust once, twice. He blocked the first, but not the second. The wound was low on the hip, bleeding but not deep enough.

He came at her again. She dropped to a squat, letting the *emari* miss, then used the chance. She came close to cleaving his right leg just below the knee, but a quick move saved him injury. *Slow!* she cursed herself, realizing how shaken she must be. She circled, centering herself. Ready . . .

The two stood parrying blows for a moment, iron striking iron, and Tasia could not help but be impressed with the *emari's* adeptness; *it's not all my shakes,* she thought. He was just good. Already, though, Rem was shouting at his advisors, telling them to take up the fallen *emari's* sword. And there was the matter of the third *emari* still guarding Rem. She decided there wasn't any time to waste. She feinted back twice, then opened her mouth and screamed, as high and loud as she could. The *emari* paused to stare for just an instant. Tasia snatched her sword around, lunging, and cut his left arm nearly off.

She looked up and found that none of Rem's advisors seemed particularly interested in approaching her, and Rem, standing there, holding a polished, barbed dagger the length of a man's thigh, made no move to send his last *emari* from his side.

Tasia was sure she could best the lot of them, but already she could see Rem gesturing with his free hand, lips moving as he sought once more to bring some dark sorcery to bear on her mind. She didn't need to take the chance.

She spun around and bolted toward the camp, hoping she had enough of a lead. Her own horse stood patiently among the others. Quickly enough she mounted the mare, then clung to the animal's neck as she sent it thundering through the trees. The morning was already well under way. It would be afternoon by the time she reached the city below, if she could get near it at all.

Rem's forces would be at the palace gates by then.

No, she thought, whatever happened in KyrPhel—whatever Tufan and the others decided to do—would happen with or without her. She could forget her intended role in the battle below, the counterforce, all of it. No doubt Adsa and Yourdon already had. Which left her only one clear, intriguing option. One chance . . .

For the first time she wondered how Yourdon had felt, during his last battle in Syttrel. But that was another world entirely, certainly, and this was no time to worry about it. No matter!

She circled Rem's position and took to the ridge again, squinting at the sun in her eyes, following the *emari* toward the high eastern hills.

❖ A CRYSTAL SWORD ❖

Flene arrived on the high hills to a warm welcome from Motan. Yourdon was pleased by this, and at finding everything still as he had left it, including the Crystal.

"I don't know which is more valuable to Rem, but I know which matters most to me," Motan said, giving Flene a gentle hug.

"I'd guard them both if I were you," Yourdon quipped.

"You are supposed to stay and help protect me," the girl said, looking to Yourdon for confirmation. "You have to."

He didn't—but he could. Pella would tell those at the palace where he had gone, the promises she had begged him to make. He could stay here with Flene, do his duty, retain his honor, and wait out the battle, altogether safe. . . .

"I am sure your grandfather needs me too," he told her, told himself.

"Not as much as I do," she countered.

"Then what of your mother? Don't you want me to look after her?" Yourdon asked, almost in spite of himself.

The girl's mood turned, her face clouded. Pella's fate now lay with that of most everyone she had ever known. He looked at Motan—whose face was unreadable now, quiet eyes looking back at him. No help at all.

"I am being selfish," Flene said, pointing her nose down.

"It comes easily to us all," Yourdon said.

He turned and put his hand on her shoulder, then he walked back out of the cave into the clearing. He wandered a bit further, enough to see down into the valley and get a glimpse of the palace and the city below. The afternoon sun shown bright and warm, revealing clear detail. Rem's forces were there by now, that was certain; the dust clouds in the city had reached the palace.

"Come, eat something," Motan requested. Yourdon was too hungry to object. He ate quietly in the cave, resting, contemplating. No matter what, his mind kept circling back.

Just after the meal one of the soldiers entered the cave and beckoned Yourdon outside. He followed, then turned as he heard a rider pound onto the plateau, a man he quickly recognized as the young soldier he had left behind in the city below. The man dismounted and hurried straight to Yourdon's side. It was clear he had tested the endurance of both himself and his mount making time up the hillside.

"So soon?" Yourdon said, a bit surprised. "What news do you bring already?"

"Rem's army is very large, and well equipped," he said, breathless. "They bring a great wagon with a heavy ram set upon it, one no gate could stand against for long."

"We expected as much," Yourdon muttered.

"Yes, but the soldiers who approach the palace are Rem's legion of dead Dral, as we feared. I watched the palace archers fire at them from the walls, but the Dral only pull the arrows out again, and continue working the ram into place."

"How many dead fight for Rem?"

"Hundreds."

"Tasia?" Yourdon asked, though he knew the answer.

"I have seen no sign."

Yourdon nodded. "Has the palace given the signal yet?"

"No," the soldier replied. "I would have seen that."

Once the decision was reached, anyone could order the man in the northwest tower to set ablaze the mass of dried kindling that had been placed there; that was Tasia's signal, if she had returned to do her duty. He couldn't imagine their argument keeping her away. Just now he didn't know whether to worry or spit.

"Any sign of the sultan's counterspells at work?"

"None that I witnessed."

Yourdon turned and looked back into the cave. In the glow of the lamps he could see Flene sitting, talking with Motan while outside a squad of soldiers milled about in the little clearing. *A safe place*, he thought, *for her*. Yourdon remembered perfectly the feeling on the battle field so many months ago, when the Syttrel had nearly killed him—when the odds had been impossible, and he had reasoned that his duty required him to find a means to stay alive. It seemed to him that he felt no difference now. No difference at all.

And yet . . .

Surely the odds were no better this day in KyrPhel than they had been that day in Syttre. Still, he felt his greatest duty now required him to oppose Rem Ana, to seek justice, to stand with those who fought against him. A duty to himself, and to Tufan.

No difference, he thought again, almost happy to be rushing to what was possibly his doom. But in a way it was different. This time, there could be no mistake. He turned from the cave and called the men to him. "One squad will remain here with Motan and Flene," he shouted. "The rest are with me!" He mounted straightaway and turned his horse toward KyrPhel.

❖   ❖   ❖

The coming sunset had already begun to blend the shadows in the woods along the eastern ridge. Where the trees grew thickest Tasia was forced to slow her pace or risk injury. The ledges and hilltops she had followed, trailing the *emari,* were easy in places but treacherous in others. Ahead the rocky edge dropped straight down to certain death, while not far back the loose earth of a steep and uneven, heavily wooded hillside forced her to walk her mount to avoid a tumble. She kept pushing as hard as she could, for those she followed would do no less.

In their haste, however, they had left a trail any child could have followed. *Even in the dark,* Tasia hoped, as she urged her mount around a fallen limb, then down a wide, dry gully that marked part of the junction between the southern and eastern walls of the valley. At last.

Here she found a long stretch of hillside covered by tall pines, their lower limbs long since rotted away. Dry brown needles blanketed the ground and made for slippery footing, but there was almost no undergrowth. She kept her head low to avoid the remaining lower branches that cluttered the way, and in clearings she pushed the horse to a trot. The pattern of hoof-torn earth was plain.

As the sun finally set and stars began to appear in the sky, a half moon to keep them company, she stumbled straight across an untidy yet established trail. She turned and followed it upward, sensing the mare's fatigue but pushing her on all the same, seeing no choice. KyrPhel lay behind her now, far below, its nearest parts littered with tiny fires. The way ahead required her attention, a fortunate thing. . . .

The trail rose quickly, but seemed to go on forever. Rains had washed small gullies into her path, and more than once she thought the mare would come up lame.

Then the earth grew level, and she found herself on a small plateau. As she worked the mare forward she heard shouting voices just up ahead, mixed with the unmistakable sound of iron striking iron.

She maneuvered as close as she dared, then dismounted and circled on foot through the trees, until she came upon the clearing's edge from the right side. Where the rock face rose again the mouth of a large cave was clearly visible, lit now by the glow of a fire built inside, near its mouth. In the clearing itself many men lay dead or dying, many of them clearly Tufan's.

But the KyrPhelian warriors had fought valiantly. She had only just missed the battle, or most of it. She decided they must have been outnumbered nearly two to one, yet they had apparently met the *emari* and stood their ground, defending the cave nearly to the last. Even now she watched two of the four remaining *emari* teaming up to strike down the last bronze-clad KyrPhelian soldier. She glanced at the other two warriors, who were checking bodies, and noticed one of those favoring his right arm.

They all converged on the sole defender at the mouth of the cave then, a flurry of swords; before Tasia could consider it further the KyrPhelian lay dead at their feet.

Yet in almost the same instant a call of defiance rose up from inside the cave. A javelin sprang from within and found the man with the wounded arm, finishing him on the spot. Another cry followed the first, then a lone figure emerged from the cave, sword in hand. *Motan*, Tasia saw, just close enough to recognize him, and feeling an urge to rush to his aid. She held back, expecting more men to follow. He charged full ahead to take on all three *emari* at once, as valiant an effort as Tasia had ever seen. But the odds clearly favored the intruders. They immediately began to force Motan back into the cave.

He howled briefly and went to one knee as one of

the attackers managed to inflict a leg wound. Another blow landed almost instantly. Tasia realized there was no one else, that Motan fought alone, as she watched him collapse on his side in the light of the cave's mouth. She leaped to her feet and started forward, sword drawn, but slowed abruptly as she saw the cave mouth fill with a soft bluish light, a glow that increased and began to sparkle like sunstruck rain as the three remaining warriors stepped over Motan and attempted to make their way forward.

Tasia crept ahead, watching. The glow suddenly became a bright blue flash, and the three *emari* were flung backward out of the cave as if launched from a catapult. They landed badly and lay dazed on the ground, stiffly groping for dropped weapons. Tasia saw her opportunity and sprang.

She reached the nearest *emari* in five quick bounds and drove her borrowed sword into his chest. Stepping over him she swung twice at the next man, who managed to lift up an arm far enough to block her first thrust, but not the second. The last of the warrior priests got to his feet in time to parry several blows. Tasia let him come, keeping her attack low in order to woo him off his guard. Instead he seemed to guess her mind, and used her own game against her.

He feinted left and high, then swung his blade in an arc and struck right. She moved, nearly astonished when his blade cut well into the flesh of her left arm.

Tasia exploded with fury as pain and blood erupted from her forearm. She laid four furious blows on the *emari*, driving him back, wobbling his confidence. When he finally flinched she capitalized, and struck him on the hip. He bent with the blow, and she found his neck an easy target.

When he lay still she turned all about, ready to move

in any direction, bleeding, seething, but she found only silence at her back.

Then movement at the mouth of the cave caught her eye. She saw Flene slowly emerging, small and defenseless, her warding spell spent now, her options gone. The girl stopped and bent over Motan, looking him over, then she softly called his name. Tasia walked toward them until she stood before them both. She looked past the girl into the cave. A finely crafted wooden box rested on a large rock a few paces beyond. *The Shreeta Crystal*, Tasia guessed, *finally. . . .*

Flene looked up at her and their eyes met. Tasia smiled at the girl, and started forward.

Near day's end Yourdon had reached the plain and begun to circle around behind the palace. He stayed wide, riding north and using the trees at the base of the shorter northern ridge for cover. By dark he was in position to lead his two and a half squads safely into KyrPhel's deserted streets.

As they approached the outskirts it was clear the invaders had long ago found the palace and, from what Yourdon could determine, had every wall under siege. There was no chance of getting close, or getting back inside. He could only hope that the troops now headed by Adsa's second commander, Suta, were still in position, awaiting the signal—and that they would be where Yourdon thought they were.

As he moved his squad down a narrow way he could hear the great, thunderous beat of the ram. Again, then again it struck, wood on wood. *Soon,* he thought, *they will be through the outer gates.*

The fact that such a pounding was proceeding uninterrupted likely meant the sultan had not succeeded in countering Rem's dark deathsway sorceries. Yourdon had watched for the fire in the tower as he had descended from the hills. No signal had been given. Somehow, he felt sure, this plan had gone wrong as well.

But another fire had caught his eye, tiny and distant, almost too faint to be sure. Even from the city's streets he could detect it, squinting into the night toward a point far beyond the city, high up on the southern hills, a small flickering no brighter than the stars that shown above the tree-lined ridge. A lookout, Yourdon thought, posted there to watch the valley and warn of any approaching forces, or a command post. This second seemed more likely; there had not been time to mount a force that would come to the aid of KyrPhel soon enough. All facts Rem was no doubt aware of.

He turned his attention back to the city around him and tried to imagine alternate plans, imagining the worst, but it proved a grim business, and one his mind sought to wander from. At length, he and his men arrived at the small arena not far from the palace itself, and here they found Suta still waiting, along with just over a hundred cavalry, the counterattack force Tasia had been expected to lead. Yourdon asked about her yet again, as soon as he had offered fair greetings.

"We have seen nothing of her," Suta replied flatly. "Nor anyone else from the palace. There has been no word at all."

"What news have you of the battle?"

"The main gates are nearly finished. Rem is using his bloodless army to head the assault, and they are nearly impossible to stop." His voice was steady, but Yourdon thought he could hear a note of trepidation in his tone, something all too familiar, all too normal, perhaps.

"I am told our weapons are useless against them."

"Our scouts witnessed hot oil being poured directly on them from the tops of the walls. When the steam cleared there was almost no effect, other than poor footing."

Yourdon doubted the other man was joking. "We have no choice but to attack from behind as planned," he said grimly. "Even without the signal. At least the rear forces are men, and can be killed."

"We stand little chance against so many," Suta said, not objecting, just making mention of the fact, Yourdon realized.

"Our appearance will rally the forces within the palace itself," Yourdon replied. "I can think of no—"

"Look, there!" a soldier yelled, then a chorus of others called out as well. Yourdon peered into the darkness between the roofs of the houses. In the northwest tower high above the palace walls a fire now burned, bright and hot against the black night sky.

"Even as you speak," the young commander shouted.

"Pray to your Gods," Yourdon shouted back, to Suta, to the rest of the men, "that they go with us!" He drew his sword and held it up beside Suta's as they led the soldiers out into the street, straight toward the palace. More than one hundred thirty in all now, they broke their walk quickly and rode at full gallop through the streets, clutching swords, axes and javelins, approaching the hundreds of troops that filled the vast, tiled square and clogged the main approaches beyond the palace gates.

Dozens of torches lit the scene well enough, silhouetting countless targets. Quin soldiers looked over their shoulders into darkness as from behind the sounds of hoofbeats reached their ears. Yourdon and the other cavalry rode straight into the Quin, scything footmen one after another as they tried to gather wits and weapons. They had been confident, resting, patiently waiting for the moment when the gates burst open and their commanders called them forward. Now they began to pay a heavy price.

The first wild Quin blows fell unsuccessfully on bronze scale KyrPhelian armor while the cavalry's swords met unprotected flesh. Yourdon howled wildly as he rode among the Quin, striking first one, then another, then the next, unable to control the lust for blood released within himself. All around him KyrPhelian warriors howled back and fought on. He kept advancing, bringing his eager battalion forward, the men struggling to stay in an already scattered wedge. Constantly he searched the night for Rem, but Yourdon saw no sign of him here. He kicked a Quin full in the face, then thrust his sword into the man's chest, imagining it was Rem the whole time, enjoying that fantasy yet again.

They drove further into the camp of living Quin with remarkable ease, closer to the palace, until before them stood the legions of the dead.

More bone than flesh, still in the rotted and tattered rags and leathers they had been buried in, they numbered several hundred in all. And all of them were pressing ahead, even as Suta reached the nearest of them and used his battle axe to cleave the animate's head completely off. They seemed completely oblivious to Yourdon and his men, singularly fastened to their task. Just ahead the massive ram towered above them, a great wood and iron wagon the likes of which Yourdon had never seen. Yourdon watched it creep back, hundreds of emaciated hands gripping it, then felt the earth rumble as it rolled forward again.

Before his eyes the great doors cracked with a sound like mountain thunder—and gave, as Yourdon realized this had been the final blow. The towering gates of the palace stood split nearly in two. Yet without pause the hordes of deathsway soldiers pulled the ram back, and pressed forward again, as if they had no knowledge of their success. Behind him Yourdon could hear many of the living rushing ahead now, swarming to either side of Yourdon's troops and the Quin who still engaged them as Quin commanders began to divide their forces according to task. Yourdon tried to count his losses. More than half of his men remained on their mounts, but the Quin cavalry was joining the fight now, turning the odds.

Suddenly everything changed.

The spell itself was not the problem, rather it was the proportions. Sorcery on such a scale was all but unheard of in modern times. Tufan had no doubt that even the Five Gods themselves would have been impressed. Hundreds of once-living Dral warriors walked the earth again, taking orders from the living, hearing with deathsway ears, responding with whatever remained of their bodies. They were slow to move and had no minds of their own, they could only do as they were told. Tufan watched them at the gates, the way they tended to wait about like drowsy oxen when some obstacle prevented the completion of a task—until new orders were given. Still, they were all but impervious to harm, and relentless once motivated.

All the while Tufan had worked feverishly, repeating freshly revised chants over and over again, finally empowering the counterspell he had been building these past weeks—building to proportions he himself could not be sure of. Such energies might go awry, might hurt the living as well as the dead, he worried, or turn into something else, a twisted invention of enchantment that no man, living or dead, would recognize. A lifetime of learning and practice had taught Tufan his limits, and they were many. He was but a minor mage, and he had never faced such a task as this, had never dreamed . . .

He broke concentration, resting for a moment, and watched as the ram was brought forward once more, listened as it pounded methodically on the palace gates below. Worry threatened to overcome him, but he steeled himself against it, and kept to his work. In the far tower one of Adsa's men waited with the signal fire, waiting with all KyrPhel for Tufan to do his part. But to rush, to take a chance on releasing the spell before it was properly defined, would likely end their one chance at victory.

He could sense clearly the essence of Rem's deathsway spell now. Rem had amassed a great deal of energy, but in order to put that energy to use among so many, he had created what amounted to an echo. Control was the key.

Once empowered, such a spell would have rushed into the earth and spread itself among the dead just as a dam might split and flood a small valley; but the result would not be the army Tufan saw before him. The buried bodies would simply have twitched and flopped about in a massive convulsion until the energy dissipated, and they were still once more.

But Rem had fashioned a means of limiting the escape of the spell's energies, then applying them to one body at a time. After that, Tufan imagined, Rem had simply repeated the final chant over and over, several hundred times, causing the spell to echo from grave to grave—from soldier to soldier—until the desired army marched before him.

Eventually the reservoir of energies Rem had drawn from the world around him would be drained, and even Rem did not have the inner reserve needed to recreate it—not for months, certainly—but that was of little conciliation now.

Tufan did not have the time to counter Rem's sorceries in such detail, nor, he imagined, the skills. But if he could interrupt the flow, silence the echo, even only temporarily, then Rem's deathsway army might collapse, at least for a time. There was no way to be sure of the chants Rem had used, but if Tufan was right, that would not be necessary. The sultan had gathered considerable energies to himself—enough, he thought, to create a brief magical clamor no chant could hope to penetrate. . . .

Tufan kept to his chants—and he prayed to the Gods, trusting in his heart that they could not be with one such as Rem, believing that he was right about Rem, and they would instead help him now in this fight against such a great blasphemer.

Finally, grown weak with hours of effort, and certain the palace would be overrun at any moment, he thought to add just one more chant to the spell. But in that same instant he heard the sickening crack of heavy, iron-buttressed wood breaking apart, and knew that he could wait no longer.

Sweat dripped off his nose and forehead as he held heavy arms out before him, braced himself, closed his eyes and gave the final chant. As the spell went forth it seemed to take every bit of Tufan's strength with it. He felt a violent wind blow up all around him and rush away, out of the tower. He tried to open his eyes but he saw only darkness, felt infinite weakness, and sensed himself falling, tumbling down.

Yourdon heard a sound like wind howling through the snowy peaks of the Tesshis—lasting only a moment before it was gone completely, leaving a brief, dreadful silence. But abruptly cheers began to rise up all around him. Then he heard the same echoing back from the distance, from the hundreds of men manning the palace walls. Yourdon looked up and bore witness as the last of hundreds of Dral corpses fell dead—*again*. Yourdon smiled to himself: *Tufan* . . .

In the next moment he saw the broken gates of the palace being pulled open wide, though from the inside, Yourdon realized, as he raised his sword to take up the fight again. He defended himself against two Quin who were snapping out of their own astonishment. All around he could hear Quin commanders ordering their men back to the attack. The battle would be won by mortal means alone now, Yourdon realized, and he intended to do whatever he could to determine the outcome.

He met the Quin blades, concentrating on the battle at hand, but with his ears he could hear what sounded like the shouts of a charge. When he dared look up again he saw hundreds of men, armored KyrPhelian cavalry, pouring out of the palace, riding over the tattered bodies of the wasted Dral and attacking the surge of living Quin. Yourdon looked to Suta and the others, those that were still alive, and saw that they had realized, too. Yourdon felt his sword arm growing unbearably heavy, but he could not rest. The only way out was through the Quin. He cut another man down before his own horse was finally felled. He stumbled off the animal, continuing the fight on foot. Blood seemed to flow everywhere. The screams of the wounded filled the night.

But Yourdon felt no fear.

No desperate urge to run. To escape.

It didn't matter that there was nowhere to go. He knew the truth. The world knew, or it would, if Suta or any of his cavalry survived.

He traded hands and managed to dispatch one more Quin soldier, but the final blow strained his left hand. The muscles spasmed and he all but dropped the sword. Two more Quin faced him now. He knew he could not best them both with no good arms and dead on his feet. He took a breath all the same, and prepared to engage them both, fully expecting this moment would be his last. Then one man suddenly arched his back and fell. The same fate found the other an instant later. No more Quin blocked his path.

The men Yourdon saw standing in front of him now wore blood-smeared bronze scale armor. Behind them another soldier rode atop a massive war horse, its chest protected by a polished bronze scale apron. The Kyr warriors greeted Yourdon as they passed, taking their fight ahead. The rider paused his mount, then pulled his helmet off.

"One day, you must explain to me how you ended here," Adsa said to him.

"That I shall," Yourdon answered, too overwhelmed to say much else lest he lose control. Adsa took a moment to look behind and to either side. Yourdon followed his gaze. Many good men had been lost, more than half those he had ridden into battle with, but the Quin were divided now, and had lost many more, while the forces of KyrPhel were united, shouting and yelping, drunk with the realization that victory lay within their grasp. Already, many of the Quin, separated from their remaining commanders, had began to run.

For Yourdon, already well past exhaustion, it was not a moment too soon. Then a horse was brought to him, and Adsa was asking Yourdon to ride along with him.

They slowly made their way through the field of dead, bloodied and bloodless, until they entered inside the palace walls.

"You didn't wait until the Dral were fallen," Yourdon said, reflecting on their original plan. "You ordered the signal fire set first."

"I saw no choice. No one did. A two-way counterattack seemed our only hope."

"If the sultan's spell had not worked, you might have succeeded only in sacrificing most of your men."

"I know," Adsa said evenly.

"The only decision you could have made," Yourdon assured him. "No commander in Detimar would have done differently. You are a man of great courage."

"As are you," Adsa said, utterly sincere.

Yourdon made no reply.

"Go to the southwest tower at once," Adsa commanded, looking up, beckoning two of his men. "If Tufan is not there, find him wherever he is and tend to him. Inform me as soon as you have found him." He watched as the soldiers hurried to do his bidding. Then he shuddered slightly, and Yourdon realized Adsa was nearly as weary as he was.

They sat for a moment on stone benches in the great courtyard, still catching their breath. Adsa called for a lantern. A soldier quickly brought one. In the light Yourdon saw the blood and gore that clung to him, and to his sword. As gruesome a sight as he had ever seen, he was sure, yet just now it did not seem to bother him.

A few moments later two soldiers slowly approached, bringing Tufan.

The sultan looked utterly vanquished. His legs were not up to supporting his bulk. His eyes were barely open. The soldiers had to help him walk. Still, he smiled when he saw Yourdon and Adsa rise to greet him, and he insisted on sitting with them. They made room, then steadied the sultan as he attempted composure.

"We would have come to you," Adsa told him.

"I made them bring me here," the sultan said, his voice as weak as his body, but clear, understandable. "Now," he added, "tell me you have the head of Rem Ana on the end of a javelin."

Yourdon and Adsa glanced briefly at each other, then Yourdon cleared his throat. "We, umm, I—"

"The men search for him even now, but we have yet

to find him," Adsa explained. "He may never have come into the city with his troops."

Tufan's haggard expression seemed to worsen slightly. "A coward, is he? I am not surprised. But I cannot accept less than his death or capture. The Kyr cannot. We must find him. We must be certain."

Adsa nodded slowly.

"Then order the men to search the dead one by one until his body is found, or until it is not. Any Quin found still alive is to be brought in and questioned, not killed."

"As you wish," Adsa replied. "We will learn of Rem's fate, I swear it. You will have peace."

Tufan closed his eyes momentarily, all the answer Adsa seemed to need. The commander stood and went among the soldiers still gathering in the main yard.

Yourdon felt the sultan's hand on his arm.

"I must tell you what happened," Tufan said, throat rasping now. "The spell I released—such an incredible spell! At first I thought I had no chance to counter Rem's deathsway spells, then I thought I might do more harm than good, but oh, by the Gods, it was a wondrous thing. . . ."

Yourdon let the sultan trail off. He looked down and examined his sword, bent and dulled, blood still dripping from it, forming a little puddle at his feet. He shrugged and tossed the weapon aside, listened to it clang on the courtyard stones as it landed nearby. *I still have my dagger,* he thought. And with that a familiar image came to mind, one that suddenly troubled him more deeply than ever before.

He took the Shetie dagger out of his belt and laid it on his lap, then looked up at Tufan, found the sultan staring back.

"What is wrong?"

"My liege, a moment," Yourdon said. The sultan eyed

him strangely, yet waited silently. Placing his hand on the dagger and reciting his spells, Yourdon concentrated on Rem, and again a vision came to him—the same vision, that of a man wearing a pleated, hooded tunic. The hood still covered much of his face, revealing only a pure white beard. The figure still held the very long dagger, its polished blade barbed on both sides. All images, Yourdon realized for the first time, that had never come to be . . .

Yet every vision he had ever conjured had been a part of an object's past. *Every one!* Why then, when he held the Shetie dagger . . .

But the Shetie were fortune tellers—

The idea struck him with a force that made his head swim. He suddenly saw the truth so clearly, a truth that had been there, right in front of him, for so very long. The only practical explanation! The visions he conjured when he used his magic on the amber dagger, the Shetie dagger, were not from the past, but from the future!

He held the dagger tightly, still repeating his special chant, and the magic grew stronger than he had ever imagined it could. He watched the young soldier striking out at the hooded figure once more, then dodging the barbed blade. But as the visions grew more complete he could see beyond the battle, could see well enough the details of a great valley just emerging behind the other man in the light of a new day . . . a city that could only be KyrPhel.

"Rem is not here!" he said, leaping to his feet, suddenly woozy as he steadied himself and let the trance dissolve. "He lives, up there!" Yourdon pointed into the night, toward the line of hills to the south, a dark silhouette outlined by the stars. The tiny spark of a fire still flickered there, high on a ridge.

"How can you know this?" Tufan asked, getting to his feet as well. They leaned on each other for support.

"It is the same magic I used when you showed me the Crystal, but the other way around."

Tufan looked a question at him. Yourdon shook his head. "It doesn't matter. Adsa!" he shouted. "Adsa!"

The commander turned at the shouts, left the men he had been speaking with, and hurried back over.

"What is it? What is wrong?" he begged the sultan.

"Not I—him!" Tufan exclaimed, pointing an accusing finger at Yourdon. "He claims to know something of Rem."

"Assemble some men," Yourdon exclaimed. "We must leave at once! He is there in the hills. I have seen it!"

Adsa looked to his sovereign, who shrugged, then nodded his approval. Within minutes a squad had been assembled and fresh horses brought. They set off through the darkness, making their way hastily through the empty streets of KyrPhel, then galloping hard across the open fields until finally they reached the hills and began to climb.

Above them the tiny fire that was their beacon had disappeared, but as he looked toward the eastern end of the valley he could almost see the first faint glimmer of sunrise beginning to show beyond the peaks. He hadn't realized most of the night had passed, that already a new day was about to begin. . . .

When they encountered a ridge two-thirds of the way up the main slope Yourdon told Adsa to halt.

"Near here," Yourdon stated, looking about him, remembering details of the images he had seen. "This is where we will find him."

"Very well," Adsa said, turning to his men, waving his hand. "Search the forest, that way, and that way." He split the men into small squads and sent them scurrying. Within minutes a man rode back with news: they had found a small clearing containing two long tents; at the clearing's center the coals of a dirt-snuffed fire still smoldered.

"They have fled through the trees, there," one of the soldiers said, calling to Adsa as Yourdon followed the commander to the sight. The soldier pointed to a battered thicket, an area barely visible in the fleeting light of the torches. They walked to the spot and the soldier bent down, placing his hands on the broken earth. "Dozens of hooves," he explained.

"We may be outnumbered," Adsa remarked, looking toward Yourdon. Then a knowing smile took over his expression. "But that seems the way of this night."

"Indeed," Yourdon said, that being enough.

Adsa summoned their horses. "Spare nothing!" the commander shouted, remounting, turning in a close circle. "They have a fair head start. We need to ride hard if we're to catch the cowards!" Determined shouts answered him, then the thunder of hooves followed him into the trees.

The agility and resolve of both horses and men were sharply tested as they made their way crashing and dodging through branches and undergrowth. They had only the light of the stars and a partial moon to guide them, and the growing glow behind the mountains, in the eastern sky. One man was lost when his horse tangled with a large sprig, sending him head over heels into a vast, unyielding oak. Adsa left a second soldier to guard the injured man, who proved to be still alive but not conscious, then the rest set off again, continuing their pace.

As the trail led them gradually downward again toward the far western end of the valley, pale daylight began to make its way into the woods, revealing details of the tattered trail. Soon the valley floor sprang into view, and with it a bit of dust clouding in the air, only a half-dozen horses and riders Adsa guessed, just making their way out onto the broad southwest road. "They must not leave this valley," Adsa decreed, and with that the column rushed forward after them.

Too late the Quin realized they had been found. Yourdon watched them turn as if to fight, then he watched them turn again as they seemed to realize they were outnumbered, or outmaneuvered, perhaps. As he and Adsa drew near panicked Quin shouts reached Yourdon's ears. Adsa drew his sword and held it skyward, and all the men followed his lead. They closed the distance, galloping faster on fresher mounts, gaining on the heavily laden Quin.

Iron clashed as they arrived in their enemy's midst, and the first Quin fell. Yourdon turned, finding himself momentarily unopposed. He heard a call for blood, then saw that it had come from a hooded man riding the lead horse.

The Quin were turning their horses, some fighting on while others attempted to bolt. Yourdon tried to push his mount toward their hooded leader, who had now begun to shout a chant Yourdon could not decipher.

Just then the man's arms went up. His hands made a strange shooing motion, and Yourdon's horse stopped in its tracks. As it tried to move it began stumbling about as if its hooves were on fire. "He's hobbled the horses!" Adsa called out, raging now.

Yourdon tried to stay atop his own faltering beast, gripping at mane and bridle with both hands and dropping his sword in the process. He watched as nearly all the Quin turned toward escape and decided he had no choice. He leaped down and ran toward them, ducking the only man quick enough to wave a sword, then pumping his legs hard as the lead rider got himself turned around and set his mount in motion. Yourdon found a burst of speed, and jumped.

He filled his hands with pack frame, then reached again and grabbed the rider's soft, pleated tunic. When he fell back the rider came with him, tumbling to the ground. They landed in a heap, then scrambled to get up and apart.

They stood facing each other now, Yourdon clutching his short, amber-jeweled dagger, the other man holding a longer dagger, silvery and barbed. In the growing light Yourdon could see part of his opponent's face—especially the stark whiteness of his beard. That didn't matter.

"Rem Ana," Yourdon said, his voice nearly steady.

The other man said nothing.

"I have come to repay my debt to you."

"No need," Rem said, a hoarse voice, not like Yourdon remembered it. His massive spells, the long night, his hurried flight, all had apparently taken a toll. Ultimately, it seemed, even Rem was no more than human, despite rumors to the contrary.

"There is a need. My need," Yourdon countered. "And the need of many others."

Rem seemed unaffected. He raised one hand menacingly. "Go while you can, or I will destroy you."

"No," Yourdon said, almost certain he knew what he was doing—even as he stared at the man the white of his beard had begun to darken. . . . "I don't trust you! Not a thing about you! Not a word you speak! You have spent your magic, I think, and you have plotted my destruction too many times already. You have nothing more to threaten me with."

Rem held fast for an instant, as if time had somehow come to a stop. Then he lashed out with the dagger, surprising Yourdon, nearly catching his arm with the deadly blade. Yourdon gathered himself and darted left, watching Rem's motion with a practiced eye. They traced a small circle, a dance Yourdon had seen times before, but Rem quickly grew restless—as Yourdon hoped he would—the mark of one not tempered by training and battle.

As Rem thrust again his hood fell back, and Yourdon could see the fury on his face, the set of his jaw as he ground his teeth together. With a grunt Rem swung wildly. Yourdon bobbed right, flashing his stubby dagger with practiced precision, and the flesh on the back of Rem's hand split open wrist to knuckle. Blood ran down the prophet's arm, and he began to shake. He dropped the heavy dagger and stumbled backward, holding his hand, a strange, twisted look on his face. It took a moment to recognize the expression, but then Yourdon understood: Rem Ana was terrified.

Yourdon grabbed him by the shoulder and pulled him along toward the others.

"You would spare his life?" Adsa said as he met Yourdon, approaching sword first. The sultan's men had been forced to slay two more of Rem's men, but the rest had surrendered, those that hadn't run off. They stood in a cluster quietly awaiting their fate. As Yourdon turned back to Rem he saw that the white in his beard had faded altogether, replaced once again by normal browns and grays.

"You should know something about the Shreeta," Yourdon told Rem, only too pleased to say so now. "It is quite powerless. As a tool of war, or one of peace, its own legend is its only strength. It's a beautiful trinket, nothing more. A crystal sword. Test it, and the myth will shatter. One day for good, perhaps." He leaned a bit closer and fixed his eyes on Rem's. "It is a fool's tool."

"Unlike you or I," Adsa said, putting his hand solidly on Yourdon's shoulder. Yourdon found him grinning.

"I do not believe you," Rem said, while two of Adsa's men pushed him to a sitting position on the ground and began to see to his hand. "The Shreeta Crystal is beyond your understanding."

"I have seen its past, and there is nothing of the Gods, any gods. I understand all too well."

Rem stared back at Yourdon, then he licked his lips. "Then I say the sultan's is not the true Crystal, which has yet to be found." He glanced up at the morning sky, the distant hills, his look despondent now, his eyes empty. "Still," he said, "Tufan's Crystal . . . would have been enough."

He was partly wrong, of course, there was no other crystal waiting to be found, but Yourdon had seen the Crystal's true heritage, had seen what could be accomplished through faith alone. In this last, Rem spoke only the truth.

"The sultan would like to see you," Adsa said, collecting Rem now. "Get on your feet."

Yourdon turned and walked back to his mount, which seemed quite able again, then he joined the others as they rode toward the streets of KyrPhel.

❖ MANY RETURNS ❖

Tufan stood on the balcony that overlooked the palace's main courtyard, watching as the prisoners were paraded before him, Rem Ana trailing the rest, then he called them to a halt as Rem arrived directly below. Despite all his ordeals and a strong, lingering fatigue that possibly eclipsed even his own, Yourdon had never seen a man quite as full of himself as the sultan seemed to be.

"You have earned this day," he shouted down to the Quin leader. Rem's lips moved, but the words went undetermined.

"What has the beast to say!" Tufan demanded loudly.

"I say the Quin will yet rise up against you," Rem howled now, straining but quite loud enough to be heard on the balcony above. This seemed to lend some small courage to the other Quin who trudged in line with him. Perhaps to Rem as well.

"I am sure, and we will be here, waiting," Tufan replied, "but not you." Rem said nothing back.

"His silence is satisfaction in itself," Adsa commented, to nods from the others. The sultan waved to his men, and the prisoners were ushered forward again.

"He will be given a speedy trial," Tufan confided to Yourdon and Adsa. "Then, once we formally pronounce his guilt, we will begin finding out just how many resurrections he has in him."

This last brought a smile to both the warriors' faces.

316

The sultan turned, and all three adjourned to the grand hall just behind them, where Pella and a handful of nobles and servants awaited them. Adsa went straight to her, and the two of them began talking quietly, standing very close together. Even Tufan seemed pleased at this, Yourdon noted, as he observed the sovereign watching them now.

"They make a fine couple, do they not?" Tufan said. Yourdon had no choice but to agree. In fact, as his mind agreed to those terms, it was easy to believe the world had meant them for each other—just as it was easy for Yourdon to believe that he had been meant for no one, like old Beken.

"That they do," he said. Then, "I didn't know."

Tufan nodded. "Perhaps she is beginning to heal. This should have happened long ago, the two of them, but she has been too reluctant, and the good commander too polite. I sense this may have changed."

"One can always hope," Yourdon replied.

The couple clasped hands briefly, then they each glanced at Yourdon and Tufan, and started toward them.

"We are grateful for what you have done," Pella told Yourdon. "Each of us."

"You have helped save our people," Adsa added, bowing from the waist. Yourdon bowed in kind, then Pella took a step closer. "But now that it is safe," she said, "perhaps you can go and bring my daughter back to me. At once."

She spoke as if she thought he should already be about it, tired or not. Indeed, Yourdon thought, he should.

"She is not here?" Tufan asked, apparently quite puzzled. Pella shook her head.

"Then where?" Tufan inquired sternly. "What have we done with her?" Pella was silent at first. She glanced briefly toward the commander. Tufan looked to Adsa as well, most accusingly.

"I have done nothing!" the commander quickly insisted. Tufan's dark gaze found Yourdon next.

"Pella asked me to take her to safety, and I did," Yourdon explained, deciding he had the least to lose in any case. "I believed she was thinking of both of you."

"It was my decision," Pella added, trying to settle the matter. "You could not have made it, and I had no choice."

"But where is she?" the sultan insisted, not the least amused. "And since when is it up to you to decide what I can decide?" he added. "I am sultan after all, and she is my only granddaughter. Do I not rule in my own house?"

"She is safe in the caves with Motan and the Crystal. I had my reasons, father. All very good ones. If you consider them, later, when we can have a proper talk, I am sure you will understand. You must trust in that. And you must allow Yourdon to leave. We all would like Flene back before another night has come."

"A proper talk would certainly be in order," Tufan stressed, nearly rigid.

"Please," Pella replied.

Tufan made a sour face, but Pella sweetened it with a gentle smile, then a kiss on the side of his head.

"Agreed," he said. "Of course. Go and fetch her," he told Yourdon. "Take what you need. And do not forget to bring the Crystal back as well!"

"I won't," Yourdon assured him, though both of them suddenly, briefly smiled.

"I will go with you," Adsa insisted. He looked up at Yourdon anticipating an argument. Yourdon made none.

"Any word of Tasia?" the sultan asked after them, as the two men turned to go.

"She is still missing," Yourdon answered, pausing. He had almost forgotten, but not quite.

"I hope nothing has happened to her," Pella said.

"I wouldn't worry about that," Yourdon said, adding a sigh. "It is my own fault for not following the good advice of a friend more often. I don't think we should worry. Just be glad she never knew where we hid the Crystal." He took a breath, then shook his head.

"Indeed?" the sultan said, eyes going wide.

"Aye," Yourdon nodded. "She is probably halfway to Dlet by now. We will likely never see her again."

"Not true," a voice called out. Yourdon knew at once who it was. He turned with the others toward the doorway as Tasia stepped into the room. Flene entered beside her, holding in her hands the box containing the Shreeta Crystal.

"You are still here?" Yourdon asked, nearly as surprised as he made it sound.

Tasia only looked at him. "Where did you think I'd be?"

Flene ran across the room to her mother. She handed the box to Tufan as she reached the two of them. He took it in one arm and put the other around his granddaughter. As mother and daughter embraced Adsa drew near and lent an arm as well. Tasia walked slowly toward Yourdon, wearing a mild scowl on her face. Her clothes were as tattered and bloodied as his own, her face was covered in dirt, her hair a mass of knots. She favored one arm. Yourdon noticed the blood-soaked sleeve of her tunic as she stood before him. He lifted the torn material and winced when he saw the wound.

When he looked up their eyes met, and held.

"Hurt?" he asked.

"Yes."

They eyed each other for another long moment, then Tasia gently smiled, little wrinkles black with grime deepening around her mouth and eyes. A very human face. An almost perfect face, perhaps, Yourdon thought, as his own stolid expression crumbled at once, leaving the two of them grinning at each other like children. He took his hands away from the wound and touched the backs of her hands; she turned palms up and held them both. The grins softened, deepened, and the air between them seemed suddenly warm enough to ignite.

"It is possible," he said, "that not all Syttrel, even you, are heathens and thieves, after all."

"Thanks," she whispered, leaning closer, "thanks a lot."

❖ ABOUT THE AUTHOR ❖

Mark read a copy of "The Sands of Mars" when he was twelve, and proceeded to exhaust the local library's supply of SF, then book stores, then magazines like *F&SF* and *Galaxy*. Eventually he tried writing some short stories of his own. Then he got interested in music, and spent the next fifteen years playing in area rock bands, writing songs (over one hundred) and recording studio demos for record companies. He also got involved in fast "street" machines, especially domestic types, like 442s and GTOs, and enjoyed building and racing his own cars. Eventually he quit auto racing and rock bands, but he still found himself compelled to do something creative with his life, so he came full circle, back to science fiction and fantasy.

He's spent the last twelve years reading, going back to school, attending conventions, and writing. He is now forty-two, and lives in Upstate New York with his wife (also an avid reader), their three children, and (of course) a cat.

Comments are welcome.
Write care of Baen Books, or you can e-mail Mark at M.GARLAND2@Genie.com

TALES OF THE WIZARD OF YURT
C. Dale Brittain

A young magician earns his stars the hard way in these engaging, light fantasy adventures.

A BAD SPELL IN YURT
72075-9 ◆ $5.99 ☐

The tiny backwater kingdom of Yurt seems to be the perfect place for a young wizard who barely managed to graduate wizard's school. But Daimbert senses a lurking hint of evil that suggests someone in the castle is practicing black magic.... Soon Daimbert realizes that it will take all the magic he never learned to find out who that person is, and save the kingdom and his life. Good thing Daimbert knows how to improvise!

THE WOOD NYMPH & THE CRANKY SAINT
72156-9 ◆ $4.99 ☐

"Those of you who have read *A Bad Spell in Yurt* will need no further notice than the fact that Brittain is at it again.... This is a fun, fast-paced, entertaining read. And it's meaty enough to keep a smile on your face." —Steven Sawicki, *Random Realities*

MAGE QUEST
72169-0 ◆ $4.99 ☐

A young wizard sets out on the road to adventure, battling evil in the quiet backwater kingdom of Yurt.

THE WITCH & THE CATHEDRAL
87661-9 ◆ $5.99 ☐

"...written in a humorous, almost irreverent style...contains romance, humor and adventure—something for everyone!" —*Kliatt*

DAUGHTER OF MAGIC
87720-8 ◆ $5.99 ☐

Daimbert's daughter is a chip off the old block—if he's lucky, she won't turn him into a frog.

EXPLORE OUR WEB SITE